Whitechapel Road

A Vampyre Tale

PAM

GREAT TALKING TO YOU AT FAN EXPO!

HOPE YOU ENJOY THE READ!

ALL THE BEST.

YOUR FRIENDS, Wayne :)

Wayne Mallows

WHITECHAPEL ROAD
A Vampyre Tale

Third Edition
Copyright © 2011 Wayne Mallows
First Publication 2010

ISBN: 978-0-9877070-0-0

Cover Art:
Concept - Wayne Mallows
Design and creation - Stef Proctor

Interior book design – Stef Proctor

Learn more about this series at:
www.waynemallows.com

Wayne Mallows
4761 Zimmerman Ave
Niagara Falls, ON L2E 3M8

Whitechapel Road is dedicated to both my family and friends, for without them and their undying support this book could never have come to be.

W.M.

Prologue

The earth, the universe in which it spins, as well as mankind itself all contain mysteries and wonders of untold proportions, the answers or understanding of which will never come to be known as common knowledge. That having been said, there are many other mysteries that come into existence simply because at the time of discovery there was neither the science nor the understanding to grasp what was being presented. In those cases the mysteries in question are sometimes solved as the advancement of time also brings with it an advancement in what had been lacking, either education, technology or perhaps both. Still, more incredibly, there are other perplexing occurrences that have taken place throughout our recorded history, and most certainly well before that time, where the body of evidence points directly at the answer, and yet the mystery comes into being just the same. This takes place despite having the facts substantiated by numerous means, means that could see the mystery laid to rest before it could even evolve. In fact the very answer that is sought by the masses stands squarely in the spotlight and yet is ignored completely, not even brought into question by those same people who seek it, for it is simply too unbelievable to be possible.

Chapter 1

Born in 1854 to a farming family in the village of Ellingham, located approximately 20 miles from the southern most tip of England, life for Aremis was, to a large extent, set out to be that of a normal farm boy growing up with his family.

Children were expected to work on the family's farm or help in running the family business, whatever that might be, until it was time to marry and even then they often did not have a choice in the matter of who was to be their life partner; the choice was made by the parents, and in many instances without the new couple-to-be having ever set sight on one another before their wedding day.

Such was the case for the boy born to the Eilbeck family who, in the fall of 1874 now in his twentieth year, was considered prime for finding a bride to marry. There had been some talk of marriage before now but it was simply not advantageous for the family to have him wed before this time. For you see, the land directly adjacent to Eilbeck farm, some eighty acres of prime farm and forest, belonged to a family who had a daughter and, despite her younger years, her parents were willing to allow a marriage to take place. By doing so, they hoped to forge a family bond that would see their two properties merge into one, becoming one of, if not the largest farm in the entire area. It was to be a most profitable venture to be quite sure.

Even though the couple not-yet-formed lived next door to one another for many years, they had not actually seen much of each other beyond their childhood years. Mary, the only daughter of Harry and Emma Smith, and who was to be wed to Aremis, had been sent away to live with an ailing aunt who had no daughters of her own and therefore needed someone to do the daily household duties for her. This somewhat insignificant fact was to present a very significant problem for Aremis come harvest time, a time in which the local farmers and their families gathered in the small town square to give thanks for the bountiful harvest and enjoy some of the fruits of their summer's labour.

This was also to be the time the two families had planned to announce the proposed marriage to the townspeople and begin preparation for the wedding. Finally, the many legal obstacles that are usually present when it comes time to officially join the two lands into one were resolved and Aremis would see his bride for the first time since she had been sent away. And yet it was on this night, the night of the harvest celebrations, that the very plan, seeded so many years earlier, began to unravel.

Dressed in his finest attire that his mother had sewn and looking quite dapper for a seasoned livestock handler, he patiently meandered around the inside of the town hall politely chatting with his neighbours. As the hours steadily pressed on and it began to grow late he excused himself from family and friends, taking leave of the hall lights and trading the claustrophobic surroundings for some space and a breath of night air out on the front steps.

As the minutes dragged by, he slowly made his way down the steps until he was standing at their footing where he remained tracing out patterns in the sandy road with the tip of his boot. As he made whimsical shapes, of no particular design, his mind was left to wonder about a future with someone he had not seen for several years. As he did, a shadow fell across his absent-minded artwork in the sand.

Startled by the sudden appearance and not yet sure of who or what had cast it, he jumped backwards wishing he had not been so foolish as to drop his guard on a dark night such as this. As his eyes came to bear on the source of the shadow, he felt a wave of relief fall over his racing heart as he saw a thin tall woman standing before him, a bright smile upon her face. Wearing a yellow dress, the colour of daffodils in springtime, but without a jacket she looked to be significantly underdressed for such a chilly autumn evening. She had long brown hair that fell freely over her shoulders, the top pulled back and clipped into place with two small ivory combs so as to keep it from her face. Her skin was pale and in the light of the moon took on a pearlescent quality, her dark green eyes sparkling as though they were somehow lit from within.

"I am terribly sorry to have startled you so," she said trying her utmost to conceal her mirth at having set such a fright onto one who seemed, at first glance, to be quite unflappable.

"There is nothing to apologise for," he replied his voice shaken by the sudden start he had just been given, "It is my own fault for being so lost in my own thoughts, I must confess at being quite relieved to discover it was you and not some beast that has found me in such an absent-minded state."

The young maiden giggled at his honest response, pleased that he had not tried to hide the fact that he had indeed been frightened by her sudden appearance.

"May I inquire as to what it is that has one such as you so entranced as to not notice my approach?" she asked with the innocent enthusiasm of a young child.

He felt the blush come upon his face, an unconscious reaction to her innocent question. "I am to meet my future wife tonight and, you see, I fear I have precious little insight as to her likes and dislikes or if either of us will even enjoy one another's company once we have met."

He looked out into the darkness that lay beyond the reach of the oil lamp's amber glow as if to find something more intellectual to say to this woman who now shared the evening with him.

"So, am I to understand that you are nervous this person will not find you attractive or interesting enough to marry?" the female stranger politely asked.

"I suppose, but it is all quite irrelevant really as it is our parents who have arranged it all." His voice was downtrodden and he plunked his hands into the pockets of his trousers as if to punctuate his displeasure. He rocked slightly on his heels in the hopes that the conversation would turn towards a topic other than that of his personal affairs.

"I think your fears are unfounded," she replied in a matter of fact voice, "as I find you quite attractive and very much a gentleman, and in fact I would be most pleased to marry you if you were to ask me."

Quite stunned by the statement just put forth by one he had only just met, he found himself flushed and at a loss for words.

"I am... I am touched you feel as you do, Miss. You flatter me, truly, so much so that I am not even sure how exactly to respond to your kind words."

The young woman laughed and spun around once, the sudden turning action sending the hem of her yellow dress floating upward like a spring flower opening to the warmth of the morning sun.

"I *am* sorry to tease you so, it is not often I have the chance, you see. I am supposed to be so proper all of the time and not partake in such foolishness, for it is seen as being quite unladylike. I am sure you can appreciate this," she said straightening out the skirt of her dress so it would lie properly.

"Yes, yes of course, I do understand, quite, and I must confess that chatting with you like this, well, it does take my mind off things. I am pleased you happened along as you did."

"As am I," she replied as she thrust her hand forward in a manner more suited to that of a man and not that of a lady. "My name is Mary, Mary Smith, and I do believe that you and I are supposed to be married this coming spring. That is, of course, if you are indeed Aremis?"

Yet again, he found himself at a complete disadvantage to this young maiden. He removed his right hand from his pocket, and in a fashion more a learned response than a conscience reaction, he took the hand offered to him. She had a firm grip belonging to someone used to working with tools and livestock and not that of a frail city girl.

"I am pleased to officially make your *re-acquaintance* Mary, you have quite a way about you. And yes, yes you are quite correct, I am indeed Aremis, Aremis Eilbeck. It has been so many years since you went away. I cannot believe that I failed to recognize you."

He released her hand removing his other hand from his pocket and holding them both out to his sides as if on display.

She smiled momentarily, quite taken in by the young man before her.

"I must admit, Aremis, you certainly look quite a bit different all dressed up do fine and all."

"True enough I suppose. My Mum made my clothes special for tonight so I would look my best for you." He turned around once, somewhat shy about what he should be doing.

"Well, you do look smashing and your Mum is quite a seamstress," she said as she gave both the clothing and the man in them a good visual inspection.

"Thank you, you are most kind." He replied, his voice carrying with it a nervous air.

With that the night and its silence overtook the pair. Mary put her hands behind her back and stared upwards towards the distant stars while he placed his hands back into his pockets and fidgeted somewhat anxiously as he looked back towards the main doors of the town hall, convinced that at any moment someone would be along to look for them, discovering them together and quite unsupervised. Realising the potential for untold trouble should they be discovered together, even though there was precious little going on beyond a good scare and some idle chatter, he thought it best to take any further conversation into the hall and, more importantly, into the public eye before something unsavoury could unfold.

"Would you like to go inside and get some food?" He asked making a hand gesture towards the double doors of the white clapboard building.

She looked in the direction he was indicating with a less than interested expression upon her face before turning her gaze out towards the roadway that led off into the forest.

"I would much prefer to go for a walk with you, if I spoke the truth." She replied quietly.

Running his fingers through his long black hair, his eyes tried to follow hers and to what she might be fixing on beyond the curve in the road. Unable to see what it might be but certain there was nothing, he put forth his misgivings regarding her suggestion.

"Really Mary, I do not think that would be such a prudent thing to do given the situation. If someone were to find out that we were together, alone, out in the dark, it could quickly become something quite shameful for both our families."

She returned her eyes to his accompanied with the faintest of smiles.

"You are a true gentleman Aremis, of that there is no doubt, but I truly wish to go for a walk. So you go back inside now and do what is expected of you and I will be along shortly to officially meet you for the first time."

She gave him a little wink and with that headed off towards the darkness that lay beyond the reach of the town hall lights.

The Harvest moon that had risen earlier that night, bold and red, was now high in the sky and, having lost most of its rouge, was quickly being overtaken by cloud making the roadway that led into the woods all the more gloomy.

"Mary, Mary come back, it is not safe to wander the woods alone at night."

His whispered pleas fell on deaf ears as he watched the pale yellow of her dress slowly engulfed by the night.

Left alone at the foot of the stairs, the sounds of multiple conversations and gay laughter, one overlapping the other as they emanated from within the walls of town hall, he was faced with a horrendous situation. If he did what was socially demanded of him, then he would go back inside and act as though he had not set eyes on her that evening. On the other hand, if he did the chivalrous thing and set off after her, if only to ensure her safety and they happened to be discovered, it would be a difficult thing to try and explain away.

With all that in mind, he knew full well that if he hesitated very much longer she would have so much ground on him that it would be all but impossible to find her in the dark interior of the forest, especially with little in the way of moonlight in the night sky. Without another soul being out on either the street or the veranda, his decision was made. With one last look about to ensue his departure would not be noticed, he bolted down the road at a full run towards the woodlands.

As he rounded the curve in the road, leaving the structures and buildings behind him for the seclusion of the wooded thicket, he called out to her in the hope she would not be much farther ahead of him; but nothing more than his own footfall could be heard. He continued on for another hundred yards until he had reached the stone bridge that spanned the narrow riverbed. Slowly he walked to the centre of the bridge breathing deeply in order to replenish his breath. When he had made the centre point, he called out to her again. Without hearing a reply, he began to call to her repeatedly, each time facing in a different direction, and with each unanswered hail his voice carried with it a more urgent sound. He was about to head off again when he thought he heard a faint reply. Distant it was, but most certainly hers, and he called out again for her to come towards the bridge, then strained his senses for any signs that she might be heading in the right direction. There was a long silence, in which the only sound he could discern was that of his own heart beating. He was about to hail again when at last he heard her call back, this time much closer. A wave of relief passed over him as he leaned against the stone wall of the bridge. He remained like that, unmoving, until the sound of another's approach sounding upon the bridge deck did cause him to look up from his survey of the blackened riverbed below.

"You scared the life out of me, dear lady."

She did not reply but continued her path towards him, a pleasant smile upon her face. When she had almost reached him, he turned to face her and she placed her arms around his body pulling him close to her, burying her face into his shirt.

Already shaken and unsettled by the events of the night, her less than appropriate behaviour now had him react in a stern manner.

"Mary, please, take hold of yourself, have you taken leave of your senses?" His voice was tempered and stern, his hands taking hold of her shoulders in an attempt to pry her away but she refused to relinquish her hold of him instead pulling him tighter to herself.

From within his layers of clothing he heard the muffled voice quietly pleading with him to simply hold her for a few moments, as she was quite frightened of the impending marriage to someone whom she barely knew.

It was a plea he could not easily deny for he himself had spent much time worrying and wondering about the same thing and so released the grip on her shoulders, letting his hands fall about her torso.

Despite the several layers he was wearing, her body felt cold and he found himself gently rubbing her back in an attempt to drive out the night's chill and instil some warmth into her before she took ill from the damp.

They remained like that, all but motionless in the solitude offered up by the night's dark veil, and even though having her in his arms felt nicer than anything he had experienced in his short twenty years, he was more than concerned about the time and their conspicuous absence. He was certain that if they were gone for much longer, members of their families would most certainly notice their absence, if they had not already.

"Mary," he whispered, not truly wanting to end the embrace, "Mary, please, we must not be foolish here. There is far more at stake than just you and I. Please, we must return to town before we are missed."

She reluctantly moved within their mutual embrace, freeing her lips from the muzzling affects of his shirt.

"You are too, too responsible Aremis, but then I suppose that is a good thing to have in a husband. Just one kiss and I will allow you lead me back to town." Her voice was soft and alluring, yet all the while retaining an unassuming innocence about it.

"Mary..." he again urged but was cut off.

"Just one, and we can go, I promise. I will not, in all likelihood be alone with you again before our wedding night and want to know your lips before I leave this woodland."

If the truth were to be known, he too felt as she, despite the stressful circumstances he found himself to be in. The idea of a stealing a kiss in a woodland dark held with it the romance the like told of by poets and writers.

"Fine, just one and we go back." He said in the most authoritative voice he could muster.

He released his hold of her as he felt her do the same. She slipped her hands under his coat and ran them up his chest letting let the tip of her nose trace a path out through the lace ruffles of his shirt to where the collar met his skin.

Her nose felt cold on his neck and he found himself unconsciously placing his arms around her shoulders in a feeble attempt to once again guard her against the chilly autumn night. He felt her nose round the tip of his chin and glide over his lips and onto his cheek. Her lips were cool and soft as she pressed them gently against his.

Having nothing in the way of practice in the delicate art of intimate courting, it was all he could do not to pull away from the sensual spell that was being woven over his lips. A passionate heat was slowly building inside him, its very existence being something that of which he had wondered about throughout his adolescent years, having witnessed only staunch distant relations between his parents as well as other married couples he had encountered.

As he returned the oral caress, he felt her lips open slightly, the tip of her tongue softly caressing his upper lip playfully searching for his. Against his better judgement, something that seemed to be very much commonplace this particular night, he let her in and met her with eager exhilaration.

Lost for many moments in both mind and body, her kisses slipping from his mouth and onto his neck laying one passionate kiss upon another as his bated breath became more and more abandoned.

"Mary, this is more than one... We must get back..."

She did not answer his continued requests for them to return to the village square, nor would he have the opportunity to ask again.

A painful cry rang out through the forest, a sharp shrill that pierced the night before quickly diminishing into nothing more than gurgle of a man drowning in his own blood. Cut clean through by fangs, quick and sharp, this throat laid open as if done by the keenest blade of a surgeon's scalpel.

His own heart now acting like a willing accomplice to the murderous attack, the rhythmic action that once sustained his life now pumped his life's blood like a crimson river into her mouth until he was too weak to fight her off any longer, his own weight too heavy to remain against the stone wall of the bridge.

Like a dog finished with the carcass of the rabbit freshly caught, she let him fall free of her support and watched without emotion as his near lifeless body slumped to the ground. The torrent of blood now slowed to nothing more than a trickle, formed a rivulet down his neck, and pooled into the dirty roadway beneath the gaping wound.

His legs twitched whilst his hand reached out towards the village as if the action could somehow pull someone to his aid.

She remained where she was, unmoving, as she watched his weak futile struggle, his fingers clutching and clawing into the stone road vainly trying to pull himself to safety. Her fascination with his efforts lasted but a few moments until, thoroughly bored with it, she stepped over him straddling his body as it lay on the ground. She remained like that momentarily before she kicked him onto his back and plunked herself upon his chest, her knees on the ground to either side of him. She reached out to his face and taking him by the chin, turned him so she might look on his features one last time while he still had life within him. She lowered her body forward so her face was but inches from his, then with lips still slick with blood she carefully kissed his quickly drying lips as she placed her hand over the gash in his neck temporarily stopping the flow from his body.

Satisfied for the moment, both in her passion and her appetite, she maintained the controlling posture she commanded above him. She wiped the smudged blood from his lips with her fingers which she then brought to her mouth, licking the ruby syrup from each of her fingers one at a time, not unlike that of a child taking great pleasure in licking melted ice cream from their fingers on a hot summer's day.

"You truly are a good man, Aremis," she began, her voice very much matter of fact, "I did mean what I said." She paused, suddenly preoccupied with his hair, playfully pushing it back from his face, combing it back with her fingers, "I would have indeed married you had you asked me."

She cast a sideways glance towards the blackened wilderness before returning her attention to her dying audience of one.

"That girl you were supposed to marry next year, you would not have liked her. A tiny, weak little thing. Hardly someone for the likes of you."

Again her attention, like a cat, was taken into the forest, this time being captured by the fleeting flight of a night bird as it negotiated its way through the woods.

"Ah but then you could not have known that," she resumed, "nor did you have any say in the matter, you were just doing what you were expected to do. Is that not what you told me? Does it not matter, your feelings, your desires, whether you even love the one who has been chosen for you? Are you not more than that of cattle or hogs being put together by their masters as so to produce the best offspring?"

She adjusted her position upon his chest causing a laboured exhalation to be forced out of her victim. Still holding his chin, she gripped it tighter shaking his head slightly from side to side.

"Does it not make you ill, to always be doing that which is thrust upon you with little, if any, say in the matter?"

Her voice carried with it a more agitated tone as she carried on with her lecture.

"I should tell you that it was her idea in actuality, the one regarding your marriage, she told me of it. When I killed her parents I had simply intended to kill her last, once I had looted her family's belongings of course, but then she kept blathering on and on about having to meet you at the town hall, something about her wedding day. Honestly!"

She threw one hand out to the wind in a mocking gesture of disbelief, "a wedding day at night, she was obviously insane. But it did get me to thinking, that perhaps if you were such a gentleman, as she had indicated, then just perhaps I could sway your attentions to the likes of me over that of a dead bride."

She leaned forward so that she was once again positioned directly over his mouth and then with a single enlarged canine fang positioned in such a fashion as to have her lower lip effectively trapped between its lethal point and her lower row of teeth, she squeezed her jaws together puncturing her lip clean through. As she released the grip in her jaws and let the porcelain dagger slip from the fresh self-inflicted wound, a pool of her own blood bubbled forth spilling out over her lip and onto her chin. As the blood continued to run freely from the newly opened hole, she lowered her face to his, taking his deathly cold lips to her own, letting the blood flow into his mouth. Through his choking sounds she continued the chilling kiss of death, not stopping until she too grew weak.

Breaking the kiss and pulling back slowly, a thin string of blood mixed with saliva still joining the two. Taxed by distance and the physics that govern its molecular structure, it finally collapsed, falling across his already bloody chin. She let herself slide off his body, gravity her only assistant and on hand

and knee she returned to the stone wall of the bridge where she propped herself up against it.

Wiping the blood from her face with a sleeve of the dress, a dress which she had stolen from her previous victim, she let her head fall into her hand. With her head supported, her elbow resting upon an upturned knee, she remained all but motionless, nestled between the body of her newfound interest and the wall of the bridge.

With the once brilliant moon now muted by cloud, she spoke to the unmoving body stretched out before her.

"You see, my dear Aremis, all this time you have been gone and no one comes looking for you. You worry far too much for those who seem to care little for your well-being."

Standing up, her legs shaking beneath her, she looked down upon him.

"You shall either die here this morning or you will recover much the way I did. The choice is not up to you in a conscious sense but will hinge on how strong your will to live is. I would take you with me and would see to your recovery best I could. Alas, I fear that I have underestimated how drained I would be in the attempt to keep you from slipping into the Reaper's icy grip. I am sure, as you have so well convinced me, that those who love you so, will soon find you, just as I am certain they will find those poor souls who were not as fortunate as you but a few miles from here."

With that, she knelt down and pressed her lips to his for a last kiss. A moment later she was gone, having crested the bridge wall and disappeared into the blackness of the ravine.

Chapter 2

Ellingham, much like any other outlying village, had experienced its share of animal attacks in the past but nothing anywhere near the likes of this gruesome discovery. Because the bodies were discovered largely intact, that is to say their flesh did not appear to have been eaten, it seemed as though there had been no purpose behind the attacks. This sparked worry and rumour that an animal of ill mind might be wandering the woods, thus several hunting parties were sent out each night for more than a week, all of which returned without a prize.

Aremis was going to be the only eye witness to what may have actually happened that night, providing he could survive the next few days and eventually recover from what could very easily turn out to be fatal wounds. With doctors and hospitals both few and far between, most being established within the big cities such as London, small hamlets and villages were considered to be most fortunate if they had within their populous a practicing physician and more so if that doctor had in any way up-to-date education.

In an attack such as this, the outcome would more times than not be fatal. The enormous amount of blood loss from such a neck wound would be the first serious issue. Injured and weak, the victim would have little to rely on beyond that of their own battered body to mend itself and slowly replenish the depleted blood supplies, completely unassisted by medical intervention.

Shock would be the next weapon in the Reaper's deathly arsenal. If the person did manage to survive such a horrific violation, shock usually claimed their mortality very soon after. Inexperienced with shock and its effects, there was little anyone could do for someone suffering massive mortal injuries and quickly slipping into shock. If left untreated, it would quickly claim the injured person.

Infection, however, was usually the deciding factor in the struggle between life and death. When the injuries sustained were cuts or tears that pierced the skin, penetrating deep into the muscular tissue, the body was left open, and vulnerable to bacteria. Bacterial infection was both swift and lethal. This was even more of a threat if the teeth or claws of an animal inflicted those same injuries. The saliva and dirt from the various beasts that were known to prowl the woods were laden with bacteria, and a bacterial infection usually carried with it a death sentence.

True to her statement, the bodies of the slain Smith family were found only two miles from the bridge where Aremis' body was left barely alive. The horses, unharmed, were still tethered to the blood-spattered wagon about a mile from where the family had been discovered. Their throats, like that of Aremis, had all been ripped open and their bodies left where they succumbed to whatever had attacked them. Mary, their only child and daughter, was the only exception, her body being located in the woods some several hundred yards from the roadway where the bodies of her parents had been found. Mary was clad only in her meagre under things, her outer clothing apparently torn from her by the animal that had attacked her. It would later come to be assumed that she had tried to flee into the woods whilst her parents were attacked but that her attempt was quite obviously unsuccessful.

There were only a few noticeable differences between that of the attack on the Smith family and that of Aremis, other than the obvious; one was alive while an entire family lay dead. All of the Smiths seemed to exhibit evidence of defensive wounds, both to their hands and arms, as well as having significantly more facial marring. Aremis, on the other hand, had only the single devastating wound to his neck; there were no other marks to be found anywhere on his body.

Eventually people grew to accept that Aremis had, like the Smith's, simply been in the wrong place at the wrong time. His life that unfortunate night perhaps saved, if but for the time being, by an act of God or possibly by nothing more than coincidence. The commotion of the approaching searchers calling out for him as they went may well have frightened off what ever had been at the heart of these horrific attacks.

In Ellingham they were fortunate to have within their citizenship one resident doctor who both lived and worked from his home just on the outside the main village. Taken to the doctor's house, Aremis was made as comfortable as possible in the living room, which at times such as these, served as the main medical suite. The bodies of the Smith family were taken to a room upstairs to await a decision on whether the local authorities felt a more thorough investigation was in order.

For the next three days, Aremis lay feverish and unconscious. His younger sister Temperance remained at the doctor's house, helping to change the dressing and continually wiping his brow with a cold cloth in an attempt to control the fever that burned beneath his skin.

Temperance was only 18 years of age, tall with long sandy hair, possessing both her mother's delicate features and her love of God. But even with all of her female attributes, she carried with her, seemingly right from her mother's womb, the fortitude of her father and, when provoked, his temper. Not many would care to tangle with either of the elder Eilbeck females under the best of circumstance. But beyond her outward appearance and potential fiery disposition, Temperance also possessed something quite removed from that of the ordinary, something that set her apart from that of her parents and siblings, a characteristic that would not readily be seen by any one person who might look upon her either in passing or under close scrutiny.

Ever since she was but a girl barely under her own steam, she had become aware of things that others in her family did not see or hear. She also became acutely conscious that it was best to keep such things to herself or incur the scorn of her parents, two God-fearing individuals who looked on such things, the like of hearing voices, talking to beings that no one else could see, or speaking of things not yet having taken place but then come into being just the same as being the work of the Devil.

Temperance, like her brother and her younger sister Iris, lived at home with her parents, tending the needs of farm and family and for the most part living out a normal if a somewhat boring farm life. In fact, this horrid incident involving the Smiths and her brother was the first time Temperance had ever been away from home without her family for more than a day. Dr. Harrington and his wife Agnes had made up a place for her in one of the bedrooms on the second floor, but she had not stayed in it for more than thirty minutes since her arrival in order to freshen up and change her dress. The rest of the time she sat with her brother, holding his hand while reassuring him when he was in the throes of fever, recording her brother's progress within the pages of her diary as she sat in the large wingback chair that stood beside his bed during times when he was asleep.

"You must rest, Temperance." Agnes said with the gentle voice of a concerned mother.

"It's alright Mrs. Harrington, I am quite fine, I assure you I am. I would not sleep if I were to go to bed now. Besides, he would be so alone and I would not like him to awaken, even for a moment, and not have any idea if he was safe or where he was. If it would be alright, Ma'am I would like to remain here."

Agnes smiled with an all-knowing glow of kindness, for she knew any further requests for the young woman to heed her advice and take her rest would fall upon deaf ears.

"Alright child, but you will be of no use to any of us if you become ill as well. I will be along shortly with some tea for you."

"Thank you Ma'am, that would be very nice," she replied as she adjusted the bed linens around her brother's chest.

When Agnes had left the room and gone off to the kitchen to set the kettle to boil, Temperance gently pulled the dressing away from the wound on her brother's neck, a devastating hole that, when he was discovered on the bridge not more than a few days previous, was as wide as the palm of her hand and deep enough that she could see both bone and ligament with clear definition. Today, however, the gaping chasm looked to be much cleaner and there was some evidence that scar tissue had begun to form about the edges of the wound.

"Oh Aremis, you are doing so well," she whispered as she let the edge of the bandage back down over her brother's neck, "I am so proud of you, keep your faith in God and you will soon be well again. I can feel it, and I will be here for you when you awaken."

Remaining steadfast to her word, maintaining her daily and nightly vigil beside her brother only leaving to eat or relieve herself, it was indeed rare to find a moment in which she was not by his side.

The week since the attack had taken place seemed to have vanished as though time itself had swallowed up the days and nights whole, effectively erasing them from existence. And although Aremis' fever had for the most part subsided, he remained unconscious and non-responsive to any form of stimulus. Despite the discouraging lack of response, no one who saw him could discount the healing that was now more than evident. A wound that was once as deep as it was wide not a full week earlier was now considerably smaller, and although still a long way from what anyone would see as being completely healed, it was certainly well on its way to mending itself.

The authorities had come by earlier in the day. Two uniformed constables from London had arrived at the house along with the local lawman, Daniel Hares. Agnes had answered the door and with polite introduction all around, the three representatives of the law were invited in. Agnes had gone upstairs to retrieve Dr. Harrington while the three men stood in the hallway before the entrance to the living room. Temperance levelled a heavy gaze in the direction of men, her ivy green eyes looking more like coal than anything resembling the shining emeralds that usually graced her face. It was a most protective look, one that had the policemen look away and talk quietly amongst themselves in short order.

Dr. Harrington soon joined the men in the front hall and, after a brief exchange; the four men entered the makeshift hospital room. Leading the way, Dr. Harrington came around the bed to where Temperance had been sitting on the edge of the chair and in a soft-spoken manner asked her if she would please leave while they went about their business with her brother. Although the request was put to her as a question, she knew well that it was not and there would be little to be gained by arguing the point. Reluctantly doing as was asked of her, she stubbornly chose to remain just outside the doorway, unwilling to abandon her elder sibling entirely to the company of strangers, whom she felt did not love or care about his well-being as she did.

Finished with the visual inspection of his neck, they turned their attention to his hands, (his fingernails to be precise), then seemingly not able to find that which they were seeking, replaced the blankets and once again spoke quietly amongst themselves before leaving the room and making their way upstairs.

When the men had passed, Temperance returned to her brother's bedside taking hold of his hand, quietly reassuring him that things would be fine, that he would soon be well and going home. She could hear the heavy footsteps of police boots on the floors above and she could picture where each of the men were as they made their way from one body to the next. They had not been upstairs very long before they returned and, thanking the doctor, made their way out. One constable stopped just before leaving and gave her what she interpreted as a caring smile, tipping the rim of his hat before he left.

It was a small gesture but one done out of kindness and she appreciated it. She had often heard tell of the police in London having little time for folks out in the rural areas, looking on them as something of a nuisance when they had to be summoned from the comforts of the big city in order to see to things that the law demanded they investigate. It was not until some time later that same day did she find out by way of Dr. Harrington that the police agreed with the findings of Daniel and himself. The physical evidence along with the statements collected from those involved led them to quickly accept that the deceased and the lone survivor, her brother, had been the unfortunate victims of an attack by an animal the identity of which had yet to be discovered.

It seemed logical enough. Mr. Smith still had his billfold with money still in it along with his pocket-watch; a gold one at that, and his wife still had her wedding band, also of gold. If the attacks had been the work of a highwayman or the likes, surely after botching such a caper would he not then go for the spoils? The only thing that was never recovered was Mary's dress and that was simply not given much consideration beyond that it was missing. Most people just assumed that it was likely the garment had simply been ripped from the body during the attack. It could also be reasoned that if the dress was blood- soaked much like that of her mother's and father's clothing, then it may have simply been carried off by a smaller creature, such as a fox after the initial attack had taken place.

Either way, the case was closed by both the local police as well as those who had travelled from London, and that worry being laid to rest meant that it was one less thing for Temperance to concern herself with. She was relieved the city police were gone and even more so that they did not wish to speak to her directly regarding the attacks. Although she felt certain she would have been able to offer up little more than what everyone already knew, the idea of being questioned about her brother had not been sitting well with her.

The hour was late and the Harrington's had already said good night and retired to their room on the second floor. She thought it odd they could sleep, seemingly without care, in the same house with three dead people one room from their own, but then she sat directly under those very same bodies without very much thought of it either.

It was well past 2:00 a.m. when she was awakened from a light sleep in the chair that had become her bed for the last six days. Her brother was once again writhing in his unconsciousness, lashing out feebly at unseen attackers and uttering sounds from a severely damaged throat, sounds that seemed quite unnatural. She had become accustomed to these nightly episodes and having regained her senses she took hold of his hands and pressed them gently back down to his chest.

"Shhh, Aremis, everything is alright. You are quite safe. You are with me, Temperance. I am here with you now, you are fine, just relax and sleep."

Her soft words gradually overtook the indecipherable sounds that had been struggling to make their way free from his throat until, after a few moments, he was both still and quiet once more.

Straightening the blanket he had weakly tossed about, she tucked it back in and readjusted his pillow. She kissed his forehead and looked down at his face, his long dark hair, a sharp contrast against his skin, which was so pale that not even the amber glow of the oil lamp could warm its appearance.

"You will be well soon, I will see to it," she whispered as she continued to look at him. She was about to return herself to the chair when she noticed his eyelids flutter slightly. She lowered her head slightly and whispered his name softly in the hopes of urging him forward from the darkness towards her voice. Suddenly his eyelids flew open revealing two blood red pools, eyes without defining pupils or iris, eyes of a hue most unnatural, void of all expression, lifeless and without soul. They were the eyes of a monster.

Temperance screamed and pulled back in horror, unable to break the stare of her brother's unnatural gaze until finally her legs went from beneath her and she fell to the floor.

Awakened by the screams of their houseguest, Dr. Harrington clambered down the stairs at nearly a full run to see what could have evoked such a harried scream from someone who was usually of stout heart and mind.

Upon entering the room he found her slumped on the floor, her upper body propped against the side of the bed. He came to her side, gently feeling for pulse and, whereupon finding it, gently slapped her face a few time while urging her to come round.

"Come on now young lady, what in God's name frightened you in such a way?" he asked in a caring but firm voice.

As she began to regain her senses she suddenly came into full awareness. Grabbing the doctor's nightclothes, terrified, she attempted through frantic breathing to tell him what she had seen.

"A nightmare my child, nothing more. Come now, there are no monsters in my house, I can assure you of that."

His voice was still firm like that of her father but with a warmth that she did not often hear from the head of her family.

The doctor let her remain on the floor clutching his robes until she had settled enough that he thought she would be able to stand up.

Once standing, with her thoughts more collected, she tried to better explain to her host that which she had seen. The doctor, as comforting as he was, continued to maintain what she had seen could not possibly be real and chalked it up to being a very real dream. The second option put forth pointed the finger of guilt to her own lack of rest, which had simply allowed her to see something that could not possibly have been there. He went on to point out that it was also quite normal for a person suffering such a traumatic injury to have rapid eye fluctuations as well as having the tiny blood vessels within the eye itself rupture. These blood vessels, as small as they were could easily turn the normally white area of the eye bright red. All of this however did little in the way of comforting her so Dr. Harrington took her by the hand and led her to look upon her brothers' face while he turned up the oil lamp. The room filled with a bright light that was far better to see by than the soft glow, which had until that moment, bathed the room in a warm yellow. With Temperance by his side, the doctor gently opened one of her brothers' eyelids, and she jumped at what she felt certain she would see. But as the lid was slowly pulled back there was nothing more frightening than a blue eye centred in small sea of white, a dilated pupil that slowly shrank away in size with the sudden introduction of light.

"Dr. Harrington, I know what I saw, it was evil, it was not my brother, that which lays there now is something else. You must believe me."

"Temperance!" He shouted, shaking her by the shoulders, "I need you to take hold of yourself! There is nothing evil about this man, he is your brother and he most certainly owes his life to you. It is because of your diligent care this last week past that he even has a chance at life and I will hear no more of this. Do you understand me?"

Temperance nodded and allowed the doctor to hug her.

"Come now, you need some sleep. Things will appear much better in the light of day, I assure you."

With that he turned out the lamp and they made their way up the stairs and to their beds.

Chapter 3

Dear Diary,

I know the love I have for Aremis as sure as I know my own reflection in a mirror but that night, the night he first returned to us from the darkness which lay somewhere between this world and the realm beyond death's gates, he brought with him death itself.

I realise as I write this that it sounds but the ravings of one quite mad. All I have to support that without evidence is my other sight, that of which I do not share, that of which has never failed me, nor betrayed me and that same sight now tells me unequivocally that my dearest brother is no longer of this natural earth. I believe so strongly this that in truth I wish with all my heart that he had perished along with the Smiths that terrible night.

I feel as though God has abandoned our family and left us to the wolves of the underworld.

Temperance, the 2ⁿᵈ of October, in the year of our Lord 1874

Temperance awoke to the sun streaming in through the windows filling the tiny bedroom with sunlight that was only slightly diffused by the lace curtains covering the leaded panes. She lay there for several moments trying to regain some of her senses, both of her whereabouts as well as a sense of time before slowly coming to the realisation that she was still at the Harrington's and that is was already well into the morning.

Throughout the week previous, she had been up with her brother for what would amount to a better part of the night. In fact this would be the first time the bed that had been prepared for her had actually been slept in since her arrival. She pulled the covers back releasing her body from the downy warmth and swung her legs out into the cool air of the room. Sitting up on the edge of the bed she took in the room through bleary eyes, taking notice of a fresh pot of warm water sitting in the face bowl upon the dresser. With a mind not quite willing to respond, it took her a moment to realise that it must have been Agnes who had brought it in some time earlier that same morning. It made sense even though she had no recollection of the woman having ever entered the room. This fact, along with what would appear to be a late morning hour only lent itself to the undeniable fact that she had been in dire need of sleep.

Taking comfort in the knowledge that Agnes would have already seen to her brother, she took advantage of the hospitality offered. Still in her dress from the previous day, she disrobed and with a soft towel, moistened in the warm water, began to wash.

Through the mindless act of washing she carefully pondered the events of the previous night with a somewhat fresh mind. Silencing her feelings for the most part, she found it difficult to dispute what Dr. Harrington had said and, even if somewhat reluctantly, had to agree that what she may have actually seen last night was nothing more than an illusion brought on by lack of sleep.

She set the small face towel neatly over the side of the bowl, then, cupping her hands, she splashed her face with the water that remained. She collected one of the dry towels from the side rail, padding the droplets of water from her face. Pulling the towel away from her eyes, intent on setting it over the rail where she had retrieved it from, she caught within the reflection of the mirror that was before her the image of her brother standing directly behind her.

His mouth appeared to be open slightly, lips and chin both covered in blood that ran from the opening, the red stain continuing down his throat onto his chest soaking through the nightclothes so that they clung to his skin. Her voice was strangled by her own fear and not a sound escaped her throat as she spun around in the tiny room clutching the towel over her bare chest as she did.

Expecting to be face to face with a monster, one that in all likelihood had already killed the Harrington's, nothing more frightening than the room's meagre furnishings greeted her terror-filled eyes. Frantically she scanned the tiny room for any evidence of the intruder she had just witnessed within the looking glass but without success. Not until several minutes had painstakingly passed did she cautiously accept that she was alone. The horrifying image she had seen must have been nothing more than a deception played out by a tired mind. Even though the room was quite empty, it did little in the way of quelling the feelings of dread that had returned, slowly peeling away any optimism that she had for the day that lay before her.

She removed a fresh dress and chemise from the hanger, part of her meagre wardrobe that she had brought with her from home when she had agreed to stay with the Harrington's, and laid them out on the bed. She looked about the room in an uneasy manner before convincing herself to drop the towel that she had, until then, kept tightly wrapped around herself and hurriedly dressed.

Straightening the bed quickly, she collected both her clothing along with the wash water, making her way from the room along the hallway to the back staircase and down to the kitchen.

Agnes was busy boiling the bed sheets in a large pot, which sat on the wood-burning stove at the back of the large kitchen where, upon seeing Temperance arrive at the foot of the stairs, she smiled and came to greet her.

"Well, you finally managed to get some rest." She said with chipper voice, "Here, let me have those things; I have the laundry well under way."

Temperance relinquished her dirty clothing to her hostess then let herself out the back door and into the cool air of the morning to dispose of the wash water. The fresh crisp air of the season set a shiver upon her and after dumping the waste-water into the grasses she set the bowl on the steps so that she could remain outside drawing in a breath of fresh air.

Even though the day was new and the air indeed revitalizing, she could not shake the feelings she had pertaining to the previous night or of the morning's disturbing vision within the mirror. She would have little time to process either of them however as Agnes poked her head out the back door, obviously aware of her guest's lengthy absence.

"You will catch your death out there dressed like that, my dear." Agnes warned in a motherly fashion. "Come back in and fetch your coat, or better yet, come in altogether, I have some breakfast set out for you."

Agnes had made porridge and had added her own touch of applesauce and brown sugar to create not only a hearty morning meal but a wonderful aroma within the kitchen. As Temperance ate, she pondered the idea of whether or not to share with her hostess the events of last night but after much personal deliberation she decided against it. Realising that Dr. Harrington had, in all likelihood, already told his wife of the events surrounding the previous evening there would be little if any point in attempting a retelling of the same events from her own perspective. She did not wish to have another chastising from someone her senior for entertaining such foolish notions. So, unwilling to run the risk of an uncertain reaction from Mrs. Harrington, she wisely chose to remain on safer topics such as the laundry and Dr. Harrington's rounds for the day.

When Temperance had finished her late morning breakfast, she offered to do the dishes but Agnes shooed her off telling her to check in on her brother. If the truth be told, Temperance would have willingly switched tasks with Mrs. Harrington for the idea of being alone with her brother in the other room set fear upon her heart. She knew it would be a moot point to try and present a case for the trading of the duties, so, she reluctantly accepted that which was to be and made her way from the kitchen, down the hallway that led to the front living area.

Unlike all the other mornings, when she awoke after willingly spending the night in the same room as her brother, she cautiously poked her head around the corner of the doorway, surveying the room and its lone inhabitant from the safety of the hallway. She watched intently as her brother lay motionless on the bed, the blankets having been pulled down and neatly folded over his chest, the result of Mrs. Harrington's care sometime earlier in the morning. Remaining at the entranceway, motionless and quiet, she tried to force the images from the previous night from her mind while she continued to monitor the rhythmic rise and fall of his chest.

So, with her courage as fortified as it was going to get, she quietly entered the room and made her way across the floor until she was at his bedside. There, with her fear bottled up tightly inside her, she looked down upon his face, much as she had done the night before. This time, though, her casual gaze of his facial features revealed nothing more sinister than the face she had come to recognise combined with his continued breathing. Unable to bring herself to open his eyelids for fear of what she might find beneath them, it was with great reluctance that she took up what had become her regular post within the red wingback chair beside his bed.

Once seated, but far from relaxed, she remained near statue-like, sitting bolt upright, her eyes riveted on the rhythmic rise and fall of his chest accompanied by the sound of his breath as it entered and left his body. She remained in this frozen-like state for a long period of time refusing to drop her guard should there be sudden cause to flee. But as the minutes slowly wore on with little in the way to substantiate her fears, she felt a calm slowly beginning to return to her.

With a quiet exhalation, a breath that she felt certain she had been holding since having first entered the room, she removed the Bible from the table that stood at the bedside and opened to the page she had marked the night before. She carefully read over the text to herself, taking solace in the printed words that lay upon the pages.

When she had finished her own reading of the pages, much of which pertained to the Divine Hand of God healing those inflicted with disease and strife, she turned the pages back to where she had begun. Standing up in order that her voice might be more easily heard without having the entire house bear witness to her unpractised sermons, she read aloud, quietly going over that which she had just read, her voice rising and falling where she deemed it appropriate in order to emphasize their importance.

When she had finished she turned her eyes upwards towards a heaven that lay above and beyond the man-made roof of wood and plaster, then following a few moments of silent prayer, turned her gaze towards the windows and to the sunlight that filtered though the pine trees in the front yard.

A longing look to the world beyond the room, she reflected on better times. But the reverie was short; she felt a hand come to rest on her hip. In a reactive state, her actions governed by survival instincts only, she flung the black book to the floor and pulled back from the bed certain she would be face to face with the creature she had seen the night before. What she saw, however, was not a monster belonging to the Devil's realm, but the face of her brother, his blue eyes looking upwards at her from within darkened eyelids set in alabaster skin.

Her fear still tight within her chest she continued her retreat from the bed, his weak grip on her dress falling away as she did, his hand dropping back unheeded onto the sheets. She continued her recoil from the bedside, her hands clamped over her mouth as if to stifle any scream that might try to escape. She watched her brother's eyes follow her with saddening bewilderment before they closed and blocked out that which he could not understand or bear to see.

Temperance stood, her back pressed against the stone mantle of the fireplace, her hands still in place over her mouth, her eyes wide and unblinking as she watched the now motionless body of her brother. She remained too frightened to move or speak, and unable to leave or to investigate further. But with nothing more frightening than what had been a distressed expression upon her brother's face forthcoming, she turned her eyes from the bed to the book that lay tossed upon the floor. Seeing the Lord's word displayed in such a manner had her quickly forgetting her fears and retrieving it from where it had landed.

Clutching the book to her chest, perhaps in the hopes of instilling the very word of God into her own being, she made her way the few slight steps back to the bedside and with much trepidation she took his hand as she had countless times over the course of the week and whispered his name.

His eyes blinked open and for the first time she saw her brother.

Still holding his hand, she lay herself over him supporting her own weight on the sides of the bed, hugging without so much as touching him. Her tears came quickly and soon had dampened his bed shirt as she told him, through a voice filled with emotion, how the whole family had thought him lost. Her emotional outpouring however was quickly brought into check when she heard him trying to speak. She knew first hand of the devastation to his neck and throat for she had seen it for herself.

She quickly pulled herself up from him, placing a finger over his lips.

"No, no, no, shhhh, you must not try to speak. It is far too early and you are far from being well enough." She said, her now voice firm but still traced with emotion.

"Mrs. Harrington, please come right away I need you!" she shouted over her shoulder in the direction of the kitchen.

Temperance reached over to the fresh hand towel and dipping into to water she let it absorb what it could before removing it. Placing it over his lips she gently squeezed the towel in her hand forcing the water from the fabric and into his mouth.

Mrs. Harrington, upon hearing the urgent call came into the room all flushed still wiping her hands off on her apron.

"Whatever is it child?" she said as she entered but did not need to wait for an answer to be provided as she saw the scene unfolding before her.

"My good Lord in heaven," She exclaimed as she rushed to the bedside. "Not too much now dear, you do not want to drown him."

Temperance withdrew the cloth and stood back to give the elder lady room to work.

"Aremis lad, do you know you what happened?" Mrs. Harrington asked with as much calmness as she could muster.

She watched as his eyes searched the ceiling for the answer and then gently and without much motion shook his head from side to side within the support of the pillow.

"What is your name, lad, do you know who you are?" The housewife/nurse urgently inquired.

This time came a positive response in the form of an agreeing head motion and darting eyes towards Temperance.

"Is this your wife, then lad?" She asked.

Aremis smiled slightly at the thought then moved his head from side to side.

"Please Mrs. Harrington, enough; he knows who he is, it is quite obvious," Temperance's agitated voice bordering on the edge of annoyance.

"Alright then, alright, fetch me some pillows from the closet in the hallway and we will see if we can get him sitting up a might."

Temperance dashed off and returned with the pillows as had been requested of her and the two women carefully lifted and adjusted the bed and the man in it until he was in a more seated position.

Once Agnes was certain he was comfortable she leaned over to Temperance and under her breath she whispered, "He looks half starved. I have some soup on the stove."

She left the room for the kitchen in order to retrieve some broth, leaving her aide in charge with her brother now awake for the first time in just over a week.

With her fear now all but erased from her thoughts, she stood by the bedside smiling from ear to ear at being able to see her older brother actually looking back at her.

At first she did not quite know what to say which seemed odd since she had spoken to him every night and day for the last seven without him uttering a word in response. It was just that now she had to be mindful of what she said as she knew he would have limited abilities in which to respond to her. Suddenly the thought that his voice might in some way be permanently damaged and that he may never be able to speak again had her once again in a tearful exhibition. She felt his hand on hers and she looked down at his quizzical expression.

"Oh, do not concern yourself with me. I am just being silly. Do you not know me by now?" she replied as she squeezed his hand in return before regaining most of her composure.

"In all truthfulness, Aremis, do you not remember what happened to you and why you are here at Dr. Harrington's home?"

She watched him strain his memories for a few moments before shaking his head slowly back and forth as he had done before.

"It is probably for the best anyway, when you are stronger I will share with you what I know, and I can assure you, that is not very much."

He smiled at his sister's unintentional double meaning hidden within her last statement, and as she caught site of his mirth she realized, quite quickly, her poor choice of wording, wording which painted her in such a daft light. She pulled her hand back quickly with a prude look upon her face.

"Oh there is nothing whatsoever wrong with this man, Mrs. Harrington, he is most surely my brother, through and through!"

Chapter 4

Dear Diary,

It has been over six weeks now, since the attack, and my brother has been allowed to return home.

Mother and Father came to the doctor's house this morning with the carriage to collect both of us.

Dr. Harrington told me upon my leaving that I would make a fine nurse if I chose to take up the vocation and, if not, then a fine wife I would someday be. He is most flattering.

Aremis has made a remarkable recovery since the attack and everyone who has been by to visit is astonished at his progress. I, having seen the wound from the beginning, am too taken aback at both the rate and degree of healing. I must confess that when I first set eyes upon the wound in all its severity, I felt certain he would not survive but a few days at best. When he had surpassed all expectation and lived on through the week and back into consciousness I was both jubilant and saddened that, although his life now spared, he would remain mute and disfigured the remainder of his days. This too seems as though it will come to pass. Although he struggles to speak as he once did - which leads to no end of frustration for him - he does have much success. As to his wound, a hole once wider than my hand across is now no more than a slight indentation, the new skin still purple and frail, is but the only evidence that still exists.

Try as I may to rejoice in his recovery as others do, there is something I cannot fully reconcile that has me feeling unsettled. I do not know how to describe that which I feel other than to say it is an unsettling sensation where there is no visible cause for such to exist.

Beyond my prayers known but to God, I have shared my thoughts and concerns with no one, for I have nothing more substantial to support my fears. For the moment I feel it would serve little purpose to share that which would surely impact everyone involved based solely on what might well be irrational thinking brought on by nothing more than extraordinarily trying times.

I will however remain vigil. For even though I write in these pages that which I think might not be anything to worry about, a part of me knows well something is not as it should be.

Temperance, the 5th of November, in the year of our Lord, 1874

For the most part, the fall and winter of 1874 were harsh. Cold, wet weather dominated the landscape that lay beneath nearly continual overcast skies and did little to uplift spirits, so to find a winter's day that was both sunny and mild was a delightful change of pace.

It was early afternoon at the Eilbeck residence on just such a day, the mid-day meal having already been served and the dishes subsequently cleared away. Outside, some of the local men in the area had gathered in order to assist Aremis' father, William with the unpleasant task of dealing with the property and belongings of the Smith farmstead. No one in town had disputed the legal documentation that had been drawn up between the Smiths and the Eilbeck's several months before the unfortunate incident.

Aremis had expected that he would be included as he was, both in the community as well as on paper, the husband-to-be of the Smith's only daughter. His father, a stern dark-haired man with chiselled jaw line and chestnut brown eyes, would hear none of it. Even though Aremis had made several passionate pleas throughout the lunchtime meal and again out on the veranda, he had been declined each and every time, the last one delivered in such a way that it left little doubt in either the one it was intended for or those standing within earshot. Though his father was trying to protect him from more unpleasantness after his ordeal and near-death experience, William was a hardened man and did not know how to express himself to his son in a tender way. The verbal rejection came like a blow delivered by that of fist or implement and Aremis recoiled in both the initial surprise and the fear of a verbal exchange possibly escalating into physical altercation with his father.

Satisfied there would be no further debate with his only son on a subject that was closed, William joined the other men, some in wagons, others on horseback, and the small group made their way off in the direction of the Smith farm which had sat abandoned since the night of the attack.

Hardly pleased with the decision but knowing well not to cross his father once he had made up his mind, Aremis paced the length of the veranda in an agitated fashion, his arms folded tightly across his chest.

Temperance, who had been privy to the one-sided discussion from her vantage point behind the curtains of the family room window, now continued her silent vigil watching as her brother walked the weathered boards obviously very much upset at the outcome.

Despite her misgivings pertaining to her brother, she still could not help but feel saddened for the situation he now found himself in. Being unable to remember what took place that terrible night, having his bride-to-be killed, and now, adding insult to injury, to be all but forbidden from taking part in the decisions regarding her family's vacant property; it must have been difficult to cope with.

She knew some of the reasons behind their father's decision not to have his only son accompany him on a grim task but also knew that it would be a pointless endeavour to try and explain them to Aremis at this point. Instead she decided to take an approach of friendship, walking out onto the porch with her apron still on, his coat in one hand and a tea towel in the other.

"Here, put this on. It is far from a spring morning out here," she said handing him the jacket.

He looked at the garment momentarily then reaffixed his gaze in the direction of the road that led to the Smiths.

"Come on," she said in a playful voice, "Do not be like that with me, if you want to brood you have every right to, but not if you catch your death while doing it. I am not about to take to caring for you the rest of my days." She nudged his arm with her elbow as she had so often done as a child when she wanted his attention. With no response she playfully repeated the process until upon the third little jab he turned towards her with a small smile upon his otherwise stern face. Taking the coat from her outstretched hand he folded it over his arm, not willing to actually put it on and validate his sister's concern for him.

She remained unmoving upon the veranda until the cold, combined with her unrelenting stubbornness, had become victorious and he reluctantly pulled on the woollen jacket.

Her mission accomplished she left him to his thoughts, shutting out the cold behind the heavy wooden front door.

Returning to the kitchen, she picked up the laundry basket full of clothes that her mother had brought in from the line earlier, the fabric still stiff with cold from the chilly morning air. Before she had a chance to do much with the heavy load, however, her mother, Evelyn, came in from the front room. Her mother, an older mirror image of her eldest daughter, had her hair down this particular day, the sandy brown flow of hair framing her face in near picturesque fashion. Tall with fair features, no one in the household risked crossing her, and this extended to her husband as well.

"Temperance," she whispered under her breath as she looked about the kitchen, "is your brother still outside?"

Temperance glanced towards the windows to confirm that of which she was all but certain.

"Yes Mum, I just took him his coat." She said in whispered voice not at all sure why it was they were whispering in the first place.

"That will be fine then," she said still whispering and gesturing for her to give up the basket and its contents. "Let me have that basket. I want you to go with him and check on the sheep that have been out in the west field."

Temperance looked at her mother with a quizzical look upon her face.

"Mum?" she questioned.

Taking the basket from her daughter she sat it onto a chair and took her daughter by the sleeve gently pulling her into the family room.

"Look at him," she said pointing towards the window that took in the front porch. "He has lost his memory, his wife-to-be and now his status within this, his very house. You and I both know why his father behaves as he does." She paused looking away, momentarily lost in her own memories of that terrible time a time that had taken its toll on the entire family. Pulling herself from her own thoughts, she continued.

"Please, Temperance, do as I ask of you," she pleaded, "I will be quite fine here with your sister Iris and I know it will do him the world of good to feel like he is contributing again, even if the task is somewhat of a ruse."

There was no real reason to refuse her mother's request. She knew that she was right. But besides it being a ruse as her mother had referred to it being, she also secretly felt that the trip out might afford her some time to try, and with some luck, find out more of what actually took place on the stone bridge that ill-fated night.

Taking leave of her mother she retrieved her coat from the hook in the kitchen and replaced her shoes with footwear better suited for walking the woodland trail to the western field. She then rejoined her brother on the veranda.

"Feel like a walk?" she inquired in a cheery voice.

"No, not particularly," he stammered hoarsely.

"Fine then, if you must persist in being a sloth, I will check on the sheep myself." She quipped as she strode off the veranda and began making her way up the road towards the point in the fence that allowed access to the trail. She had thought about taking the horses and accessing the fields via the roadway but that would require getting saddles and tack and then putting it all away upon their return. However, that aside, the whole purpose of the outing was not to complete it in short order but rather make it one of importance for her displaced brother.

He watched her leave the porch but before she had gone more than a few yards from the house he called after her.

"Temperance wait, you should not go off on your own like that! It is... it... it is not... safe..." His voice trailed off into a deafening silence that engulfed his mind.

Continuing to walk away, she heard his firm warning trail off and she looked over her shoulder half expecting to see her brother in some manner of pursuit. Instead what she saw was not that of her older sibling giving chase but of him leaning on the porch rail, his legs giving way beneath him, one hand holding his head as though gripped in pain. She turned around immediately, running back to the house, arriving at the veranda's edge in time to catch his fall as he dropped to his knees directly in front of her.

"Aremis, what is wrong, what is the matter?" she screamed.

He did not respond to her distraught pleas for information but remained on his knees, both hands now supporting his head, his fingers entwined in his long hair.

"Aremis, please, you are frightening me! Tell me what is wrong!"

With her second request failing, she got up with the intention of retrieving her mother from the house, but before she could leave she felt his hand take hold of the hem of her coat.

"Wait, please, just a minute, please do not leave me..." His voice was low and weak and if not for his hand upon her coat she felt certain she would not have heard him.

Evelyn arrived at the door, alerted by the commotion on the front porch, but Temperance waved her back into the house. For the moment, and so long as he was talking, there was no need to have her mother's worry adding to the crisis.

Her mother closed over the front door at her daughter's urgent request and Temperance knelt down at his side, putting her arm around his shoulder hugging him tightly. They remained like that for some time before he finally spoke.

"I remember something." He said at last, breaking the tense and worrisome silence.

"Oh my dear God, you frightened the life out me," she replied with relief in her voice, "I thought you were having a relapse or the like."

As his breathing began to return to normal, Temperance decided to try and coax this flash of memory into the light of day. Remaining as they were, she rested her head on his shoulder, her arm still around him, as she softly made the inquiry.

"What was it that you remembered?"

There was another long silence, one that had her soon thinking she may have made a choice based on selfish desires and not the welfare of her brother. With an answer not forthcoming she was about to try and change the subject, or at the very least make some attempt at apologising for being so intrusive, when he began to speak.

"There was a woman... she, she was like you, walking away..." He trailed off again as he searched through the fog that separated his splintered memories of that night from that of his conscious mind. Looking for some clue, anything more than what he currently had, some piece, or tiny fragment that might be able to bridge that gap and allow him a more precise view of his missing past.

"What woman, who are you talking about?" Her voice strained by her need to know, she pressed him, perhaps harder than she ought. Frustrated, unable to provide the answers she wanted to hear and ones of which he himself wanted to know, he lashed back at her overly eager inquiry.

"I do not know, damn it! If I did, do you not think I would tell you?"

The sudden outburst and the cussing, both of which were quite out of character, frightened her so much that she recoiled, releasing him as she did so. Standing up she continued to back up several steps, folding her arms across her chest as her own horrifying memories burst into her mind. It was in that briefest of moments that she felt it might well be prudent to leave alone such things that God himself may have deemed better stricken from one's thoughts rather than risk the discovery of something far more unpleasant than a few missing hours in a loved one's life.

The sight of the startled look upon his sister's face, accompanied by her actions, cooled his temper in short order.

"I am so sorry, Temperance, please, forgive me," His tone now more like that which she knew and trusted, he continued on in an attempt to calm his sister and to explain his unusual behaviour.

"I am so frustrated that I am unable to recall my own thoughts, to have my own memories elude me like a rabbit through the thicket, especially when I know so many people have a desire to know what happened that night out in the woods, no one more than myself"

His words, even though compelling, could not erase the feelings that were once again well established within her, feelings and memories of a terrifying night at the Harrington's several weeks prior, an event that had left her questioning both her brother's identity as well as the foundations of her faith itself.

Seeing her unaffected by his apology or his explanation, he turned his eyes from his sister, focussing them instead on the roadway that lay a few feet beyond the fence.

Another silence had erupted between them, and for a few fleeting seconds it seemed as though that was how the day was to end for the two of them, when Temperance broke the quiet stalemate.

"This has been a very trying time for us all, you more than anyone. I want to help you, help you find out what happened out there that night but you have to be patient with me and with yourself." Her voice was quiet and unassuming and she hoped that her words would reach him without enflaming an already volatile situation.

She waited patiently, not sure of what reaction might be forthcoming and not willing to seriously consider reducing the distance she had put between them until she had more certainty.

"You have already done so much, far more than I deserve when I treat you so. Mother has told me as did Dr. Harrington."

She smiled.

"You have been through quite an ordeal, dear brother, nothing more. I am willing to share with you what I know if you promise not to damn yourself for things, those of which the Good Lord may have blocked from your mind with reasons known but unto Him."

Feeling as though he had already done enough damage with his intemperate blasphemies, he remained silent but nodded his understanding, if perhaps not his agreement, to his sister's last statement.

"I am pleased," she said her voice again sounding cheerful, her words belying how she was truly feeling inside. She stepped off the veranda then cautiously waited at the foot of the stairs for him to join her so as not to initiate a repeat of what had just happened. She remained there for several minutes in isolated silence until, with a reluctant smile upon his face, he descended the few steps and stood alongside her.

"That is more like it," she said giving him a quick hug before leading him by the hand towards the opening in the fence, "do you remember when you used to race me to this spot?"

"Yes," he stammered, then coughed, but managed to continue with more clarity than which he had first started out with, "you would cry when I beat you to the finish."

She slapped his arm, the heavily padded woollen jacket absorbing the blow.

"You would hold me back so I could not get past you; that is the only reason you won all the time."

She watched his smile broaden as the comforting childhood memory gently replaced the fragile and fragmented images from a dark and evil night, the details of which were so terrible that God or frail human subconscious saw fit to keep them a secret.

Even though the walk and subsequent empty task of checking on sheep would net her little in the way of information, it would be a good remedy for her brother's down spirits, so much so in fact, that the two of them made the task somewhat of a routine over the next few days. Heading out shortly after breakfast, they would talk as they made their way to whatever field or barn that was to be the destination of day.

In addition to having seen progress in his emotional state, she had also noticed a marked improvement in his voice. He no longer seemed to be struggling in the way he had earlier in the week and at one point he even managed to laugh. For her, thinking back to that day at the Harrington's when she first realised that he might never be able to speak again, to now hear him laugh was nothing shy of a miracle.

About the only oddity that struck her, and her alone, was that even though he was eating much better he did not seem to be gaining any weight. This in conjunction with the fact that he always seemed to be tired had her wondering if would not be prudent to see Dr. Harrington. She had mentioned this idea to both her mother and brother getting, for the most part, similar answers, answers that to her seemed to be underwhelming at best given the severity of the original injuries.

The lacklustre responses by her two closest family members had her seriously wondering if she was the one that ought to be paying a visit to the doctor to inquire if there might well be something amiss within her mind. For whatever all those around her might say and truly believe, she still held fast to the feelings that told her simply that something was not as it appeared to be.

Chapter 5

Dear Diary,

It has now been just over four weeks since Aremis has returned home and although life here seems to have returned to normal, I still have reservations as to whether it actually has.

My brother's voice has returned to him, a blessing to be certain, and he now only stumbles over the occasional word. Both Mother and I worry for his well-being. Even though he does seem to be healthy enough, he has not managed to regain the weight that he had lost during his recovery. This is made more of a concern by his constant complaint of feeling tired. He has told me of being unable to sleep and is troubled by nightmares, but he will not elaborate on what they are about, only that they prevent him from returning to sleep once he has been roused from his slumber.

As to the night of the attack, I have been unable to retrieve any more useful information from him other than that of a woman, a person my brother claims to have seen walking away from him. However, I cannot even be certain that this is something that can be looked upon as factual.

There is something else that I find disturbing but which may also come to be nothing more abnormal than that of nature itself and completely unrelated to my brother.

I had discovered the body of slain sheep in a small wooded area of our property two days ago. I had happened upon it on a morning when my brother had requested to remain in bed, as he was not feeling himself. I went for what had become our routinely morning walk, in order to keep Mother's ruse of checking on the livestock convincing. I had no intention of checking on animals, which, for the most part, tend to themselves and so went to the creek where as children we all used to play. It was there in the undergrowth that I did find it.

This, as I say, might simply be an unfortunate result of straying too far from the flock and falling victim to a predator.

I wish that I could put into words all of the feelings which I have within myself. I find them all quite impossible to sort out much less attempt to describe them in writing.

Temperance, the 6ᵗʰ of December in the year of our Lord, 1874.

Now it could be said that it was rare day indeed that one would see William and Evelyn Eilbeck partaking in a social get-together beyond that of church on a Sunday morning. That having been said, it was not to say they shunned the idea of a social evening with their neighbours, but such a visit was usually reserved for anniversaries and other special occasions. It was, in fact, one of those rare occasions that saw the two of them get dressed in their Sunday best and head off to the Brookes' place, located on the other side of the hamlet, leaving the house in the care of their three children.

Temperance had helped her mother prepare an apple pie earlier in the afternoon with apples preserved from that summer so they would not arrive at their host's home empty-handed. She hoped that they may well stay the night and upon seeing her father carrying out a small overnight bag she knew that it meant that she would not likely be seeing her parents until the following morning after church. Even though she loved her parents dearly, she very much enjoyed the odd times within the span of a year in which they would be away.

Standing on the porch, the night's ebony curtain already draped over the landscape, she cast her thoughts back over the day's events enjoying the fresh memories that came to her through her happy recollections. Her day already off to a good start knowing that her parents would be out for the evening was made even more joyous when her father requested his son's assistance in making ready the horses and carriage for the trip to the Brookes' home. It was something she knew he could have easily managed on is own but may have thought it time for him to set aside his fears and let Aremis begin to take a more active role within daily work routines.

She waved to her parents as she watched the buckboard wagon, its makeshift canvas top set over the single bench seat; disappear around the bend in the road. When it had disappeared completely from view she turned to go back inside and that was when she caught sight of Aremis returning from the barn, a small oil lamp in his hand to guide his step. She held up at the front door and waited for him a wide smile on her face.

"What has put you into smiles?" he inquired as he arrived at the front steps.

"You teamed the horses today." She replied still smiling.

He smiled and even blushed slightly, lowering his head in order to conceal it from her.

"Aremis Eilbeck, are you blushing? Dearest Lord I can now return home knowing that I have truly seen all there is to see." Her hands raised up in prayer-like fashion, her voice full of mirth at her brother's expense.

"He could have managed it, you know it be true. He only did it out of pity."

His words snapped her from her moment on the imaginary stage and that of her little performance.

"Out of pity!" she exclaimed, her hands now set square on her hips, "Is that what you honestly believe?" Her once playful voice now so removed from her words it was as though it had never been there.

Aremis looked about sheepishly for a moment before responding and being cut off before he had even begun.

"Well..."

"Well nothing. I will not stand here and listen to this tripe. You have no idea how this family has suffered. Do you think it is but you and you alone that had been dealt this misfortune? We all thought you lost. Mother was at church everyday praying for your soul. Father hardly spoke a word for fear of breaking down and instead immersed himself in work until he was so exhausted that when he did finally lie down, sleep took him quickly. With God as my witness, I can tell you most solemnly that our father does nothing born from something as lowly as pity, and you, Aremis, should be ashamed for thinking in such a way."

Her words were as cutting as they were accurate and he wished in silence that she had struck him hard upon the face, for the pain from such a blow would have already started to wane.

With little more than his own self-pitying beliefs to support his point of view, he knew that he was not in any position from which to make an adequate stand, especially when confronted with his sister's honesty backed up by her temper. So with victory not possible and no real option of retreat, a truce-offered apology seemed like the only choice left to him. But before he could put his thoughts into action, he watched mutely as Temperance turned abruptly and stormed into the house, slamming the heavy front door behind her.

He remained there, unmoving, for quite some time before finally setting the oil lamp down on the steps and setting himself down along side it. Sitting quietly on the step, his legs drawn up to his chest and his arms wrapped around them, he stared out into the forest that lay beyond the road that ran past the driveway's end, pondering what had just unfolded between himself and his sister. He began to wonder if coming face to face with the spectre of death does not simple impact oneself but that it also impacts those around you as well, sparing not even the ones who love you most.

He shook his head as if to dislodge the very thoughts from his mind. There could be nothing that could cast doubt, in either word or action, on that of the love his family had for him.

With little left to do outside besides more thinking, he turned out the lamp and set it up on the veranda behind him before making his way back into the house to meet whatever cool reception might be waiting there.

Upon hearing his entry Iris called out to him from the kitchen.

"I made tea, would you fancy a cup?"

Unable to be certain as to whether Temperance had told her of what had just transpired outside and not wishing to make an enemy of his youngest sister, he quickly accepted the offer with as much grace as he could muster before he had even entered the kitchen.

"Thank you, yes, that would be lovely."

He hung his coat onto one of the five hooks that were mounted on the wall by the back door then plunked himself, unceremoniously, into one of the wooden chairs that were set about the large kitchen table. He folded his hands together and placed them in his lap as he watched Iris warm two cups with the steaming water from the kettle.

Noticing that there were only two teacups out on the counter, he inquired gingerly as to whether Temperance would be joining them, knowing full well what the answer would be given the state of mind she was in when she left him on the veranda.

Iris looked over her shoulder at him with a half smile upon her face before she returned her attention to the task at hand.

"No, I think she will be choosing to remain in her room tonight if I know her at all." She replied.

Iris, while shorter than her older sister, still retained all of her facial features and if not for the height and age differences (two years in the case of Temperance and Iris) it might prove difficult to distinguish all three of the Eilbeck women from one another.

Momentarily at a loss for words, he looked about the kitchen aimlessly in the hopes of finding something new to discuss hidden within the all too familiar surroundings.

Iris brought the tea to the table on a small wooden serving tray, the edges of which were decorated with ornate vines and pristine pink flowers hand painted by their grandmother years before. She set the tray with its consignment of tea, milk and sugar along with two small spoons upon the table, then pulled out a chair closest to her brother and took a seat beside him.

"You do look pale," she said in a concerned voice that easily belied her young years. "Perhaps Tempie is right, you ought to consider seeing Dr. Harrington in the morning."

She stirred a teaspoon of sugar into his tea and then followed it with a splash of milk. When the ingredients were evenly mixed within the confines of the porcelain chalice, she removed it from the tray, complete with saucer, and placed it before her brother.

Aremis unlocked his fingers and ran them through his hair, combing the loose locks back from his face as he did.

"I am fine, truly, I am simply tired, nothing more. You both worry far too much. Based upon how you both carry on so, I figure the two of you shall make fine mothers some day."

Iris shot him a dirty look as she began to dress her own tea.

"That may well be true, but I do not hear you raising complaint about my making your tea the way you like it now, do I?"

He smirked at her comment than laughed slightly despite his best efforts to conceal it.

"No, no you most certainly do not, that is true enough," he replied his voice still carrying with it the humour caused by his sister's quick retort.

"I must confess, Iris," he began, the mirth that had been so prevalent in is previous words being replaced by a tone more worrisome, "I have in truth been feeling a bit queer the last few days, not sick per-se, just, well not like myself, and frankly have no clue what to make of it."

He picked up the teacup and gently sipped the warm beverage, letting its aromatic flavour fill his senses. His confession of not feeling well now out, he felt certain that in less than a moment he was going to find himself on the receiving end of another scolding from yet another female, all within an uncomfortably short period of time.

Iris, like her older brother, had just taken her first sip of tea while she listened to him attempt to explain away her fears, the conclusion of which did little in the way of setting her worries to rest. Gently setting her teacup down, she reached across to him she touched his arm and softly rubbed it through the heavy cotton work shirt.

"Have you even stopped for one minute and allowed yourself to grieve?" she asked in a soft-spoken voice.

Perplexed by her inquiry, he too set his tea down but chose to keep his hands wrapped about the white ceramic vessel for warmth.

"Have I grieved? Grieved for whom? I do not follow you."

As the words left his lips, as they became real and no longer mere thoughts but sounds that he could hear and process within his own ears and mind, he suddenly realized what his sister was alluding to.

"Are you referring to Mary? Have I grieved for Mary?"

Not wishing to intrude into what she felt was a deeply personal matter; she did not answer with words, but simply nodded to convey her intention.

He once again looked about the room as if to find the answer hidden in one of the corners or on top of the cupboards, but when the answer was not forthcoming from any of these external sources he returned his gaze back to his sister.

"Of course I have grieved for her, for the whole family. It was a horrible loss of life."

Iris shook her head and moved her hand from his arm so that it rested on his hand as it still cradled the cup nestled in the saucer.

"I do not mean in that way," she began in the same unassuming voice, "what I am speaking of is; have you thought about your loss, the loss of Mary and her alone? She was to be your wife, your life with her, your future, all suddenly and quite mercilessly altered forever. Have you allowed yourself to feel the sorrow of all those losses?"

He thought about what she was saying for what seemed to be a long while before he pulled his hand free of hers and let the teacup free of the hold he had on it. Leaning back in the chair he rubbed his eyes for several seconds before returning his hands to the tabletop, folding them one over the other and staring off in silence at the darkness that lay beyond the glass of kitchen window.

"How do you expect me to grieve for someone who I hardly knew?" he asked in a quiet but annoyed tone.

Iris would not be provided any real opportunity to present him with the answer he had solicited from her.

"Was it not enough that I was at the burial, still unable to speak? Forced by my own will to stand there mute and on show like some abomination that travels with the gypsy caravans, to be unable to say anything even if I wished it, to find some words of love or compassion for a person who I had but met in passing and yet was expected to have taken her hand in the holiest of vows before God!"

His elbows still on the table he raised his hands and let his head fall into them so that his forehead was supported by his upturned palms, his fingers entwined into his hair that had once again fallen forward.

The kitchen fell into silence and remained so for some time as Iris felt that, even though her motives where ones brought about out of kindness, she may well have poked a wound within her brother that was still painfully fresh. As the seconds quickly ran into minutes and the silence within the room grew heavier, she felt compelled to try and force another avenue of conversation rather than run the risk of the night ending on a sour note.

"Alright then," she said in the best uplifted voice she could muster, "It is, after all, none of my business and we should not dwell on that which we can neither alter nor erase."

Her words seemed to have little impact on him as he remained unmoving, his position unchanged since taking it up at the end of his last statement. Feeling as though she had really stepped on a nerve, Iris again tried to bring about a more amiable conversation, starting with an offer to top up his tea for him.

"I think I should fix you a fresh cup. That one must be getting cold."

She reached over to retrieve his cup and saucer but just before she could actually pick it up, he grabbed her wrist and held it fast with a vice-like grip.

"Aremis, you are hurting me!" she squealed as she tried to pull away.

"Does it not make you ill, to always be doing that which is expected of us?" he said, his voice low and unfamiliar to her, "To go about our lives so blindly and without so much as a question. Are we no better than obedient dogs?"

Iris pulled frantically at her arm with her free hand as the level of panic increased within her, tears welling up in her eyes as she stammered for him to release her.

"Aremis, please, let go, whatever is the matter with you? You are really hurting me!"

Lifting his head from the hand that had still supported it, he looked directly at his sister who remained struggling within his unyielding grip. Her focus remained upon the hand that held her; she did not immediately notice his change in position from that which she had last remembered him in.

As he continued to watch his younger sister struggle within his grip, he felt a horrible conflict erupting within his mind, a single intellect but with diversely opposed origins of thought; one knowing without a doubt that he was hurting her, the other truly not caring about it. As the conflict raged on within the silent battlefield of his mind something more interesting took his attentions, almost like a previous oversight, one that is at first missed but then is discovered and suddenly becomes blatantly obvious.

He could see a glow of sorts all about his sister's neck and face.

This flush was unlike anything he had ever before witnessed. The crimson hue seemed to emanate from beneath her very skin as it pulsated with a life of its own, extending more than an inch beyond that of her body. The aura that now surrounded her head and neck only seemed apparent where her skin was visible, its translucent red light diminishing where her clothing concealed her skin.

With this new observation permeating his thoughts, oblivious to his sister's frantic pleas for release, he turned his sights to her wrist, which he still held firmly in his grasp and noticed a similar glow from the skin that was exposed below the cuff of the dress. Unable to explain this phenomenon and without thinking, he found himself moving as though in a dream, aware of his actions but unable to have power over them. He stood before her, pulling at the collar of her dress, tearing it open violently exposing her left shoulder down to the top of her breast, instantly revealing more of the mysterious ruby aura. The sound own heartbeat pounding so loud within his ears it all but obliterated the frantic screams of his sister. It was not until she turned her eyes from her trapped hand to that of her brother's face did all attempts to free herself suddenly cease as she fainted from consciousness.

Suddenly, as though a blinding shroud had been lifted from his head, its removal allowing him to see and hear all that was around him as if witnessing it for the first time, he took stock of what was happening.

The sensation of his sister's body slipping from his unfastened grip had him unexpectedly clutching at the air between his hand and hers in a vain attempt to avert her collision with the floor. Iris now lay slumped on the kitchen floor, motionless before him, her dress laid torn open, her silken chemise having been ripped along the seam. He felt, more than he could actually account for, that he had done something terrible but had precious little recollection as to what exactly it was.

He knelt down over her unmoving body as panic began to set in on him. Not sure of where to begin, he had barely enough presence of mind within the entanglement of thoughts which overwhelmed him to press his two fingers against her neck. It was something he had been shown many years before by a then much younger Dr. Harrington. His mother had taken him to check up on a persistent cough and, in a trade for the fidgeting boy's cooperation, the doctor had told him how to find a person's heartbeat with just two fingers. It seemed ages before he finally felt the slight throb beneath his two fingertips.

With a relieved sigh, he rocked back so that his heels supported his weight. Remaining there, crouched beside his sister, he tried to piece together the lost fragments of time. However, his foggy examination would have to wait as his thoughts were interrupted by the sound of Temperance calling out as she raced down the stairs, obviously alerted by the commotion that had emanated from the very room in which he now sat.

The elder of the two sisters arrived into the kitchen already dressed for bed in a long flannel gown and stocking feet, the shock upon her face as she entered from the hallway told him that things were probably much worse than anything he could have imagined.

"What happened here, what have you done?" she demanded, her voice sharp and accusing.

He stood up from his crouched position on the floor and faced her, preparing to answer her questions with what little he had to offer.

"Do not move, I want you to remain where you are," she ordered more than asked.

His movement suddenly halted, Temperance grabbed a carving knife that had lay upon the countertop closest to her and pointed it at her brother.

"Move away from her!" She demanded.

"Temperance, please, there is no need for such theatrics, she fainted is all. I was merely checking for her heart beat, nothing more."

His words were calm and reassuring, but rather than risk further agitation on the part of his knife-wielding sister, he did as she had asked and stepped back to the door that led out to the back porch.

She watched him closely as he backed up, his hands raised up before him in a defensive manner. His words made sense and she knew if it were not for the memories of what she had witnessed that night at Dr. Harrington's home, she thought she would easily have believed him.

When he was as far back as he could go, she took her eyes from him to survey her younger sister who still lay quite unmoving upon the kitchen floorboards.

Seeing the torn dress and camisole beneath rekindled her suspicions that her brother was something more than what he now presented.

"Tell me what happened, exactly." She demanded returning her sights to where he still remained all but motionless by the back door.

"It is as I have told you," he began. "We were having tea. She was asking me about Mary and the funeral, my feelings and other things like that. I suppose, the thoughts of such unpleasantness overwhelmed her, for she fainted and fell from the chair."

"What of her dress then? How is it that it has come to be torn away like this?"

In the same relaxed manner he gave her a description of the events, based solely on what he believed to have taken place.

"As I said, she fell from the chair. I dropped my tea when I tried to break her fall. As I reached for her shoulder I only managed to grasp the dress. It was not strong enough to support her weight, thus it tore."

Temperance rubbed her forehead with her fingers trying to make sense of what she was feeling and that which she was hearing. She would later describe this moment in her writings as *'the words not matching the music'*.

"Swear before God that what you say is the truth."

"Temperance, please!"

"Swear to it or I will kill you where you stand!"

His eyes grew wide at this sudden and very real threat made by the same woman who had only weeks before nursed him from near-death and who now stood before him seemingly determined to dispatch him to the very place she had brought him back from.

"I swear it. It happened so fast, but with all my knowledge I swear that is what happened."

His voice was trembling and he had taken hold of the doorknob in case his explanation was, for whatever reason, not to be believed.

"What in God's name is the matter with you Tempie, have you taken leave of your senses?" he asked, his voice still distressed by the standoff.

With tears beginning to well up in her eyes and her hands trembling uncontrollably, she felt as though she could hardly function let alone try to separate what she was feeling from what she was now witnessing. With everything that had happened over the last few weeks, she felt as though she was lost within the walls of an enormous maze, a labyrinth from which there existed no means of escape.

Iris began to stir at her feet, the sounds of returning consciousness quickly driving out the feelings of despair from her elder sister.

"Get out!" Temperance demanded, directing her renewed determination over the point of the knife still aimed towards her brother.

"Temperance," he retorted but was immediately cut off.

"Get out! Get out now before she awakens!" She was shouting at him and slowly making her way around her sister towards her brother, the knife held between her two hands, thrust out ahead of her.

With little room for negotiation and nothing more compelling to work with, he thought it best, for the present, to do as she demanded. Without taking his eyes from her he turned the door handle releasing the latch and let himself out into the crisp night air. He waited on the back porch, his back to the rail, watching as his sister locked the door, pulled the curtains over and disappeared from view.

Figuring that she would next make her way to the front door as so to lock it as well, there was little for him to do but wait out the tense situation. Grabbing a wooden chair, one that used to belong in the kitchen, he walked it to the end of the veranda and positioned it so his back was to the house. There he remained, alone and still, looking out at the moon, and as it rose above the tree line he wondered, with some distress, exactly how this situation would end up being played out.

Inside Temperance was doing exactly as her brother had imagined, making her way directly to the front door and locking it, but unlike what he had envisioned as she made her way back towards the kitchen she entered the front family room. There, reaching behind the corner cabinet, she removed her father's rifle from its secluded hiding place. Holding it for a few moments, reacquainting herself with the heavy weapon, the same one that her father had taught her how to use when she was but a girl of thirteen, she opened the breech and checked to see that the cartridge in the cylinder was not a spent round. Satisfied with her quick inspection, she closed the weapon and with it held firmly in her right hand she pulled open the drawer in the cabinet. Lifting the lid to a small wooden box that lay within, she removed several more rounds.

Returning to the kitchen armed with both rifle and knife, she stepped over her sister as she made her way to the back door. Cautiously she pulled back the curtain edge with the barrel of the gun peeking warily though the slight gap, not certain what might be on the other side. Allowing her eyes to adjust to the darkness, it was several seconds before she could at last make out her brother sitting motionless in a chair near the end of the porch. She let the curtain fall back over the window and returned to where her sister lay upon the floor.

Setting the weapons along with the extra shells upon the tabletop, she retrieved a cloth from a shelf on the far wall and quickly submerged it into the pail of fresh water that sat on the counter nearest the stove. Ringing out the excess water from the rag she went to her sister and knelt down beside her. Keeping a watchful eye on the back door, she gently tamped her forehead, talking to her as softly as she could manage under the circumstances.

"Iris, come now, you will be fine, wake up. It is me, Temperance."

It took several minutes of continued persuasion before Iris did begin to come around, slowly at first but then, as if awakening from a vivid nightmare, she grabbed onto her older sister's nightgown as she frantically looked about the kitchen in a terrified manner.

"Where is he?" she asked frantically as she kicked at the empty air, her feet sliding on the floor as she did.

Temperance grabbed hold of her and held her firmly to her.

"Where is who? Who are you talking about?" She asked firmly, already certain of what the answer would be.

"Aremis! Where did he go?" Iris answered, her voice full of terror.

Temperance continued to hold her tightly, reassuring her that she was safe.

"Shhh, now it's alright. He is outside and the door is locked. You had a dizzy spell is all, and it would seem that you have been out for a bit. Just try and calm down now, you are going to be fine."

Iris, still in her sister's arms, began to cry hard. Her tears, falling from her eyes, rolled off her cheeks and landed on her sister's flannel nightgown, disappearing into the warm fabric. Temperance stroked her sister's hair and tried to console her, while keeping her eyes trained on the back door and her ears tuned to the sound of a window should it be opened somewhere else in the house.

After several minutes of inconsolable grief, Iris began to regain her composure, enough that Temperance felt she would be able help her to her feet and into a chair. She knew that being huddled together on the floor was no place from which to make a defendable stand should such action suddenly be required.

When Iris was comfortably seated, wiping the tears from her eyes with the sleeve of her dress, she noticed the rifle on the table and became immediately upset again.

"Why is father's gun out? What is happening?" she pleaded.

"Nothing, it is but precautionary. When I heard the commotion from upstairs, I thought there was someone in the house. I thought it best to have it with me."

Her words were designed to be comforting but even she herself did not believe them. She pulled up a chair so that she was seated directly opposite Iris while Iris would have her back to the door and she could keep an eye on it as she tried to determine what exactly took place while she had been upstairs.

"Tell me what happened." She asked firmly, most of the soothing voice now gone.

Iris looked about the room briefly. Then, realizing her shoulder was bare she pulled the torn dress over the exposed skin as she fought back her fears to recount what had happened.

"I had just made tea," she began. "Aremis had just come in and you had already gone upstairs so I asked him if he fancied a cup. I knew you and he had a bit of a row outside so I thought it might be a nice way to try and smooth things a bit."

She looked back to the door that led outside.

"Are you sure he is outside?" she inquired with a shaken voice.

"Yes, I am quite sure. Now please Iris, I need for you to continue, it is important." She tapped her sister's hand in an effort to both reassure her as well as encourage her to continue.

"Well, I think I may have upset him, for you see I thought that perhaps the reason for his feeling so down of late was on account of him not grieving the loss of Mary, you know, on the night of him to be meeting her in an official manner and all, I am certain he has not shed a single tear for her."

Temperance nodded her understanding as Iris picked up the overturned teacup that had held her brothers tea and set it upright on its saucer as she continued on with the events that followed.

"I think it must have touched on a nerve because he took to being real quiet and put his head in his hands. At first I thought I was right in my assessment of why he was feeling off and that maybe all he was in need of was a good cry and things would seem a might better, but the silence was so long that I began to feel uncomfortable in it, do you know what I mean?"

Temperance again nodded and Iris continued on.

"I was feeling a tad guilty about having asked him something that was really none of my business so I reached for his hand and told him that I should not have broached the subject and I went to take his cup to warm it up..." She paused, her lip trembling as she pulled the tatters of her dress tighter to her chest. "He grabbed my wrist, Tempie, really hard. It hurt so much."

She showed her sister where he had taken hold of her arm and to the surprise of both women they could see the skin was already quite bruised.

Upon seeing the discolouration Iris began to cry anew, and it was several minutes before Temperance could get her calmed down enough to continue.

"When he took hold of you, was that when you fainted?" she inquired as her sister gently rubbed her wrist while stifling back tears.

She shook her head, not looking up as she continued to wipe the tears from her face with her sleeve.

"No, I was still trying to free myself from his grip all the while telling him that he was hurting me. It was then that I actually looked at him. He was looking back at me, but..." She paused, a frightened tremor running through her.

"You are fine," Temperance reassured her. "It's alright now."

Iris swallowed hard, trying to quench her throat, which had become dry from crying.

"It was not him, it was not Aremis," she stammered, obviously still affected by what she had seen. "It was a demon!"

Iris was now trembling so badly from the retelling of the horrific experience that Temperance had little doubt what was being told was, in fact, the truth. She felt she would have believed her younger sister even if she herself had not experienced a similar demonic-looking creature within the face of their brother some weeks back.

"Iris, tell me, did you see his eyes?"

Iris nodded quickly, a look of complete and utter terror taking over her facial expression.

"They were red, all red, no whites, no pupils," she shivered violently. "That is when I must have blacked out, for the next thing I can recall is you being with me."

"Alright, that is fine. You're safe now. Nothing else will happen tonight."

She pulled the gun from the table and walked to the back door.

"Where are you going with the gun?" Iris asked in a frantic voice.

"Nowhere. I need for you to just sit still for a minute whilst I check on something." Her voice was now calm and sure as she drew back the curtain that covered the back door.

Aremis still remained seated on the chair, possibly unmoved since the last she checked on his whereabouts. Letting the curtain fall back over the glass she returned to the table.

"Now, you must listen to me, I want you to go upstairs to Mother and Father's room, I want you to go inside then lock the door behind you. Do not open it unless you know for certain that it is either our parents or I. Do you understand?"

"But what of you? I want you to come with me."

Temperance shook her head.

"No, I cannot. I have to deal with this, and in order to do that I need for you to do as I ask of you."

Iris began to get upset at her sister's request, desperately trying to get her to reconsider and accompany her to the second floor.

"Iris!" She shouted, "I need for you to take hold of yourself!" Temperance took the knife from the table and presented it to her younger sister handle first. "Take this with you and do not let anyone in unless you know it is our parents or myself. Do you understand?"

Trembling, Iris took the knife and nodded her understanding.

"Good. Now go." She as much ordered as asked, pointing in the direction of the stairs. When Temperance heard the door on the second floor close, she removed her coat from the hook on the wall beside the pantry and slipped it on. Picking up the extra shells from the table she placed them into one of the pockets then, for the second time that night, lifted her brother's coat from the same row of hooks on the wall, laid it over her left arm and then, unlocking the door, she stepped out onto the porch.

The cool night air caressed her bare legs and she felt the resulting shiver travel the length of her spine, making the hairs on the back of her neck rise. Still in stocking feet, she cautiously padded along the short distance that separated them until she was directly behind where her brother remained seated and unmoving. With the gun in her right hand, her finger poised on the trigger, she levelled it at the back of his head.

"Are you going to shoot me now?" he asked in a quiet voice.

Although it was her brother's voice true enough, she did not respond immediately, for she could not be certain of exactly who it was that was addressing her. A long silence ensued, one she felt must have been similar to the one Iris had described, and she felt a cold of another origin than that of a winter's night in the woodlands suddenly take grip of her heart.

"We need to have a talk, you and I," she announced in a voice that belied her fears and effectively broke the silence.

"I would very much like that, the truth be known," he replied, a near chuckle seeming to follow his initial statement before continuing. "Do you want to go first or would you rather it be me?"

She tossed the heavy coat to the floor beside the chair he was sitting in.

"I brought you your coat. It is cold and you have been out here for quite a while."

She stepped back a few steps as she watched his arm reach down and retrieve the coat from the grey planking of the porch.

"Thank you. I am cold." he replied quietly.

Once he had the coat on and done up, she told him to stand and face her.

Not figuring he had much choice in the matter, he did as he was instructed and slowly stood up from the chair, then turned to face his sister, his hands open and at his sides.

"Now what?" he asked, not daring to move.

Temperance readjusted the weight of the rifle so that is sat more comfortably within her grip before she replied.

"Other than feeling cold, how are you feeling? Be honest with me or I swear by all things holy I will end your life where you stand."

Aremis swallowed hard as he knew with most certainty that she was quite serious in her charge to him. Biting his lower lip in a nervous reaction he thought about his current situation and how he was feeling both in the moment and of late before he dare utter a word. After what seemed like several minutes of stressful silence he spoke. The sound of his voice breaking the stillness made her jump slightly, causing her to unconsciously clutch the weapon's stock tighter to her shoulder.

"To your question, other than quite chilled, I began to tell Iris that I have been feeling somewhat off of late, but I truthfully do not know as to the reasons behind it. I know I have no illness to speak of, I do not feel fevered or chilled other than that induced by the climate of the day and other than my memory, which seems to fail me regularly, I feel much as I always have."

Another silence followed the forced self-assessment as she thought about all that he had just said, weighing it against that which she had heard from her sister. Before ordering her sister to their parent's bedroom and leaving the kitchen she felt convinced she would be able to shoot and kill whatever had possessed her brother. However, standing face to face, not with some red-eyed demon from the nether world, but the face of her beloved older brother, she found the idea of extinguishing his life unthinkable. This thought safely tucked away, far from anything he could know, she inquired further to that of his memory, or more precisely lack of same.

"Can you remember anything more of the attack that happened that night at the bridge?" she asked sternly.

"For the love of God," he began, in an agitated manner.

Temperance levelled the rifle and drew the hammer back with a pronounced click.

"P..., Please, wait, I am trying, I cannot recall much, only trappings and ghostly images, all of which make little if any sense at all.

"Try harder." She demanded, unmoving in her stance.

Tears began to well in his eyes as he strained the darkest recesses of his mind, searching for anything that might shed some light into why this was happening to him.

"I can remember a woman. She was tall like you. She, she, was walking away from me, in the woods..." He paused, his eyes half closed, the trickle of tears tracking down one cheek, "no, wait, not in the woods, not yet. She, she was on the road, I can remember the road near the town hall."

"Who is she, what is her name?" Temperance demanded.

"I have no recollection, please, I swear to it." He fell to his knees sobbing.

She lowered her aim so that it followed his progression to the floor.

"Temperance, why, why is this happening? Why do you not believe me? What do you know that I do not?" His plea was sorrow-filled and his kneeling posture continued until he was nearly a ball upon the floor of the veranda crying into his hands.

For the second time that night she was faced with the tears of a loved one, both directly caused by the actions of another family member. She wrestled with his question pertaining to her knowledge of the event and whether or not it would be foolish or productive to share with him that which she not only knew but the part she guarded from everyone else.

"Alright, God help me that I do the right thing here and am not being played by the Devil's misleading ways, I will share with you what I know."

With that and while her brother remained at gun point, she told him all she knew pertaining to the attack, right up to and including the night she had witnessed his return from death's doorstep. When she had finished her recount of the events she paused, and in the quiet that ensued, thought deeply on whether or not to carry on with the information regarding her other sight or leave well enough alone. It was obvious that he was both shocked and intrigued by her observations to this point as he had ceased with the emotional outpouring and was now kneeling with upright posture. His face told her without a doubt that, for the most part at least, her words were making some sense and possibly filling in some of the gaps within his mind.

"So am I to understand that you believe me to be some sort of monster?" he asked, snapping her attention away from her own thoughts.

"That would be too simple an answer," she replied quietly. "A monster I could kill, like the wolf that preys on the live stock, for I know it is a wolf when I look upon it through the gun sight. I do not know what it is that I look upon presently."

He slouched backwards in a more contemplative state, his bottom resting upon his heals, and his hands on the tops of his thighs as he looked off over the railing of the veranda towards the smaller of the two barns that occupied the space just west of the house.

"How can you be so sure of what you see?" he asked flatly not bothering to look her way but continued staring off into the distance and the darkness. "Perhaps it is as Dr. Harrington had said: that it was nothing more than a waking dream, a delusion brought on by long hours without rest."

"And what of what has just taken place inside? Do you think it coincidence that Iris has described to me the exact same features in you that I had seen that first night you awoke but told not a soul beyond that of Dr. Harrington? Or perhaps you think she a victim of over work and poor sleep, as well as I? Do you forget that which I have just told you, of the police from London, how long they spent here in the village, with Dr. Harrington? I am sure they had initially thought you to be the murderer, whom in the struggle was himself injured. Not until the extent of your wound was revealed did they think otherwise."

"But they did think otherwise!" he exclaimed, cranking his head back to face her, his patience obviously growing weary of having his sister holding him hostage. "For heaven's sake Temperance, those men, by your own accounts, are professional investigators, from London no less! If they think me but a victim in this heinous act why then do you cling so to the idea I am not?"

She shifted her weight from one foot to the other readjusting the heavy weapon as she did so.

"I never said you were part of killing the Smiths, I very much look on you as a victim, much as they were. The difference is that you are still alive, quite miraculous as that might be, and to that miracle I do not know if I should be grateful or view myself cursed."

Aremis hung his head tired and cold.

"There is something else, something I hesitate to reveal to you, something I have not in my entire life confided to another soul."

He raised his head to listen to whatever confession-like statement might be forthcoming.

"Aremis, it is not the body of evidence that has been collected, along with eyewitness accounts of your actions that has me stand like this before you. It is my own feelings."

Her brother snorted in a mocking disapproval of her words.

"So, am I to understand that I am to be tried here, like this, at the end of gun, based entirely on nothing more than your intuition? Is this what you are telling me?"

His words and displeasure at her statement were not without foundation. In fact she felt more assured by his disbelief that it was actually her brother she was talking to and not some poet-tongued serpent from the underworld.

She paused but a moment to gather her thoughts, thoughts of which she had never imagined ever divulging and certainly not in this manner. Then with her mind clear she took what she felt would be the most believable account within her memory and with caution thrown to the wind she put forth a question.

"Do you remember when you were about ten years old and you fell through the ice on the pond?" she asked, the topic seemingly having taken an unexpected turn.

Looking momentarily perplexed by the direction of her question he lost all look of disdain as he now searched his memories for some distant shred of childhood.

"Yes, I remember that, you came with Father and fetched me out. I thought I was going to die out there that day. Why do you ask such things at this time?"

"Have you even wondered how I knew to get Father from his work in the barn that day, how I knew where to find you, or that you were even in trouble?"

Her voice was calm but it wavered slightly with the chill in the air that was slowly taking hold of her body.

"I have no clue, I was lucky is all. Perhaps God was looking out for me that day."

"Perhaps, that is the case, but what of the time I told you the Smiths would have a baby and that it would be a girl, and more precisely that she would be your wife, what of that?"

"Lucky guesses, nothing more. A girl's telltale game of who marries whom; I have witnessed many a child play such guessing games. You best be careful of who you are telling such tales to as it could very easily lead to your damnation."

"It is not *my* damnation, as you so put it, which I worry for, but yours. I have told not another soul until this very moment, and as I stand here with you I know most certainly that, one way or another, my secret will remain safe."

There could be no mistaking the meaning within his sister's words. He knew without a doubt the seriousness surrounding her convictions as well as the repercussions if such news were to fall on the ears of those intolerant of such thinking.

"It is with this other sight, something of which I do not pretend to understand, other than to trust it, that spoke to me that first day at the Harrington's when you first awoke. It's with that same sight that screams to me now and tells me to fear you. On that morning, the morning you first returned home from a darkened world, I am convinced you left a part of your soul there within the darkness and brought back with you, in its place, death itself."

Probably for the first time in his life, Aremis felt real fear. Fear manifested from the idea that some unnatural predatory being might now inhabit his body, that he had no recollection of it coming to him, or having it in some way enter him. When he combined this with not having any conscious memory of many of his actions throughout any given day, it caused a coldness within him that was far more chilling than the frigid night air could ever have been.

"So, what is to happen now?" he asked, shivering slightly, "If I am now some sort of dark creature from Hell and you be an oracle of sorts, what of us, what are we to do?"

She raised her eyes to the heavens momentarily but saw only dusty spider webs stretched over the rafters of the porch before returning her gaze to where he was still kneeling.

"I am hardly certain," she began, but paused as she stared blankly at him. "I know that I can no longer trust you, Aremis, not anymore. I do not know what remains of my brother whom I know and love and what is steadily replacing him with something of which terrifies me. I truly do not wish to have my hand forced by nothing more than a feeling, a feeling which I could never substantiate in any court of law, never mind that of my own family."

"Really, Temperance, I cannot help but feel that you make too much of something that may not be as bad as you make it to be."

It was perhaps a last ditch attempt at coming to some truce in order that they might discuss this further by the fireside rather than continuing on in the frosty early-December air, but all it did was light a fire within his sibling.

"You feel I make too much of this, you feel that I have indeed gone mad. Iris too, mad the both of us and you, the one who has been touched by death's own hand, you are fine and with all your faculties? Does this not sound like the trappings of someone who is mentally diminished, one who thinks all those around him are mentally unstable while he himself remains of level and sound mind?"

She did not give him time to form a response to her query.

"Where were you last night, and the night before that? Tell me if you know."

He pondered for a moment before raising his hands up in surrender.

"I assume in bed until sun-up then to breakfast."

She narrowed her gaze gripping the rifle tightly.

"Get up." She demanded.

"But..."

"Get up, now! I have something to show you, maybe you will believe your own eyes if not my word."

Reluctantly he stood up on shaky legs and waited for instruction as to where they would be going. Using the barrel of the gun as a pointer she directed him to descend the stairs and make his way towards the front of the house. As he began the walk she stepped in behind him keeping several feet between them as they went.

"You are in your stockings you will catch your death out here." He remarked as he looked back at his sister following along.

She did not bother with a reply, but instead ordered him to make his way to the gate that led to the field where the sheep had been for the last two days.

Following her instruction he made his way to the gap in the fence and then through it, continuing along the well worn dirt pathway that led from the road through the forest to the fields, the same path they had taken a few days earlier while carrying out their Mother's clever ruse.

When they were both through the forest and standing at the leading edge of the field, the near full moon casting down a silver glow on the frosted dew-covered grass, he again inquired as to the purpose of this plan.

"Across the field, by the stream, move." Her voice was without emotion, much like a military man in charge of a new recruit.

The two moved out over the field, guided by the limited light offered by the moon in a sky that was dotted with quickly moving clouds and their familiarity of the land in which they travelled. When they reached the stream that ran through a small cluster of trees she told him to walk to the large oak that stood about 50 yards up the stream and that she would wait for him.

Not wishing to argue with her further, he took his leave and made his way up the bank towards the tree. When he arrived he stood there looking upwards at the branches as the stretched skywards towards the stars.

"What am I doing here?" he called out to her.

"The answer is on the ground, not in the heavens!" she replied.

He turned around to look back on her in an attempt to see what she was talking about and that was when he noticed the carcass of a sheep in the undergrowth.

"A dead sheep, this is what I am to see?"

"Two, in as many days, both together, a bit odd would you not think?"

He looked down and spotted the second body only a few feet from the first under heavier undergrowth.

"It is winter, the pack animals take out the ones that stray, it is not all that uncommon. Surely you should know this. Honestly, I fail to see the significance between these dead animals and what we were discussing back at the house."

"Odd to not eat what they kill," she called back.

Her words having pricked his curiosity, he moved the underbrush aside to afford a closer inspection of the dead animals. True to his sister's short statement, what he discovered were two completely intact fully-grown sheep with not a stitch of flesh removed from their bodies.

He grabbed the one that lay closest to him and dragged it from the undergrowth into the moonlight so as to better investigate this finding. He rolled the dead sheep over, checking with his hands and eyes for any signs that it had, even in part, been a meal.

"You are right. Not so much as a mouthful has been taken from this animal."

"The other one is the same if you care to see for yourself." She replied.

Looking into the thicket and not fancying crawling through wet mud to retrieve it, he thought it best to take her word on it. She apparently seemed to know much pertaining to the matter.

"No, that would fine. I believe you. Now what?" he shouted back questioningly.

"Look at the neck," she replied, still unmoving from her location.

Stepping over the animal, straddling it, he pulled the head back and forth until he found the dark discolouration of blood in the wool. Following the bloodstain back from the lower neck of the beast he discovered the source, a gaping hole in the throat.

"Good heavens, the flesh has been cut through as though it were nothing more than warm butter." He commented, mostly to himself, but loud enough that she could hear him. "I cannot recall having ever seen a wound such as this before. I wonder what manner of creature it was that made it."

"I have seen a wound like this before, exactly like that one in fact." she commented.

"You have? Where?" he asked, as he stood, up letting the animals head fall with a thump to the ground.

"On you, when you first were discovered and brought to the Harrington's house." Her voice was nearly as emotionless as the night was still.

"My God!" He shouted, suddenly distressed by what he had just heard, his voice, setting a start upon her, for the second time that night. "You knew this and you brought us up here just the same. Whatever it was that did this is likely still out here!"

"I am quite certain that it is." she replied, her voice still chillingly cool.

"Have you taken complete leave of your senses?" he shouted. "Knowing full well what has happened to these animals, to me, you, seemingly without regard or presence of mind, brought us both up here where we could both be in immediate peril?"

His words bordered on hysteria but did little in the way of making an impact on her.

"I think we are both safe for the moment," she replied, in a voice that was very much matter of fact and far removed from that of her brother, "I want you to walk towards the stream, there you will see the old fallen log we used to pretend was a pirate ship. I want you to reach inside and tell me what you find."

Fearful and annoyed he lashed out at her in an appeal to end this dangerous game of hide and seek.

"Temperance, this is absurd! Would it not be prudent to return in the light of day? I am sure this can all wait until then."

His words fell on deaf ears, and without a response to his request he threw his arms up in the air in a fit of exasperation before wearily trudging off in the direction of the pirate ship log.

Approaching the old fallen elm he was, for a moment, transported back in time to where he had once been the captain of The Emerald as he named the log, for it was so completely covered in moss that it looked more a shade of green than that of brown bark. There were so many emotions connected to the log that it was difficult to separate them all. For a few moments all he desperately wanted to do was simply sit down and go over each of them, one by one, savouring each moment as though it were fresh and new again.

He was not to be granted his desire, however, as the sound of his sister's voice calling after him to retrieve what was in the hollow of the log broke into his mental wonderings.

Wrenched violently from his thoughts of a happy childhood into the present situation, one of which held a future where he felt he might not see the coming dawn, he knelt down and then reaching into the open end of the log, he padded about in the darkness with his hand. It was several seconds before he touched upon something soft and not of the forest. Taking hold of the item, he cautiously removed it and held it out before him. At first he was unsure of what it was he held in his hands other than it was made of material but as he began to unravel it he realized what he held were in fact two different bed shirts that had been bundled together. As he continued to disengage one garment from the other, the moon's silver light, hidden for the most part behind ghostly clouds, made the process that much harder. The once pristine white fabric now soiled and wrinkled, he saw what he felt what he first thought to be nothing more than dampness combined with dirt ground into the fabric was, in actuality, blood. Both shirts were soaked through, front and back, with blood.

Kneeling at the foot of the stream, one shirt draped over each of his upturned hands, he studied them: the fabric, the pattern of the crimson stain that ran from the neck line, heavier near the collar, spatter on the sleeves and cuffs, trailing off near the waist. He looked back at his sister who still held the rifle trained on him.

"What is all of this, what does it mean?"

There was a short silence before she answered with much sadness in her voice.

"Look at the inside of the collar."

Frustrated at her lack of information, he turned his attention back to the shirts, unfolding the dirty cotton further and straining without success to locate that which he was supposed to see. About to give up, unable to see what was apparently hidden from his eyes only, the moon slipped free of its cloudy veil and in the milky white light, the thing that had eluded him until now, became quite horribly apparent. For there sewn into the inside seam of the collar, two letters, *A.E.,* his own initials placed there by their mother to keep check of what belonged to whom at laundry time. As the horror spread through him like fire through dry wood kindling, he turned his eyes towards his sister in some unlikely hope that she might have a logical explanation for what he could not fathom himself.

"I watched you leave the house the last two nights in nothing more than the shirts you now hold in your hands. Mother has not seen your nightshirts in either your room or in the laundry basket, nor would she for they were in neither place. You hid them in the log. Who else but you could know of this place, of the log and its hollow, to walk amongst the sheep as not to startle them, to be strong enough to carry them off with little effort?"

She paused momentarily then continued.

"More so than all of that, tell me what beast that you know of that kills another only to have its blood and not its flesh? No beast of natural creation I can assure you."

He stared back at her, the bloodied shirts still in his hands, crying out, as much to her, as to the heavens above him.

"My God, what have I become?"

She watched him through tearful eyes, his body hardly moving, still positioned on his knees by the log, his hands now clenching the nightshirts as if to wring the blood from the very fabric. She could hear his mournful sobbing softly emanating from him, the sound floating on the air but a moment before being swept away by the nearby stream as its waters cascaded over the rocks.

Never in all her years could she have envisioned this moment. For her to be here in the place where she, as a child, had played with her brother and younger sister, to now be here again faced with an impossible task of having to end the life of one she loved most dearly.

"Heavenly Father, if there be another way, other than that which you have now presented before me, I ask that You, in all your kindness, show it to me for I fear that I do not have within me that which is needed to end his life."

She wiped the tears from her face, and then pulled the gun's stock tightly into her shoulder. Taking a firm grip on the barrel as to steady it, she drew back the hammer slowly so as not to disturb the deathly quiet. Her index finger slipped into the trigger guard and lighted upon the cool curved steel of the trigger.

"Please, Dear Lord, if there be something in my brother that is still of Your hand then please show me... I beg of you."

Her whispered pleas fell on the silence of the night with little in the way of an answer forthcoming. As she cleared her mind of her prayers and prepared herself for the sound of the rifle's deafening blast followed by its powerful kick back, she suddenly noticed Aremis standing up very slowly his hands up in a defensive manner as he stared off towards the stream. She was about to call to him, to tell him to hold up where he was when she saw what it was he was recoiling from. From out of the underbrush, almost lost within the shadows themselves, she could make out slow stealthy movement advancing on her brother. Squinting into the moonlit darkness it was another few seconds before she realized it was a black wolf. As the creature left the thicket and hopped through the water to the other side, closing the distance between itself and her brother, she squeezed the trigger.

In that instant the forest erupted with a thunderous roar that sent all manner of slumbering bird and mammal to flight both in sky and over ground. As the smoke cleared she pulled a second round from her pocket and quickly reloaded the weapon without so much a looking at it. She took aim through the dispersing smoke in case she may have only wounded the animal, or worse, missed it altogether. As she scanned the area through the slit in the view finder at the end of the barrel she found that the wolf lay still from what appeared to be a fatal wound while her brother sat, his back to the large oak, his eyes still fixed on the dead animal. Seeing the object of her aim dead upon the forest floor brought her immediate elation but it was to be short lived as she realized she very well may have killed that which only moments before she had been praying for.

"My God, what have I done?" she said aloud but, not with enough voice to carry any measurable distance.

A horrible feeling descended upon her and she truly felt sick to her stomach as she brought the rifle to bear once again on her brother.

Still with a look of fear upon his face, he turned his attention towards his sister. Seeing her standing as she was, the freshly fired weapon now directed towards him he knew well what was coming.

"Do you think there might be any hope for me, some other way? I have not asked for this affliction, surely to God there must be some answer other than that which you now present."

His voice was shaking to the point of it being nearly indiscernible.

"I have no understanding of what it is that you are, beyond that of terrifying stories about unworldly creatures, thus I have no way of knowing what, if anything, can be done for you."

He huddled against the tree, as a cowering child hides from that which threatens its safety.

"What of Dr. Harrington, might not he have something to offer other than an execution?"

"And what do you propose to tell him is ailing you? You yourself attest to not being in anyway ill, by medical standards. And what if you have," she paused, trying to think clearly in a situation that was completely void of normalcy, "what if you have another attack or whatever it is that seems to take you so? What of that? What of our family? Am I to let you back home? Knowing full well, that it may well result in the death of one or more of our family, including that of myself?"

He looked about the darkened forest as the moon slipped behind a cloud but for a moment before returning to the night sky and illuminating the ground below in a milky glow.

Aremis drew a heavy ragged breath before speaking,

"You are right. I fail to see another way. I put myself in your place and I would, as you do now, be making the same choices."

She pulled the hammer back until it clicked into place and took careful aim so that the bullet would pass through the centre of his chest, ending his life quickly and without suffering.

It was at that moment she caught sight of a raven, perhaps frightened off by the first blast, return and land upon a branch of the tree her brother now sat propped up against. She watched it for a several seconds, recalling the stories pertaining to the raven being the bird that could bring back one's soul from the land claimed by the dead.

Perhaps, she thought, the wolf was but a test, a means for which to know my heart most certain, and now the raven is the true sign for which I have asked. Her eyes darted from the large bird within the trees branches and her brother's unmoving form at the base of its trunk.

His sister's hesitation to do that which he had no doubt she was about to do had him follow her gaze to the branches above his head and when he could not locate that which had her so transfixed he, with much hesitation, called out to her.

"What is it that you see?"

"A raven." She replied.

He returned his sights skyward but still could not see the bird she made reference to, and even though the bird's feathers were sure to be quite black he felt as though he should be able to, at the very least, make out its shape given the light cast by the moon.

As she continued to watch, unbothered by her brother's inability to see, that which seemed so obvious to her, it took to flight and pursued a northerly direction until it was gone from her sight as well.

Whatever thoughts and reasoning may have run through her mind during that instant, no one will ever know. Perhaps it had been the raven's sudden appearance, or that her brother was unable to see it. A more realistic possibility was she could simply have had second thoughts about carrying out what would certainly be deemed a premeditated murder. Or, it might have been something else entirely, something beyond that of mortal comprehension. Whatever it was it though; it had Temperance do the unthinkable.

Lowering her aim on her brother, she let the hammer back slowly then dropped the rifle until it remained supported by only her right hand. She made her way slowly up the gradual slope to the tree and her brother, whereby she knelt down directly in front of him. If he was the beast she believed him to be he would have surely seized the opportunity, quickly ending both her life and the threat she posed. But he did no such thing.

"I asked God if there was something still left within you that was still of His hand and if so then to show it to me this night and prevent my having to carry out such a cruel task. He has given me this and I now believe that, despite my feelings, that there is a part of you that is still good."

Tears began to well in his eyes and he looked away to hide his fears and relief.

"Come, do not look away. I need to see your face, your real eyes. Let me see you."

He returned his eyes to hers and remained like that while she finished her words to him.

"I love you, dearest brother, perhaps more than my own life for I find myself like this with you now. I fear that you must take leave of this place for if there is an answer to this horrible affliction that has besieged your soul then it is not to be found in this little hamlet. Of this I am most certain."

He stared at her through watery eyes for what seemed to be a long time, unable to grasp what she was saying, or more true to the point not wanting to face that which she was conveying.

"I am to leave, leave our home?" He paused briefly, "And of the family, what will they think of me? It would look for all as though I had abandoned everyone for my own selfishness. Afraid of work is what they will all say. I will bring disgrace to our home, to Father; he would never forgive me for such a thing. Surely you cannot be serious in this? Are you?"

Even though he posed the question he knew well the answer: the only other action that would ensure his family's safety would see his sister sentenced to hang for his murder. Better, he thought, that the family need deal with one loss and not two and so, without much choice, he reluctantly agreed to the second of the two options.

"You must go tonight before Mother and Father return home for then it will be far more complicated to explain your having to leave."

"Tonight, but I have no clothing but that which is on my back..."

"Tonight," she interrupted, "you will go to the Smith's farm; it is still quite empty. Wait for me in the barn. I will bring some of your things out to you in the morning after church."

She paused; making sure what she was saying was getting through to him before she continued.

"I will write a note for you and leave it upon the table for Mother and Father, then explain to them that you felt you needed to work in the city for a while, until the memories of the accident and the loss of Mary had eased some. I know I can ease at least some of the pain they will feel more than if you end up killing someone we know."

She took hold of his hand and squeezed it tightly in the hopes of making the painful words feel more peaceful within his mind.

"Does it not bother you that this, which you now propose, may very well be setting a monster loose on some other township?"

It was something that had more than crossed her mind since she had first thought of the raven as some heavenly sign, and she wavered on whether to speak the truth or say that which she hoped for.

"I have to believe that God has shown me the way, and if not killing you *is* to be that way then I must have faith in His wisdom and in you that I have not done exactly that which you concern yourself with."

The lie born from hope sounded better to her than the truth built on fear, fear that she would in short order hear tell of untold death, all of which could have been averted if she had been willing to do what needed to be done here on this very night.

"You must hurry now," she urged. "I have to get home and get things ready and you have to get to the barn before sunrise, otherwise risk being seen."

She stood up and held out her hand for him to take it, and when he did she pulled him, with his assistance, to his feet. Wrapping her one free arm around him she hugged him closely.

"I know you will do what is right, Aremis, you have overcome death which tells me without a doubt you still have God with you. Perhaps if you travel to London to a priest or physician there, perhaps they will have encountered such things before and will know what it is that has stricken you so."

Her body felt warm against his and he shivered from a renewed cold that seemed to come from within more than from the chill night air. Returning her hug he felt the blood begin to pound in his ears and the strange ruby-like aura began to appear above his sister's head as it lay against his chest. With what resolve he had left he pulled himself free of her embrace as he looked out towards the direction of home so as to hide his eyes from her.

"You are right in that I must be off. It will indeed be sunrise soon and we both have much to do if this mad plan of yours is to succeed."

A shudder ran through her body as his words, no longer sounding like those of her brother came to her ears, and she realized with a renewed sense of fear that she may well be on borrowed time, and that it was quickly running out. Without another word she clutched the rifle tightly in her hand and ran for home leaving her brother, or what might remain of him, alone in the wooded enclave.

When she had completely disappeared from view and he was sure she would not be returning, he fell to his knees and let his head fall into his hands. He wept openly for several minutes before, on hand and knee, did he crawl over to the wolf, shot dead only moments earlier. There, crouched over the animal, its body still warm, did he further open the wound left by the bullet and begin to lap up the blood as gravity pulled it from the gash.

Chapter 6

14th of December, 1874, I have precious little time to write to you today other than to say it is a grim day unlike any other I have experienced.

T.

Standing before the wooden gate which barred the driveway to the Smith homestead, Aremis, his hands resting on the top rail, stared up the wheel-worn driveway towards the house that stood in a clearing just beyond the trees that lined the front of the property. Having made good time, making the choice to cut through the fields and woodland rather than risk the main roads, he had arrived well before the sun had begun to breach the eastern skies. With only a few hundred yards standing between him and the prearranged destination he found himself suddenly unable to continue.

Alone in the chill air of pre-dawn, there could be little doubt still left within his mind that something sinister had indeed happened to him on that fateful night well over two months ago. Having been forced at gunpoint to see the evidence with his own eyes, the terrible images, but a precursor to the frightening realisation. Both were now etched into his mind with a permanency of which he felt would remain with him until his own mortality withered and ultimately failed.

Despite the gnawing cold in the air and having been out the entire night, it was the first time in many hours that Aremis actually felt warm. Similar to the cold that had gripped him earlier, a bitterness that seemed to originate from within his very being, this warmth also seemed to have its origins from within, unaffected by the surrounding temperature.

Fleeting memories flitted though his mind, like pieces of a puzzle that had been scattered by the wind, pieces that slowly, as if by magic, began to drop into place until they formed a picture. He strummed his fingers absentmindedly on the top rail of the gate as he mentally organized these newly recalled memories into sequential order based on a delicate timeline, slowly putting together the series of events that had unfolded the evening of the Harvest Festival.

It was during this moment of careful reflection that he first noticed his fingers whimsically strumming on the wood of the gate. His fingertips were stained dark with blood so thick on some fingers that it had become caked beneath the nail.

Momentarily pulled from his thoughts by the new discovery, he found himself holding his hands before his face, much as a baby does when it first makes the discovery that the hand it is looking upon is actually its own. Slowly turning his hands, studying every detail with a macabre interest, his thoughts began to gradually spin backwards.

Feeling neither disturbed nor frightened by the grim discovery, knowing full well how the blood had come to be upon his hands, he cautiously wiped his lips with the sleeve of his coat to discover, upon removing it from his mouth, a similar red stain now upon the fabric.

Without much of a reaction to that which he felt should repulse him, he felt strangely serene, a calmness he had not felt since the attack. Turning his sights inward, he watched as the fragmented images came together, the lost events from his past slowly connecting to one another, each snippet of memory falling into place behind the next in a choppy motion.

Suddenly, as if struck by a hot poker, he cried out and clutched the side of his neck with his hand. Dropping to one knee, driven down by some unseen implement of discomfort, he cried out through clenched teeth. Through the pain, its intensity growing to the point where he felt he would no longer be able to remain conscious, things within his mind became crystalline.

Like a voyeur standing but a few feet away, and yet seen by no one he watched, he found himself mesmerized by that which he was witnessing. Bearing silent witness, he watched the tall brown-haired maiden come before the image of himself outside the town hall, her gentle and relaxed manner taking him off guard but not enough to cause alarm. As he continued his silent vigil he watched her turn, and with a casual smile cast back over her shoulder, she began to wander up the road disappearing into the darkness. He remained with his likeness, sharing his torment at what to do next, being forced to choose over that which was proper and that which was right. Then, as though tethered to the three dimensional mirror image, he followed along, without footfall, behind the man, who was himself of a few weeks earlier, as he ran into the darkness after her.

Upon reaching the stone bridge that spanned the narrow river, he watched himself shout mutely into the darkness then listen deafly for an answer that no one could hear, and as they waited for a reply he saw her return from within the blanket of night, slowly making her way across the bridge. Unlike his twin-likeness who seemed both relieved and elated at her return he, perhaps like his sister's feelings towards him now, knew there was something quite unnatural about the woman who now drew close and embraced his likeness. Her sensual embrace, although being relived from an external point, rekindled the memory of awkward feelings, feelings that slowly grew into ones of passion. Watching with a morbid fascination, unable to pull away from what his own thoughts were now showing him, the tender embrace gently turned into a lover's first kiss, he felt a fear unlike anything he had ever known sweep over him. With an urgent need to warn his double quickly mounting within him, he could do nothing more than reach out to him in a silent scream that had no more volume to it than the unmoving air within the stillness of that night. A prisoner within his own mind, all he could do was look on in horrified silence as her mouth slipped from his double's lips and onto his neck, and then with the tiniest of kisses completed, there was a flash of white. Pale lips, soft and sensuous, that had not moments before rendered such delicate affections onto another's skin were now clamped tightly on his throat as blood, his blood, streamed from either side of her mouth as she held him firmly against the stone walls of the bridge with a strength that belied her slight stature.

Much like a young child might observe a fox as it stalked and snatched a chicken that had strayed from the safety of the yard, unable to prevent the attack or assist the victim of it, he watched, helpless, as she let his double fall free of her arms, then stand over his unmoving body as it lay upon the bridge.

Desperately trying to hear what it was she was whispering to her unconscious victim, he found himself gliding, without physical assistance, until he was directly beside her. His eyes riveted on her he watched as she lanced her own flesh with a wolf-like fang until her own life blood seeped up around the tooth trickling over her lower lip. As her own blood pooled in her mouth, she leaned over and let it run into her victim's mouth, first from above him then directly through a blood smeared kiss that went on for several minutes. Wiping his mouth with her fingers then bringing them to her lips she licked the blood from her skin until, without warning, she abruptly took her gaze from his look-alike and stared directly at him with eyes burning red, void of all human contrast. For the first time since the waking nightmare had begun, she spoke in words that he could actually hear.

"And now, my dear Aremis, you can remember. I sincerely hope that it was worth it."

Terrified that he was no longer in some vivid recollection of buried memories and lost accounts but actually reliving the event within the present moment, he began to gag and choke on the red syrup she had let flow freely into his mouth more than a month earlier. The taste of iron enveloped, and then overwhelmed his senses, until he could no longer suppress that which seemed so real, he was forced into vomiting. A torrent of blood spewed forth from his mouth and pooled within the wheel ruts cut deep into the wet, packed earth of the driveway. The blood, its rich ruby colour defined further by the morning sunlight, created an illusion that looked as if the very ground had been slashed open and left to bleed out through the wound.

Shaking, his skin soaked with a cold sweat, the terrifying vision withdrew, retreating back to where it was nothing more real than a memory. Even though the sickening events were still fresh, lost to him for more than two months, they felt more like something that had taken place a very long time ago.

As the minutes trickled past he slowly began to regain his senses, focusing on the present moment and all around him rather than on the thoughts and images within his mind. The debilitating pain which had struck him so suddenly and with such severity, all without form or means was vanishing as quickly as it had first set on him, leaving in its wake a numbness that left most of his neck largely void of feeling.

Struggling to regain his legs, he pulled himself to his feet with the assistance of the fence rails. Clutching the rail for several minutes until he could be certain he would remain standing, he pulled his hand from what had been the source of several minutes of intense discomfort. Convinced that his hand would most certainly be covered in his own blood, he was both surprised and relieved, albeit somewhat confused, that there was nothing more disconcerting than that of blood belonging to a dead wolf upon his hands. He touched his neck several more times, each time inspecting his fingers for any evidence that he had indeed suffered a genuine injury, but nothing more than sweat mixed with animal blood ever materialized

Closing his eyes in the hopes of shaking off the remaining memories of over a few months ago, as well as those of only a few hours previous, he placed his arms, folded one over the other, on the gate's top rail and let his head hang down between them. He remained like that for several minutes, lost in the sound of the breeze as it rustled the few remaining leaves that stubbornly clung to the skeletal branches of the surrounding trees.

He felt his stomach growl and with that sensation was reminded he had not eaten since well before he had gone to assist his father with the horses. He opened his eyes, and as he stared down at the driveway, he noticed the blood he had expelled still pooled in the wheel ruts.

Momentarily mesmerized by the ruby coloured puddle at his feet he stared at it for several minutes, seemingly unaffected by its being there, before carefully beginning to disperse the blood pool along the length of the narrow gully with his boot so as to make it less obvious.

Surveying his work, not fully satisfied with his efforts, he made his way the short distance to where the driveway met the road. There he gathered a few handfuls of loose sand from the roadside's edge and returned to the bloody puddle, now more of a reddish stain within the wheel track, and poured the sand from his hands, completing the job of concealing what remained of the bloody smear behind a mask of sand and mud.

Dusting his hands off, he looked about in a somewhat nervous manner just in case someone may have been privy to what had just transpired. Satisfied that he was indeed quite alone in the early light of daybreak, he hoisted himself over the gate in one quick agile movement, landing steadfast on the other side.

Acting more like a thief than that of a trusted friend and neighbour, he darted up the driveway, sticking close to the trees rather than simply walking up the middle of the private roadway.

At the top of the driveway, where it crested the hill and broke free from the cover of tall elms that lined it, he came to a clearing that separated the family home from the main barn. The barn, its rough-cut timber planking weathered by years out in the elements, lay off to the left, nestled into a slight valley while the house, a white two story clapboard over field stone, very similar in many ways to that of his own home, stood off to the right at the top of another small hill.

He had only taken about half a dozen steps towards the barn where he had been instructed to wait for his sister's arrival when he stopped and turned his attention back towards the house. Standing there chilled and hungry, he took in the empty home's layout, its faded green trim, the slate roofing, the laundry line strung from the back porch to a post set near the wood shed, the patterned curtains still drawn over the windows.

Folding his arms across his chest, he continued to stare at the home wondering about the family who had built it, and lived there for so many years, more years in fact than he himself had been alive. Now, to have it standing empty, void of life altogether, made him sad.

Casting a look back towards the barn and then to the sun that was only just above the trees he discarded the original idea of waiting in the barn for what could easily amount to several hours and made his way towards the house in the hope of finding something to eat.

Climbing the front stars, the planking creaking under his weight, he found himself before the front door. A modest wooden nameplate with the name S.D. Smith carved into it was set high and in the middle of the door. He ran his fingers over the engraving before unconsciously knocking on the door. As the first then second knock echoed back, his third knock became more of a tap as he realised that no one would be there to answer his hail.

He waited several minutes nevertheless before trying the door's handle, which was, as he expected, unlocked. Releasing the bolt, he swung the door open and stepped across the threshold into the small foyer containing two doorways, one on each side, and a narrow hallway that led off towards the back of the house. The house was cold and felt empty. There was no fire in either the fireplace or in the firebox of the stove, nor had there been since the attack.

Closing the door behind him, he made his way through the living room towards the kitchen. It felt odd to be in someone else's home when they were not there to welcome him. And even though he knew the Smiths themselves could not possibly be there, there was still an eerie presence within the house that had him wondering if in fact they might still, in some way, be present.

Mrs. Smith's knitting bag was still set by a chair in the living room, an unfinished cardigan laid over the arm of that same chair, a book, its page marked by a scrap of yarn, still sat upon the table, its cover now covered in a thin layer of dust. In another corner of the room sat another chair with a similar wooden table beside it, a tobacco pipe set on a glass ashtray, a tobacco box next to it, that when seen taken together like that, told a silent story of winter evenings by the fire, a husband and wife chatting about the day's events or tomorrow's hopes and dreams.

Other than the thin dusty layer that seemed to cover everything, there was not much else that seemed out of place. It was probably fair to say that Mrs. Smith would have been similar in many ways to his mother, in as much as her kitchen was as immaculate as it was functional. His memories and mindful comparisons were soon replaced by a need to find some real food, and not just fantasy-filled ideas of fresh baked pies such as the one his mother and sister had made the day before. Figuring there would be little in the way of edible food remaining in the kitchen he looked for the door that would lead down to the cold cellar. It was several minutes before he discovered it. Unlike the home in which he had grown up having within its design an actual cellar door, this house simply had a trap door set into the floor of the kitchen which in turn was hidden by a small rug.

Hoisting the heavy door up and letting it fall back on the chain that held it from continuing backwards, he stared down into the blackness that lay beyond the wooden framed square cut out of the floor. There would be little point descending into a room that would be without windows and subsequently without light, and so the task of locating a candle and then matches became the next obstacle to overcome.

The candle was not much of a problem as there were many about the house; the matches, on the other hand, were proving more of a challenge. Not until having searched the entire kitchen twice over without success did he recall Mr. Smith's pipe and tobacco on the table in the living room. A quick search of the small table yielded a small metal tin, the contents of which was a small stash of wooden matches.

Returning to the kitchen with his prize he lit two candles, one to take with him and one to set at the opening to the cellar in case the one in his hand should fall victim to unforeseen drafts and be blown out.

With the single candle in hand, he cautiously made his way down the ladder-like stairs to a space that was barely 5' high, a tight fit for almost anyone. Rooting about in the dim light he quickly found several baskets containing both pears and apples from the summer just past. Setting the candle and its holder upon the edge of shelf he removed a pear, quickly feeling for bruises or burrowing holes left by insect invaders looking for a winter home, and upon finding neither, he took a much anticipated bite. The first pear was devoured in a manner of seconds followed by two apples ingested in much the same fashion.

His hunger abated for the moment, he plucked two more of each fruit from their respective resting places and tucked them into his coat pocket for later. Retrieving the candle he continued his search of the cramped storage area beneath the house but after finding little else of interest he returned to the kitchen, closing the trap door behind him.

Making his way back to the front door he peered out through the glass, scanning the driveway and road beyond the fences for any sign of his sister. He remained like that for several minutes before pulling his attention away and returning it to the interior of the home.

Standing in the small foyer, the family room off to the right and the modest dining room to his left, he still felt peculiar about being in the house without its owners present. He was about to make his way back to the kitchen when a picture hanging on the wall near the staircase caught his eye. Photographs being still in their infancy and certainly by no means commonplace, he was immediately curious about its subject. His parents had only a few such photographs in their home and they were of his parents on their wedding day and one of each child at the age of about 5 years.

He stood before the black-framed picture studying the three people as they stood all looking very proper within the glass covered ebony border. Carefully removing the picture from the hook, he took it over to the front windows so as to see the images more clearly in the light. There in the sunlight, captured within variation of grey, was Mr. and Mrs. Smith, and between them their daughter Mary looking to be about age 13.

He stared at the picture for many minutes, taking his time with each figure, looking into their eyes, starting with Harry then moving to Emma and finally settling on Mary. As he stared at her features locked away forever within the chemicals and paper, he placed his finger onto the glass over her cheek and softly caressed the smooth cold surface.

A drop of water spattered onto the glass and was smeared beneath his finger. He withdrew his finger from the glass then directed his attentions towards the ceiling before realising that the droplet of water had in fact been his own tear which had fallen onto the picture.

'Perhaps you are right Iris,' he thought returning his gaze to the portrait, 'I have not grieved for this family, for this girl who was to be my wife, for my own life that been lost to me also.'

Thoughts of this family and of his own, both before as well as after the attack whirled about inside his mind. Taking a final quick look at the picture within his hands, he tucked it under his arm, pushing the thoughts from his mind as he did so.

With the portrait secured beneath his arm, he made his way up the stairs and quietly went from room to room. Starting at what was surely the bedroom of Mr. and Mrs. Smith, the bed still made, a basket of folded laundry set to one side of it ready to be put away, a series of books on one night table while another pipe and ashtray was set on the other. As he took in the room, its contents began silently telling the story of the people who had once lived there, their habits and routines of daily life, without so much as a single word having been spoken.

Opening the door to the next of the two remaining rooms, one that may have once been designed for a second child - a child that for whatever reason never came into being, had been converted into a sewing room. Even with his untrained eye for such matters, he could tell very quickly that Emma Smith must have been quite an accomplished seamstress. There were numerous works partially made, both for men and women. Rolls of material had been stacked up on a table next to the far wall, while on the other side of the room a very modern foot pump sewing machine that appeared to be at best only one or perhaps two years old. Anyone involved with thievery would have most certainly seized the opportunity to pilfer an item such as that and have it sold, if not the same day, then most certainly before the dawn of the next one. It would have been an easy deduction to make for the detectives investigating the murders that robbery could not possibly have been the reason behind the attacks that night.

The last room was located at the end of the hall on the backside of the house and with only one other occupant residing within the home, it could only be that belonging to Mary. Gingerly pushing the door open, sunshine streaming from the enclosure into the hallway filling it with a warm glow, he stepped into the room and for the first time since arriving at the house, felt as though he was indeed trespassing.

Looking about the room from its threshold, not quite willing to violate it further with his uninvited presence, he took in what he could from his place at the door. As it had been in her parent's room, her bed was made and her bedclothes were laid out on her pillow for that evening's retirement. There was an oil lamp on her nightstand and a small dresser with a mirror set to one side of the room's single closet. A small book with a red ribbon wrapped around its cover caught his eye. A point of curiosity, one he could not seem to quell, he drew a deep breath and quietly entered the room, making his way to the nightstand.

Carefully lifting the book from where it had been placed, in all likelihood by Mary herself, possibly only a few hours before she and her family were killed, sent a shiver up his spine. He knew before he pulled the ribbon that held the covers tightly closed that this book was her diary. He knew this firsthand, for Temperance had one very similar, if not exactly the same.

He sat down on the edge of the bed and carefully flipped through the pages that were filled, for the most part, with Mary's handwriting separated by little pictures highlighting points of interest in this girl's life. As the pages slipped past his fingers, he suddenly stopped the procession of paper with his thumb and flipped backwards through several pages until he had arrived at the thing that had caught his eye. A wide smile broke over his face as he looked down at an artistic rendering of a man on horseback, a small arrow pointing to the man, the words Aremis above the arrow, the name encircled in a heart.

He pulled the picture, which he still had tucked under his arm, free and placed it under the diary so he could look upon her face and the drawing, which she had created simultaneously. The smile that had taken his features so suddenly was quickly fading as he gazed at the photo image and the hand-drawn rendering. His emotions welled up within him, flowing freely from him as he broke down, slipping from the bed onto the floor as he clutched both the picture and diary to his chest crying.

Chapter 7

Dear Diary,

I am writing from the barn, where I have been packing some of my brother's things whilst my parents are at church. Mother insisted that I stay home in order to keep watch over Aremis. I feel as though I am trapped within a horrible nightmare, one from which I cannot awaken. My darkest fears have been realized: that my brother is not completely himself. But nor is he completely of the darkness, that of which I do not understand but know most surely contaminates his being. I came upon him last night in the midst of attacking Iris. If she had been alone, had I not intervened, I cannot say for certain the outcome would have ended as it did.

I have shown Aremis the evidence of his actions: the sheep he himself had slain, his nightclothes blood-soaked and hidden in the woodland of our very property. In fact, I very nearly ended his life last night.

I have no idea if I have made the right choice in doing what I have done, what I still plan to do, but feel I have little, if any, choice. My other sight does not show me the answers I so desperately need and I feel no connection to God, no guidance as to what is right or wrong. I feel alone and yet I would not wish to share this with those I love for they would not understand and I would not wish to burden them with this horror. Soon I must begin to spin the web of lies to those I feel most close to, all so that we may one day be a family again. I must close for now. I hope by this time tomorrow I will, at the very least, have some better news to tell you and perhaps even something genuinely uplifting.

Temperance, the 15th of December in the year of our Lord, 1874.

It had been a dreadful twenty-four hours for Temperance, most of which no one would ever come to know. Having set out the night before with the intention of killing her own brother to now being charged with telling her parents that their only son had suddenly decided to up and leave the farm in order to seek out work in the city had all but brought her to the brink of a breakdown.

Her sister was another matter entirely. Iris was still in their parents' room when Temperance arrived back from the woods. She had to call out for her several times before she emerged and came running down the stairs so fast Temperance felt certain that she would lose her footing and crash headlong into the floor. She had managed to set the rifle down in the nick of time before catching her younger sibling near full flight at the bottom of the stairs, her eyes all red from crying, her speech barely discernible.

"I heard the gun shot!" She wailed, "Did you kill him, did he hurt you, is he dead, is he dead?"

"Hush now, it is alright now, hush. I need you to calm down, we have much to do, you and I, and we have precious little time in which to accomplish it."

Her voice was low and relaxed and it was not long before her sister had gathered herself into a more composed state. With Iris settled, as much as could be expected given the ordeal of the last few hours, Temperance told her of her plan, one that initially did not sit well with her younger sibling.

"It is the only way, Iris, I swear, other than killing him in cold blood, an act of which I could not explain and one of which would certainly see me hanged. I am sure you would not wish that on me would you?"

Iris shook her head violently trying to contain a new level of anguish that was building up within her.

"Good. I need you to be strong now or this plan will fall apart as surely as the coming sun will rise in a few hours. Can you do this?"

Her sister nodded wiping her eyes as she did.

Temperance then began to tell her of what had happened in the woods, of the wolf and of the raven, of her prayers and, finally, of her plan to let her brother live in the hope that he could find an answer to his affliction in the city, far from those he loved and cared for.

"All I need for you to do is agree with me. If Mother or Father put any questions to you all you have to do is say something to the effect 'Aremis spoke to Temperance of it mostly, he only told me as he was leaving'. Do you understand?"

"I understand Tempie, I do not like lying to Mother or Father though, it is a sin you know."

Temperance smiled at her sister as much as the statement itself for if lying was a sin then what was setting a monster loose on the city of London considered to be in the eyes of the Lord?

"It will be alright, sweetie, sometimes our faith will have us do things that might seem wrong but are done for the right reasons, and not having Mother and Father worrying about Aremis right now is most certainly right."

She hugged her sister tightly as she continued the rest of her address within the privacy of her own thoughts.

'...and dear sister it is far better not to have the Devil's minion living in the room next to that of our own, and of that I know, that I am most certainly correct.'

Although still unbelievable to her, that her brother would no longer be living with them, the news was received remarkably well by both parents. Her mother, as expected, had taken the news the hardest, unable to fully understand why the decision was made so suddenly and without so much as a word to anyone during lunch or before they left for the evening. It had taken some clever bending of the truth to convince her mother that he had only been toying with the idea the last few weeks, not really taking the idea all that seriously, but when the men happened by that night on the way to London to help build some of the new rail lines he simply could not pass up the opportunity or the free ride.

Unlike the reaction of her mother, her father's response was one of quiet understanding. He seemed to appreciate the reasons within the tale she had spun regarding her brother. His desire for some time away, both from the farm and the family, but most of all to distance himself from the pain he felt at the loss of his bride. For her father, there was something bravely honourable to choose to work for a stranger over that of kin in order to find closure.

Iris had kept up her part of the bargain, maintaining a level of composure fit for the situation, explaining away a sudden tearful exhibition as a result of missing her brother which sent their mother over to comfort her and removed Temperance from any further questioning at that moment.

The second part of the plan, getting her brother's things to him, was to be far trickier than Temperance had initially realized. Forgetting that it would be Sunday morning and that all the shops and feed stores would be closed, she had not foreseen the difficulty of trying to get the wagon ready for an alleged trip into town. By the time the lunchtime meal was over she was in a state of internal panic that was nearing the breaking point. It was not until

Iris, now well aware of the plan and all that was at stake, wandered into the kitchen from the living room and in a matter of fact voice asked Temperance if she had forgotten that she had told Mrs. Harrington that she would lend a hand doing linens after church.

Temperance, looking somewhat bewildered at the question that had been put to her knowing full well no such plan had ever been made, suddenly understood the meaning behind her sister's careful words.

"Oh heavens," She exclaimed "with all that has gone on around here the last little while it must have completely slipped my mind. I hope she will not be cross with me."

Temperance pulled off her apron and ran upstairs to get changed and was back downstairs in short order.

"Temperance," her mother called to her.

She stopped in her tracks, certain that the careful ploy had somehow been found out.

"Yes, Mum,"

"You know the importance of keeping one's word now. I know that you have been preoccupied with your brother that last few weeks and currently, but do not let something like being forgetful tarnish your good name."

Temperance smiled back at her mother's attempt at stern warning, which got a slight smile from the woman who just levied it.

"Do not worry, Mum. I will still be there in good time." She replied in an up-tempo voice.

"I should hope so, be off with you. Give our regards to the Harringtons and be sure to tell them of your brother going off like that. I am sure they will be interested."

"Yes Mum, I will."

And with that she bolted out the back door and raced to the barn where she had stashed as many of her brother's things as she thought he could use as well as comfortably carry.

As she entered the barn she was now relieved that it was Sunday for it would be the one day of the week she could be certain her father would not be someplace close by. Sunday afternoons, for her father, were spent in the living room reading the bible or chatting with her mother in the kitchen, and on occasion even helping with the dinner.

Grabbing the small satchel from behind a toolbox, she set it upon a workbench then went about saddling up a chestnut mare named Velvet. Velvet was her favourite horse and it usually served duty with another piebald mare named Trinket when her parents needed to go to town or went visiting as they had done the night before. She had not been out riding in some time as it was deemed more ladylike to ride in a wagon than on horseback.

The saddle securely in place upon the mare, she pulled herself up onto Velvet and raced out of the barn, turning the thundering mare towards the road.

Her mother came out onto the porch shouting and pointing at her as she galloped by. Temperance felt certain that it was yet another warning regarding her less than ladylike behaviour, but there was no way to know for sure as the sound of Velvet's hooves combined with the wind in her ears effectively blocked out all auditory communication coming from her mother, and so she simply waved and shouted her goodbyes before making the gate and turning out onto the roadway.

Following the short trip to the Smith farm, made even shorter by the speed she had pressed Velvet to maintain, it was not long before she found herself at the driveway of the abandoned farmstead. The familiar fifteen-minute ride she had come to know as a child seemingly taken only a few seconds.

Not feeling comfortable leaving Velvet tethered to the gatepost, she sought out another means of entry. Following the roadway a short distance she came upon a break in the fence large enough to allow both her and her ride passage.

Once she had negotiated the makeshift means of access through the stone and split rail fencing, she carefully plotted a path though the unkempt wind-whipped weeds that, despite the short time period, had all but taken over the once-tidy area.

Riding slowly up to the barn, its large wooden doors closed over and securely latched from the outside with a heavy wooden beam, she suddenly felt uneasy. Knowing that it would be impossible for someone to get inside the barn and then place the beam between the iron holders on the doors, she looked about the landscape nervously.

"Damn it, where are you?" she whispered, her hand up to her brow in order to shield her eyes from the mid afternoon sun her mind full of dark possibilities. Perhaps he had thought better of her idea. Perhaps he had run into another wolf whilst making his way through the woodland and not survived the encounter. More frightening however, was the thought that he might very well be there now, watching her from some secluded spot, waiting for an opportunity to take her unawares.

She forced the thoughts from her mind, focussing instead on making her way around the small scattering of out buildings, and upon finding them as secured as the barn she turned her attentions to the only structure left, the house itself.

Leaving the horse un-tethered by the front stairs leading to the veranda in case she needed to make a hasty exit, she patted the animal softly on the neck telling her to behave and not run off as she removed the gunnysack from the saddle.

"You be good now Velvet. I will be right back." She said with a voice very much hushed.

She crept up the front steps then stopped in her tracks as she noticed the front door ajar.

"Aremis?" she whispered.

There was no reply to her purposefully muted hail.

She swallowed hard and removed a small knife that she had concealed in the duffle bag before setting the loaded satchel down on the veranda.

She gently pushed the front door open and let her eyes adjust to the dim light within the interior of the home. In a hushed voice she once again called out for her brother, and once again the only answer she received was that of silence.

With the point of the knife leading her way she slowly made her way around the rooms of the first floor, the cold still air within the quiet living space making her feel as though she were in a tomb and not a house at all. Continuing to navigate the main floor for signs of her brother she found little that would indicate he had been there, until she entered the kitchen. There she suddenly had her fears confirmed that she very well might not be alone, for there on the counter was the core of an apple, its white flesh now, for the most part, the colour of cider. She inspected the discarded fruit knowing well that if it had been there for more than a day it would have been dried and dark while this one she now held in her hand was still fresh.

She set it back down on the counter and looked about her surroundings before making her way down the hallway that led from the kitchen and to the staircase leading to the second floor.

The stairs creaked one by one as she slowly made the ascent to the upper floor with the knife still held tightly in her grasp, her heart beat pounding in her ears.

The sunlight beamed through the thin sheers that hung over the window at the far end of the hallway, its light capturing tiny dust particles that hung suspended in the still unmoving air.

Temperance surveyed the hallway from the relative safety of the stairs, casting her eyes through the balusters while she remained unmoving, still three steps from the top. From her vantage point she could see all four doorways belonging to the upper level rooms, all but one of which had their doors open, the exception being that of the linen closet located between the two bedroom doors closest to the stairwell.

With little in the way of choices, she quietly mounted the last of the steps until she was standing in the upper hallway. She stuck her head into the first and closest of the bedrooms only to find it empty. Relieved, while not in the least bit comforted by the discovery, or lack of same, she cautiously moved past the linen closet to the next room and peering in found it to be the same as the first one, furnished but void of life. Turning her attention from the second room back to the hallway and the last room that lay at the end of it, she took a deep breath while reaffirming her grip on the knife. She hugged the wall that was opposite to the door she approached, giving her the most visibility into the final room.

Through the open door she could only see a small portion of the room as the door itself actually blocked the rest of the interior from her, which meant she would have to actually enter the room in order to inspect it. She crept in, holding her breath; she peered around the edge of the door. The breath she had held slowly slipped past her lips when she found her brother fast asleep on the small bed, a book beside him and what appeared to be a framed picture held to his chest.

She thought about calling to him from where she was in case she needed to retreat but then thought better of it. She knew that if he were no longer the brother she remembered then it would be foolish to think he could not easily overtake her before she could reach the front door and mount her horse. Without much in the way of safe options from which to choose she quietly made her way to the bedside and with the knife held tightly in her grip, her thoughts of using it planted just as firmly in her mind, she eased herself onto the bed beside her brother.

Her weight on the bed not seeming to disturb his slumber, she watched his face for several minutes remembering back to simpler times with him. Times where she would sneak into his room on Christmas morning and shake him from his slumber in order to tell him that Saint Nicholas had come in the night. Or the other times when she went in looking for consoling after having been scolded for some indiscretion or wrongdoing. Now as she looked down on him, a tear trickling down one cheek, she longed to have those times returned to her once again.

She turned her face to wipe the tear from her eye then noticing the book on the bed she picked it up, closed it over and read the word 'My Diary' embossed in the cover.

Setting it back on the bed she returned her gaze to her elder sibling and softly whispered his name.

"Aremis, wake up."

She watched his eyes flutter open, close again and then open fully

Relieved they were the crystal blue she had grown to know and not the red she had witnessed that night at the Harringtons, she rubbed his hand that lay clamped down over the picture upon his chest.

"Temperance, what, where are we, what happened?" His voice was sleepy and he sounded quite disoriented, almost panicked.

"Shh, I am with you now. I was worried when I could not find you. I thought something dreadful might have happened."

His eyes looked about the room as he tried to align his thoughts with the surroundings he now found himself in.

"Where are we?" he asked in voice more like his own.

"We are at the Smith farm," she said concerned, "do you not remember?"

He squinted at his sister as if to somehow try and recall the memories she was describing either in his own mind or someplace in between her thoughts and those of his own.

"The woods last night," she continued, "the plans for you go to London..."

"Yes, yes, of course, forgive me, it would appear that I am still quite asleep."

Temperance, a nervous smile upon her face, was relieved to discover that he seemed to be very much himself.

"What do you have there?" she asked tapping his hand softly with her fingertip.

He raised his head from the pillow to see what it was that she was referring to and then closed his eyes, letting his head fall back into the silken covered softness.

He removed his hand from the picture so that is remained unsecured upon his chest and told his sister to look at it. As she took it from him and slowly rolled the wooden frame over to see the contents that lay behind the glass, he explained what it was she was looking at.

"That is Mary, there in the middle..." his voice trailed off, and as it did he placed his hand over his eyes to try and hide what he was feeling as much from himself as his sister.

As she stared at the three figures, their near emotionless faces staring back at her from beneath the glass, she did not know what she could possibly say to her bother that could in any way ease how he might be feeling, or to convey that she too was feeling sorrow for a loss most terrible.

"Aremis," she began, but was cut off before she could even get her the whole of her thought out.

"I read her diary. I know it is private but I thought since she was dead then what harm could there be in it."

He paused to make eye contact with her before continuing.

"She had liked me for a long, long time. Did you know that?"

Temperance shook her head.

"There are pictures of me that she had drawn, her thoughts about how she felt, her dreams of marrying me some day, her whole life is laid out in that little book. It is all that I have left of her. There is nothing else, no future with her. I shall never know her voice, her laughter, her sorrow, nothing. There will never be another entry in this book."

There was a long pause in which time, at least within the confines of the tiny bedroom, seemed to stand still.

"I will kill the woman who has brought this upon me!" he shouted.

The sudden unprovoked outburst took Temperance by surprise and she jumped from the bed. Even though quite startled she managed to keep the knife concealed from his view.

Seeing his sister leap from his side, obviously as a result of his voice and words calmed him immediately.

"Oh Tempie, I am so sorry. I did not mean to frighten you so, you of all people, I could never harm in any way. I would sooner take my own life before I would allow that to happen."

Relieved by his words as much as his tone of voice, she relaxed her guard if but marginally as she gathered her thoughts.

"I know you must be very angry, and with just cause, truly, but killing another to avenge those senseless deaths will serve them no purpose or provide them any measure of comfort and would most surely stain your hands for all eternity. I would not wish that for my dearest brother."

He looked away for a moment, not happy that his own flesh and blood did not share his desire for justice by his own hand but quickly returned his thoughts and eyes back to her.

"So now what?" he inquired in a voice that lacked any enthusiasm.

"Well, we have to get you to London but before that we have to get out of this room and house. I am afraid that I have little time to spend before I shall be missed."

As the two made their way downstairs and onto the front veranda, Temperance explained to her brother how she had broken the news to their parents regarding his sudden decision to leave. The whole idea still did not sit well with him, but there did not really seem to be any other option available. The problem of how he was going to travel the several hundred miles that lay between his home and the city of London presented an obstacle more daunting than the distance was great.

Outside the sun was already well across the mid winter sky which left little doubt in the mind of the plan maker that time was short at hand.

"We will have to hurry now," she said over her shoulder as she hopped down the stairs and with careful deception slipped the knife into the top sleeve of the satchel as so not to draw his attention to it.

"I have brought all that I thought you might need. I hope that it is going to be enough to carry you through until you get yourself settled."

Her voice was artificially uplifted but she thought it better that way rather than portray how she was really feeling inside. She could not afford for him to rethink the whole scheme, or worse yet, simply to refuse to leave. She knew that without the rifle as her insurance it would be all but impossible for her to force him to do something he did not wish to do and, with nothing more than a kitchen knife for persuasion, she would quickly find herself at what could turn out to be a deadly impasse.

Removing a bag she had tethered to the saddle, she handed it to her brother to hold while she began to root through it. Not bothering with his sister's actions, lost in his own thoughts of a situation both of them found to be nothing short of unthinkable, he pondered an uncertain future.

Finding that which she was in search of, she paused and looked into her brother's eyes before she spoke. She needed to be sure she had a long-established connection before continuing. His far off look diminished as he focused on her face,

"What?" He asked in quiet voice that was almost unfamiliar to him.

"I have brought something for you," she began, then stopped, not pleased with her choice of wording. "This is so awkward."

For the first time since arriving at the Smith farm, and perhaps since the whole horrid situation began to unfold, she felt her resolve fading away like a child's sand castle against the incoming tide until she could no longer maintain her composure. Tears filled her eyes and she hid her face from him so as not to look vulnerable. As she cast her eyes down, watching the tiny drops fall from her cheeks and land in the arid winter soil, she felt his free hand light upon her shoulder. Softly he began to rub her shoulders and upper back until she was in a warm embrace. She cried openly on his chest unable to form any words that would soothe the way she felt or ease the horrible situation.

Minutes seemed to slip past before her sobs began to ease. She heard his voice from somewhere above her, soft and familiar, his words drifting down to her like so many other times in her life when she found herself at some impasse.

"Come on now," he said in a voice most gentle, "everything will be fine, you will see. No need for all this outpouring." He paused and squeezed her tightly to him. "Besides, if you keep on you will soon make your shoes all muddy."

Her sobs turned to a momentary giggle at his words before she fell silent, a silence formed from sadness and loss, a loss that in reality had not yet taken place for he still stood before her, holding her tightly to himself. There was indeed a loss, however, perhaps one not readily seen but one just as real, and having him still there with her made that loss much harder to cope with.

With her hand still in the satchel she pulled herself together and eased away from his embrace. She was still unable to make eye contact with him as she began once more, that which she found so hard to contemplate, much less make conversation about.

"Aremis... I have no easy way of saying this, to tell you that what I do now is out of love and concern for you. Please do not think me as wicked."

With that said she pulled a wine bottle from within the bag and pressed it into his hand.

Momentarily bewildered by the bottle in his hand he looked first at it then at his sister in the hopes of understanding the meaning behind both the bottle and her hardship over giving it to him.

"I do not understand," he said quietly, the confusion more than apparent in his voice. "You of all people should know I do not drink, and how Mother feels about alcohol, why do you give me such a gift?"

She looked up at him the tears still in her eyes,

"It is not wine. It is..." She paused, looking away briefly, then brought her eyes back to meet his. "...blood."

Aremis took a step backwards as if pushed by the very words uttered by his sister, a gasp slipping from him as he did so.

"Blood!" he said sharply holding the bottle out in front of him. "You have gone mad."

Temperance pulled back from him, taking with her the satchel so she might have the knife close at hand. She took several steps back putting more distance between herself and her brother.

"Please, do not be cross with me," she pleaded. "I fear for you and I do not wish you to harm anyone or anything on your way to London."

He glared at her, as he held the bottle more like a club than a container of liquid.

"What do you think I am, some animal, void of thought and reason?"

But before she could even form an answer his face suddenly softened and he looked away from her, turning his gaze off to the woodland that lay beyond the barn.

"Forgive me," he said under his breath, not bothering to look at her as he said it.

"The sheep, do you remember? I am only trying to help." Her voice was cracked and dry.

"Yes, I remember," he put a hand to his face and rubbed his eyes with his fingertips. "How can I forget?"

"I am so sorry, Aremis, I do not know what else I can do."

He turned to her, his hand now away from his eyes.

"This is fine, you have been remarkable all things considered, there is nothing more for you to do; the rest will be up to me."

She held the bag in front of her like a protective shield as she nodded her agreement with his statement.

"There is one more bottle in the bag, I hope it will be enough to last you." She said in a solemn voice.

When you were ill, Dr. Harrington gave you willow-bark water for your fever and pain. He said he could not give you too strong a mixture, as it would thin your blood and slow the healing of your wound. I have made a strong mixture, as he described, and combined it with the chicken blood so as to prevent its clotting.

He chuckled almost sarcastically,

"It will take me some time to walk to London, it does not lay just over that hill." He pointed off in a vague undefined direction towards some unseen escarpment beyond the trees.

"You shall not be walking to London," she announced with a renewed firmness in her voice.

Somewhat annoyed at his sister's tone he turned to face her with his arms outstretched to his sides.

"Is that indeed fact? And how, might I inquire, do you propose I get there? On Velvet? Where do you think I would manage to find a place within the city that would have accommodations for a horse, and how would you explain the absence of one of our horses to father a full day after I was to have left?"

He folded his arms over his chest at the conclusion of his rant.

More irritated than frightened at this point, Temperance launched back with a simple reply, but one that carried with it little doubt she was serious and not willing to negotiate.

"I am taking you to the train station, you will be taking the 7:00 o'clock to London tonight. You will, under no circumstances, be making your way to London on foot, is that understood?"

"A train, I am to take a train?" he mocked. "And how am I to afford such lavish means of transport, have you even given this plan of yours any real thought at all?"

Nearly enraged by his attitude, convinced that he had no real idea of how much she was risking in order to help him or how serious the entire situation was, she nearly threw the satchel at him but then thought better of it.

"Aremis Eilbeck you are nothing short of impossible at times! Do you not see that I am trying to help you?"

She waited for some sort of a reply but when none was forthcoming she carried on.

"I have been doing a number of jobs for Mrs. Harrington as well as the Johnstons and I have managed to save a little sum of money. I am going to buy you a ticket and give you the rest to go towards rent and food. Hopefully it will be enough to get you through until you can either speak with a minister, physician or find employment."

Another awkward silence ensued that lasted several minutes before it was broken by a meek sounding voice.

"So, what happens now?" he asked.

Still quite put out with her elder sibling, she ran her fingers though her hair brushing it back from her face then turning away she looked out towards the trees.

"Temperance?"

"What?" She snapped, her irritation more than apparent in both her tone and posture.

For the fourth time in less than a quarter of an hour he found himself shamefully apologizing to his sister.

"I am sorry,"

"As am I," she replied. Pausing for a moment to take a breath then turning back to face him she continued.

"Do you think I want you to leave? Do think I find any of this easy, that I am not dying inside knowing that I am the one who is providing you the means to leave me, leave our family?"

"No, I mean yes, of course, I understand. I just cannot believe this is happening, that it has to be this way. I never thought I would be leaving this village, not like this anyway, under a curtain of lies and darkness.

Temperance nodded, grasping the depth of his feelings and what he was forced to deal with. The thought of being in the same situation he now faced, essentially cut off from all she had come to know, had her feeling like finding some other way to deal with this. She had become so preoccupied with arranging his leaving and worrying about protecting her family that she had lost sight of the human part of her brother, a part that she was hoping desperately to save, a part that now must feel alone and frightened.

She quickly pushed any notion from her mind, shaking her head slightly as if to deny the existence of any new idea she might have given birth to before it had a chance to develop.

"That is alright, there is little point in you and I exchanging harsh words with each other. This situation is neither your fault nor is it mine but it has become ours, and together we must try to seek out a remedy with not much more than our wits to work with."

Her voice was firm but kind, her words finding their mark and producing the desired effect.

"True enough," he replied, his free hand rubbing the back of his neck. "So do we make our way to the train station in Totton?"

Temperance held her breath at hearing the question put to her, not wanting her answer to incite another outburst or further discourse between them.

"Well," she began slowly, trying to think of a delicate way to say what needed to be said, "I guess that would depend on when you last had blood." She blurted out the last word that seemed lodged in her throat.

Her words suddenly conjured up memories of his ordeal at the gates to the Smith farm some hours earlier were he had thrown up whatever blood he may have had in him at the time. He felt certain that at that moment, at the gates, his mind was clear, but standing in the front yard now he had no recollection of how or where the blood had come from, nor did he really want to know.

"Do you think I should drink some of this now then?" He asked in a voice that was startling matter of fact for the task being posed.

"I think it might be wise," she replied

He brought the bottle up before him and tilted it around slowly, watching the thick crimson liquid glide around the inside of the glass. He thought he would find the idea of actually drinking blood repulsive, but as he watched the fluid as it slowly continued to spin within the makeshift chalice he found himself drawn in by its color and, more surprisingly, the scent, even though the bottle remained quite sealed.

"Where did you get this from?" he asked, his thoughts still immersed in the unfamiliar senses that were awakening within him.

The question brought back vivid memories of the night before where, upon her return to the family home from her ordeal in the woods, her plan already near completion, she had gone out to the chicken house and there, releasing the flock to night and possible predators she tore out one side of screening installed to allow fresh air into the hen house, then grabbing four of the older hens she snapped their necks. Pulling off handfuls of feathers from the dead birds she let them fall to the ground for the wind to scatter about before making her way to the barn in order to cut and drain the birds into the two bottles she had brought with her.

"I took it from some of the chickens," she said at last.

Aremis took his eyes from the bottle and looked at this sister.

"I feel certain that someone will figure out what is going on." He said in a cool voice.

She shook her head in rebuttal to his statement.

"Sometimes the fox gets in no matter the efforts taken." She replied in near identical tone to that of her brother's.

He half-chuckled, knowing full well that if his sister has put her mind to something then whatever it might be it is sure to have been done to polished perfection and nothing short of that, even if, as in this case, the purpose was to deceive.

He pulled the cork from the bottle and brought the open end to his lips. Then, without much thought, he let the syrup-like substance fill his mouth.

The first sensation was one of iron, a taste that almost hurt his tongue to the point he was afraid to swallow for fear it might in some way harm him. But as the seconds flashed by, the harsh taste began to diminish, transforming into something similar to that of cider, both bitter and sweet together and yet not. Then, before he had time to think on it further, he had swallowed it. The sensation afterwards was one of sweetness in his mouth and a warm comfortable feeling in his stomach, a warmth that seemed to progress throughout his body until he was quite unawares of the chill still within the air.

He took another mouthful, this time tasting only the sweet as it flowed over his tongue. He swished it around in his mouth, savouring the new sensations that seemed to be coming one upon another now as he moved the liquid back and swallowed it.

He felt as though he could drain the rest of the bottle's contents in one last gulp but thought it wise to save the remainder for sometime later. If it be true that he needed this ubiquitous liquid that, was indeed everywhere but for obvious reasons not easily available, then it would be prudent not to drink all of what he had before his journey had even begun.

He forced the cork back into the bottle and ran his thumb over his lips to ensure there was no sign left to give silent testimony to his morbid choice of beverage.

"Are you alright?" Temperance asked with much concern.

"Quite fine," careful not to sound too elated about how he was feeling inside. It was not difficult to tame the newfound sensations when faced with the reasons behind their existence combined with a future that was far from desired.

"Do you think that will be enough for now?" he asked, holding the bottle up, shifting the focus from himself and that of his feelings back the situation at hand.

"I have no idea, in God's name. How could either of us know what is enough?" she replied. "I would imagine if you feel more like yourself than you have of late then I guess it will be fine for the time being."

Aremis looked himself over as though he was scrutinizing the fit of a new overcoat, then announced that he was indeed feeling as fine as any other day in his memories, memories of a time well before this nightmare had besieged him.

The two then spent the next few minutes sorting out some of the other details of his leaving so their stories matched. She told him that he was to write as soon as he had arrived in London and was settled; otherwise, their parents would worry themselves sick. He was to then write her separately and keep her informed about what was happening in regards to his illness. He was to post the letters to her with the Harrington's address upon them. She would then collect the letters from there when she went over each week to help the doctor and his wife. This was as so not to raise suspicions that things may not be as normal as they appeared to be.

Not exactly sure of how she was going to accomplish having to collect her mail from the Harrington's, she was all but certain that Agnes would not see her stuck and if need be she was quite prepared to simply tell her the truth, as bizarre as it was, although she hoped that it would not come down to that.

She asked Aremis if he would ride to the train station and let her sit behind him. She said that she was feeling exhausted by the entire ordeal and wanted to rest a bit before having to ride home again. The truth be known, she felt safer with him in front of her than she would if he were at her back. She'd not come this far to then fall victim to whatever might lay in wait just below the surface of her brother's familiar features.

He agreed and mounted the chestnut mare. Then, holding out his hand to her, he pulled her up behind him in one smooth movement.

"Are you comfortable?" he asked, his head turned slightly her way.

"Yes, fine thank you." She readjusted herself slightly then directed his attentions towards the fence where she had first made her way onto the property.

"I found an opening in the fence just over there."

Following her direction he guided the horse through the undergrowth to where the fence was in disrepair and out onto the road.

The train station was some 10 miles away, and on horseback they would arrive well ahead of nightfall. If luck held out, they would be in time to catch the last train leaving that evening.

As they came out from beneath the canopy of intertwined tree branches that, in summer would be filled with leaves creating a living ceiling of green overhead, they crested the hilltop that overlooked the township of Totton, which was considerably bigger than their own little hamlet.

There on the hill, looking over the town, they stopped, taking in the landscape of rooftops and stone buildings that all but filled the valley below, the truth of what must be done now staring back at them with a stark, cruel reality.

Temperance placed her arms around her brother and tightened the grip but for a moment, before she relaxed her hold of him, not wanting to fuel any ideas he might have of staying back.

With a soft clicking sound and a gentle tap of his boot heels on the animal's sides he urged Velvet to motion once more, following the road's gentle curves as it led into the town.

He had only been to Totton once or twice during the course of his life, but despite this time related obstacle, he found his way through the narrow, business-lined streets, with relative ease. The maze of homes and businesses leading to a cobble-stone clearing, a small open courtyard of sorts, its perimeter lined with wagons and carts, some empty while others lay burdened with the spoils of local labour, the fruits of which were to be loaded into train cars then shipped off to distant places. Beyond these worn looking wagons were parked one or two finer looking carriages, their black paint and polished brass lamps gleaming in what was left of the vanishing afternoon sunlight. Their well-groomed horses, some with ornamental decoration upon their harnesses, stood fidgeting restlessly, eager to be on their way, while others drank from the numerous water troughs apparently enjoying the reprieve from their duties.

This was the Totton Township Train Station, a single wooden building with a large overhanging roof extending out in either direction that covered a large platform placed parallel to the double lines of steel rails. A building that served not only as the main junction for rail service for both the passengers and freight alike but was also home to the local post office.

"Looks busy." Aremis commented as he carefully guided Velvet through the myriad of obstacles in search of a place to tether their horse.

Temperance did not reply until they had come to a row of cast iron hitches set in the ground near the far end of the building.

"Yes, it is. I cannot recall seeing so many unfamiliar faces in one place at a single time," she said looking about the area before she continued.

He offered his hand to his sister who took hold and let herself down, then stepped back as he dropped down beside her, quickly lashing the reigns to the iron ring in the hitch post.

The two made their way along the wooden boardwalk that ran along the front of the old building, its yellow paint peeling in a number of places, until they were standing under a white sign, upon which was simply written 'TICKETS'.

Temperance stepped up to the small window that had a circle cut in the middle of the glass and another rectangular cut out at the bottom. She looked through the glass into the lamp glow of the small ticket booth. A man of slight build, wearing thin wire glasses, his grey hairline well receded sat in a chair directly before the window looking down at papers that lay upon his desk.

"Excuse me," she asked politely as she leaned towards the glass so as to be heard.

The man behind the glass looked up momentarily, then returned his gaze to the paperwork that covered his desk.

"The train arrives at 7:00 PM," He said without thought or query to her reasons for being there.

Trying not to look put off by the man's inaccurate assumption or the discourteous manner in which he had delivered it, she began again.

"Excuse me," she asked again in the same polite manner.

Again the man looked up from his work with a face most weary.

"Yes, miss?"

"I would like to purchase a ticket for the next train to London, if you please?"

The man looked at her through the window for such a long time before speaking that it was actually starting to make her feel quite uncomfortable. She was about to repeat herself when he at last spoke.

"Will it be just you travelling, Miss?" He asked looking past her to her brother standing off to one side, his back to the window and the goings on.

She followed his gaze then returned it to him.

"Ah, yes please, just one, thank you."

The man frowned, perhaps at her answer, perhaps at something completely unrelated, then opened the drawer in the front of the desk and removed a single strip of manila-coloured card with some red and black writing on it. Taking a pen from the glass holder he dipped it in the ink and began to write something on the face of the card. When he was done he pulled a silver pocket watch from his vest, opened it, and checked the time on the watch against the large clock that hung on the wall behind him. Then, satisfied that the two times corresponded with one another, he entered the time on the card before placing the pen back in its glass holder upon the desk.

Writing the amount out on the receipt, he slid the thin strip of paper under the glass without so much as a word pertaining to the amount. Holding the receipt in place so as not to have it taken by the wind, Temperance read the figure then retrieved the tiny hand purse from within her coat pocket. Opening it she removed the coins summing the total requested. She counted it twice before placing it on the window ledge, and pushing it under the glass. An arthritic hand pulled the coins through the space between the glass and the windowsill and then, as she had done just a moment before, the same coins were then counted twice before being dropped into the money drawer below the counter top.

With a final inspection of the ticket the man placed it on the windowsill and slid it towards her. She barely had the ticket in her grasp before he was back to his work, not bothering with pleasantries or manners.

Aremis had gone back to the horse and was softly stroking the animal's neck as she came up to him, the newly purchased ticket in her hand. She tapped him on the elbow, handing him the ticket as he turned to meet her.

"Here you are," she said in an uplifted voice that belied her true feelings. "one ticket to London. You will be well rested by the time you arrive."

She smiled, waiting and hoping for some sort of artificially positive response, but when none seemed to be forthcoming she pulled the satchel from her shoulder and took it to one of the many benches that sat outside the station. There she sat down, setting the small backpack-like bag across her knees. Once opened, she began to go though the contents, much as a mother might do before sending her child off to the first day of school.

"I've put in three changes of clothes, two for work and one for church," she called out to him, still checking as she did so. "There is some food, and your toiletries in the side. I will put my purse in there for now, don't you lose this," she warned in a voice that sounded so much like their mother it made him smile, if only for the briefest of moments.

"I have also tucked the diary and photograph you showed me back at the farm in here as well. It seemed like the right thing to do under the circumstances."

She looked up and tried again to enlist a smile from her brother with one of her own, but with little success. She could not fault him for it though. She knew it would be impossible if the tables were turned and she was the one who would, in less than an hour's time, be heading off into a completely uncertain future. She began to buckle the satchel closed, trying hard to focus all her thoughts on the simplest of tasks rather than allow the feelings and recent events to take over.

"Thank you," he said softly.

She looked up to see the smallest of smiles peeking out of an otherwise worried face.

"I think it best if you go back now," he said, any evidence of the smile now erased as though it had never existed.

"No, I want to stay until you get on the train." She protested.

He sighed and shoved his hands into the pockets of his coat.

"It would serve no purpose for you to remain here for what might be some time. You know as well as I do that trains are more often late than they are on time. Besides, it is getting dark and I would feel much more at ease knowing that you were home safe and not out on the roadways."

He had a valid point and if the truth be known she too would have preferred to be home than where she was at that very moment, but he was most certainly wrong about her having no purpose in being there. She was going to be sure, without any question, that her brother and whatever else he might be, would be on that train before it left Totton Station that very evening.

"I am not going to see you for some time, and I am not forfeiting my time, time that I can spend with you, just so I can ride home with what little is left of the day's fading light."

Her voice was plain and to the point, carrying with it little room, if any, for negotiation.

Aremis drew a long breath as he looked at his feet. He moved a small stone in a circular pattern in the sand with the tip of his shoe.

"Sometimes, dear sister, it is you that is the impossible one, not I."

She smiled, at both his comment and his unwillingness to press her on changing her mind.

She finished buckling the top of the satchel closed then held it out for him to take. He plucked it from her hand and in one motion threw it over his shoulder, letting it settle at his side. Other people had begun to arrive, both by carriage and on foot, until the once quiet station was bustling with activity.

"We should wait on the platform before there is no room to move," she said, taking in he crowds that were steadily forming around them.

Without any more being said, they made their way along the wooden walkway to the end of the building, then up the few short steps to the covered platform. Walking to the edge, Temperance poked her head out over the tracks and looked south down the rails to where they disappeared from view around a curve lined with leaf-bare trees.

She felt a firm tug on her arm as Aremis pulled her back from the edge of the platform.

"Please stop doing that," he said as he pulled her away. "What if you were to fall?"

She squirmed free of his grip, a most annoyed look upon her face, one that quickly softened as she looked back at him.

"I am not a child of five, you realize." She said with more mirth in her voice than annoyance.

He chuckled under his breath, "Sometimes I do wonder."

She slapped him on the arm, as hard as she dare, the result of which made him laugh all the more.

She had missed his laughter most of all. It seemed like it had been years since she had heard it, and it made her smile despite the circumstances. Seizing the opportunity to keep things on a light and uplifted note, she spoke to him of times he had teased her and other times still he had down right scared her to death, jumping out at her in the barn and the like. She would scream and he would fall to the ground laughing. These were the times she wanted him to remember and not dwell on what was to be. For the most part, her simple plan born from opportunity more than it was conceived, seemed to be working as he chatted with her, sharing his memories of times, both silly and awkward, and despite her best efforts to maintain her composure, she found herself laughing along with him, quite uncontrollably at times. She wanted these stolen moments to go on forever, to be lost in a crowd of strangers, none of them knowing the terrible secret that both he and she shared. But she knew it would not last forever. In fact, it would not last out the hour. The distant shrill of a steam whistle brought the cacophony of multiple conversations to an end, setting upon the crowd a momentary silence, as everyone on the platform turned southward in unison to face the direction the sound had originated from. She knew the end was now close at hand.

The approaching train not yet in sight, the crowd of people slowly resumed their conversations, but Aremis and Temperance remained quiet, lost within the unmelodiousness of indecipherable speech that surrounded them.

The whistle sounded again, this time much closer; the plumes of grey and black smoke now visible above the trees that shrouded the rails from view.

"What of Christmas?" Aremis asked suddenly in a voice that was quiet concerned.

Temperance returned her attentions from the sooty cloud in the distance back to her brother and his question.

"What of it?" she replied.

"I've not got anyone a present." He stopped perhaps lost in the reality of the situation.

She almost laughed out loud at his worry over a holiday, given the grave situation he now faced.

"Christmas is still almost two weeks away. You may be back before then." She interjected positively.

Even though her words were encouraging he did not share her optimism and it showed in his face.

"Do you think this, whatever it might be," he paused, "do you think it can be sorted out?"

She stepped into him and hugged him tightly.

"Of course I do. If not by someone of the church, then most surely by one of the many doctors within the city. City doctors must see more peculiar things in the course of a month than what poor Dr. Harrington would likely see in a lifetime out here in our little corner of the world."

She made a good point but he found little comfort in it as the train slowly rolled up, its thundering engine belching out white steam while its black smokestack spewed ember laden soot and ash into the air like some monstrous mechanical dragon.

Men in uniform jumped from the moving train as it slowly ground to a halt, quickly setting down small wooden step stools upon the platform directly in front of the doors to the coaches.

"Whatever you do, do not lose your ticket or they will throw you off at the next stop," she paused, "and that is if you remain lucky."

"Thank you, and no, I shall not lose it."

She was about to say something else but her thoughts were interrupted by the voice of the conductors commanding that all who were going to London should now board the train.

"So this is it then," he said solemnly.

"Yes," she replied. "You are off to get well and I am off to the Harrington's to cook up some well thought out tale. Wish me luck, will you?"

"Good luck. I fear you will need it if I know anything about Agnes and Mother."

She laughed at the thought even though there was precious little that was funny about either the situation or her having to lie outright to the two people she both loved and respected.

Fewer people were now on the platform and the conductor again called out for those boarding to do so.

"I have to go, or all you good intentions as well as your savings will have been wasted."

She stepped back to allow him his space but as she did, he grabbed her by the shoulders and gently kissed her forehead.

"Thank you, for all that you have done, but more importantly for believing in me."

With that he let her go and ran the few feet to the train. Then without looking back he hopped the two iron steps and disappeared into the coach.

A tear ran down her cheek as she momentarily lost sight of him then, as she wiped the droplet from her skin, she saw him sit down and open the window.

"I will write you as soon as I am settled," he shouted, his voice barely audible over the hiss of the steam.

She waved her acknowledgment as she watched the men who had initially put out the step stools pick them up then jump upon the iron platform and into the foyer of the coaches.

The whistle screeched out its warning that the train was about to begin its journey and a moment later the steel framed monster slowly moved forward, gradually picking up speed as it did.

It had been a long time since she had actually seen a train and she had forgotten how loud they were. She covered her ears, removing one hand to wave, then, placing it back quickly in an attempt to block out at least some of the noise. A part of her wanted to run along side the train but she refrained. There was no need to make the difficult situation that much harder than it already was. So she watched in silence from her spot on the platform as the train left the station. She could still see him waving until the curve in the track caused the coaches themselves to obliterate him from her view.

She remained on the platform for a short time lost in her thoughts, of all that had taken place during the course of the last few months as she listened to the sound of the train growing fainter with each passing minute.

When the station had been reclaimed by the silence, she made her way back to Velvet who stood patiently where she had been secured.

Temperance unlashed the reigns and turned the leather over in her hands, slowly studying the areas he may have held less than an hour ago.

"God, why do you test us so?" she asked in a whisper before pulling herself up and seating herself into the saddle. She turned the mare around and with a hastened trot she made her way back through the streets dressed in their twilight colors until she was clear of the mortar and stone, and back on the hilltop. There she stopped and looked back at the swath cut by the railroad that lay beyond the town, a man-made slice that ran through the forest and hillside, all but lost in the ever-increasing darkness.

There, in the privacy of both the location and the darkness, emotion overtook her. She lay forward, resting her head on Velvet's soft mane and she cried hard. Although she would never voice her thoughts beyond that of her private writings, she knew in her heart that in all likeliness, she would never see her brother again. For if he could not find a cure and quickly, then it would not be long before his thirst would drive him to take a life, and in a city where people outnumbered the animals she feared that life would undoubtedly be a human one. She knew that if he were apprehended for murder he would be hanged for his crime. That was her back up plan, as morbid as it was. It was a near certain failsafe, for if he could not find resolution to his affliction then he would be sentenced to death. One way or another, the chances were high that he would not be coming home.

A night owl screeched from someplace deep within the woods, woods that still lay ahead of her, and she jumped slightly at its sound, a sound not dissimilar to the whistle that was on the train. Velvet moved from side to side, restless to be on the move, rather than standing still in a strange part of the countryside far from the comforts of her barn and oats.

"Alright," she said softly to the animal as she pulled her face from the now wet mane.

Wiping the dampness from her cheeks with the sleeve of her coat she patted the horse's strong neck.

"Come on girl, let's run. I need to get to the Harrington's and come up with a pretty convincing story before I am found out."

She stopped her verbal address to the animal, a creature as smart as it was, would not possibly be able understand all that she was conveying to it before she started anew.

"I need to get away from this place." She stated flatly.

Sitting bolt upright, suddenly with purpose, she snapped the reigns and tapped her heels into the animal's sides. Like a shot from a gun it was not a second before the two were in flight down the road. She leaned into the furious forward motion to steady herself, the brisk night air caressing her face, a near-full-moon on the rise above the trees lighting their way like the ghostly rendition of the daytime sunshine.

Chapter 8

Dear Diary,

I believe today to be the saddest day in all my years, for yesterday I bade farewell to my only brother and closest friend. It has been through my actions that he has gone and will, most likely, never return home. Mother and Father have been led to believe that he has gone to work in London. They know nothing of the true nature behind his leaving. All the deceit that makes up, and supports this ill-gotten ruse, exists by my hand and mine alone. My greatest of all hopes, in fact the only thing I can take comfort in, is that he might find a cure, some resolution to this terrible affliction someplace within the well read, well schooled medical establishment within the city, either through the doctors or through someone of faith who may possess some knowledge or have had some similar experience that might be able to shed light on what has taken hold of my brother.

Failing these hopes I fear that I have knowingly dealt my own brother a death sentence.

Temperance, the 16th of December in the year of our Lord, 1874

The train ride from Totton had been far less exciting than Aremis had hoped. It was to have been his first ride aboard a train as well as being his first time away from home, and even though the circumstances surrounding both were less than desirable he thought he would do his best to make the most of the new experience. Once it had grown dark however, his lack of sleep over the last few days accompanied with nothing much to look at beyond his own reflection staring back at him from within the blackened glass of the coaches window, he had quickly succumbed to sleep. So deep was his slumber, in fact, that he had not awoken until the train began to slow, the steel wheels squealing on the rails as they negotiated the various curves and switches on the approach into London Station. Aremis spent the rest of the night on an inconspicuous bench in the station.

The dawn had broken into day, not much brighter than the previous night had been. Overcast skies sent down heavy rains that combined with a relentless west wind that whistled around the black soot-stained buildings, making the task of keeping dry close to impossible for those unfortunate to be traveling the roadways and sidewalks of downtown London.

He now found himself, like so many others around him; standing under whatever shelter was available, looking out at the weather that was most inhospitable.

'Well this is a nice way to be welcomed,' he thought to himself as he tried to get his bearings within the unfamiliar landscape.

There was little point in making a dash for it as he had no idea where he would be dashing to, so instead, he stood where he was and simply took in the dreary day with all of its soaked inhabitants, many of them on some mad flight to someplace or another.

As the rain continued he began to formulate a plan of action. It was better than standing there cold, lonely and feeling sorry for himself.

The way he tried to envision things was that the sooner he found some answers to some of the questions he had then the sooner he would be able to return home and that was most certainly something worth spending time on.

Looking out from his temporary shelter it was difficult to determine exactly where he was in relation to the places he needed to get to. The surroundings were all made up of tall buildings, some of them six floors or more in height, which made visual navigation much beyond a few hundred yards all but impossible. He thought it best to seek out the church before a doctor, simply based on the idea that he had no real identifiable symptoms for which to describe to a physician. That being the case, he also had no idea how to go about telling someone of the cloth exactly what it was that he felt was wrong with him either. In fact, he himself did not know, or understand, what exactly had afflicted him in the first place. All he had to go one were a few sparse memories of what had happened to him the night of the attack, with the exception being the vision he had experienced while at the front gate of the Smith farm, something of which he now looked upon as being a waking dream of sorts.

Other than his wounds, which were now quite healed, there was precious little more than what Temperance had told him and she of course was not there with him now to back up the claims. He pondered this situation for several minutes, trying to put the pieces of this strange puzzle into some sort of sensible order, or at least in an order he would be able to sensibly relate to another person. As the minutes slowly accumulated and this mental manipulation having come no closer to making any sense at all, he unknowingly chuckled out loud. His sudden audible amusement, with no apparent reason for it, caught the attention of a few people who were standing close by, all of whom moved back just a little allowing themselves a bit more distance between themselves and the odd laughing fellow.

Not wishing to further appear the fool, or worse yet one quite mad, he opted to take his chances with the weather. The rain had slowed somewhat, but it was far from stopping, as he dashed across the cobble stone courtyard to where it met the street. There he quickly negotiated the many carriages, their drivers all hoping to pick up a fare on this bleak morning, and quickly crossed the street. On the other side of the road he again found shelter, this time beneath one of the many canvas awnings that hung out from the shops that lined that side of the street.

Another man ran in close behind him shaking the rainwater from his thin jacket and complaining bitterly about the weather as he did so.

Somewhat taken aback by both the man's sudden appearance as much as his colourful language he used to describe the day, Aremis simply nodded and quietly agreed.

The two men then stood silently watching the renewed force in which the heavens delivered its watery onslaught on those unfortunate to have been caught unprotected out in the open.

Pondering his next move Aremis began to wonder about his family and what might be happening back home, whether the rain he was seeing now was also falling there. He was on the verge of feeling quite sorry for himself when a clap of thunder rolled across the overcast skies and snapped him from his downhearted thoughts.

"Excuse me, sir." He asked of the stranger standing beside him. "Would you happen to know where the nearest church might be?"

The man glanced over at him then looked away, not answering for what felt like a very long and uncomfortable period of

time. Without bothering to look back, but instead continued to stare out into the sheets of rain he replied.

"A church ya say? What faith would ya be seeking, then?"

Aremis pondered the simple question, wondering if it would be prudent to reveal such personal things to a complete stranger. He had often heard his father speak of topics to avoid in conversations, especially with strangers, one of them being politics and the other religion. Besides, at this point he did not really care. Whatever denomination of religious order could best help him would be his new found place of Sunday worship.

"To be frank with you, sir, it does not much matter to me, any one will do."

The man gave him an odd look, then broke into a wide nicotine-stained smile that was there and gone before a few seconds had passed. Without so much as hinting at what he had found to be so amusing, he pointed down the street.

"You're going-ta-take this here street for a ways, now, you with me? Then, when you see the bank buildin' you turn to yer left. Don't recall the name of the street. You stay on that one about nine, maybe ten cross roads or so and you'll come to a church, Catholic I believe."

With that the man removed a pipe from inside his jacket and plunged it between his teeth before lighting it.

Aremis watched the cloud of grey haze envelop the man's head before it was whipped away in a gust of wind that also sent the rain in a diagonal direction.

"Thank you very much," he said politely, "I very much appreciate it."

The man gave him a quick once over, then darted off into the rain, the pipe still tightly clenched between his teeth as he ran.

The brief encounter had left him feeling even more alone that he had been before meeting the stranger. But that aside, he had made some small progress in this unfamiliar place, and for that he had to be grateful.

With little signs indicating the weather might be letting up, Aremis decided to make the most of it and began to make his way down the main street in the direction he had been told to take. Sticking close to the buildings, and keeping under awnings and overhangs wherever he could, the progress being made was anything less than quick.

Despite the weather and the slow pace, he eventually arrived at the previously described cross streets. Turning onto the side street, the store fronts, with their protective awnings which had been providing him shelter up until then, quickly gave way to modest residences. Their tiny front yards bordered in both stone and iron fence work and as he made his way along, he found himself quickly running out of shelter. With his protective cover all but gone he was faced with having to wait out the storm that showed little in the way of subsiding or carry on without shelter. Not wanting to lose time waiting for something he had no control over, he resigned himself to the weather forging on through the rain.

He had pulled his collar up around his neck and held it closed with his one free hand, his head down as he walked smartly up the dingy narrow road that was hardly wider than a laneway. He was making better progress now that the rain was no longer a predominant factor, his progress now only slowed, on occasion, when he had to step aside and allow the passage of a carriage or wagon.

It had been quite a few streets beyond that of the stranger's estimation but the destination to his quest was now in sight. Even with the low cloud cover and rain he could make out the stone bell tower and several of the adorning steeples that rose up above the surrounding buildings.

Upon seeing this spiritual landmark he felt immediately lighter even though logically he knew that in all likeliness the answers he was seeking would not be easily discovered, even within such a sacred place. He had told himself several times, both on the train and once having arrived in this dingy city, that it may very well take several visitations to places such as this, and through many denominations of faith, before he might be fortunate enough to find some relief from that which had besieged him. That being said, he felt positive about having made a start, and that was better than how he had been feeling back at the train station.

Approaching the man-made House of God he was taken aback by the grandeur of its architecture, so much so that he stood in the middle of the street in a state of motionless amazement while fellow, pedestrians passed him by as though he were quite invisible. It was not until a gruff voice yelled at him from atop a work cart being pulled by two enormous horses was he pulled from his wonderment.

"One side or t'other!" shouted the less-than-patient lead as he sat holding back on the reigns, quite unprotected from the elements.

Aremis quickly moved towards the church, then watched as the horses and the wagon loaded high with wooden crates continued past. The driver scowled down at him and touched the side of his head several times with his finger before returning his attentions to his team and the road ahead.

This, his second interaction with someone from this dirty place, was not helping him feel welcomed or in any way comfortable in his new surroundings, and he suddenly longed for home.

It was just then that he felt a light touch on his shoulder followed by a soft voice, the combination and unexpectedness of both made him jump.

"Oh I'm terribly sorry dear, I didn't mean to be setting such a fright upon ye like that."

He spun about abruptly before the person addressing him had even time to finish her sentence to find a woman, a nun to be exact, standing there before him, her traditional habit sheltered from Mother Nature's wrath by a small black umbrella, which she held down close to her head. She spoke with an Irish accent and seemed to be in her mid 40's, but it was difficult to tell given her attire, stature and the gloominess of the day.

Being not of the Catholic faith he had never set eyes on a person the likes of her before this very moment, and he suddenly found himself quite unsure how to address such an individual. Back at home in his own little parish, one that was constructed from wood hewn from the very forest that surrounded it, the same church his father had helped build, he would simply address the resident priest as Reverend on Sundays and Mr. Tucker on most other days. This however was not home, as he had been harshly shown on two other occasions that day, and with a poor record of interactions since his arrival he found himself lacking in voice.

The nun smiled and tilted her head slightly to one side.

"Are you lost?" she inquired further, having not managed to solicit a response from her first attempt.

He shook his head slightly,

"No, no ma-am, I am not lost. Well not really that is. You see, I have come here to get some advice on a problem I have, and I was directed to come here by a man at the train station."

Aremis pointed back down the road in the direction from which he had come, in the hopes of making his words that were nothing less than the truth seem more believable.

"Ah, I see," the nun said in an understanding voice. "Well then, if this is the place you should be then we have to assume that you've arrived then, shaunt we?"

She smiled again, trying to win the trust of another in a way he felt she must have done countless times before.

"Father Dudley will be back later this afternoon. I'm sure whatever it is that you find so troubling he'd be the one to help you. But for now, you can't be standing out here like this in the rain, you'll be catchin' your death before too much longer."

She took hold of his forearm and motioned him towards the opening in the gates.

"Come along now, I'll get you a towel and I may have something warm to feed you."

Her mannerisms were not unlike those of his mother, kind but with an underlying authority that one knew better than to cross. He let himself be led along the stone walkway, and it wasn't until he was almost to the doors that he found the words to speak.

"Thank you, ah, Ma'am, you are most kind."

"Ah, it's alright lad," she said with a well-versed chuckle, "just call me Sister Jillian."

The two unlikely companions made their way to the front doors without further conversation, and with a hefty pull on the iron handle Sister Jillian persuaded the heavy wooden door into motion, allowing them entry to the church's blackened interior.

It took several moments before his eyes could adjust to the contrast in light from what was already a dark day outside to that of the churches inner sanctum. Sister Jillian on the other hand had no need for sight as familiarity guided her through the darkness towards a faint flickering flame on a distant wall, leaving her rain soaked stranger alone in the vestibule.

An orange glow quickly illuminated the front area, banishing the darkness into the farthest reaches of the buildings structure.

"Good heavens," she said softly, "one would think it was the middle of the night in here."

Aremis did not respond to her statement, but nodded in agreement as he turned his gaze upwards towards the ornate ceilings far above his head. Pillars of white stretched skyward crowned off with golden leaves that supported an A-frame roof, its timbers as wide as the kitchen counter in his parent's home. The walls, all of cut stone, were nestled between these pillars, each one containing a huge window of coloured glass set into lead and iron frames.

He had not seen anything so grand in all his years, and his bewilderment at such magnificence could easily be seen upon his face.

"This place is astonishing. It is beautiful beyond words, I am utterly overwhelmed, Sister Jillian."

The nun looked up and about the grand building, her familiarity with the place perhaps obscuring how beautiful it truly was.

"Aye, it's a special place to be sure. It's been home to me fer quite a few years now."

They remained there for some time, simply taking in both the visual splendour as well as the ominous presence that let it be known to all who entered that if this was indeed the House of God then God was, without question, great.

Some time had passed before the nun urged her guest to follow her. The made their way through the church to the back, entered a doorway that connected to a long hallway that was as dimly lit as the rest of the church, this hallway eventually opening up into a large kitchen area. It had all the look and feel of a place designed for the preparation and serving of food, along with some things not normally associated with same, such as cots and bedding.

Sister Jillian went to a long cupboard, and after rooting around in it for a few moments she closed it and came to where he was standing. She held out her arm, which had over it, a towel, a man's shirt and trousers along, with a sweater and a pair of socks.

He looked at her with a quizzical expression.

"Come now," she said firmly, "Out of those wet things. You can have these while I hang those you've got on to dry by the stove."

He took the garments and laid them on the table, then watched as she left the room through another door. It was the first time since his arrival earlier that day that he had been met with kindness. A chill ran through his body, almost as a physical expression of her words of warning earlier whilst they were still outside in the rain. Not wishing her foreshadowing to come to fruition, he placed his satchel on the stone floor beside him, disrobing quickly and, with the towel provided patted himself down. Standing completely naked within the large room he, with as much speed and grace as he could manage, pulled on the temporary gift of dry clothes, successfully averting embarrassment should the nun suddenly return.

He took the wet clothing to the table by the coal stove and there found a small dish, that contained within it, a small number of wooden clothes pegs. Carefully, he began to place the clothes one by one on the string that ran from the wall to a wooden beam, clipping them in place with the well-worn pegs. He had almost completed the task when he heard the door open, and looking over his shoulder he saw the nun re-enter the room.

"Oh, aren't you a dear," she exclaimed at seeing her guest hanging his own clothes on the line. "You must come from a good home, you must. Not many like you pass through here, I can assure you of that."

Aremis smiled at her, finding it somewhat amusing that she would think the minuscule task was something in need of such praise.

Carrying a small iron pot, she placed it on the stovetop with a clank.

"There, we'll let the soup warm for dinner. I'm sure you've not eaten yet today." she said looking back at her guest before continuing.

"Father Dudley will be along later this afternoon. In the meantime, you and I can have a wee bit to taste with our tea."

With that she moved the black kettle to the middle of the stove, checked the water level within the metal vessel, then, motioned for Aremis to follow her to the long wooden table that sat in middle of the room.

"Come and sit with me until the kettle boils. I'd very much like to know a bit about why you be here so far from home."

They sat down opposite one another near one end of the table, and Aremis went about the business of telling the nun all about his family and his life on the farm, taking much care not to allude to the events and circumstances surrounding the last few months. He felt there was little need to share such detail with someone who had shown him nothing but kindness since his arrival. He felt strongly that she would, in all likelihood, dismiss him in short order if she were to learn about all that had been going on since the attack. Even when she asked him outright what it was that brought him so far from home he did not feel the need to lie, but instead simply told her the tale, as all in his community knew it to be. That his bride-to-be, along with her family, had been killed, and he himself injured to the point of death by an animal that had, to this day, never been caught. It seemed to satisfy the nun's curiosity for the time being as she wiped the corners of her eyes with a handkerchief, pressing her lips tightly together in order to produce a tight lipped smile.

After some time had passed the kettle on the stove began to whistle and its merry little song filled the room. Sister Jillian got up, touching his shoulder as she made her way back to the stove.

"It'll be alright lad, you'll see. No one more than I knows that God moves in mysterious ways. Things'll be just fine."

Her words, offered up in both kindness and comfort, did little in the way of providing either, as he watched his hostess pour the boiling water from the kettle into the teapot. Having retold much of his life, touching on some of the most painful things he had ever experienced, he was left feeling there was little that anyone would be able to do for him, at least anyone of mortal standing.

Sister Jillian returned to the table, setting the teapot upon an iron trivet before making her way back to the stove. She had made several trips to and from various drawers and cupboards before Aremis absentmindedly inquired if he could assist her. But by the time he had posed the question she was all but finished, returning one last time to the table and setting down a small plate of bread to complete the modest meal.

She seated herself in the same chair as before. Then, with a brief smile, she closed her eyes and bowed her head to say grace.

It was a simple prayer of thanks, similar to the one his own family would recite before mealtime, and whether it was the prayer, the way in which it was said or some combination of being warm and within caring companionship he felt somewhat grateful for having taken the direction from the coarse-mouthed, smoking man back at the train station. It was also the first time since this whole ordeal had begun that he felt that his path was, just perhaps, being directed by a higher power, and if that were indeed the case, then just possibly that path would lead him to restitution.

Both the meal and conversation had been light and he had been grateful for both. He had cleared away the dishes, amidst much protest from Sister Jillian. He had taken the dishwater out to the curb that ran along the edge of the laneway that snaked in behind the church as well as the surrounding buildings, taking in the many gravestones that dotted waterlogged grass as he did so.

The rain had let up but the sky showed little signs in relinquishing its hold upon the heavens, and it looked as though it would remain a day without sunshine.

Arriving back in the kitchen, he found Sister Jillian in conversation with a stout man dressed all in black, his near bald head, trimmed only at the sides with short white hair.

"Oh, excuse me for interrupting," Aremis began, setting the dishpan down on the counter. "I did not realize you were with someone."

He turned to leave by the way he had entered but heard the nun's voice calling after him.

"No, no, it's all right Mr. Eilbeck. Please, come back, there's no need to run off like that," She paused and waited for him to return to where she was standing.

"This is Father Dudley. Father, this is the young man I was tellin'-ya-of ."

The rotund priest smiled, his teeth bent and crooked as an aged picket fence.

"Sister Jillian tells me you are quite the gentleman, Aremis."

His voice boomed through the kitchen as though God himself was speaking though this man of flesh and blood. Yet despite the intensity of his voice, it still carried with it a softer manner than one might think to be within such a man.

Aremis smiled back somewhat sheepishly at the compliment, not sure how to respond or what to say.

"He's a bit shy, Father. Took me a spell to get him to come round it did. But he's a good lad, you'll see."

"I'm sure he is, I'm sure he is," the heavy-set priest repeated as he set his meagre belongings down on the table and folded his long coat over the back of a chair before sitting down.

He motioned for Aremis to join him at the table, while at the same time he silently motioned Sister Jillian to leave them alone.

Making some excuse pertaining to her requested departure, she set a bowl of soup along with a small plate of bread before her superior and then without, a word, she disappeared through the door that led back to the church.

Aremis sat down at the table directly opposite the priest and remained quiet, not sure of what or how to begin any sort of conversation, much less one that was as strange as the one he was supposed to relay. It was not until the man before him was well into his late, midday fare, did he begin to speak.

"So, Aremis," the priest began as he carefully spread a small amount of butter onto a piece of bread. "What is it that troubles you so that it brings you all way to London? Surely your place of birth would have a pastor that could help you, as well as I, no?"

His words were kind, despite the inquiry Aremis suddenly felt his throat go quite dry, so much so that he wished he still had some remnants of his tea from earlier in the day for which to ease his parch.

"Well, sir, Father, it is not that we do not have a church or a priest at home, we do, and he is most kind to be certain, but..." he trailed off looking for the words that would adequately describe why he was there, but could neither find them nor bring himself to actually describe the true nature of his plight to this stranger sat before him.

Seeing his difficulty with what could only be described as a simple question, the seasoned man of God began to reassure his guest and urged him to find strength in the Lord so he might find the words to carry on.

"Now, then, my son, you need not be ashamed of difficult circumstances. We are all tested from time to time, and many of those tests God puts before us we do not understand. Perhaps it is His will to have you come here today, to see me. Who can know for certain?"

Aremis nodded politely, even though he felt certain the holy man had no real idea of the severity that lay behind his pilgrimage to this church.

"Perhaps it is so, Father, but the only thing that is true is that I do not understand why it is that I be so stricken with such a thing when I feel that both I and my family have been good and devout people our entire lives." Despite his voice being nearly choked dry the message was still delivered with a painful fluidity.

"Is it this sickness of which you speak that brings you here, or something else?" the priest inquired, biting off the buttered end of the bread.

Aremis looked down at the table in the hopes that perhaps the answer might somehow appear upon the well-worn wood before returning his eyes to the man opposite him.

"I cannot entirely say for certain, Father. You see, I had an accident of sorts, the only survivor..."

"Yes, yes, dreadful bit of business that," The priest suddenly broke in, "Sister Jillian explained it to me briefly, terrible. But you must believe me when I tell you that those people who lost their lives are in a far better place now. They are with God. And you, my son, you must also be grateful for having been spared"

The room fell silent again, the only sound was that of the soup being cleaned from the spoon in a steady fashion.

"To be honest, I am not sure whether I am grateful or not," he replied solemnly. "With all I have been witness to of late, I feel that it might well have been better if, I too, had perished alongside my neighbours that night."

The priest set down his spoon upon the table with some authority that set a start on his table guest.

"It is not you who is to decide who lives and who is to die my son. It is God who makes such decisions. We, as His humble servants, are simply to abide by His word and know without doubt that it His word and that it is right. It is healthy to grieve for those who have passed on, but it is not wise to pine over them, for it is God's will they have been called home. Self pity or self loathing will only bring sorrow and hardship upon ye, lad."

The priest, his short, hard throated sermon now done, punctuated with a stern look of warning, one of which Aremis felt the elderly man had used to close many a Sunday mass.

Fairly certain that his words had found their mark; the priest retrieved his spoon and resumed his lunch.

The room, again consumed by silence, as Aremis pondered the words that had all but been thrust into his mind but a moment ago. There could very well be some truth in what was said, if not in its entirety then at least in part, that he had been feeling sorry for himself but not completely in the manner in which Father Dudley had been alluding to. He knew it was one thing to lose friends and family to accidents and the like. It was quite another to have your own life snatched away, not by death itself, but by a harbinger of death, a messenger sent out from within the Reaper's dark kingdom, one that does not in fact kill you but ends your life just the same, turning you into something that is a far cry from anything God himself had created.

"Father, with all due respect, I do not question God or His will, for it is not God that I fear." He paused but a moment before continuing. "It is something else."

The priest looked up from his meal and motioned for him to continue.

Not wanting to divulge too much or too fast, or implicate himself as someone in need of commitment to an institution for the mentally infirm, he chose his words carefully.

"There are some, not many however, back home in my village, that believe the attacks that took place on that night were not committed by a dumb animal," he paused to make sure he had the priest's attention, "but something more sinister."

The priest shook his head from side to side slowly as he wiped his mouth with the soft cloth hand towel which had, until then been, lying upon the table.

"This is foolishness," he began with a firm voice, "foolishness brought on by superstitious people living in a backward community. We are not living in the Stone Age, or a time governed by fantasy filled tales of dragons or imaginary monsters, which lurk beneath bridges. These things simply do not exist!"

He slammed his open hand hard upon the tabletop causing the cutlery to bounce.

Aremis did not take kindly to his friends, family and neighbours' being referred to as being backward in their thinking, but it was difficult to put up much of an argument when he was only willing to divulge a limited amount of information.

He was in the midst of pondering how to defend his point further without making an enemy of the man opposite him, when the priest again spoke up in a voice only slightly reduced in volume and potency.

"My son, Aremis. Please, please listen to me. Do not let the ideas of a few cloud your mind and convolute the facts." The elderly man paused momentarily eyeing up the man whom he shared his table through scrutinizing eyes before continuing, "The main fact, as I would see it to be is this: you yourself were there, were you not? Did you not see with your own eyes that which attacked you?"

The room fell silent as Aremis looked about the kitchen in search of an answer that would be different from those within his mind, one that may lie somewhere beyond his own thoughts and memories, that could somehow account for his beliefs without damning him into looking like a fool or worse.

"Well, were you there when this attack took place or not?"

The priest's words carried with them an air of irritation.

"I was there, not directly with the Smith family. They fell victim before I, some few miles up the road."

"So," the priest continued, "I put it to you again. What pray-tell was it that attacked you?"

Aremis touched his neck, running his fingertips over the area where the near fatal wound had been inflicted while his mind tried to filter through the fog of disjointed memories and second hand accounts of that fateful evening, the most recent being the terrifying hallucination or vision that had taken place outside the Smith farm only one day previous.

"It was a woman…" he said softly under his breath as if afraid that by saying it too loudly his own words might somehow bring the all too real memories to life once more.

"I beg your pardon," the priest inquired, "what did you say? Are you claiming that it was a woman who attacked you?"

Aremis now rubbed his forehead then let his fingers run through his hair,

"Yes," he said with slightly more conviction. "I believe it was a woman, yes."

Now it was Father Dudley's turn to fall silent, leaning back in his chair and tossing the napkin to the table before him. He remained like that, arms folded across his chest, without so much as a word being said for what felt like several minutes. Finally, still quite motionless, he inquired in a voice far removed from the one used only a few moments earlier, which could have easily been described as bordering on being confrontational.

"I find that difficult to believe, given your stature lad. I would think it be most difficult for a man anything less than one of stout build being capable of taking you down. But a female, surely you must be mistaken? Perhaps what you saw, or more accurately, remember, is that of a nurse, or some other lady figure tending your wounds after the attack. Your mind is simply trying to fill in the gaps of your unconsciousness."

He raised his eyebrows at the end of his proposal in hopes of enlisting a positive response from his guest, but it wasn't to be.

"Father, I am near certain of what I saw, and to your thoughts, I do remember all those who came to my aid in the days and weeks that followed, none of whom am I now confusing with the person I recall as the attacker. In addition to this, I have had dreams, horrid dreams, both of that night and of things I do not recall having happened. They are all of, or have something to do with her, this woman. She attacks other people, some now in this time and place and some in other places, different from here. And yet, in my thoughts, the ones that come to me upon my awakening, it is as though I know these places and people as if I myself had seen them first hand."

With a look of astonishment and bewilderment upon his face, a look that quickly faded into something that lay between anger and disappointment the priest again tackled the problem posed to him.

"You are bound to have dreams, terrible dreams. Even I have such terrors in my sleep, as do young children, and neither I nor most who suffer such nighttime horrors have experienced the likes that you have been through. These dreams are just that: they are dreams, nothing more. You cannot let these images that come to you in your sleep contaminate your life. Otherwise, I fear you will drive yourself quite mad."

There was a slight pause before he began again, but this time he took a different approach.

"Do you pray to God? Do you ask for His divine goodness to help you with this problem?" he asked flatly.

The truth be known, he had not much thought about God of late, and if he had it could not be said that it was in kind to be sure. His family had been the ones that had been seeking God's intervention in his near death encounter, and his sister who had carried it on since his return to the land of the living.

"No sir, I mean not directly. I do pray most every night in fact, and I have been attending church on Sundays, once I was well enough to do so. I do pray for my family and such but as I do not know exactly what, if anything, ails me, and so I have no idea how to ask for help."

"Ah, I see," he said softly as he leaned forward folding his hands together then resting them outstretched upon the table. "So if you claim to not know what it is that troubles you then may I ask what do you *think* is wrong with you? Why come all this way to seek an answer to something that you yourself are unclear as to whether it even exists?"

It was a valid question, one he himself had asked several times since arriving in this dirty dank city. Rather than waste time trying to formulate a new self-created response he opted for one he already knew, the one his sister had given him.

"I had hoped by coming here, to a place such as this, more established and more worldly regarding such oddities that I might find someone who has encountered things such as that which I have described."

Father Dudley shook his head slightly, as if attempting to sort out what had been said. The old priest gripped the bridge of his nose with his thumb and forefinger, poised to speak, but before he could even form the first sentence Aremis burst out a final statement.

"Father, I feel I may be turning into the very thing that attacked me!"

The priest looked startled at the sudden outburst, but quickly regained his composure.

"You feel that you are becoming a woman?" he asked, not in any way serious.

Not catching the old man's attempt at humour at his expense, Aremis went on in a frantic attempt at explaining that which he feared most.

"No, no, you do not understand! I was bitten by this woman, this creature. She killed the Smiths but left the horses only several feet away without so much as a mark on them. The bodies were left without even an ounce of flesh having been removed. What sort of animal do you know in existence today that kills its prey, takes only its blood while leaving bigger game untouched?

Seeing his agitated tone and elevated speech, Father Dudley raised his hands in a calming motion while requesting for Aremis to take hold of himself.

"I am sure all of this is very much troubling to you, and, as I am by no stretch of the imagination a biologist I would not have even the slightest inkling as to what manner of beast hunts as you describe. But that does not mean such an animal does not exist, or that, in due time, a natural reason for these attacks will be discovered."

He paused momentarily; to be certain his audience had indeed regained his composure before continuing.

"As to this beast of yours being thought of as some sort of demonic female abomination, I can set your mind at ease right here and now. For although I profess to know precious little regarding our Lord's animal kingdom, I can tell you with all certainty that the thing which you believe attacked you and your neighbours has no foundation in the realm of reality much beyond tales of mythical lore. The creature that you are loosely describing was known in older times as Nosferatu"

"Nos-for-at-too?" Aremis repeated clumsily, attempting to reproduce the ancient Latin word.

The look on the face of his guest told Father Dudley that further explanation would be required in order to clarify the few known details pertaining to this unsavoury legend.

"Yes, Nosferatu, it is the Latin name for a mythical creature that, as the story would have one believe, fits that which you describe, more commonly known by its European name; a vampyre. The modern day vampyre is a *fictitious* human-like creature that is said to be without a soul. One who walks the night in search of human victims for which to feed upon. Once finding that victim, it is said they drain and consume that person's lifeblood in order to procure its own existence. It is but a fairy tale, the likes of which were created to keep little children in their beds at night, nothing more."

He stared at his guest without the slightest hint of emotion, and then in a stern voice he finished off the explanation with a factual punctuation.

"It also does not exist outside the imaginations of superstitious old women."

"Are you certain of this?" Aremis asked, an air of urgency in his voice, "Are you sure that this creature cannot possibly exist? For it sounds very much like that which attacked me."

"I am quite sure!" Father Dudley shouted, "I will not lend myself to this ridiculous conversation any further!" his face turning a shade of red as he roared his displeasure at the continued interest in that which, in his mind, was nothing more than fiction.

"You were attacked and injured by an animal, just as your neighbours had been! You survived, they did not, and what you are experiencing now is guilt for having been spared when you should, in fact, be most grateful and thankful unto God for having spared you. Running about seeking answers to something that does not exist, fuelled by irrational thoughts will only serve to be your undoing!"

It was at that moment that Sister Jillian returned to the kitchen, alerted by the elevated voices that had obviously travelled from their point of origin to where she had been until then.

"Oh, in Heaven's name now, what be all this commotion in aid of then?" she asked as much as demanded.

Father Dudley burst forth in colourful expletives, describing the last few minutes of conversation he had been having with their guest. Sister Jillian, apparently not particularly bothered by his outburst, the volume in which it was delivered, or the topic matter within that delivery, simply listened as she went about her business in the kitchen acknowledging him where she felt it necessary.

This odd, almost one-way conversation went on for several minutes until, like a locomotive that has had its fire go cold, the elderly priest soon ran out of steam as well.

"Yes, well that's all fair to say Father, but you know as well as I that the Good Lord works in mysterious ways and this is no different than one who is trapped by drink or gambling, you know there's no talking sense to them until they themselves are ready to hear it."

Father Dudley shot a heavy look at Aremis as he reluctantly agreed with what she had said.

"Besides all that Father, you should get a move on, else you be late."

His stern looks suddenly vanished, being replaced by one of quizzical inquiry.

"Late? Late for what, Sister?" He asked in a voice that very much matched his facial expression.

Sister Jillian glanced over her shoulder as she responded in a matter of fact voice.

"Tonight is your regular visitation at Providence Row Convent, do you not recall? Father Richards is coming by to fetch you. Actually, I'm surprised he's not here already."

She turned her head towards the clock that rested upon a shelf at the end of one wall.

Suddenly, as though a dense fog had lifted, the look of puzzlement was gone from his face and he all but jumped from his chair.

"Good grief, my mind, it is bad enough of late without all this talk of ogres and goblins, I assure you."

"Yes, yes, I often hear you mention that, but mind you, without such things as *goblins*."

The priest gathered up his things, leaving the rest of his soup on the table and made his way to the door that led back to the church.

"Sister Jillian, if you please, will you talk some sense into this man before he leaves us?"

"I'll do my best Father. You best get yourself along now."

Her voice was like that of a mother shooing her children off to school in the morning. If not for her attire and the person she was addressing, the scene could have easily been mistaken for exactly that.

Father Dudley left the room and padded down the hallway until his footfall could no longer be heard. The nun quietly made her way over to the door and closed it, then returned to the table where the two men had been disagreeing more than discussing the circumstances behind their visitor's arrival.

"Now don't you mind Father Dudley. He's a good and kind man but a might set in his ways, he is. Similar to a good physician, he may very well know his practice but lacks bedside manner, that's Father Dudley."

Sister Jillian smiled and tapped the backs of his hands with hers.

"Now then, do you have lodgings for the night?" she asked.

Aremis shook his head,

"No, ma-am, Sister, I fear as yet I do not. As I have mentioned earlier, I have only just arrived and this was my first priority. I will have to make inquiries as to a place to stay while I am here.

Sister Jillian nodded her understanding, then after a few moments of silent contemplation, she quietly offered him the opportunity to remain there for the night.

"You seem like a nice lad, Aremis, truly ya do, so I'll make this exception and offer you one of the cots here for tonight. But you must promise me one thing, no more talk of ghosts or unworldly things in front of Father Dudley.

Even though his feelings were sharply divided by the offer put before him he gratefully accepted it, for despite the restriction being placed upon the one thing he needed to know most of all it was still better than spending his first night in London out on the street.

"Thank you Sister, you are most kind. I am sure my Mum would be most grateful for the kindness which you have shown me, much as am I."

"That's fine lad, not to worry," she began as she gathered up the lunch dishes Father Dudley had left on the table, "but tell me, what's all this fuss and goings on about goblins and ogres? It seemed to have set the good Father on his ear, it has."

Not sure if he understood the question that had been put to him since it fell directly on the heels of being told not to discuss such things further, he politely asked her to clarify what it was she was asking of him.

"Did you not just tell me I was not to speak of such things, Sister?"

"Not around Father Dudley," she said as she got up from the chair and carried the near antique dinnerware to the counter. "There are many things in this world we do not fully understand, just as I'm certain there are things that still lay undiscovered. I think it foolish to make one's self blind to such things. Ignorance is the real sin here, my boy."

A bit confused by her contradicting statements but not wanting to lose the opportunity to tell his story to someone who might be able to help, he quickly began to tell the tale from the beginning with as much detail as he could remember or choose to put in. He did, however, take some precaution in leaving out both the near attack on his own sister and the discovery of the dead sheep in the woods of his family's farm. He had precious little, if any, recollection of either of those accounts and he felt certain that if not for Temperance having both shown and told him of the incidents he would not have any memory of them at all.

When he had finished the telling of his patchwork tale he sat deathly still at the table and waited for Sister Jillian to put forth her thoughts or ideas on what she had just heard. The nun sat equally as unmoving as her guest, in the chair opposite him, her head turned towards the wall where a wooden carving of Jesus on the cross was hung predominately in the middle of the white plaster. She seemed to be lost in her own thoughts and he wondered for a few moments if she had even been listening to what he had been telling her.

After what felt like several minutes of silence had passed between them, he pressed her to share with him her thoughts on his situation.

"Sister Jillian?" he asked quietly.

His voice breaking the silence and her fixation upon the crucifix she turned to face him folding her hands over one another.

"What do make of what I have told you Sister? Do you feel that such a creature could exist or am I simply confused as Father Dudley would have me believe?"

She looked away briefly, perhaps pondering the question or possibly trying to avoid having to answer it, but then returned her gaze to face him. Her look was one of concern and ill ease, which had Aremis questioning whether he had in fact made a fatal mistake in trusting this woman.

She looked back towards the crucifix one last time then with a laden voice she spoke.

"Well, it's quite a tale, to be certain. As to whether I believe you to be confused on the facts of that story matters little. Does it really matter whether an animal killed your wife-to-be and her family, and very nearly did the same to you, or it was the work of a highwayman, male or female? The fact is that three people are dead and you survived. The cause has yet to be discovered. Can you not live with that and know that all matters pertaining to this will be sorted on the Day of Judgment?"

Her words were far kinder than those of Father Dudley, and he mulled over what she had said wondering if he may simply be seeking some sort of revenge for the loss he had felt. That it was possible the dreams and apparent sleepwalking episodes were nothing more that fuel to feed the need for retribution but it wasn't long before he dismissed the notion entirely.

"Sister, I assure you with all of my being that it is not through an act of malice or retribution that has me so far from home. I fear that whatever it was that attacked me and left me for dead - beast, or creature of ungodly design - it has contaminated my being with something that it carried, like a disease of sorts."

Sister Jillian narrowed her gaze, then relaxed it again as she thought about his words.

"Have you been to see a doctor and expressed your concerns to him?"

"I have been to see my doctor back home, the one who first tended to my wounds, but he can find nothing abnormal with me and assures me that I am both fine and worrying for naught."

"Perhaps then he is correct in his diagnosis and you may indeed be fretting over nothing."

He knew or, more accurately, he felt that he was not simply fretting over something that lacked foundation that what he was grappling with was, without a doubt, a real threat. How to go about proving this was becoming increasingly difficult and he soon found himself in a conundrum of unprecedented proportions.

"Aremis, you must understand, that sometimes people who have come face to face with death often feel as you do, that there was some reason behind why they were spared, that perhaps they were somehow unworthy of receiving entry into the Kingdom of Heaven and so go down this path of critical self examination seeking out the slightest, and in many cases, completely unfounded reasons for their otherwise fortunate survival. You have had a horrific experience and have been dealing with an incredible loss, of that I have no doubt. It's not a wonder to me that you feel as you do, but without any evidence to support some of these other fears you have voiced perhaps it is, as I have said. The simplest of answers quite often prove to be the correct ones."

Aremis nodded his understanding, if not his agreement, with her statement then shifted his weight in the chair, changing his position and his inquiries as he did so.

"Have you been," he began immediately losing any measure of tact regarding the question he was about to pose, "have you, well, been a nun for a long time?" he managed after his initial stumble.

She smiled and nodded her head,

"For as long as I can remember, dear. I don't have much recollection of a time before I was with the Church. In fact, the Church is more a home to me than my own birth place could ever have been."

"So, in all your time here, doing God's work surely you must have come across some people that were, how do I say this? Not right."

Sister Jillian brought a hand to her chest in feigned shock, amplifying the impact of her words.

"Oh my, yes, lad. So many souls lost in one way or another, most due to hard times or self-abuse. These are troubled times we live in, make no mistake about that."

"In any of those instances did you ever suspect that there might be something more sinister than what was on the surface, something evil?"

His query was well thought out, designed to take the focus away from himself and his so called imaginary troubles with the hope that it might jog her memory into recalling some person or event, things within her own day-to-day duties, one of which, she may have dismissed as nothing more than another unfortunate person falling on hard times, but it was not to be. Her answer, although it most certainly had trappings of unnatural things within its context was more of a general Sunday school response, not at all what he was hoping for.

"My son, all manner of discourse and unhappiness we see today most certainly has its roots running through the Devil's hands."

Aremis hung his head slightly as though his last ditch effort for something tangible had delivered, instead, the final blow to his quest.

"I'm sorry I can't be of more help to you, Aremis, but I truly feel there is nothing more sinister afoot here than a man with a broken heart and a number of unanswered questions."

Although disappointed in the outcome, he again reminded himself that the likelihood of finding a conclusion to his predicament on the first attempt would be highly improbable and with that understanding serving as his crutch he forced a smile, reluctantly agreeing with his host. He took a small amount of comfort in knowing that despite not getting much in the way of an answer, or even a direction for which to pursue an answer, he was not going to have to shell out any of his limited money for either accommodation or food on this his first night in the city.

The remainder of the afternoon and on into the evening was spent helping Sister Jillian make a meagre dinner of potatoes and carrots in a large pot and tending the various duties within the church. As the evening wore on and darkness reclaimed the city he was surprised to see how many people, both men and women, had made their way to the back door of the rectory in order to receive a small amount of food that his hostess had made up and had simmering on the stove.

Seeing these derelicts of society, cast-offs of a big city, a city too busy with all manner of things deemed to be important to worry about the hungry, the homeless, or those in such desperate need made him realize how cruel life can be. He had never before seen such hopelessness and shame in another person's face before that night, and he teetered back and forth between feeling good about doling out the meagre rations and wondering, if things did not pan out for him in short order, if it would not be he who would find himself standing at the back door of this or some other church, his very survival hinging on the kindness of a single person on the other side of stone wall and wooden door.

The last in a long and steady line of these persons left about 8:00 p.m. that night, and with their departure, Sister Jillian bolted the back door and turned down the oil lamps until only a faint glow illuminated the kitchen. She set out a blanket and pillow upon a cot, then, set a small washbasin and hand towel on the table.

'Thank you so much for all yer help tonight, Aremis," she said in a tired voice. "You certainly made my evening's load a bit lighter, you did."

"You are most welcome. It was hardly difficult work. I believe I found seeing all those poor people more of a challenge than the work itself. I do not know how you find the strength and still remain so faithful. To know that God must see such suffering and yet He does nothing to ease it."

She smiled faintly at his observations and quickly drawn conclusions.

"He does intervene. He sent them here to us and so tonight they will not go hungry."

Her simple answer left him speechless, the obvious answer, one he himself had been participating in for a better part of the night had eluded him which left him wondering what other things of late he had been blind to.

"Father Dudley will be back about eleven tonight. He rarely comes in here after his visitations so I'm sure you'll be undisturbed. I'll be saying good night to you now. I trust you'll have a good night's rest, lad. God bless, and the peace of the Lord be upon you."

She turned and, like a ghost or angel without weight, she slipped across the stone floor without so much as a sound and disappeared up the staircase at the far end of the kitchen.

The sound of a heavy wooden door being unlatched, swung open and subsequently re-latched at the top of the stairs was the only sound that carried back to the kitchen, and then it was quiet again.

Plucking his satchel from the floor, he made his way over to the cot. Suddenly feeling quite weary, he sat down upon its edge letting the bag fall back to the floor between his feet. Unbuckling the clasp that held the satchel and its contents secure he pulled back the top and peered into the bag. In the dim light of the kitchen the first thing that appeared to him was the wine bottle containing the blood his sister had given him. He pulled it out and held it up before the dim glow of the oil lamp that sat nearest to him. He tilted it slowly, watching the viscous liquid move around the inside of the vessel, leaving bright red wash marks upon the glass as the elliptical wave moved about the transparent container. Unexpectedly revolted by what he was doing he set the bottle down by cot and pulled out small amount of writing paper, along with a quill and tiny inkwell. Setting everything down on the cot he got up and retrieved a cutting board that hung by the stove and returned to the makeshift bed. With the board carefully set upon his knees creating a compact desk, he began to compose a letter to his sister and parents just as he had promised. He had no idea when he would be able to mail them but thought it best to have the day's events recorded before the details fell casualty to busier days and fading memory.

Perhaps not realizing how taxing the day had been on him or how tired he truly was, he awoke in the cot, his first letter still unfinished lying upon the floor along with the cutting board, inkwell and pen. It took a moment for him to get his bearings as to where exactly he was. He lay there motionless on his side, staring down at his things on the floor as his thoughts of the day's events slowly drifted back through a foggy mind. It was just then, as things were starting to fit into place, that he noticed something, or more accurately, a lack of something. The bottle his sister had given him, the one that contained the blood, was not sitting upon the floor where he had left it before starting his letter. He quietly peered over the side of the tiny bed, searching the area beneath it in the hopes of finding the bottle toppled over and having rolled just out of sight, but it was not to be found. Not sure of what might have happened, and hoping that Father Dudley had not varied from the routine Sister Jillian had mentioned, he swung his legs out and sat bolt upright searching the area around the cot.

"I hope I didn't wake ya lad," came the now familiar Irish voice of Sister Jillian.

Startled by the unexpected sound of another person in the room with him, he scanned his eyes across the kitchen. There within the dim light he could make out the shape of the nun by the table.

"Oh, Sister Jillian, you did give me a startle. Not your fault at all though, I must have nodded off."

"A-see, well, too much of the drink will do that lad," she said in a scolding voice as she held up the wine bottle.

His heart began to race and he felt beads of sweat forming upon his brow.

"Now the truth comes out, I can now see the reason why you might think the things that you do. It's nothing but the Devils poison fillin' yer mind with such outrageous thoughts!" she said her once kind voice escalating.

"Sister Jillian," he stammered, "it is not as it would seem,"

"Oh it's not is it," she retorted her voice annoyed, "I took you in, I believed in you and now I find you to be nothing more than a man besieged by the bottle. If you think me a liar then I'll gladly listen to yer explanation. But I warn ya, I've heard the lot before you ever happened by, I can assure you of that."

Aremis clasped his hands together in a pleading fashion as he began to formulate a response to a situation that he felt had little chance of coming to any sort of reasonable conclusion.

"Sister Jillian, I know what it must look like but I promise you that it is neither wine nor spirits of any kind in that bottle."

He watched as she titled it back and forth apparently watching as the contents of the bottle swirled and sloshed about.

"Then what might it be if not wine, and why do you have it?" she asked calmly.

He swallowed hard, not entirely sure if the words that were in his head would even come out when summoned, and for a moment he thought it might be best to bolt, to grab the bottle from her and make for the door. He could easily overpower the woman and make his getaway but then he would be on the run in a strange place without friends or lodgings. It would be no time at all before he would be apprehended, and all without having found out the slightest thing about what was happening to him.

"I'm waiting lad." She said without so much as a hint of emotion.

Aremis took a deep breath and formed the unthinkable phrase. Then with an equal lack of emotion he answered her.

"It is blood, Sister."

He watched the shadowy shape of the nun again lift the bottle and hold it before her face.

"Blood?" she replied in a voice mixed with shock and curiosity. "Who's is it? Where did you get it from, and for what reason do you have it?"

Letting out the breath he had been holding since the words left his lips he replied,

"It's not a person's blood. It came from a chicken, so I was told."

"A chicken? What in God's good name would you want with the blood of a chicken?"

She paused, still inspecting the bottle and its contents.

"You're not drinking this stuff, are ya lad?"

For the first time since his arrival in both the city and the church he was faced with having to deal with the horrors behind his strange actions or outright lie to the one person who had shown him any measure of kindness since his arrival. With the seconds quickly slipping by he took what many would have viewed as the coward's choice rather than face what very well could be harsh consequences to an unsavoury truth.

"No, no, Sister, not at all," he said with some air of confidence, an air that quickly began to vanish as he went on. "I brought it with me, to, to... For, I mean in the hopes that doctors might be able to see if the bird was killed by the same beast that attacked us."

The lie now released before a jury of one and set to stand trial based on its validity he held his breath and silently awaited the verdict.

Without much warning Sister Jillian turned her back to him and set the bottle back down on the table with a slight thud, the sound of which made him jump slightly.

"Well, I must say, I'm pleased to hear that," she said in the softer tone that he had come to know and trust.

He watched in the dim light as she raised her hands to her head and then, in a somewhat surprising act, she removed her headdress, setting it down upon the table.

"I was worried about ya lad, I truly was. That chicken blood is a most foul tasting drink."

There was a sudden silence within the kitchen that was so thick he felt his lungs all but choked off by its very existence. There was no possible way that he could have misunderstood that which had been said, but there was no other explanation for what he had heard. He was just about to inquire as to the meaning behind her bizarre comment when she burst out into laughter. The volume of her mirth gave him chills as he watched her turn up the wick of the oil lamp that sat on the table in front of her. As the glow in front of her grew it cast her body, still wrapped in her long black robe, into a dark shadow.

"Have you taken leave of your senses, my dear Aremis?" She asked, her Irish accent having a near melodic quality about it.

"Whatever do you mean Sister? I am afraid I do not follow you?" He asked, puzzled and quite taken aback by her sudden odd behaviour.

"What I mean," she began, as she slowly turned around, the light from the oil lamp momentarily illuminating her face so that it revealed her features awash in a ruby-rich syrup that covered both her cheeks and chin, running down her neck, disappearing beneath her clothing, "is this. Are you such a fool as to go and tell a priest and a nun that you believe yourself to be some sort of unholy, blood drinking, Hell-born abomination? Do you have any idea what they would do to you had you succeeded in convincing them?"

Her voice was now hard and pointed, all traces of the gentle melodic tongue having vanished as she stood before him, her hands on her hips, her eyes, now void of any diversity in colour other than a single hue of red that encompassed the entire eye, a colour that burned like hot coals, glaring out at him.

"You!" He shouted jumping up from the bed, "What are you doing here, where is Sister Jillian? He demanded as he took up a defensive posture.

"Oh Aremis, is it not obvious? I have come to save you," she replied seemingly not the slightest bit bothered by his words or his actions.

"Save me! You cannot be serious. You are the thing that has wrought all this misery upon on me. You have all but ruined my life!" he screamed at her.

"Oh please," she said throwing one hand into the air in a carefree manner that matched her tone of voice, her enlarged canine teeth now quite noticeable as she spoke, "theatre hardly becomes you."

A tremendous rage engulfed him, and he launched himself at her with every intention of killing her by whatever means it took. But before his hands could find their mark upon her neck she quickly sidestepped the attack and then, with one almost effortless motion, sent him careening through the air, crashing to the floor beside the table. Winded, he laid there, his body momentarily stunned by the blow. It was several seconds before his eyes slowly fluttered. His vision temporarily blurred it was another moment or two before he could actually focus, and as he did what greeted his eyes shocked him. There under the table, wearing only her under garments now soaked in blood was Sister Jillian, her throat torn open, her eyes still wide, staring in terror at the last thing she had seen.

He reached out towards her face to close her eyes as he cried aloud.

"Aremis, Aremis!" The words filtered though his grief and began to force the horrific image from his mind. "Aremis lad c-mon now," the voice called to him again from somewhere within the ebony blanket that muffled sounds and obscured familiar things from view. "Wake up. Yer havin' a terrible dream ya are. You must wake up now,"

His eyes fluttered open, Sister Jillian's face mere inches from his own, a worried look upon her face.

"I could hear you all the way upstairs. You gave me quite a fright you did lad. I felt certain that someone had broke in."

Slowly regaining his senses, the realism of the nightmare still at the forefront of his mind, he sat up quickly looking around the kitchen in search of the invisible intruder he now knew all too well.

"Are you all right Sister?" He asked.

"It's I that should be asking that of you, lad" she replied as she stood up. "You sounded like you were havin' a time of it, and it weren't a good time, by far."

Aremis sat on the edge of the cot as Sister Jillian went over to the cupboard.

"I'll get you a cup of water. You just breathe deep now and try and relax a bit."

Looking down, he noticed his things on the floor as he had left them, including the wine bottle. Without wasting a moment he quickly snatched it up and, without a sound, placed it into the satchel, flipping over the bag's top cover so as to conceal it from view.

Sister Jillian was just making her way back as he was picking up the letter he had started, along with the tools needed to compose it, and set them on the blanket.

"Here ya go lad," she said as she handed him the cup of water.

Thank you Sister, you are most kind."

She smiled and sat down on the cot beside him. She noticed the letter on the bed.

"Ah, I see you're writin' a bit of letter there, to your family then, I'm figurin', no?" she inquired.

He nodded his head as he swallowed the mouthful of water.

"To my sister actually. I promised I would try and write most every day if I could. She keeps a diary of sorts and she wants my time away to be recorded as some sort of keepsake. I am not totally sure as to why exactly."

She smiled and nodded her understanding of womanly things not easily understood.

"We girls do odd things like that, it be true" she replied, perhaps recalling a far off time when she too may have done such things for reasons known but to her.

"Do you think you'd be able to sleep now, or would ya prefer me to stay with ya a spell longer?" She asked in a motherly manner.

"No, no thank you Sister, I'll be fine now. These dreams are more commonplace than I care to admit to but I will be fine. Please go on back to bed. I will try not to trouble you further tonight."

She rubbed the back of his hand softly then stood up to go.

"It's no trouble at all lad. You try and get some rest now,"

He watched her leave, and when he was certain she had gone, he hung his head cradling the weight in his hands, trying to find some significance to the nightmare while at the same time block the horrible scene from his mind. The dreams, if they could be called that, were getting more and more realistic. Often, like this latest one, they related directly to the most current events that were taking place in his life at the time. For most people this would simply be looked upon as the events of one's day being played out in the unconscious mind, mixed in with the things that are most important, upsetting, or in this case terrifying. But for some reason he did not feel that this was the case. Something had him believing more and more that these night terrors were more than the sum of his subconscious thoughts playing back a collage of images, memories and experiences in a random format. Unlike his childhood dreams, or even more recent ones that had occurred before the attack, all these latest visions, both sleeping as well as the one that occurred while he was fully awake, were as real as if they were unfolding as any other day-to-day happening might do, void of all the usual dream-like accompaniments that are, more often than not, unrealistic sounds and images.

If it had simply been but a one-time occurrence, or if they had been spread out over a wider time frame, then he could have more easily dismissed these events as nothing more than vivid dreams brought on by a frightening experience, much as Father Dudley had suggested, but with the escalating frequency and a violent recurring character, a person whom he could barely remember but was beginning to become all too familiar with, he felt certain that there was more to these dreams than simple subconscious flights of fantasy.

Chapter 9

Dear Diary,

Today I received a letter from my brother. He has been gone only a week in full and yet it feels like an eternity since I watched him leave. I have worried so for his well-being even though it was I that all but forced his leaving. I found his letter to be such a welcome and much needed lift to my spirits, which in all honesty have been very much down since his departure. His words however carry with them mixed feelings.

Having been fortunate enough to have been welcomed by the priest of the first church he visited, having been granted temporary accommodations within the same in return for doing work for the nun who so resides there, a Sister Jillian, all of it was better news than I could have hoped for. However, the good news seemed to end there. Neither the old Pastor nor the kindly Sister who had befriended my brother could provide any further information pertaining to his disturbing condition.

I do not wish to dwell on the negative points, for that will serve no purpose other than to worry me further, but he tells me of his worsening dreams, and of this female creature, the one he now believes to be responsible for the attack. I fear that which grips his body so, whatever it might be, may very well be starting to affect his state of mind as well.

The blood I had provided him is by now most certainly gone and I can only assume by the time I had actually read his letter that he would be in need of a new source. I hope with all my heart that he may find some way of acquiring more by honest means. (I have no idea how that can be accomplished in such big city.) Otherwise, I do not wish to think on what the consequences will be, not only for him, but also for those around him.

I am very grateful for him finding such kind people while so far away from home, but at the same time I worry for their safety as much as I worry for his. I must trust in God that He and He alone will keep my brother and all he may encounter safe.

I pray that I will soon receive another letter giving me more positive news.

Temperance, the 25ᵗʰ of December in the year of Lord 1874

It had been nearly a week since he had posted the letter to Temperance and as he walked along the side street, the same street that he had first found himself navigating that day in the rain, he wondered if she had received it yet. This day was a far cry from that stormy first morning when he had arrived at King Cross station, for today the sun was bright and the temperature far more comfortable. Most of the people he encountered on his way to the market were in a light mood, and some even greeted him with smiles and, on occasion, a verbal solicitation.

Despite feeling as though life had dealt him a terrible blow these last few months he had, through good fortune (or perhaps through a similar intervention, the likes of which were explained to him by Sister Jillian that night he had helped her dole out the meagre rations to the downtrodden) managed to find both a friend and a temporary roof within this enormous city where, at least in part, he felt as though he had a home.

Originally having been told that he could stay but one night, Sister Jillian quickly discovered that having a strong and reliable, as well as trustworthy, pair of hands around the manse was most beneficial and so offered to let him stay on a few more days until he could find suitable accommodations as well as employment. The night terrors that had besieged him on his first night at the church had not reoccurred and he was cautiously optimistic that perhaps he had seen the last of them.

Even though the day was indeed bright and his mood for the most part light, he had not lost sight of the serious problem that currently existed. On the previous evening he had attempted to drink the last of the blood that was left in the bottle his sister had provided but found it to have gone bad, and so had to discretely discard it in the garden. He was now burdened with the arduous task of locating and securing more, something he felt certain would be a difficult acquisition at best.

Earlier that morning, Sister Jillian had asked him if he would make the short trek to the market in order to purchase some bread, along with a few vegetables, with which to make the daily soup. She had offered up a basket for the task but he had refused it, explaining that he would prefer to use his own satchel to which she had made no rebuttal. He had emptied most of what his sister had loaded into the satchel, stowing the contents that now represented all he had in the world, beneath his cot in the kitchen. With the bag empty, the bottle that once contained the chicken blood lying flat on the bottom, he set out, the well-seasoned sack, slung over his shoulder.

As he made his way along the thoroughfare, his mind began to sort out where he might best be able to acquire that which he needed, and there was little doubt in his mind that he did indeed need it. He had noticed, or more accurately become aware that, even though the conscious act of consuming blood repulsed him, there was no denying the feelings of calmness that came over him soon after he had done so.

Short of capturing and killing an animal of sorts, something he thought could prove to be quite challenging within a city such as London, he felt that the two best places that he might find blood would be either a butcher shop or an infirmary, the latter being less desirable than the first for many reasons, all of which disturbed him greatly.

As he was already going to market, a place he had not yet been to, he thought it might very well be the ideal place to locate a butcher, even though he had not the faintest idea how to go about asking for the blood and not actually the flesh.

The market was a busy bustling place with people moving about in chaotic patterns while vendors called out and flaunted their wares to those passing by.

In such a place it was not long before he had both the vegetables and bread he was sent out for. With his appointed task completed he began to plot his own course through the stands and carts, carefully eying up each table that had meat on display. As he had envisioned, however, all the meat that was for sale on this day was of the dried and salted variety, nothing fresher than several weeks at best. Most of the meat peddlers were busy dealing with several customers at any given time, so any chance of being able to strike up a casual conversation with any of them was effectively eliminated before it had even begun.

He was about to call it a morning when, as chance would have it, he saw a few stands hidden away in a side alley which ran perpendicular to the main street of the market, the vendors and their carts nearly unnoticeable amidst the awnings and crowds that all but obscured the tiny laneway's entrance from view.

Squeezing though the tight space afforded by the street vendors, he left the crowded main market and quietly meandered up the less congested alley. The first two stands carried bats of material piled one on top of another, so much so that the tables looked as though they might well fail under the burden. The women tending them looked up momentarily delighted at hearing his footfall, but then quickly returning to their conversation when they realized that it was a man who approached. Beside them was an unlikely partner to these female venders of fine fabric, a chimney sweep. Dressed all in black, a top hat upon his head, one that had most certainly seen far better days, he greeted the lone stranger with a wide smile quickly accompanied by offers of a safer home and family protected through the application of his services.

Now, almost to the end of the lane, Aremis at last came upon another display of dried meat along with a splashing of vegetables. A boy, no more than ten years of age, sat quietly behind the wares, playing jacks and humming to himself, all the while quite oblivious to a potential customer looming over his wares.

The opportunity, location and merchant were almost ideal for which to engage in what could easily turn out to be nothing short of an odd conversation. With no one close enough to be within earshot he would not be overheard, and the lack of other customers in the isolated laneway meant the chance of interruption would likely be slim. The age of this shop-keep being that of tender years was simply an added piece of good fortune. If this lucky streak were to continue then the questions he had to pose might not arouse suspicions, and if by chance they did then he would simply deny them, dismissing any such misgiving as nothing more than a child's misunderstanding of his query.

"Excuse me, young man," he asked in a firm voice.

The lad behind the table jumped at the sudden interruption that sent his jacks scattering.

"Yes sir, sorry sir, I was daydreamin' I was. It's bin a terribly slow day it has"

Aremis smiled and nodded in order to reassure the boy and gain his confidence.

"That is quite all right lad. What is the name of this shop?"

"It's me dad's shop sir, "Quinn's Meats". Anthony Quinn is me dad, I'm David Quinn."

"Well then, I am most pleased to make your acquaintance David," he said smartly, as he surveyed the various dried meats that lay upon the table.

The boy watched carefully in the hopes his customer might tip his hand and reveal what it was he was in search of.

"Is there something in particular you be seeking, sir?" he asked, eager to make a sale.

Aremis paused, carefully configuring his response.

"There just might be," he replied setting his eyes on the sausage links at the end of the table. "I would like six of your links if the price is right, ten if you make it worth my while"

The boy beamed at an offer that may well have been his only one that day.

"Yes sir, they're very good, my favourite, truth be known. They're a half pence each, five pence if you take a dozen."

Aremis smiled at his eagerness, as much as at his upping the quantity.

"Ah, I see you father has schooled you well in the importance of customer satisfaction"

The boy beamed with pride at the unsolicited compliment from a complete stranger.

Aremis slipped his hand into his pocket and carefully pulled out four pennies taking care not let the boy know there was more hidden within the confines of the pocket. He slowly counted them out and set the coins on the table's edge.

"It would seem that we have a problem young Mr. Quinn," he said in a glum voice, "It would appear that I can only produce four pence and I require five to meet your generous offer." He paused to watch the face of his young adversary before continuing. "I really do only need six links but perhaps you'd sell me ten for the same bargain you would apply to twelve. It is but one pence short and ten be a tad better than six. What say you?"

The boy narrowed his gaze, pondering the proposed transaction like a seasoned merchant, weighing up the extra sales over the loss of the full penny on the ten.

After what seemed like a longer time than it probably was, the boy agreed to the transaction.

"Fair-nuf," he said as he pulled ten links from the pile and placed them into a paper sack. "That'll be four p even, if you please, sir."

Aremis plucked up the coins and dropped them into the boy's hand waiting while he counted them out before taking his purchase from the table.

"Thank you very much sir. You won't be disappointed, you'll see."

"I am sure they will be most delicious, and if they are as tasty as you say they are then I will most surely be back to pay you another visit"

The boy smiled at the prospect of future business from a new customer, a customer whom he had secured without his father's presence.

Aremis turned to go then, almost as an afterthought; he turned back to the table with a finger raised as to add credibility to his ruse, he plied his quickly rehearsed line.

"Tell me young Mr. Quinn, per chance, does your father keep live chickens?"

Momentarily taken back by the sudden interest in chickens, the boy seemed somewhat dumbfounded by the question.

"Chickens sir?" he queried, "Yes, we have chickens. Is it eggs you be after then? For if it is I'm afraid I don't have any here with me today."

"No, no, that is fine. I am not interested in the eggs and truth be told, it is not for myself that I ask. The inquiry is for a friend who insists on killing the bird herself, a disgusting bit of business if you were to involve me. I could not see myself having to deal with it personally, you understand?"

The boy, still a bit confused nodded his understanding even though he didn't fully follow the story.

Aremis continued, "Something about it being fresh and all, better tasting. Who am I to say for a cook I most certainly am not, as many would attest to. All I know is that I am new in town and you have been most fair in your dealings with me. I think it only proper that if you or your father were to be so inclined as to sell a bird to me then I would most definitely be inclined to continue our business further."

"Oh I see, sir, yes sir. It's not common to sell em live an all, but I don't see a problem with it, just I don't know what me father would be chargin' for such a bird. I can find out when he comes by, and if it pleases you to return tomorrow I can tell you of what he said."

Things had gone better than he could have hoped for and he extended his hand towards the boy in a friendly business gesture.

The unlikely pair shook hands on the deal as though a major transaction had just been struck, the boy's tiny hand all but disappearing within his customer's grip.

"You are a good man David. Your father should be proud of you, and I will most certainly tell him of your diligent handling of my business should I be fortunate enough to make his acquaintance."

"You're most kind, sir, Thank you. I'll get you a good price, you'll see. Come back tomorrow and I'll do right by ya, I will."

"Of that I have no doubt." Aremis replied in a cheery voice releasing the boy's hand and bidding him farewell with a casual wave.

"I will be back in the morning young Mr. Quinn, until then."

With that, Aremis made haste down the alleyway and back into the mayhem of the main market.

He felt he had done well this day, having not only accomplished the task set on him by Sister Jillian but also establishing a good lead on a fresh blood supply. The purchased sausage links would not go to waste as a casualty of bargaining but would be used to thank his hosts for their hospitality and, with some luck, secure a few more days lodging.

The following morning, good to his word, Aremis made his way back to the market in hopes of striking a deal with the young vendor. The sausages he had purchased on his previous outing had been well received by both Sister Jillian and Father Dudley, with Sister Jillian serving them up for breakfast with fried potatoes and onions. Whether or not the morning fare he had provided would indeed secure him a longer stay had yet to be discovered, but for now he took some comfort in knowing that his hosts were pleased with him.

He had only been walking for about ten minutes when he thought something had gotten into his eye, although it did not hurt as such. He continued along at a slower pace, rubbing his eyes in unison in an attempt to alleviate whatever the problem might be, and finally stopped in order take in his surroundings. Thinking for the moment he had resolved the issue it was not until he brought his eyes down from the rooftops and high windows did he realize that it was more serious than he first thought.

As people passed him on their early morning flights to destinations known but unto them, it seemed as though they had a glow of sorts around their heads and necks, a red aura-like radiance that extended several inches out from any area of skin that was not covered by clothing. Momentarily captivated and somewhat confused by the phenomena, he stepped back from the main sidewalk so that he could study this visual anomaly without being conspicuously in the way of those he was watching. Lost within his own observations, it was several minutes before the conversations he had with his sister that night in the glen forced their way to the forefront of his mind and he found himself suddenly gripped with fear. For he knew it to be the same glow which he had seen about his own sister's skin moments before he had told her to return to the house leaving him alone in the secluded wood. As the memory continued to develop, another more frightening representation burst into his mind. The vivid imagery quickly unfolded over the original thought, replacing it completely. An image of him holding Iris firm in his grasp, the same ruby glow emanating from her skin, and a hunger within him unlike anything he had ever experienced consuming his thoughts.

Tempted by the urge to run from the scene, to escape the street and its many people, he forced himself to stand his ground and take stock of that which he was feeling as well and witnessing. He had already been shown, quite clearly, that the answers one is seeking are often right before one's own eyes.

Looking about cautiously, not wanting to draw attention to himself, he tried to relax. Leaning against a wall he took up a posture that looked as though he may simply be waiting for someone. He passed casual glances over the pedestrian traffic as it passed, making sure not to focus too long on any one person. Continuously moving his eyes from one person to another and, on occasion, with a look of boredom upon his face, he would simply turn his eyes towards the heavens, taking in the clouds that were moving gently across the sky high above the slate rooftops. After a few moments had passed he returned his gaze to the flow of people moving past and immediately the red glow was present.

Looking down at his own hands he made another discovery. Despite his hands being bare they did not emit the same glow as those around him, but appeared to be quite normal under his casual inspections. Not sure if he was happy in the discovery, he plunged them into the pockets of his trousers and continued to take in the various strangers as they anonymously passed him by.

Other than the affect being wholly disturbing, the visual anomaly did not seem to have any other adverse affect on him and after several minutes of inconsequential observations, he decided to carry on with his plan and continue on to the market.

By the time he had reached the alleyway where he had purchased the sausages the day before he had become somewhat accustomed to the red halo that enveloped everyone around him. Rounding the corner, he entered the laneway, quickly making his way up the shallow incline towards the butcher's little stand. As he drew closer he could make out the distinct shape of a crate sitting on the end of the table nearest him, and within that crate was a chicken.

'You have done well young Mr. Quinn', he thought, as he made his approach to the table, his hands still in his pockets, his fingers playing with the loose change he had within one of them.

Arriving at the table he could see the boy, David, his back to the alley bent over with another man as they routed through several bags that were stacked against the stone wall.

"Young Mr. Quinn," Aremis hailed as he stepped up the table's edge.

The boy jumped and spun around smartly, the older man following suit but at a much more mature pace.

"Sir," the boy replied upon seeing Aremis standing at his table, "You've come back!"

Aremis smiled at the boy's jubilant reply.

"Of course I came back. Why would I not? I should tell you as well, that I was most impressed with your links, you were indeed quite correct in your claims."

The young boy was once again beaming, but it was to be short lived as he caught the watchful eye of the man beside him.

"Oh thank you, sir, that's most kind of ya to say." He paused and stepped to one side slightly before continuing in tone more reserved, "This is my father, Anthony Quinn, sir, I told him of yer request and he's brought ya a fine bird."

David's tiny hands directed his customer's attention to the caged bird that sat on the table.

"Yes I see that. Brilliant, I must say, and for such an odd request I'm sure."

Aremis turned his attentions from the boy and the bird to that of the father and knew immediately he would not be as easy to deal with as his son had been. Nevertheless he felt that a kind and open approach would be best and failing that he would navigate those waters when he arrived at them.

"Mr. Quinn," he began in a cheery voice, "I must tell you first off that you lad here is well on his way to being a shrewd businessman not withstanding having a fair rapport with your customers. He is a good man up and coming. You should be most proud."

The boy looked up at his father for a moment then turned his gaze back towards the jailed bird upon the table's end. The man's look never softened, nor did it change in any way for that matter. He stood behind his table, for all intent, a stone carving of a store-keep, one that was completely void of mortality, that was, until he spoke. Even then his mouth hardly moved, the lines etched deep within the skin of his weatherworn face taking on the appearance of time etched fissures within the stone of an ancient statue, his voice gruff and marred as though a verbal representation of his hardened features.

"Good for nothin'," he grumbled not taking is squinting eyes of the man before his booth, "Eats more than he can sell. Be better if I sold him instead."

The way in which he spoke of his own son were so appalling it was all Aremis could do not to dress the man down right there. He knew the importance of discipline and respect, as well as the difference between that and abuse. Many times he had been scolded for various things he himself had done, things that, for whatever reason, did not measure up in his father's eyes but he had never been addressed in the manner in which this father addressed his own flesh and blood.

He tried to remain calm and not let his anger get the better of him for he knew it would ill serve him to make an enemy of someone who had access to something he required. Still in an uplifted voice, but tempered with caution, he continued on,

"Ah, well, Mr. Quinn, he is but a boy. I am most certain that he will grow past whatever short-comings you may find to be so distasteful."

"And what do ye know of such things?" Mr. Quinn grumbled.

Aremis smiled and gave the lad a wink before answering,

"I was a boy once too, and none too polished, I can assure you of that."

Without so much as a second's thought, the gruff man mumbled through his obvious disapproval of this stranger's assessment.

"The boy tells me that you want a live chicken. Why is that, Mr...?" his thick voice trailed off leaving his inquiry to hang in the air as though suspended on a string.

Momentarily fearful he had been found out, his cleaver ruse discovered, he fumbled for an answer. Not wishing to divulge the truth, for obvious reasons, but in need of closing the deal, he selected is words carefully but before he could reply he was again pressed for an answer.

"Yer not one of them gypsy types into sacrificing things to the devil is ya, now?"

The curt shop-keep's rude allegations were all that was needed to put his answer into play. Looking up from the cage that held the bird he put on a most quizzical look, a look that quickly transcended into one of annoyance.

"I beg your pardon?" Aremis demanded more than asked, his voice more than a little elevated.

His tone and body language obviously taking the brusque older man by surprise and he backed up slightly and his eyes, eyes that had remained until that moment scrutinizing slits, were now peeled open as Aremis continued.

"Am I to understand you correctly, that you think me to be some sort of roaming bandit that is somehow liken to that of the devil? Is that what you are implying?"

The older man cleared his throat about to explain his way out of his comment but was cut short.

"I will have you know, Mr. Quinn, that I have been a faithful church-going man since I could walk, as was my father and his father before him. I do not know which I am more appalled by, the way you treat your boy or the way in which you treat a new customer! I should take my business elsewhere for it is obvious to me why you are sectioned off from the rest of the market. Good day to you!"

It was a bold move, one that had him wondering as he made his way back down the laneway if he had just committed a mistake most costly. He was just about to round the corner when from behind him he heard a tiny voice shouting out for him to hold up.

"Sir, sir, please wait!" It was the boy David.

Aremis paused just at the corner so that it would be quite visible to all who watched from within the alleyway that he was but an angel's breath away from leaving.

"Thank you sir. Please, I'm so sorry. Me dad's not a bad man. He's just a bit ruff on the edges is all. Me Mum passed on a year ago and, well, he's not bin right since. Please, sir, let me make it right for ya, please."

The boy's plea, be it nothing more than a conjured tale of pity designed to pull at his heart stings or be it truthful, had Aremis feeling poorly for the boy, and even though he would have gone back regardless of the manner in which he was asked, the boy's heartfelt request made the whole business all the more believable.

"I do not take kindly to being referred to in such a manner, young Mr. Quinn. It would serve your father just if I simply went elsewhere,"

The boy's head dropped at hearing his words.

"However, I am still very much impressed with you and your manners, so it is for you and our business arrangement that I will return."

"Oh yes sir, thank..."

The boy's appreciations were cut short.

"But I warn you lad, any more allegations such as I have had to endure here today and I will most definitely take my dealing elsewhere. Is that clear?"

David nodded frantically, his hands still clenched tightly in prayer-like fashion before him.

"In addition, I think it best if I deal with you from now on young Mr. Quinn. I think you may wish to inform your father of that."

"Yes sir, he won't be none too happy 'bout it though." David replied, casting a glance over his shoulder towards his father's makeshift shop.

"Well that may well be true, but I will remind you that I too am unhappy at being addressed in such a manner, and if your father wishes to make a sale with me today it will be done through you, otherwise...."

David nodded again and turned, running fleet-footed towards the top of the lane.

Aremis watched the as the boy ran the entire way up the alley, only stopping when he had reached his father's booth. He continued to observe the distant negotiations from his position at the corner of the building, all the while ensuring that his body was poised in such manner as to lend itself to the illusion of flight should his proposal be rejected.

He swallowed hard, the dire feelings melting away as he saw David wave for him to return. Nearly in unison with the boy's beckoning he watched as the youngster's father step out from behind the table and head off in the opposite direction.

Retuning to the point where the whole ugly altercation had first unfolded, Aremis found David alone behind the table, his small hands resting on top of the cage, which was now positioned front and centre upon the table top.

"I'm terribly sorry for the way me father treated you sir, but as I promised here is the chicken. Do think your friend might fancy it?" The boy's voice was all business but not without sincerity, much as it was on their first meeting the previous day.

Not interested in the bird much beyond what it contained within its veins he was forced to continue on with the lie he had initiated, carefully eyeing the prize within the small wood-framed cage before answering.

"Yes, I am sure that it is quite fine. You may remember my telling you that I have no understanding of such things, my young friend, but if you tell me it is a good bird then it must be so, is that not correct?"

David smiled and nodded in agreement,

"Oh yes sir, all our chickens, pigs, goats, all of em, are top notch they is. Just like them links you had, the best you've had I'd wager."

"That they were," he laughed through his words before settling down to the matter of payment. He knew his financial situation was slight but not yet dire, having with him only what his sister had seen him off with. He knew all too well that if that meagre stash were exhausted before he could procure suitable employment he would be facing a harsh reality indeed.

"Right then, young Mr. Quinn, what have you to say about a price for this bird, keep in mind that despite the rudeness shown by your father I am quite serious about keeping my business with you. I am a man of my word."

"Yes sir, you 'ave bin most kind, I'll do right by ya as I promised"

The young entrepreneur paused but a moment, perhaps to weigh up something his father might have said or perhaps to size up the man before him. Either or it matter little as the young boy of ten quietly put forth a price of 10p.

Aremis nodded his head slowly as he gripped his chin with his thumb and fingers, pulling on it gently as if pondering the price put before him by this youngster. He thought the price might be on the high side given the altercation, but that was something he could find out at a later date from any of the other merchants in the market place. For now, though, he thought it prudent to let the boy have his day. He needed the bird, the boy needed to prove himself worthy to his father, and perhaps this was the very way to forge a new relationship that all involved would surely benefit from.

"That would be fine, lad, I shall take it with me now." He said, his words both kind and caring, words he felt certain had their roots planted firmly in days when he would spend hours talking to his mother about how he felt he would never be able to measure up in his father's eyes.

"Beg yer pardon?" The boy asked, nearly stumbling over his own words.

"It seems to be a fine bird and you to be a fair young man. I will let you know what my friend thinks. No matter the outcome I will return to let you know, but for now, the price you ask is fair."

The boy was elated, and even though he tried his best he could barely contain himself.

"Right sir, thank you. You won't be disappointed."

"I am quite sure." Aremis replied as he counted out the coins carefully for he could ill afford an error either way and when he was done he counted it out again before handing it over to David.

"Perfect," the young lad announced, putting the coins into a small wooden cash box that was hidden beneath a few bags of vegetables.

"Well then," Aremis began, "if all is in order, I will bid you a good afternoon and I hope to see you again in the very near future."

With that he plucked the small cage from the table and tucking it under his arm he turned to go.

"Thank you again, sir, if you please, I'll be needin' the cage back when yer through with it. As for anything else, anything at all, you just come and see me, I'll do right by ya."

Aremis did not bother with a reply this time but simply gave a cheery wave as he left the lane. He thought it best to leave on professional terms and not one that was overly friendly, for if second visit was required and finances had not improved some negotiations would need to take place before another transaction would be possible.

Walking along the busy street, a caged chicken tucked under his arm, he felt a bid odd and thought for the first little while that people were staring at him. But this feeling, like the odd red aura that had suddenly appeared earlier in the day, also became less noticeable as the minutes wore on.

Safe in the knowledge that Sister Jillian would not need him for several hours, he made his way towards the waterfront where much of the city's industry was established. He thought it best to use this free time to scout out some possibilities for employment, as well as seeking out a quiet place where, undisturbed, he could carry out what a few months ago he would have considered unthinkable: to kill the bird and steal from it its life blood.

He knew that taking a live chicken back to the church for dinner would more than raise an eyebrow or two, and not wishing his reasons be known or appear to his hosts as a thief or someone unstable, he thought it best to kill the bird while making his rounds for work. He would then hide the cage and simply retrieve it at a later date, whereby he would return it to David as arranged.

The morning sausages had been a welcome addition to the otherwise humble meals served within the walls of the church kitchen, so he felt that providing a fresh bird for dinner would not go without its appreciation. This in mind, it was not to say that everything he was doing was all part and parcel belonging to some elaborate scheme to procure lodgings, far from it in fact. He was already feeling quite fortunate for having happened onto Sister Jillian, or more accurately her having happened onto him. This in of itself was grand indeed, but then to have her take a liking to him, so much so as to offer him temporary sanctuary from both the weather and the night, was really more than he could have hoped for. If the links and the chicken just so happened to net him a few extra days whilst he sought employment then it would have been all the more worthwhile.

The docks and warehouse district of East London could be described, at best, as a seedy place full of rundown buildings, narrow streets, and claustrophobic laneways, all of which bordered the wharf. Its numerous docks and spits lined with all manner of ocean-faring craft, none of which looked worthy of sea travel on even the calmest of waters. The light-hearted and friendly people he passed in the market place were now gone, replaced instead by a scattering of dishevelled-looking dockhands, and delivery men, along with an assortment of drunks and prostitutes. Women normally associated with conducting their business well after nightfall, meandered along these dirty streets in search of men with whom to ply their trade, well before the stroke of noon on any given weekday.

Most of the men he passed eyed him with suspicion, while the women he encountered would often call out to him in the hope of soliciting a response and perhaps a coin or two, but he paid them little mind as he searched the windows and doorways for any signs that might indicate the business that resided within was in need of help. After several hours had passed he had become quite familiar with this dismal part of the city, and even though he had searched quite thoroughly he had come up empty in his quest for work. Feeling a little downhearted he tried not to dwell on it, instead focused on what he had discovered, and that was an abandoned sail shop at the very end of a dead-end alley. He had wondered down the empty back street to see if it actually led anywhere beyond the curve which effectively hid the rest of it from the entrance, but found it stopped abruptly at the water's edge, the only thing of any significance was the abandoned shop. He had looked though the window and after cleaning a small portion of the glass found the inside to be quite barren, and by the looks of things, it had been that way for some time. There was now nothing more than a few old crates along with plenty of garbage and debris within what may have at one time been a busy establishment.

This abandoned and forgotten shop would provide the perfect place in which to carry out the deed and would also be an unassuming location in which to stash the cage.

With a sick feeling in his stomach, he made his way towards the secluded little back street, passing, as he did, a woman who appeared to be in her late thirties. Wearing a long black skirt, a similarly coloured jacket, quite threadbare in places, her long brown hair drawn up and tucked beneath a once stylish hat, she smiled at him as he approached and inquired first, to where he might be going, and secondly, if he might fancy some company. Looking up to see who had addressed, him he noticed immediately that the red glow that he had become somewhat used to earlier in the day was now far more prominent around this woman, and he unknowingly starred at her as he continued his approach. Taking his longer than normal look to mean something else, the woman stepped directly in front of his path, placing her hand upon his chest as she did so.

"Hallo luv," she said in sultry tone that carried with it the smell of gin, "a wee bit lost are we?"

Her actions and question taking him completely off guard, he found himself momentarily unable to form a response.

"What's a matter hon, cat got yer tongue, or is ya just a bit shy?"

Her voice swirled in his mind, her words, the meaning of which, lost before he could comprehend them. The barely coherent sounds mixing together and becoming completely undecipherable before being swallowed up entirely by the soft thumping of her heartbeat. He felt her moving her hands over his chest, the warmth of her touch penetrating his coat and shirt all the way down to his skin. The red glow that now surrounded her made it appear as though she was on fire and he pulled back startled by what he was both witnessing and feeling.

"Oh, come on then, luv, don't be like that. I don't bite... not unless you want me to." The woman said finishing off her statement with a giggle that was more suited to that of a schoolgirl and not a grown woman.

She tried to close the small gap that had opened up but he pulled back further.

"Please, Ma'am, I have neither the time nor the inclination for this now. I must be on my way."

His voice was shaky and lacked its normal confidence, but it was still enough to tell his monetary suitor that she would not be getting a shilling or two from this gentleman.

"All right luv, another time then," she said quietly and passed by, and continued on her way, leaving him alone on the street.

Trembling, his thoughts cluttered, he stumbled down the sidewalk, turning onto the back street that led down to the old sail shop. In the seclusion of the tiny laneway he leaned hard against the wall of a building in order to compose himself.

After a few moments had passed, and on unsteady legs, he slowly made his way down the secluded cobblestone roadway until he was before the front door of the shop he had found earlier.

Looking about suspiciously to ensure no one had followed him or could see him from the few dirt-covered windows that looked out onto the shop, he tried the handle only to find it secured, as he figured well it would be. His first plan now abandoned, he slipped from the front stoop and silently made his way down the narrow passageway between the buildings. Forcing open the gate at the end of the passage, which led into the back of the abandoned storefront, he quickly negotiated the debris-filled backyard until he was at the rear door. Once again he took a cautious look about before trying the rusted door handle. Just as with the front door, this point of entry seemed to be locked as well. Annoyed at having been thwarted a second time he slammed his hand hard upon the old wooden door and to his surprise a small gap appeared between the door and door-jam. Pushing with considerably more force, the old hinges, nearly frozen with rust, groaned loudly as the door gave way and swung open into the darkness within.

Choosing for the moment to remain outside, he cautiously hailed into the blackness to see if anyone might already be inside. The last thing he wanted was to be accused of being an intruder, or worse, to have a witness to that which was to take place. When no one responded to his hail, he carefully crept inside and called out again, with nothing more than the same silence coming back to his query. Setting the cage down on the floor he carefully made his way around the first floor. Then, with the same care, he quietly ascended the staircase to the single upper level, which he found to be in much the same condition as the first level had been. What once may have been a tidy little waterfront apartment was now left derelict, in horrid disrepair, with broken windows, water damage from a leaking roof and evidence of an obvious rodent infestation.

Satisfied that the place was indeed empty he quickly descended the stairs to the first floor, retrieved his purchase and returned with it to the upper level.

He placed the cage on the floor in the middle of the second floor flat and pulled his satchel from his shoulder. Setting the bag down beside the cage he pulled the knife from its hiding place and held it tightly in his hand.

He stared at the bird trapped within the cage, its own fate incomprehensible but guaranteed nevertheless.

Aremis had killed many an animal back home and had little difficulty doing it beyond that of his early years, but for some reason the bird he was about to kill made him feel ill.

He knelt down and before opening the cage he prayed to God that this thing, which gripped his life so completely, would soon end so that he might one day leave this dark and forlorn place and return home to his family. His prayer finished, the soft-spoken words giving way to the all-consuming silence within the room, he remained motionless for several seconds waiting, or perhaps hoping, that some divine intervention would occur and he would be spared from having to do the unthinkable. But as the seconds quickly grew into minutes, the minutes adding up one upon another, his head thumping softly from an ache that had been steadily growing behind his eyes since early morning, he snapped open the latch on the wooden cage and with one hand grabbed the bird from within. Holding it down on the floor, its body pinned tightly between his knees, its head pressed to the floorboards, he quickly slashed the steel blade over the struggling birds stretched neck. Blood burst forth from the wound, a wound that was quickly sealed over by the hand that had held the knife and then, with eyes shut tight, he brought the flailing bird to his face. He placed his lips over his own hand then released the pressure over the gaping incision. Blood shot from the bird's neck, spattering his face before he could get his lips tightly over the wound he had just inflicted. The warm syrup-like liquid entered his mouth so fast it almost choked him, not just by volume but also by its very existence. As his mouth quickly filled to capacity he forced himself to swallow, driving the contents down his throat into his stomach, leaving the now familiar iron-like aftertaste in its wake. As more blood pooled in his mouth, he had to fight off the feelings of nausea, which, if allowed to continue, would send all his hard work back into his mouth, and onto the floor. With his mouth again nearing capacity he forced the second mouthful down, the aftertaste of iron that had once been so strong that it actually stung his mouth now carried with it a taste most pleasant. The fierce struggle that had been going on was quickly fading, the life blood all but drained from the bird, its heart rate slowly fading to the point of collapse, its weak contractions unable to keep pumping what little blood was still left within the dying animal's veins. Aremis found himself sucking hard on the wound, drawing up all he could get before what little was left would be trapped within the dead carcass.

The entire macabre scene was over in less than a minute.

Still kneeling, Aremis gradually released his grip on his prey, its now lifeless body slipping from his hands and falling to the floor with a quiet thump. He remained there, unmoving, his hands still up to his face, blood trickling down between his fingers and disappearing beneath the cuffs of his coat.

His stomach had wrenched several times but he had forced himself to hold down the viscous contents until the involuntary spasms had subsided. Fairly secure in the knowledge that he was not about vomit all his careful planning out onto the floor, he slowly slumped onto his side and pulled his knees to his chest.

He remained like that for quite some time, hardly moving, the only indication that he was not unlike the blood-covered chicken that lay but a few inches from him was the gentle rise and fall of his chest as he drew in then and expelled breath.

A loud peel of thunder roared over the roof of the second floor flat. Its sudden and violent arrival set such a start upon him that he jumped, so hard in fact, that he actually left the wooden floors where he had been lying. With eyes open wide, he crawled in a near state of panic through the dimly lit room until he had reached an inner wall where he propped himself up and took in his surroundings. Trying to take stock of the situation, it was several moments before he realized he must have dozed off. It was another few moments before he could recall what had happened and where he was.

A brilliant flash of lightning suddenly illuminated the second floor flat in a blue/white light allowing him to see, if but for an instant, the body of the bird lying in a small pool of blood upon the wooden floor.

Another clap of thunder exploded right above his head, so loud as to make him think that it was God himself beating upon the roof in an attempt to break in and dispose of this vile abomination that had taken up within a being He himself had created.

Aremis hid his face in his hands, trembling in the corner of the room, crying out for forgiveness as the rain pelted down upon the roof and what glass still remained within the window frames.

"Oh Father in Heaven, I have begged You to lift this curse from me and yet You have not, I do not wish this to continue but what am I to do?" his sobs carrying on through his words.

Aremis looked up from his hands staring out into the darkness of the room, possibly in search of an answer to his pleas, when another flash of lightning lit up the room along with something else.

In that instant, a moment lasting no more than a few precious seconds strung together in the never ending fabric of time, he saw a figure ascending the stairs, its form rising above the floors as it made its way up to the small abandoned flat.

His eyes now momentarily blinded by the brilliant white and subsequent blackness within the room, he strained into the darkness trying to make out shapes and attempt to find the person who by now would most certainly be on the same floor as he.

Straining to find some discernable shape within the inky confines of the room, it was not until another blinding flash had again illuminated the space did he see the form that had been, but a moment earlier, upon the stairs now crouched over the dead bird.

He pulled his hands to his mouth and clamped them down tightly over his lips as he watched the person's hand reaching down to the corpse before the whole image was once again lost in the enveloping darkness that ensued.

Terrified, and still straining into the pitch without seeing much beyond the spots and flashes left by the last lightning bolt, he heard the sound of footsteps moving about the floor. It was impossible to tell, with any accuracy, where they were coming from due to the torrential rains that effectively cloaked most of the stranger's footfall. Then, in the deathly chill brought on by a night filled with cold rain, he heard the unmistakable sound of someone breathing directly in front of him. Before he could clamp his eyes shut, blocking out whoever might be before him, the dark room exploded with light.

He stared directly into the red eyes of the creature who had delivered him into this hell, her mouth partly open, her blued lips dressed over fangs lit pearl-white in the flash, her opal skin spattered with blood, its sticky residue trapping strands of her hair against her face.

He turned his face from hers squeezing his eyes shut tight.

"Leave me alone!" he screamed, his words lost in the thunder above.

He felt her cold hand grip his face firmly and force it back so that he had no choice but to look on her in the aftermath of the lightning, most, if not all of her features now lost in the darkness, leaving only the red pools that burned from within her eye sockets set above the lethal white knives of her mouth.

"Look at you," she said in firm whisper that was more frightening than if she had simply screamed the very same words, "You are truly pathetic. Hiding in the dark like a child afraid of the storm, honestly!"

He tried in vain to pull away, but her grip on him was too great and he was left powerless to look elsewhere much less escape her entirely.

She glanced back over her shoulder into the darkness at the chicken that still lay upon the floor and continued her verbal attack.

"You are disgusting, you nauseate me to my very core... A chicken? I will wager that you even paid for it, did you not?" She said waiting but a second for an answer she really had no intention of listening to.

"You did!" She shouted and thrust her head upwards laughing forcefully.

"I cannot believe it! You had the chance to take the blood of a useless woman back in the street, someone who had nothing in life to speak of, and who would surely not be missed, and instead you choose a filthy chicken!"

Her grip on his face increased, her knee on his chest holding him against the wall as she forced his head back until he was looking straight up. Forcing her thumb in between his lips she wrenched open his mouth until he felt sure she would dislocate the mandible from the joint.

"Well my dear Aremis, not all is wasted here tonight for I have come to help you."

She knelt hard into him forcing what little breath he had left in his lungs to be expelled, until he was desperate for air.

"Since you are unable to end the life of someone as pathetic as a common whore, it was left to me, and I assure that I do not share the same desire to preserve such loathsome creatures."

She paused, watching as he neared unconsciousness.

"Now my love, you will taste the difference."

She opened her mouth and let a crimson river flow from her lips into his mouth until it overflowed and emptied down his chin and cheeks.

Trying to swallow while gasping for breath at the same time, he choked on the warm syrup that ran down his throat. The taste in his mouth was immediately sweet, unlike the blood of the chicken, but even so the heady candy-like flavour was not enough for him to keep from gagging.

Unable to breathe with his mouth overflowing he swallowed hard gasping for air as soon as the sweet syrup passed by his airway.

Above him he could he her continued laughter, and her mirth enraged him so that he lashed out with his right hand, grabbing hold of her exposed neck. He heard as much as felt the laughing abruptly end as though a switch had been turned off, and he squeezed even harder pressing his fingers deeply into the soft flesh of her throat.

Effectively cutting off both her air and voice he quickly felt her strength fading, and he was finally able to break free of her hold, effectively turning the tables from the hunted to hunter.

His hand still clamped tightly on her throat he pulled her down to the floor, pinning her kicking legs beneath his. Positioned over her, he placed his second hand over her throat doubling the pressure he was exerting on her neck. He felt her hands trying to dislodge his grip but there was little movement and in a last ditch attempt she pounded on his chest before those blows soon grew weaker, until finally, her arms fell lifeless at her sides.

With victory his, he refused to relinquish his grip for fear she was plying some sort of unworldly trick, and so continued to squeeze and shake her violently, her head bouncing on the floor like that of a rag doll.

Several more minutes passed without any signs of life coming from beneath him and so finally, with much caution, he released his grip and stood up. Brushing the hair from his face he drew in a ragged breath, trying to regain some of his composure. The room was still and dark as he stumbled, still weakened from the struggle, over to the windows in order to get some fresh air and clear his head. The violent storm which had raged only a few minutes before had begun to move on, its fury still making its presence felt someplace in the far off distance. As the dark rain clouds that had covered the sky began to break up, leaving in their wake only a more uniform covering of grey, he caught a glimpse of his face in a broken pain of glass. He stared at his ghostly reflection, his pale skin spattered and smeared in a dark ruby red that ran from his lips, over his chin and down his neck. He wiped at the stain on his face with his fingers, transferring some of the sticky paste to his fingertips. Looking down at his fingers he noticed that the same stain also covered parts of his brown coat and he cursed under his breath.

"Damn!" he said in a hushed whisper as he slipped his fingers into the little puddles of rainwater that had collected in the rotted wooden sill of the window.

"I cannot possibly return to the church in this state. There would be no explaining it."

Rubbing his fingers together quickly, adding more water as he did, the ruby syrup began to thin and slip from his skin until only an alabaster white remained.

Having turned the once clear rainwater into something more akin to that of red paint, he moved to another window, and similarly broken panes of glass. Finding more pooled water from the storm, he continued to wash the evidence from his face.

Removing his coat, the one his mother had bought for him as a birthday present a few years earlier, he laid it in the thin covering of water that had soaked all the floors beneath the windows. Moving it around in the water in an agitated fashion he was able to effectively remove most of the blood while at the same time darkening the material enough to hide any of the red stains that still remained.

He carefully, but with haste, checked his appearance in the makeshift mirror of broken glass, making sure there were no visible traces of blood he might have missed. Satisfied as he could be, given the poor quality of the reflection, he turned his attention to his dead adversary. Looking back at the body lying on the floor at the far end of the room, he eyed it cautiously for any signs of life or whatever it was that propelled her body into movement. He still could not quite believe that he had indeed beaten the thing that had all but destroyed his life. But after several minutes of careful observation he was fairly certain that whatever it was it was most certainly dead, or at the very least gravely wounded.

He walked in a semicircle towards the lifeless form until he was within striking distance of the body.

He nudged her torso with his foot using enough force to ensure she would most certain feel it should she still be maintaining the illusion of death, but she did not move.

"I wager *you* never factored this into your plans did you... whatever you are." He said with a tone that bordered on being sinister.

Not expecting an answer, and now certain the thing that lay on the floor was indeed dead, he reached down, and taking hold of her flimsy jacket he pulled her towards the windows so that he might have a better look at her. What greeted his eyes horrified him and sent him reeling backwards, his hands raised to his face.

"No, no, this cannot be. It is not possible!" he shouted as he continued to reverse until his back was against the wall.

He remained there unmoving, his hands still brought before his face in such a fashion that they covered his mouth, and gave an appearance of one who might be in prayer. Prayer, however, was the farthest thing from his mind at that point as he stared back at the body that now lay bathed in the grey light of both a fading day and retreating storm.

He frantically went over the events of the last few moments, events that had him convinced that he was being mortally attacked by that which had attacked him so many months earlier and felt so threatened by as to end her life in order to preserve his own. It seemed so quick, so forced, that there was little in the way of detailed memory from which to draw on, and unfortunately for him it was that detail he so desperately needed.

Was this another dream or a vivid hallucination which had somehow managed to transverse the boundaries between imagination and reality, distorting it so effectively as so that what actually was could not be recognised from the vision's dark possession of it?

His head began to spin, unable to make sense of anything he was seeing. Unable to resolve the situation before him, or the recollection of events that led to its being, he had no choice but to investigate it further in the hope of finding some clue as to what might have happened. He made his way across the floor with much trepidation to where the body still lay, not sure of what he should be looking for or how to proceed.

He stood over her for a few moments, taking in her face, the colour now gone from her skin, her lips pale and blue, her eyes still wide open, unfocused on the ceiling. The small blood vessels within the whites of her eyes, having been ruptured during the struggle, the blood had gradually pooled, turning the majority of each eye a brilliant red. Her jaw lay slack, her mouth hung open, looking as though she was still gasping for air, her neck already showing signs of bruising from the massive trauma that had been inflicted on it. Her hat lay off to one side, and her shabby overcoat torn open, the buttons scattered about the floor.

He pulled his hands from his face, clenching them together tightly, twisting and wringing them with much force as tears welled up in his eyes. Shaking uncontrollably, he now looked down not on a vicious creature from the netherworld but on that of the prostitute he had run into in the street not more than an hour earlier.

"Oh God," he whispered through a voice that was cracked with tears. "What have I done?"

He paced around the corpse trying to formulate a plan, a plan that seemed to have no solution beyond seeing him hang for his crime or, should his incredulous act somehow go undetected, live out the rest of his life in a lie with the burden of what he had done weighing forever on his soul. The prospect of either brought him to the brink of sickness.

With the light of day having returned from the retreating storm only to be fading anew with the onset of nightfall, he knew he would soon be missed by Sister Jillian. If he did not wish to add to his already bleak situation by having to fabricate another story to explain being late he had to think quickly and accurately, for any mistake no matter how minuet, might well lead to his undoing.

His original idea of cleaning the bird after he had killed it now seemed to be out of the question. If the authorities discovered feathers belonging to a chicken it wouldn't take much time for them to do a quick check of all the market merchants to see if anyone had sold a live chicken. Since that was a most unusual request it would not take them long to figure they were on the right track. As much as it pained him to waste that which he had only just purchased, he had little choice and quickly gathered up the bird along with a few feathers and made his way to the south end of the flat where a single window looked out over the river. Carefully looking out over the dismal surroundings he took stock of the area, and when he was sure there was not another soul around the abandoned dock he let the lifeless bird fall unceremoniously into the black water below. He watched for a few moments as the chicken floated amongst the debris that had gathered with the tide before it slowly drifted beneath the surface and was gone.

Returning to the body, he routed through her pockets and removed several coins and a comb with several teeth missing. Placing all but one of the coins into his own pocket he tossed the other one, along with the comb, onto the floor near the stairs a short distance from where the body lay.

Picking up the knife he used to sever the chicken's throat, he placed it back into his satchel and closed it over. Grabbing the cage, he let it fall from a rear window into the secluded, garbage filled backyard. Given the location and the state of the grounds he figured that it could remain there undisturbed and unnoticed until he could fetch it at a later date, sometime after the eventual investigation had concluded and public interest had subsided.

With the cage lying on its side, partially hidden by overgrowth, he scooped up a handful of water that had settled in the eaves just outside the window then ran back to where the chicken's blood had initially spilt on the floor. It required several trips to the window before the blood was all but unnoticeable and in a room that was peppered with rooftop holes it might easily go amiss during a police inquiry.

The last task, however, made him feel vile, but he knew that it had to be done. He paced back and forth, finally placing a finger between his teeth and biting it to the point of nearly breaking the skin. Removing the wounded finger from where it had been painfully pinned he tugged at his hair as the dilemma he faced tortured both his mind and soul.

Aremis closed his eyes tightly while blindly reaching out with one hand grabbing the dead woman's blouse. Tugging at it with considerable force he pulled it down and away exposing her left breast. Horrified by his actions, his progress momentarily stalled, before applying an equal, if not greater amount of mental strength, he pushed his feelings aside. Keeping his single-minded focus at the forefront of his mind, he pulled at the hem of her skirt until it too gave way. He continued on with the violent attack, until the garment had been pulled clean off and tossed into the corner. The same was done to the tattered slip until her lower half was completely bare.

Unable to look upon her or face that which he had done, he rolled her body over leaving her face down. Then, in a small act of humility, he pulled the tails of her threadbare coat down over her hips so that she would not be discovered in such an undignified display.

He took one last look around a room that he hoped he would never set eyes on again, then grabbed his satchel from the floor, quickly descended the stairs and left by the way he had entered, taking care to leave both the gate and the back door ajar in order to simulate a hurried departure.

He had taken much care in leaving both the sail shop and the laneway itself to ensure that no one had actually seen him leave either the building or the lane.

Once back onto the main streets and further from the warehouse district, Aremis quickly lost himself in the pedestrian traffic that was still thick in the late afternoon that followed the storm. Although now camouflaged by those around him, he felt the weight of stranger's eyes upon him as they passed. It was as though his very guilt was as visible to those around him as if he were carrying the dead woman's body in his arms. It took much effort for him to carry on walking at a relaxed pace and to maintain a look upon his face of one who had not a care in the world much beyond that of simple means. For even though the storm which had just passed over, a force of nature that had left the cobblestone roadway wet and shimmering in the late afternoon light, there was another storm of equal force and violence raging on within the confines of his mind.

It was not until he had nearly reached the front gates of the church did he first make the discovery. With all the horror that had befallen him in the last few hours, the torment within his thoughts of doing what was right and what was required in order to survive, he had not noticed that the red aura that had surrounded everyone he encountered that day had vanished without so much as a trace.

He sat at the wrought iron entrance-way leading to the church grounds and tried to look about casually, taking in as he did the few people that were still out and about. None of them had the previously ubiquitous crimson glow of earlier in the day. He looked down at his shoes, wet from the long walk back from the wharf, trying to understand what it was that was happening to him. Then, with singular clarity standing out within the confusion of his thoughts, he pressed two mental puzzle pieces together and they fit.

For the first time since he had looked down on what he thought was a killer of demonic proportions, only to find himself staring at the body of a harmless woman laying dead at his feet, were his thoughts not consumed by what he had done.

'This glow might represent some sort of indication as to my need for blood,' he thought as he sat down on the stone step to ponder this further.

Water from the earlier rains soaked through his trousers as he worked through the validity of this new discovery. Recounting the steps from the time he first noticed it, pale and translucent around the heads of people that passed him by on this very street earlier that same morning, to the time back home when a similar glow appearing around his sister in the forest, only to have it disappear entirely only a few hours after drinking the blood of the wolf, and lastly, seeing a much brighter, more vibrant hue of red, around the head of the prostitute in the warehouse district. The memory of the streetwalker suddenly broke him away from his mental study of the newly discovered facts. He pulled his legs up to his chest and hugged them to himself resting his chin upon his knees, trying to forget what had taken place only a short time ago. After a moment of silent grief for one he had dispatched without knowing and without cause, he forced his thoughts back to the glow and what it might mean. The more he thought about it the more he was convinced that it was some sort of hunger pang. It was clear that the intensity of the red auras changed gradually. That is to say, even though it appeared quite suddenly on every person, the colour was pale and muted, but as the day wore on that colour became stronger, more vibrant. It was like a coloured similarity to those feelings of stomach pangs. When one is hungry, the longer one is without food, the stronger the stomach discomfort becomes. So he concluded, for the moment at least, that the stronger the color in the aura the greater the need for blood. Of course, without any way of backing up this discovery he would have to wait and see. If and when, the mysterious red glow appeared again, he would pay close attention to both its shade and intensity, than compare that information with how he was feeling otherwise.

If this new-found evidence actually panned out there might be some forewarning, a way of predicting when he must drink. However, the only way he would find this out would be by playing a very dangerous waiting game that, at its conclusion, could bear witness to another deplorable act, one of which could see him led to the gallows.

Chapter 10

Dear Diary,

It is the New Year and it has been many weeks now since I received my brother's first and last correspondence and I must confess that I fear the worst. Both Mother and Father have also felt that something may be amiss, although they have not let on to Iris or myself much beyond wondering how he was fairing in the city. I have not shared with them his first letter to me, nor do I intend to, for there are too many details that could raise questions as to the true reasons behind his leaving. Even though it pains me greatly to see them worry so, it would be far more upsetting to them if they were to learn the truth behind their only son taking flight so unexpectedly.

I tell them not worry, that he is, in all likelihood, busy working and has had little time or spare money for which to buy stationery and postage. I remind them, too, that he is smart, strong and very likeable, so that it is quite unfounded to think that anything more than a busy life has kept him from writing. I wish, more than anything, that, I too, could believe my own misleading tales and find comfort in the words that tell of prosperity and a life full, but I know them to be nothing more than lies, wishful thinking created and told in order to comfort my family and those around me.

I have searched my thoughts many times in an attempt to see that which my other sight so often provides, but this also fails me. I know I still possess the sight, for I see things which I know I am not privy too, like Mother making me a new dress for my birthday, but for my brother there is no hint about what might be.

I can only hope and pray in silence, for I can share this burden with no one. I pray that he is indeed all right, and that I will soon hear word of his well-being, but for now all I can do is worry.

Temperance, the 22ⁿᵈ of January in the year of our Lord, 1875

It had been exactly three weeks since he had unwittingly killed the prostitute on the second floor of the flat in the abandoned sail shop, and today, like every other since then, Aremis made his way down to the train station to hear the headlines called out to passers-by from the local news boys. And, like every day since that dreadful afternoon, there was no news whatsoever of police finding a body or any mention of a missing woman. Oh, there were murders, gruesome and numerous to be sure, but nothing pertaining to a crime he knew all too well existed. Three days after the killing, he had retrieved the cage from where he had tossed it and returned it to the butcher in the laneway. He didn't risk venturing into the building or returning to the second floor. He was there to fetch that which he needed, and do so in the shortest amount of time. There would be nothing that could be gained in revisiting the room that, in all likelihoods, still contained within its walls a severely decomposed corpse. That covert midnight visitation was to be his last connection to a place, a place he wished with all his heart could be erased from his mind.

Truth is, if not for that one unspeakable deed, he would be hard pressed to discount the fact that things, on a whole, had gone remarkable well since first arriving in London.

He had, with the help of Father Dudley, secured employment as a cleaner at a hospital located in the district of Whitechapel and was managing to do well at it. Both his boss, Mr. Thompson, as well as the rest of the staff, including the doctors and nurses, all seemed to like him well enough and he had not received one complaint since arriving there. He had also found lodgings, again in part to a good word put forth by the well-known priest, with one Mrs. Doherty, a heavy set Scottish widow who ran a small rooming house near the district of Whitechapel. Father Dudley had spoken kindly of him to her and so Mrs. Doherty gave him a much reduced rent in exchange for him doing odd jobs around the place. The arrangement was working out marvellously, and his landlady was quite pleased to have a strapping young man around the house, especially in the evening hours, as it would seem his presence had quietened down the rowdier tenants who lived there.

His first two weeks' salary had set him up with enough money to pay his first month's rent early, much to the delight of Mrs. Doherty, as well as leaving him enough for food and a new spring coat, which allowed him to finally hide away his old one with the odd stains upon it.

His room upon the second floor, although sparsely furnished and small, afforded him a place to sleep, privacy, and a view of the street. There was a bed, a small table for a nightstand, another small table and one chair for meals and a dresser with an oval mirror. It was certainly far from high class, and it most certainly was not home, but it was shelter with a friendly soul tending upkeep, and for now that was about as much as he could hope for.

On his second week at work, he had spoken to a doctor at the infirmary, under the ruse of not feeling well, and had managed to get an appointment to see him the following afternoon. He had held high hopes of finding out a bit more regarding his condition, but just like his colourful first meeting with Father Dudley, his ideas that he might be something other than wholly human were met with almost humorous rebuttal by the young attending physician. Humorous disbelief was still far better than the near confrontational conversation he had with the priest just over a month prior, but it still net him little if anything in the way of useful information.

His eyes and hearing were both good, and his heart and breathing also seemed to be quite normal for a man of his age. Although it was good news, he still felt strangely disappointed that the doctor had not found anything out of the ordinary.

Despite a good bill of health, the curious red glow he had experienced, did in fact, return to him on or about the third day after drinking the chicken's blood.

He had made a decision of sorts that if the medical world was unable to cure him, and the world of spirituality could not identify that which he felt stricken by, he would take it upon himself to find out what exactly was wrong with him. Failing that, he hoped he would at least come to some understanding of what was happening to him, and then with that knowledge, be able to control it. He felt it was a better plan than doing nothing, and with some continued good fortune either plan could see him able to return home from his self-imposed exile.

He had purchased a small paper calendar from a local shop to keep a record of when he last drank. He had marked the day that he had killed the bird with a little crucifix, more to mark the human life he had taken than for the animal. He then put a tiny 'X' in the corner of each subsequent day thereafter. He also wrote meaningless notes and meetings as so to disguise the otherwise bare calendar, just in case someone might see it and inquire as to the meaning behind the notations.

On the day the red glow had returned he had gone back to see the butcher's son, David, and to his delight, found another chicken ready to go. He had brought the bird home, along with a small amount of feed and then stealthy took it to his room. With his next blood supply already secured he began the test, an exercise that had him carefully recording the amount of red he saw, the depth of the colour, how far the colour extended past one's body, along with his pulse, his eating habits, how much sleep he was getting, all the while keeping in mind that which his sister had told him that night in the woods. She had seen him leave on several nights, presumably to kill the sheep in the glen, events of which he could not remember having happened.

It was on the fourth day, not wishing to duplicate a walk through town similar to that of the one he had taken back home. A walk he could not remember having taken, but one that ended in the death of two sheep in the secluded glen of his family's farm, Aremis locked his door, placed his lips to the throat of the chicken and, with the knife, opened up a deep wound, drinking the warm liquid that gushed from it.

He had already concluded early on in the experiments that a chicken a week, no matter how lucrative it might be to the vendor, had the potential for attracting unwanted attention, and that was something he could ill afford. He knew that he either had to have multiple vendors willing to supply him with chickens or he would have to find other sources of blood. There were numerous stray animals about London, cats and dogs were always in supply. There were also the unwanted creatures, such as rats and mice he could pick from if the need required it. Draining a chicken of its lifeblood was ghastly enough, but the thought of doing the same to an animal he viewed as a pet or worse yet, to vermin made him feel more and more like he belonged to some other species, far from that of human.

Nevertheless, no matter what his feelings were, he had resigned himself to the task of cornering a cat one wet evening when few people were about on the streets. There, within the seclusion of the back alley, he opened a skinny cat's throat and emptied its life force into his mouth, leaving the carcass for the rats to enjoy.

Although the consumption of another living creature's blood disgusted him on a core level, he could not deny the feeling of wellness that followed almost immediately after taking in the last drop.

He noted his feelings, both physical and emotional, relating to this latest kill upon his calendar, taking good care to hide the true meaning in cleverly-worded abbreviations and references to family and work, so that any who might happen to notice his notations would see nothing more than a man who longed for his home or a diligent employee.

Two notable observations he had made after ingesting the feline's blood were, firstly, that it did not seem to sustain him as well as the blood of the chicken had done, for the red hue had returned one and half days sooner than it had with the chicken. This was both troubling as well as an inconvenience, for he could not be sure whether it was the size of the cat that had made the time line so much shorter, or if it was the blood itself. Either way, it was going to present a problem at some point. If the size of the animal had to be that of a chicken or larger, or worse yet, that some blood by its very composition might be unable sustain him for more than a few hours. Both were serious issues on their own, but they would quickly pale in comparison after an early morning discovery yielded something far more severe. Aremis had awoken on the morning of the second full day of having the red hue surround all things living, experiencing significant oral discomfort. The pain that he felt was the sole reason behind his sleep being prematurely interrupted. The sun not yet risen, he sat up in bed and turned up the lamp that sat on his makeshift nightstand until the smoky yellow flame illuminated the tiny room.

He rubbed his eyes, trying to force the sleep from his mind and rekindle his senses as he took stock of the irritation within his mouth and lower sinuses in an attempt to understand the source of the low throbbing pain.

Not recalling having received any sort of injury that could account for the pain, he thought that perhaps a tooth had become decayed and would require removal. He opened his mouth and shoved a finger inside in an attempt to locate the source of the discomfort. No sooner than he had done that, however, he quickly withdrew the digit, now bloodied from what appeared to be a singular puncture wound to the very tip.

Confused, his mouth and finger now in pain, he jumped to his feet and made his way the short distance to the mirror affixed to the dresser. The dim light did not afford him anything in the way of usable light and so he returned to his bedside to fetch the lamp. Back at the mirror he set the lamp upon the dresser's worn top and turned up the wick as far as it could safely go. Then again, with his mouth open wide, he lifted his upper lip and starred.

What he saw startled him so that he jumped back from the looking glass as though the flame of the lamp had burnt him.

Breathing hard and doubled over, his hands holding his weight on his knees, he tried to make sense of what he had seen within the mirror. After several long minutes, he regained himself enough to again approach the looking glass. Sweating and visibly upset, he pulled the lamp closer to the mirror and then, leaning in towards the glass, he carefully lifted his upper lip with his finger, revealing an elongated canine tooth that projected down from his upper gum line. Moving his lip higher still, he could see the abnormal tooth had split the gum in two distinct places causing it to bleed and the entire area was red and swollen. The same enlarged fang and gum damage was to be discovered upon the opposite side of his mouth. In addition to this hideous deformation that seemed to have occurred on its own through the night were also the consequences left by such oral weaponry in a mouth not designed or accustomed for such things. Both his lower lip and tongue displayed numerous cuts and abrasions, a result of having come into contact with the knife-like points at the end of each tooth.

Still in a state of shock by what he now looked upon, no longer able to believe that it could simply be some trick of a tired mind, he turned his attention to his wounded finger. Holding his hand so that the light of the flame gave him the best illumination possible, he inspected the fingertip. The wound was clean and still bled openly, the single puncture looking to have penetrated the flesh to a depth of 1/8 of an inch. He squeezed the area just below the injury and watched as the blood pooled in the hole momentarily then, unable to sustain its own weight, rolled out of the opening and dropped in a tiny splatter upon the floor.

As a second droplet began to pool where the first had been, he placed his thumb over the hole and pressed down tight, effectively closing off the flow.

Turning the lamp down he carried it with him to the table and, pulling the calendar from the wall, he made the latest entry in a bizarre string of events that had him convinced he was slowly progressing further and further away from humanity towards something he dare not even think about.

The rest of the day was spent in his room. He had told Mrs. Doherty he was feeling poorly and would she please let Mr. Thompson know he would not be into work that day but would work an extra day at the end of the week to make it up. He hoped this decision would not end up costing him his job, but he had little choice. There was no possible way he could make his rounds through the infirmary during the light of day, knowing full well that anyone wishing to speak to him would surely notice a bloodied and sore-looking mouth beyond which were teeth more akin to that of beast than that of human being.

Mrs. Doherty, with much concern in her voice, told him that she would indeed go see his employer about the situation and told him to rest assured she would put in a good word for him. It would stand to reason that it was in her interest, as well as his, that he kept his job, for without it he would be on the street and she would be out the rent money.

Pacing around his tiny apartment, looking in the mirror nearly every time he passed it, he began to formulate a plan to get more blood before anything more could happen.

For the most part, the majority of his outward appearance seemed to be unchanged with the exception of a lower lip that looked somewhat bruised and swollen. His thoughts were to wait until late afternoon and make his way to the market and see David. If his luck was good there would be a chicken waiting for him and, if not, then he would have to seek out some wayward stray within the narrow back streets and winding laneways then use the fading light of the dying day to provide the veil he would need to cloak his actions.

He pulled a handkerchief from his satchel and folded it so that it adequately covered his lips. He would use this to feign symptoms of a cold when talking to David or whomever else he might run into on his route there. He practiced in front of the mirror, lowering his voice so that it mimicked someone with sore throat, then watched, much as a strict schoolteacher might do, to ensure his actions matched that of his act. There could be no slipping, no possibility that the daggers within his mouth might be seen.

With that thought in mind he let his hand, the hanky still within his grasp, slip away from his face as he looked at his mouth. The porcelain white points were more than visible even though his lips were only slightly parted.

'What if this is not temporary?' he thought, as he stared blankly into the mirror, studying the grotesque new look within his own mouth.

He pressed his lips tightly together, but even so, he could still make out the outline of the teeth as they pressed against his upper lip, forcing it to protrude slightly, altering his facial appearance.

A part of him wanted to give up right then and there, to lay back on the bed and let whatever was to become of him just happen. He contemplated the entire series of events: Mrs. Doherty finding him, her calling for the police, the constables arriving, him being led away in irons, confessing to the killing of a woman he did not know, the consumption of blood to maintain his normality, to his final moments before execution and wondering if his family would ever know all that had befallen him.

However, the other part of him would be victorious on this day, and he pushed the thoughts of surrender from his mind with firm fist levelled upon the top of the dresser.

"No!" he said with a firm voice, but well under his breath so as not to set alarm through the house. "I will beat this thing, or hold it at bay, if only to find that which made me this way and kill it. I swear this unto God!"

He stared long and hard into the mirror, noticing as he did, a faint red ring circling his blue irises. He had been so involved with the horrors of his teeth that he had not taken much notice of his eyes. Looking at them anew, and with critical scrutiny, he could definitely see a band of dark red that ran about the outer edge of the blue. Unlike his teeth, however, this new found variation was far less obvious. Taking a step back from the mirror, the reddish halo was no longer visible; try as he might to see it.

With a better part of the day having been whittled away in his room, late afternoon was well upon him. Mrs. Doherty had been up and called through the door as to inform him that Mr. Thompson, although quite displeased with his absence, said he could make up the time at the week's end, providing he was in as promised by 8:00 a.m. the following day.

He had thanked her through the closed door with a gruff voice that sounded thick with illness.

Satisfied, she returned to her first floor apartment in the back of the house. When he was sure she was quite settled, he quietly made his way down the stairs and out the front door, taking care not to let it slam shut.

With a purposeful walk he made his way swiftly to the market place and to the laneway that led to the boy vendor who, with luck, would have that which he needed so desperately.

But this day was not to be his, for when he arrived he found the table, usually filled with meats, completely vacant without so much as a hint that anyone had been there in several days.

He looked about the laneway as he pulled the handkerchief from his coat pocket and forced a cough into it, hoping to catch the attention of the lady in the stall next to the one he now stood before.

When she did glance his way he called out to her, inquiring as to the whereabouts of the butcher. The woman shrugged with a complete lack of interest in his query, turning her attentions back to her task of repairing trousers.

"Not bin here in about three days now." She said quietly, not bothering to look up from her task.

He looked about; both up and down the lane, in search of another option while he formulated his next step.

"There's other meat vendors back the way you come in if ya fancy a look about." The seamstress offered up, again not taking her eyes from her work.

"Yes, I know of them, thank you. I was really quite comfortable with Mr. Quinn's little establishment." he replied, looking over his shoulder as he cleared his throat in the cloth hanky in order to hide his mouth from view.

There was no reply this time, only a slight up and down motion to her head indicating that she had both heard him as well as understood his desire to continue business with the absentee merchant.

Other shop stalls were already beginning to close for the day so, with a polite acknowledgement of thanks to the lady for her help, he made his way back to the market, knowing full well the possibilities of finding a live bird, or any other beast for that matter, would be slim at best.

He had walked the entire market area several times, taking in everything and everyone with vision that was sharper than it had ever been in his life. Although the images were indeed precise everything he looked upon seemed as though he was taking it in through red panes of glass. The red aura that had only seemed apparent around those with exposed skin now seemed to be everywhere, both on the few people who remained in the market as well as inanimate objects.

He knew that if he made it though the evening and managed to get back to his apartment he would have another observation to add to his calendar, but for now he had more pressing things with which to occupy his mind.

With darkness settling in on the city, and most of the people now gone from the once busy marketplace, he wandered alone down dark alleyways in search of some hapless creature to slay and hopefully, with that animal's lifeblood, reverse what was happening to him. But as the minutes slowly accumulated, one upon another, the twilight gradually being swallowed up by the blackness of the coming night, he had come up empty. Feeling panicked by his failed mission, and quite uncertain of when he might lose his capacity to remain sentient, he turned for home, all the while keeping a watchful eye for anything that could yield even a drop or two.

Keeping to the darker side streets he quietly crept along, constantly searching for any signs of movement within a gutter or beneath a stoop. Thinking he might have better luck down by the waterfront he turned down a dark roadway, the only light being that of lone gas lamp at the far end of the street. He had only managed to transverse about half the distance when he was suddenly confronted by a short stout man in dark clothing, brandishing what appeared to be a knife.

"Right then, guv, that's far enough, now," the man ordered, "all I want is yer purse and I'll be on me way, no trouble."

Taken quite by surprise, it took a moment for what was happening to actually register with him, all the while looking quite dumbfounded by the whole situation.

Obviously annoyed at the lack of response or compliance by that of his intended victim the would-be thief flashed his knife around so there would be little doubt he meant business.

"Money, jewellery, the lot, or I'll stick you here and now, no word of lie," he demanded with as much malice in his voice as had been in his first address.

Still standing not two feet from his attacker he could hear the man's heartbeat pounding inside his head as he watched the blood moving in rivulets beneath the skin of his neck, as though his very outer shell was translucent. He felt his mouth become dry and he found it difficult to swallow, but he managed to clear his throat, bringing the handkerchief to his lips as he did.

"Look here, my good fellow. I have neither the time nor the wealth to meet your demands. If I did I would most certainly bow to your wishes and avoid any further dealings with you, but I am new to this place and without means or property, so if you please, I have a matter most pressing to attend."

His words fell on either unsympathetic or uncaring ears, for as he tried to continue on his way the bandit stepped out before him, effectively barring his way.

"I'll not warn ya again, friend. I'll take your pack and have ya empty yer pockets, then you can be on yer way to whatever is so urgently awaiting ya."

Aremis took a step backwards and raised his hands to his temples as the throbbing within his mind pounded a beat so loud that it bordered on the threshold of pain, its rhythm all but obscuring the thief's final demand.

Then, without further warning or provocation, the bandit thrust the weapon forward plunging it into his victim's stomach.

The pain was searing and Aremis unconsciously grabbed at the hand that held the knife, its blade deep within him, the hilt pressed tight against his abdomen, in an attempt to dislodge it. Blood began to soak his shirt, the excess running down the handle of the knife and onto the hand of his assailant.

As he continued to struggle with his attacker, still trying to displace the blade within him he noticed the steady stream of blood begin to flow from his body, blood that took on an appearance more in common with that of molten iron than of blood, the centre of the stream glowing so brightly that it actually seemed to give off sparks.

Forcing the man's hand backwards, withdrawing the blood-covered weapon from his body as he did, Aremis grabbed his attacker's face with his free hand, clamping it hard over his mouth, effectively sealing off any attempt at further communication or a cry for help. At the same time he drove the man's head backwards exposing his unprotected throat.

What happened next was lost in a cacophony of sounds that were all but unheard in the calamity that began with the snapping of bones within the wrist of the knife-wielding aggressor.

An anguished, muffled cry came from the bandit's muzzled mouth as his forearm snapped as though it were winter-dried kindling. The two bones now shattered at the joint, the knife fell from his limp hand, bouncing on the cobblestone and coming to rest several feet from the struggling men.

Continuing to push the man's head further back, all the while retaining a firm grip of his broken wrist, he backed his quarry across the narrow roadway and into a covered breezeway between two businesses, in the row of small industrial buildings and shops that lined the deserted street.

The stocky man felt like nothing more than a marionette in the hands of an accomplished puppet master as Aremis manoeuvred him with near effortless precision until they were both well along the covered walkway.

There in the seclusion, concealed within darkness, the prey having become the predator, Aremis pressed the man against the laneway's back gate so hard the wood began to bend and splinter under the force. The struggling man's feeble attempts to free himself of the vice-like hold produced, little if any, meaningful effect other than to reinforce his own helplessness.

With the stocky thief pressed against the fence, Aremis was barely aware of the repeated blows being delivered to his right side and upper body in an attempt to have him release his grip, for his focus was not on the feeble attempt at escape but on something else entirely.

Everything within that laneway, in that very instant of time, had seemed to slow to a near standstill as he took in all that surrounded him in finite detail. A spider went about the task of creating a trap that was both delicate and deadly for any insect unfortunate enough to become entangled within its sticky strands, a rat scurried along the ground just beyond the fence in search of scraps, while above, in the night sky, flew a sparrow hawk, out late in the hopes of happening upon something to eat. In that moment he felt a strange sort of kinship with this assortment of night creatures, all of them working under the cover of night, all with a common goal: to find their next meal, just as he was.

He brought his attentions from the dark, cloud-covered heavens above and back to the man who was still struggling frantically before him, his head, still pushed back his throat fully exposed. A tiny pattern of intertwined lines slowly began to immerge over the tightly stretched skin. Looking at first like the intricate designs one might expect to find on finer lace trimmings and such, the pattern soon began to change and grow, the lines becoming more complicated, the canvass of skin in which they had first seemed to be laid upon slowly vanishing. The web of minute red and blue lines which crossed back and forth, one upon another, creating a colourful veil, both concealing and connecting larger lines of similar complexity, which lay just beneath this intricate, covering. These connections, in turn, leading to conduits even greater in size, their near translucent walls carrying within them liquids of ruby-rich red and darker plum-blue that moved along with pulsating bursts that caused these flexible pipes to expand and contract with a rhythmic beat that matched the sound within his own mind.

Without conscience or fear of reprimand, his actions now governed by something older and far stronger than that of mindful thought, he slowly turned the man's head to one side noticing as he did so that two of the larger conduits became easily visible. He watched as the veins and arteries that carried blood to and from the man's brain expand and contract at an ever-increasing pace, in keeping with the man's continuously elevating heart rate.

Then, like a cobra striking, he lunged towards the unprotected neck, sinking his enlarged dagger-like teeth deep into the soft flesh. With the two fangs embedded deep, acting like anchors, his lower teeth came together in a scissor-like fashion severing tissue, tendon and blood vessels alike, tearing out clean the entire section of flesh that had covered them.

A geyser of blood burst forth from the gaping wound as he spat the mouthful of skin, and muscle onto the ground. Bringing his head back to his victim's neck, the hot syrup soaking his face and hair as he again sank his teeth into the area just behind the chasm he had just created. He pressed his lips tightly against the warm flesh as condemned man's heart pumped his blood supply into the mouth of his executioner.

A taste not unlike that of apple cider with a consistency of thinned molasses or maple syrup, it was a far cry from the rusty metal taste he had experienced within the blood of the animals he had killed. As the warm semi-sweet liquid filled his mouth, he drank with both force and desire until his victim fell weak under his own weight.

The once fiercely struggling criminal now suddenly heavy within his grip, Aremis released his hold, letting the heavy man slip away. His lips made a slight sucking noise as the bloody seal was broken, his teeth pulling free of the wound they had inflicted, as the body that barely contained life within its shell slumped down the side of the fence into a heap upon the stone walkway.

He stood over the body of the dying man watching, as though in vivid sunlight and not muted darkness, the blood stream, continuing to pump from the massive trauma while, in a weakened state, his victim tried to cover the wound with his one usable hand in a vain attempt to stop the inevitable.

Filled with something similar to contentment, Aremis dropped to one knee as he continued to watch with morbid fascination. The blood, no longer exiting with rhythmic pulsations, but pooling in the crater he had made before gradually escaping between his victims fingers placed over the wound in weak attempt to prevent its exit. Upon the stones where he lay, the gradually expanding blood slick formed a shallow pool that shimmered in the limited light, a dark puddle that had a look similar to that of warm chocolate spread over fresh shortbread.

Aremis remained like that until, finally, with a ragged breath that sounded as though it was taken through a medium of liquid and not one of air, he watched the thief's body go still, and the final trickle of blood come to a stop. A final droplet hung in the balance, suspended on a triangular protrusion of flesh for several seconds before finally, under its own weight, was pulled free of the coagulant's grip and dropped into the crimson puddle.

The night was as still as death itself and yet he did not feel particularly frightened. He remained quietly crouched over the body, carefully listening to all that was around him for any signs that he might not be alone.

With little more that the scurry of vermin along the back lanes and that of boisterous conversations within the run-down town homes that backed onto the rear of the secluded breezeway, he carefully went through the pockets of the man whose life he had just taken.

Removing the contents and laying them on the ground, he was surprised to find a large number of coins totalling a tidy sum for such an unsavoury character to be in possession of. He assumed, quite quickly, that these coins were simply the spoils of illicit deeds, some of which may have been carried out that very night. Thinking of this made any thought of guilt at what he had done dwindle to a point that was for, all practicality, nonexistent.

Keeping a watchful eye on the mouth of the breezeway, Aremis plied his newly-acquired skill, the one he had taught himself back at the old sail shop, taking most of the coins and thrusting them into his pocket while leaving a few smaller denominations scattered about on the ground. Unlike the unfortunate business with the prostitute though, he knew that this fellow would most certainly be discovered come first light, and so he carefully went over the scene looking for anything that could possibly lead to his undoing. The only thing, the obvious thing, was of course a giant hole in the man's neck, and even a blind fool would easily be set to wondering as to what sort of midnight criminal in the business of stealing would use their mouth as a weapon. As far as he knew, the beasts in the woods that lay far beyond the city had not invaded London to take up monetary thievery and so something would have to be done and done quickly.

He stood up, wiping the blood from his face with the sleeve of his coat as he did, when he felt a sharp pain in his side. His memory suddenly aligning itself with the conscious part of his brain remembered the initial confrontation and stabbing, a recollection that had him grabbing at the source of the discomfort.

Setting aside, for the moment, the matter of a dead criminal in order to inspect the extent of his own mortal wound, he pulled his coat open and yanked up the blood-soaked shirt, exposing his stomach to the limited light within the awning covered lane. With the virtual daylight he had experienced just moments before now all but gone he was forced to carefully poke around the skin, searching for a wound he knew was there. But after several minutes all he could find was a spot that was very tender to the touch, but where no incision seemed to exist.

Not satisfied with his initial inspection within such a dimly lit environment, Aremis felt certain if he had indeed missed the wound caused by the knife then he could quite easily end up like his attacker, having slowly bled to death on his way home. So, cautiously making his way to the entrance of the breezeway, he carefully poked his head out to see if anyone was on their way down the deserted back street. When he was certain the way was clear he stepped partially onto the roadway and pulled his shirt from the bottom, holding it out in front of him. The moon, in its ¾ phase, had broken clear of the overcast skies, casting a dull silver light over the entire area. Even in the diminished light offered by the moon he could easily tell that his manila coloured shirt was soaked with blood, a large cut visible within the middle of the crimson stain. A matching tear within the fabric of his coat was also quite visible. Since his coat, which had been done up at the time of the attack and during his own violent retribution, had stopped most of the thief's blood from even reaching his shirt, Aremis had little choice but to conclude that the blood he was looking at was indeed his own.

While still bathed in the wash of lunar light he continued to run his fingers over his stomach, sliding them through the blood that covered his skin, as he searched for the source, a hole within his own body, which could account for the pain he had felt and the blood that now saturated his shirt. But, just as moments before, he came up with little more than a sore spot where he felt the initial penetration of the knife had taken place.

For a moment, standing there alone, his own thoughts being his only sounding board, he seriously began to question whether or not the whole knife-wielding incident had simply been another vivid hallucination. Suddenly panicked by that thought, he quickly ducked back down the breezeway to where the body of the stocky man still lay in a pool of blood. He took some odd comfort in finding the man he had just killed still lying there exactly as he had left him.

Relieved for the moment, he was still left pondering the validity as well as the nature of the attack. He walked back up the narrow lane towards the road, softly rubbing the tender area to the left of his navel, trying to recall the serious of events that seemed to be lacking in detail, despite the enormity of the situation.

It was at that moment, having reached the roadway for the second time, he noticed the knife lying on the cobblestones. With the quiet back street still void of pedestrian traffic, he darted out and retrieved the weapon, returning with it to the protective covering between the buildings.

Slowly turning the short weapon over in his hands, studying as he did, the crude cutting implement's limited features, most of the weapons surface, both blade and handle, still slick with blood, he ran a finger through the ruby-red syrup that coated the blade, the now semi-congealed substance sticking to his fingers as he did. Pulling his fingers from the blade, the thick liquid clinging to them as he did, he placed his thumb and forefinger together before his face and rubbed them in a circular motion, the blood acting like a morbid lubricant of sort and he knew that there could be little doubt that the knife he now held had in fact penetrated his body. As to how there could be no injury of any significance was still quite perplexing.

Unable to reach a conclusion, one that made some reasonable sense, he resigned himself to leave it as yet another mystery, something else that he would have to add to his notations when he returned home. With limited time to finish a task most gruesome Aremis, with the knife still in hand, made one final trip back to the body where, without emotion or hesitation, he slashed with violent repetition at the neck and facial area of corpse until the original wound was barely discernable amidst the mutilation and disfigurement.

Tossing the knife onto the ground he stepped back, inspecting his work as an artist might do, examining his latest creation in paint or stone for flaw before the gallery would open to a plethora of critics, the difference being, that his artistic medium of expression was in flesh, his connoisseurs and critics that of the police and curious onlooker. He wiped his hands on the front of his coat as he continued his grim survey, the garment's dark navy colour effectively hiding the excess blood.

Slicking his hair back from his face, the long black locks looking no more sinister than if he had been caught in an isolated rain storm, or had just stepped from the barber shop, his hair set down with a fancy pomade or tonic, he tucked his shirt tails into his trousers and fastened his coat, then calmly exited the breezeway.

He made his way, as his original plan was to do, towards the waterfront. With his need for blood satiated, the purpose behind continuing the trek was no longer about finding food, but more to take a path where it would be unlikely to meet anyone who could either recognize him or have legal backing to question him on his reasons for being out. Along the rough harbour front there would be little chance of either, and so he walked along in a manner that was almost carefree and convincingly belied the horrendous act he had carried out not thirty minutes earlier.

The walk home had been, as hoped, uneventful and, as luck would have it, no one was about the main hallway.

Not wishing to press his good fortune, he quietly locked the door behind him and leaped up the staircase two at a time, arriving at his door and managing to get inside just before he heard Mrs. Doherty's door at the foot of the stairs open and then, after a moment, close again.

Inside the sanctuary of his tiny room he was at last able to breathe, for it had felt as though he had been holding his breath since he first ventured out of the breezeway and onto that back street for the walk home.

He slipped the coat off and hung it over the chair, then went over to the mirror. Unbuttoning his shirt he pulled it off as well and inspected his wound more closely under the better lighting afforded by the oil lamp.

Still, to his amazement, despite the blood that covered his skin and soaked his shirt, there was not a trace of a wound upon his body, not even the smallest of scratches was visible.

"Unbelievable," he said to himself under his breath as he continued to look for something that simply could not be found, and that was when he discovered something else. As he had uttered that single word unto himself he noticed that the fangs, teeth that had been so prevalent earlier in the day were now much reduced in size and nearly normal looking in appearance. Along with that his gums did not seem to be as raw looking, the ache that had been there for a better part of the day had also subsided greatly, and even the red within his eyes had completely disappeared.

With all these new findings coming one upon another he almost leapt from in front of the dresser to the wall where he had hung the calendar and, pulling it from the nail, he placed it on the table.

With ink well and pen he made careful entries on to the day, crossing out previous notations pertaining to the horrific mutations he had seen that very morning.

He was feeling positive about the remission of these horrid anomalies until he came to the realization that the reason behind their retreat must have something to do with the blood he had consumed. There was no other logical reason he could come up with to explain it otherwise.

Suddenly what he had done hit him like a hammer. Not only had he wilfully killed another human being, he had done so, in part at least, to drink the man's blood.

The confident carefree killer that had so carefully created a misleading crime scene to disguise the true nature of the offence, as well as his identity, now lay upon the floor, his eyes shut tight, legs drawn to his chest and shaking violently, until finally his conscious mind fell victim to sleep.

The following morning he had been roused by both the diffused sunshine streaming through the thin veil of curtain that covered the lone window and that of his landlady, knocking on his door to remind him that it was her good word that would be in question if he did not soon make haste and get himself to work.

Her warning had been friendly enough, but he knew that it could easily change if he were foolhardy enough to lose his employment.

He had washed carefully that morning to ensure that any traces of blood were removed from both his hair and beneath his nails before dressing in a new shirt and trousers. He had made the choice to leave his coat behind, even though the dried blood was even harder to see than it had been when it was fresh. He simply was not willing to take the chance in the light of day that someone might notice. The day was bright, and the sun carried with it a hint of warmth as he made his way towards the infirmary. Following much the same path as he had taken the night before, he dropped his blood-soaked pants and shirt in a rubbish bin he found tucked beside a busy textile shop, covering the bundle with loose scraps of mismatched fabrics until it was well buried.

At this point he could have simply turned north on the next street which would have led him back to the busier main street some four blocks up, but instead he chose to continue on, tracing out his footsteps of a few hours earlier. There was a part of him that needed to know if the body had been found and if so what, if anything, was thought of the crime.

Coming upon the back street he had walked out of several hours earlier, the sight of a large crowd gathered around the entranceway to the covered lane suddenly took him aback, and he knew without a doubt the reason behind why they were there.

His first thoughts were simply to turn and find some other means of getting to where he needed to go, but he forced himself forward towards the crowd, the whispered voices becoming more discernible as he approached.

Trying to maintain a look of idle interest, he arrived at the outer ring of what appeared to be approximately twenty-five or so people all talking amongst themselves. He tried to catch bits and pieces of what was being said about what had happened, but it was all so sporadic.

Unable to make any sense from this intermingled chatter, he tapped the shoulder of a man who stood, his back towards him, and inquired as to what had happened.

"Looks like a murder, from what I gather," the man replied. "The constables were called in early this morning, they have been in there since I arrived."

The man's voice had almost an elated tone to it as though he was speaking of a travelling show that had arrived in town and not that of a murder.

"A murder you say?" Aremis replied with an alarmed tone, "Dreadful business that."

"Yes, true-nuf," the man said in agreement before starting anew. "Must be something special though; they sent for an inspector some time ago and he arrived not long after me."

A bolt of fear shot through him as the words of the stranger lingered in is mind. Had he forgotten some detail? Was his attempt at disguising the wound not good enough to conceal the truth? All of this ran though his mind as he carefully maintained his composure. He was about to enquire further about the arrival of the senior law-man when two constables emerged from the laneway and ordered the crowd to move back. As the group complied, moving back in stumbled unison, the uniformed beat constables talked quietly between themselves.

With the crowd now well back in the street, the man he had been standing with broke away and approached to the two uniformed lawmen inquiring of them had what happened.

"Nothin' that would be concerning you now, be on yer way or stand back."

The tone made it clear that the constable was serious in his address and was not someone to be trifled with. So without acquiring any further information the man returned to the crowd and took up a place beside Aremis.

"Sodder," the man said under his breath as he plunked his hands into the pockets of his trousers. "They all act so bloody high and mighty, they do."

Aremis nodded in agreement, even though he did not share the man's viewpoint but did not think it was something worth risking a disagreement over.

The constables went back to their conversation, and as the throng of spectators, some of whom had grown bored with the lack of new information, began to disperse, he found that in the relative silence that ensued he could actually make out the whispered words that were being said some fifteen feet away.

Intrigued and a little shocked by this, he strained to catch every word he could, as the two constables carried on with what they thought was a private conversation.

"... had it comin' he did, crook like that, deserved what he got, just a matter of time it was."

The other policeman concurred with his counterpart, nodding his head once then adding his own thoughts on the matter.

"One less for us to have to be dealing with. Must have picked the wrong man last night, that's pretty much a given. Inspector thinks he probably came on a sailor-type, perhaps returning to the docks from one of the local public houses, bloody shame it was."

There was some hushed laughter between them, which effectively drowned out the next few words before he was again able pick up what was being said.

"...either way he's dead and good thing too. I hope the bloke who did it is back on his ship and out to sea. I would hate to have to arrest a man after me own heart."

There was more muted laughter before a man in long grey trench coat appeared at the head of the breezeway and motioned for one of them to return with him, leaving the other constable alone to watch the thinning crowd.

With the investigation still ongoing, and no indication when it would conclude, Aremis felt there was little to be gained by remaining there any longer. In fact, he felt that being seen as overly interested might very well draw unwanted attention to himself.

"Well, it would seem there will be little else to see for some time yet so I must bid you good day, sir," he said to the man with whom he had shared the last few minutes, "I fear that if I do not soon get to work there will be no job waiting for me when I arrive."

His words brought about a short burst of laughter and heartfelt understanding from the man who then wished him a good day.

'Have a pleasant day,' he thought to himself, repeating those departing words in his mind as he made his way along the back street and out onto the busier main thoroughfare. It seemed such an odd thing to say to someone you have just spent the last few moments with, standing not a hundred feet from where a murder had taken place, all the while discussing the little known facts and formulating possible hypotheses. More important than that of the peculiar farewell, however, was the conversation that had transpired between the two policemen. It was obvious there was little if any regard for the victim. By their blatant disdain for the fellow, one could easily deduce that he must have been nothing less than a well-known criminal in the area, one of whom the local constabulary were happy to be rid of, no matter the means. He wished he knew what the inspector might be thinking, whether he also shared similar feelings, that this murdered thief had indeed got his just deserts, or if he was the sort of man who would see to it that justice was served no matter the victim's background or previous history.

For now though, it would seem that he had been afforded some time, due to how the whole brutal scene was being viewed by the popular opinion that day. The murdered man's unsavoury past meant that he was held in poor esteem by those in the community as well as within the local law enforcement, and his untimely death hardly creating much of a moral outcry from either societal, or professional sect.

For the first time since waking that morning, he walked along with a mind much less weighted down by the act he had committed the night before. Even though he knew all too well that which he had done was wrong on every level, he felt it fair to think that if that man had not accosted him then, in all likelihood, he would still be alive this very morning. With that serving up as justification for his actions, he continued on to work feeling better than he had in days.

Chapter 11

Dear Diary,

My prayers have been at last answered as yesterday I received a letter from my brother. Mother and Father also received a similar posting the previous day. We have all been so worried these last few weeks, I more so than that of my parents, for I know what they do not.

I am pleased to hear tell of his finding both accommodations and employment, neither of which he claims to be luxurious but serve their intended function quite well.

I am disappointed to discover that neither the priest of the Catholic Church nor the first doctors he visited have been able to shed any light on that which holds him hostage within his own body. I had secretly hoped and openly prayed that he would be able to find someone or some way to either cure him or drive out this thing within him, but for now it seems that is not in keeping with God's intentions.

He has indicated to me his plans to keep seeking out, within the time offered to him as his own, other denominations of the church as well as other physicians, with the continued hope of discovering some answer. In addition to this, he has also confided in me that he intends to make inquires of the local gypsies in the hope that their odd ways and beliefs might somehow be of help. As I know nothing of these people or their beliefs, I can only hope that if he does indeed follow this path that it will lead him to meaningful answers.

He talks of the blood I had given him and of its expiration, but tells me little of how he is continuing to survive without it, or if he has found some other source for which to acquire it. I feel certain that if he no longer needed blood then he would have surely mentioned it in his letter. The absence of this only makes me worry all the more.

The letter he sent me was far more detailed than that of the one addressed to the family, for which I am grateful. He has kept to the truth, as much as possible saying the work on the rail lines had not panned out but had found meaningful work at a local hospital. He spoke of finding lodgings through his contact with the priest at the Catholic Church, the same man, who, in goodness and kindness, was also responsible for helping to find him his current employment.

This letter and its news have pleased both Mother and Father, knowing that their son is doing well while so very far from home.

Even though there is much in his writing that is indeed uplifting, it is what is not said that I find most troubling. I feel, more than know, that there is something still horribly wrong, and simply because he does not speak of it does not mean that it is not there.

In short, he tells us of his small room within the home of a kind landlady, and yet he does not provide, either our parents or myself in privacy, an address whereby we might visit or write.

I have no other choice but to sit by and wait for his next letter in the hopes that things will be made clearer to me at that point.

Temperance, the 19th of February in the year of our Lord, 1875

Chapter 12

Dear Diary,

Hello my old friend, I am certain in fact, that if you be in actuality, a friend of flesh and blood and not one of paper and binding you would not easily wish me well, what with my horrid lack of correspondence these many years.

Nevertheless I am here now and I will endeavour to convey to you all that has happened since my last entry. I must confess that I know not where to begin as so much has taken place, most of which is still quite unbelievable to me despite seeing it with my own eyes.

Something that is quite normal, but still quite upsetting to me is the passing of my mother two years ago now. It seems to me that it was only yesterday, and I still am moved to tears when I realise she is, in fact, with God and no longer with us. I must clarify that it is not that I am angry that she is gone, only that she passed before Aremis could be with her. Although I miss her terribly, I know with all my heart she is with God and in that she is happy. Father suffered though through her passing and he, like I, has found difficulty in coping with her death.

The farm continues to do well, so much so in fact, that father has taken to hiring on extra help in order to meet the demands of both the livestock and crops.

Iris is still at home and has taken on the role of mother and housekeep. She is seeing a young man, much to father's disproval. He is one of the men father had hired. I have met him on several occasions and find him to be quite likable, despite what father has to say about him when out of earshot.

I myself married a year before mother's passing and am content in my life now. I live in a small home within our tiny community. My husband, John, is a blacksmith by heritage and has now taken over the small shop once run by Mr. Harris.

John is a good and kind man but that having been said, I do not trust him with the knowledge of my other sight or the truth regarding my brother. John is a church-going, God-fearing man who would not hear tell of the things that I have borne witness to. Truth be known, he would, in all likelihood, have our marriage annulled and me viewed as one quite insane if he were to know the truth.

As to my brother, Aremis, as I left it last, things did not appear to be good. Well, things are different now, by no means better or even close to what I would consider normal but I suppose it is the best I could have hoped for, given the grave circumstances that have surrounded him.

I must confess that I was both annoyed and relieved that my brother did not attend my wedding for as much as I would have loved to see him there with Father, in truth, it would have given me one more thing to be concerned about.

When I watched Aremis leave, that dark afternoon 14 years ago, I felt certain it would be the last time I would ever set eyes on him but I was incorrect in that belief. With the exception of the first year he was away, when there was precious little in the way of correspondence, much less a visitation, he has arrived home each and every Christmas and often comes out for a short visit during the summer months. Failing that, he would come during the month immediately preceding the harvest.

I still receive regular postings from him on or about the middle of each month in which he tells me of his weeks and various happenings within his life so far away.

From all I have gathered, as well as witnessed firsthand, he has managed to do quite well for himself over the years, finding work and dressing smartly whenever he arrives home. His arrival always brings with it not only himself but a smattering of gifts, no matter the season, and yet despite all of this I am still as wary of him as the day I confronted him on the porch.

He has spoken very little to me of that which caused his exile, only confiding in me that what had stricken him so many years ago remains with him still, albeit he now maintains with conviction he understands how to control it.

He had confided in me through letters received at the onset of his second year in London that he had exhausted every avenue of hope for finding either a cure or redemption. He wrote, at times in detail, of carrying out macabre tests upon himself and keeping detailed notes on the results, He has, however, never disclosed to me what the end results of those experiments were.

When we are together and alone, something I do not encourage, he will not discuss with me anything to do with his condition, the experiments, or what I feel must still be a need for blood. Anytime I try to establish a conversation or a line of gentle questioning that might lead me towards a better understanding, he tells me, quite curtly I might add, that he has it under control and then changes the subject.

To say that I am unhappy to see him when he arrives would be a lie, but it would also be fair to say that I am greatly relieved when it comes time for him to return to London.

It is spring here now and I am looking forward to summer. I am with child, my first, and I wish with all my heart that Mother were still with me so that she might see her grandchild when the time arrives. I must be content that she will see all from her place in heaven and I hope with all my heart that the view she may enjoy is not privy to things unholy, in this way she might be spared knowledge of what I feel her only son is committing on a frequency most regular.

Temperance, the 3ᵈ of April in the year of our Lord, 1888

Having posted what had become something of a regular monthly letter to Temperance and his family, Aremis stepped from the small post office at the north end of Commercial Street into an April morning filled with sunshine. He pulled a small silver pocket watch from within his light jacket and flipped open the delicately engraved lid.

It was just after 9:30 a.m. and after viewing the time, as it was told to him by ornate black hands, he snapped the lid over concealing the face of the tiny timepiece from view before tucking it back into the pocket from where he had first retrieved it.

He took in all the sights and sounds that surrounded him as he reminisced about his arrival in London some fourteen years ago, on a morning that was far different than the one he was enjoying currently.

It had been a difficult few months during that first year, and many an evening had passed where he found himself alone within the confines of his room, contemplating the consequences of taking his own life rather than continue on in the way he was being forced to exist. He longed for home, for a life he could no longer be a part of, and one that would certainly not tolerate that which he had become. He found himself stranded between two worlds, worlds that could not have been farther apart from one another if he, himself, had designed them to be that way.

But life can be a funny thing, funny not in the sense of humour but in oddity of circumstance, for often things that come to us in our day to day lives that are viewed as detrimental can, in fact, carry within their cloak of misery and despair the seeds of change. The misfortune of having, quite by chance, a run-in with a would-be thief on a deserted back street so many years ago had provided him, in the ensuing short and violent few seconds, more information regarding his condition and how it worked than all the following months of persistent inquiry had net him collectively.

Had he not taken that lonely back street as he frantically returned from the market square, or if had been more diligent about his experiments with the blood of animals, he possibly would have never have had to kill another human being and take from them their life's blood. But it was through those series of events, a string of miscalculations and unfortunate circumstance, which had inevitably led him to commit such a heinous act, and in doing so did he come to realize human blood held his afflictions at bay longer. In addition to this, it was also obvious that if he exercised caution in choosing his victim, the local constabulary put little effort into discovering who had actually done away with someone viewed as nothing more than a troublesome nuisance.

The life he was now forced into living, one painfully carved from the rubble of his former life, revolved around precision time keeping. He knew all too well the dire consequences that would result if he should become negligent of the steady progression of days, or ignored a simple mathematical calculation, a calculation based on what creature the blood he had ingested came from and how long it had been since he consumed it. Failure to abide by these two factors could easily see him reduced from a rational thinking being to a single-minded predator, something that, in this day of increased science within the police forces' investigative processes, he could ill afford.

On the day that had preceded this one, he had run into Sister Jillian as she made her way about town running her various errands, and she had all but insisted that he stop by and visit a while, providing of course he could afford the time. She went on to explain that Father Dudley had been feeling poorly of late and felt that his time in this world would soon be drawing to a close. She thought it would do the old man good to see someone he had helped so many years ago, and with her final words sounding so grim he found it difficult to refuse the kindly nun.

He had promised himself sometime ago that he would do his best to distance himself from those he encountered in order to keep them safe and to keep his identity as obscure as possible. Accepting the invitation would mean he would have to go back on that promise. It had been several years since he had been back to the old church where he had first arrived that rain-filled day so he felt reasonably safe that not many, if any, beyond the old priest and nun, would take any notice of him.

The post office he had just left had net him little in the way of newer employment news. His interest in searching out employment opportunities was not due to being in a dire situation regarding finances but more for reasons of requiring a change.

He had discovered early in that it was to his benefit to move about from one job to another as frequently as the market could provide so as not to become too well known to those around him, as well as keeping him from forming any sort of long-lasting friendships. He wanted little in the way of personal attachment or connections in case the time came when he might have to leave suddenly.

Aremis was always vigilant to ensure he had enough money with him at all times so that he could walk the night time streets without fear of being arrested for vagrancy, a serious fear for all those living a more transient nature, for even if he were to be stopped he had with him both means and proof of lodgings that ensured he would be neither detained nor placed in such appalling working conditions as the penal workhouses. This was all-important to his survival since it was under the black curtain of night that he sought out his prey. For it was when the world was without the light of day, did those of unsavoury backgrounds and ill-gotten trade did so venture. Where these vile predators of the darkness plied their trade, he would also go to reap his unholy bounty from those very people who preyed on the unfortunate or the careless.

On this bright and sun-filled morning he had set off to accomplish a number of things that required his attention, and as the day progressed he was making good headway on meeting those self-imposed goals.

It was approaching 4:00 p.m. when he again removed the pocket watch and noted the time. He had managed to complete all that he had set out to do, but in doing so had left himself a bit shy on the time which would be needed to walk the distance to the old church where he was to meet with Father Dudley and Sister Jillian.

The ever present teachings of his mother regarding the importance of being punctual poked at his brain like that of a child who will not leave an insect bite alone, scratching at it until it becomes far worse than it had been initially.

He quickened his pace and darted down a laneway that joined two main thoroughfares, in search of a cab. Luck seemed to be with him that late afternoon, for as he emerged from the small connecting lane he spotted a Hansom Cab at the far end of the street. He raised his hand and stepped out into the roadway in order to make his intentions known to the driver.

Keen to make a fair, local cab drivers were always on the lookout for a customer and it was but a moment before the black stallion was turned and the horse-drawn cab was making its way towards him.

As the two-wheeled Hansom Cab pulled up, its single black horse, dressed in matching black tack trimmed with red ribbon and brass hardware, looked as proper as the carriage it was tethered to. He gave the driver brief but detailed instruction to take him to the Catholic Church that was just north of King's Cross Station.

With the directions conveyed and understood, he opened the door, stepping into the cab's luxurious interior, closing the door behind him. The interior of the coach was as fine as its exterior suggested. The seats and armrests made from soft red velvet stretched over well-padded cushioning, that looked as rich as they were comfortable. The small glass windows, draped over in black tapestries, drawn open and tied back, the walls and doors all adorned with gleaming brass appointments so rich and detailed, that one could have easily believed they were seated within a booth of a fine hotel restaurant and not in something designed for transportation.

Once he was comfortably seated within the coach he pulled the black twist rope that hung through brass eyelets, that in turn connected to a bell located above that cab's roof near the driver's seat. When rung, it signalled the cab driver that his passenger was ready to proceed, or if already moving, a need to stop.

The carriage lurched slightly before smoothing into a steady forward motion that saw the closing stores and businesses slip past the plate glass windows, one looking much as the last one had, before disappearing from view.

It had been a short ride, one that had saved him a considerable walk, and it was not long before he found himself parked on the street in front of the church. Lost in a daydream of sorts he had not even realised that they had come to a halt. In fact, it was not until the driver opened the small porthole within the roof of the cab to inform him they had arrived did he notice his surroundings.

Aremis stepped from the mobile sanctuary and stood on the road's edge looking at another more traditional sanctuary, one he himself had taken refuge in many years earlier.

The driver informed him of the fare. Aremis reached into the inside pocket of his long coat, pulled out a small change purse, removed several coins and placed them into the driver's outstretched hand, telling him he could keep the overrun.

Pleased with the gesture as much as the amount, the driver tipped his top hat then snapped the reins on the horses back.

The black horse and cab moved off, continuing up the narrow street until they had crested the hilltop, turned left and disappeared from view.

Standing before the grand stone house of God he could not help but remember standing in that very spot, several years prior, soaked to the skin and wondering what was to become of him. He looked down at the step where he had sat not a more than a few days after his initial arrival, the place where he had come to his first realisation, the first real solid evidence that what he was or was on the way to becoming, may have within its origins clues to its design and function.

The solitary walk down memory lane was serving up bitter-sweet recollections for him, and so, with little more than slight exhalation that sounded more like a snort, he forced a tight-lipped smile as he made his way to the rear of the church, leaving his many thoughts and memories to swirl off like autumn leafs in the coming breeze of the approaching nightfall.

Arriving in the small backyard behind the church, a place he had become all too familiar with during his first weeks at the church: a place where each night without fail, a tattered, disjointed line of people would make their way up the stone path to the back door of the rectory. The unfortunate and the abused, they would all come, in the hopes of receiving not the word of the Lord but something just as important, a small cup of whatever Sister Jillian had put together earlier in the day, along with a thin slice of bread. For those people, forgotten or, in truth, shunned by society, the afterlife was something that could not be reconciled. A near dream-like conception that lay far from the harshness that was their existence here in the material world, where things like starving to death or seeing their family taken and separated from one another was a far more realistic belief than that of the so-called eternal love of an unseen God.

As he approached the old wooden door that led into the kitchen he pondered his last thoughts, the ones pertaining to God, and it struck him, quite suddenly. Perhaps it may have been because of his location, within the grounds of this religious place, or it may have been nothing more than mere coincidence brought about by idle thoughts and memories, that had him thinking about how he had lost much of his respect for his Heavenly Father since having come to London. This disillusionment he felt did not have its roots in truancy, far from it in fact, for he had prayed most every day for some sort of salvation or Divine release from his plight. It was not the lack of diligence in his devotion that had damaged his relationship with God, but the lack of response he received to those heartfelt prayers. So deep was the spiritual injury, in fact, that he was beginning to think God did not even exist. But if he was mistaken and such a being did so be, then he hated him for turning a deaf ear to such desperate pleas.

For the second time that night he forced his thoughts and personal beliefs from his mind so they would not interfere with the social evening that still lay ahead. Knocking once in order to announce his arrival, he let himself in, closing the heavy door behind him, effectively shutting out the chill night air along with his feelings.

The evening spent within the company of old friends, the first and only ones he had made and chose to keep, had been delightful, more so than he would have lent the possibility to, considering his current state of mind regarding all things religious. The only down side to the entire night was that Father Dudley had indeed deteriorated considerably since he had last seen the old priest, and even though he still maintained a portly physique, it was plain to see he was suffering. His movements were laboured, as was his speech and breathing, but amusingly enough his appetite did not seem to be adversely affected by any of his medical afflictions.

An unexpected addition to the kitchen that night was that of a much younger priest, obviously sent in by the Catholic Church to learn the ropes from his much older predecessor and then ultimately replace him upon his tutor's passing. He would later come to remember this somewhat morbid ascension to leadership and would often wonder how Father Dudley must have felt about having this up and coming young man there with him, living in his house as it were, for the sole purpose of having him teach the young man all he knew so that he could be simply be replaced at the time of his death, before if need be.

Sister Jillian had also aged some since he had thanked her for her kindness at the front steps of the church and made his way to his first rented room, but she wore it well. She still retained the sparkle in her eyes that seemed to be even more brilliant when she smiled or laughed, and she had certainly not lost any of her Irish tenacity when it was called for. This had been quite apparent early in the evening when the young apprentice unto God had indirectly agitated his older mentor and Sister Jillian was forced to step in and settle the old man down, much in the same way she had done on his own first dealings with Father Dudley, using a combination of old-school firmness that was well wrapped in kindness, mixed with a dash of wit for good measure. However the formula might be summed up, the outcome was always the same: a restored calmness, delivered in short order.

The remainder of the conversation around the diner table that evening was light and, as he had been instructed many years before while at that very same table, Aremis stayed well clear of things pertaining to the unnatural, even though he now knew well, through first hand experience, that such things most certainly did exist. What he was, however, still remained a mystery, and for that night, it was most certainly going to remain that way. He was not about to bring ruin upon the pleasant social gathering by trying to again prove that which he could ill prove without damning himself in the process.

The evening's gathering being what it was, a rekindling of old friendships and an introduction of new ones, it was not surprising that time had run away with them and the hour had grown late in short order. It was well after 11:00 p.m. and Father Dudley had already excused himself for the night some two hours earlier. Sister Jillian had gone with him to ensure he would be settled in his bed, but returned to the kitchen shortly thereafter.

With morning drawing ever closer, the present day's final minutes close at hand, Aremis decided it best to take his leave and begin to make his way home. He no longer lived a mere six streets over and, if he were unable to hail transport at this late hour, he would be looking at forty minutes or more before he would be home.

So shaking hands with the new priest and giving a Sister Jillian a warm hug, he bid farewell to his hosts and made his way back to the street by the way he had arrived, several hours earlier.

Out on the street, it was as he anticipated, the roads were barren and quiet without so much as a glimpse of a taxi. It was much the same way out on the main street. If he chose to go in the direction opposite to that which he needed, he would find himself back at the rail station. He thought there might well be a cab there, but if not, he would have easily added twenty minutes to his walk.

Resigning himself to the fact that he might very well have to walk the entire way home, he set off east towards the docks and the more notorious part of town. He knew he would stand a better chance of flagging down a late night entrepreneur hungry for one last fair in a place that would still be serving both ale and female company. Besides, the seedy part of town also provided him the perfect hunting ground, a place where he could walk in complete confidence and complete anonymity, where those whose lives he snuffed out would neither be missed nor mourned in the light of day.

He still had nearly a full week in hand before he would once again need to seek out an appropriate victim, but if the opportunity presented itself he was not about to turn a blind eye to the offering.

Following the main streets for the better part of the journey home with little luck in finding either a ride or suitable blood supply and not particularly bothered by the lack of either, he turned down a service lane that would cut several minutes off his trip.

It was a laneway he knew well, but one he chose to stay clear of mainly due to the inhabitants who wandered its tight, claustrophobic length. It had numerous turns and sharp corners, fences and alcoves, all of which prevented anyone who entered it from seeing either end at the same time no matter where you stood along its length. But with the wind blowing in, what felt like another spring storm, the idea of remaining dry outweighed the ghosts and bygone memories

Although the lane itself was a well-known haven for the criminal element, which in turn provided an ideal hunting ground for those whom he preyed upon, it was also well known as a place where women could, and often did, peddle their feminine charms. It was these ladies of the night, women forced into a life of prostitution by either need or circumstance, which kept him from negotiating the narrow corridor unless untimely hunger dictated otherwise.

Ever since he had, in grave error, taken the life of just such a woman, he found himself unable to even make eye contact with her sisters of the trade. That, and the fact that he never knew for certain what had become of the body or the investigation, made those feelings within him that much harder to deal with. So, with answers not forthcoming and absolution not being an option, avoidance had become the medicine of choice in this matter.

He had, after several months, whether driven by guilt or perhaps a morbid curiosity, in fact made a pilgrimage back to the abandoned sail shop only to find nothing more than a building in dreadful disrepair. There was no evidence, nothing whatsoever that would lend itself in supporting the memories, thoughts and recurring nightmares which were a constant reminder that he had indeed taken someone's life within that forgotten, derelict room upon the second floor.

Most who commit such crimes are elated when nothing of their insidious deeds ever comes to light, but for Aremis, that fact alone, the idea that the person whose life he had taken through nothing more than a mistaken identity may never have been identified and in all likelihood went to her final resting place quite unknown, was the worst of it.

The thieves and swindlers whose lives he took he did so without pity or remorse, for he felt it was through their evil deeds that they found themselves face to face with their own demise. But when it came to the life of the prostitute, he carried a wound within him that penetrated deeply, and no matter how fast his body could mend itself from physical trauma it could not seem to heal nor erase the feeling or the memories surrounding the untimely death of this woman so long ago.

Making his way smartly through the narrow passage, he passed numerous drunkards already bedded down for the night's impending weather in whatever shelter they could find for themselves. Although easy targets, he did not often prey upon those addicted to the drink, for as easy as it might be to locate, dispatch and have little in the way of repercussions upon the discovery of their remains, their alcohol-saturated blood often left its affects on him, much as it had done in the one who had consumed it originally.

Beyond the wayward alcoholics, he continued to make his way towards home, negotiating the numerous turns and directional changes that were the hallmark of this dingy lane, the sporadically spaced gas lights the only illumination to an otherwise ebony world within the stone and brick-lined passageway.

From within the darkness, the objects of his deliberate forestalling could be seen lurking in covered doorways and beneath bay windows. Almost with a predictable occurrence came the gentle inquiry as he passed, all sounding similar, all made with the intent of luring one lonely soul to seek the paid company of another. Just as the hail was predictable so was the response he would give, never harsh or belittling, but always firm and always, no thank you.

He had passed a half dozen of these women, some of them well past their best years, and he was nearing the point where he would be free of the laneways confines. With less than fifty yards before him he passed a fenced-off lot, which at one time might have been a residence or shop. As he did, he spied a lone woman standing just behind where the fencing ended. He turned his head slightly as he passed, taking in as he did her clothing, a milestone better than her sisters in the trade were wearing that night. A knit shawl around her shoulders, burgundy in colour, covered a blouse that was lighter, its pale hue patterned with some sort of delicate floral design, perhaps embroidered. She had on a long black skirt that bottomed out at her ankles, her shoes polished black lace-up ankle boots. Her hair was draped in a scarf that looked to be silk and she had it pulled around so it hid most of her facial features from view.

Initial eye contact having been made and any form of threat to his person eliminated, he returned his attention to the task of getting home.

An Irish voice softly called out to him from behind as he continued on his path, the combination of feminine tone and delicate accent created a most alluring sound within the stillness of the night.

"Could I interest you in some lovin' before you make yer way home, good sir?"

Without looking back, he replied in his usual unfeeling manner, giving a nonchalant wave to emphasize his answer.

"No thank you."

Usually that would suffice and there would be little, if any, further conversations, however in this instance it was not to be the case. The brown-haired woman stepped from the shadows and called to him again.

"Do you have someone special then, or is it just me that's to yer dislikin'?"

Her voice was still soft and gentle, and if not for the accent he could have easily thought her to be any number of women whom he had encountered in the various shops that surrounded his apartment. Whether it was her charms, her voice or a combination of both, it had done enough to have him give her a more emotional response.

"No, there is no one else. My answer is my own and has nothing to do with you. I am late and have no need for company, female or otherwise, so I shall bid you good night."

He turned to face her and gave her a short gentlemanly bow, then turned to go, satisfied his answer, along with the gesture, would dissuade any further communication from the solicitor.

"Well that is a shame," she said quietly, her words barely reaching his ears, "for I find you quite attractive and very much a gentleman, good sir, in fact, if the truth be known, I would even agree to marry you if you were so inclined to ask me."

Her words, even as faint as they were, stopped him cold in his tracks and turning around slowly he found himself not twenty feet from where she was standing, her shoulder pressed up against the brick wall, gently supporting her weight in an off balance stance, her hand still holding the scarf over her face.

The very same words he had heard so long ago, words that had taken him so by surprise that they left him not knowing what to make of the one whom, then, had stood before him in the darkness, in much the same manner as this stranger now stood before him. Nearly exact in their height and stature, the only discernible difference being the voice. Far different from the one that had spawned over a decade of night terrors, there could be little chance this was simply a remarkable coincidence. The possibility of that would be nothing short of staggering.

His mind raced in an attempt to come to some reasonable explanation or understanding of that which was before him, even though he had long ago given up lending reason to things that were connected with or had anything to do with what he had become.

If it were nothing more than mere coincidence then it would indeed be incredible, and if not, it would be nothing short of terrifying.

He studied her stature, trying to compare it to what little he had in the way of memories regarding the woman outside the town hall. There was no shortage of ghoulish imagery within his mind's eye, dream-like renderings of what he thought the originator of his illness might be like, but in actuality he'd had only one brief encounter with her and that was a long time ago, in darkened conditions not dissimilar to the one in which he now found himself to be in.

If this person or thing was indeed one and the same as the one who had attacked him that night in the forest, did she look on him now as simply another unknown victim or did she know whom it was that she was actually soliciting.

Stalling for time in order to think through what was happening, he took up the position of one dumbfounded by her statement, in hope of either proving his fears to be true or dispelling them as nothing more than words of similarity playing on a tired mind.

"Excuse me, but why on earth would you say such a thing to me when you do not even know me?"

His words were smooth and confident and hid well his misgivings about dealing with something that could easily prove to be nothing short of the very daughter of Satan himself.

There was a long silence that followed his query, but it would not be words that would tell him what it was he searched for. As the woman slowly spun side to side as she pondered the question, much as the one who had claimed to be his bride had done outside the town hall. She lowered her head and pulled the scarf from her face, letting the one loose end fall over her bosom. As it did she raised it again and stared back at him with eyes that glowed red, a slight smile that more than revealed a pearlescent fang.

Fear and rage welled up inside him as he, for the first time since their last meeting, was standing face to face with that which had wrought this curse upon his life.

"You," he hissed, his voice molten with rage, "what in God's name are you, what have you infected me with?"

Acting as though nothing more than a polite introduction had just been initiated; she simply tossed her hair to one side, a wide smile upon her alabaster skin.

"Oh Aremis, please, do not be such a prude," she said with an air of one quite casual and without so much as a trace of accent in her voice. "I am a woman just as you are a man, honestly. And to think, I once thought you quite bright."

The waking visions and lucid dreams he had once experienced, the same ones that had inadvertently caused the death of a prostitute years before had subsided not long after the unknown woman's death, and he had reasoned that it was due, at least in part, to a more regular diet that did not see him going long lengths of time without blood as he had done in the early days of his affliction.

He rubbed his forehead with two fingers, trying to determine whether what he was seeing before him was, in actuality, what was really there, all the while keeping his eyes trained on his adversary. He did not want to make the same mistake twice, to be duped by an illusion into killing an innocent, but by the same token if what he was looking at was real then he may never get another opportunity to exact retribution for a life stolen from him. He hastily decided that further communication might dislodge the clues he would need to make that decision one way or the other.

"You did not answer me. You at the very least owe me an answer." His voice was low and well tempered, unlike his first interaction had been.

"My dear Aremis, I owe you nothing," she replied, playfully spinning around on the spot where she stood. "And, as to what we are, I have no more idea of that than you."

She finished her slow pirouette and straightened her skirt before carrying on her conversation.

"I cannot understand why you are so annoyed. You seem to have done well enough for yourself. Fine clothes, very proper and all, living here in the big city, it's quite an improvement from the man-boy I met at some ridiculous harvest festival, all dressed up in his Momma's mediocre attempt at tailoring. Do you truly believe you would have found happiness with that wisp of a girl?"

She shook her head from side to side as if in disgust as she recalled the distant memory.

"She was nothing like you, or her parents for that matter, they at least made an attempt at defending themselves, but not her. What was her name again?" She playfully asked, tapping her index finger on her lower lip, "Ah yes, I remember now, it was Mary. Same name as my own, in fact, how could I forget?

She paused but a moment a half smile creeping across her lips.

"No, not Mary, no fight in her, she just crawled through the woods bawling like a newborn. If she had kept quiet I may not have even found her out there..." She paused, letting her finger stray from her chin down her throat onto the top button of her blouse where, with little effort, slipped it though the buttonhole. She repeated the action three more times until the blouse fell open exposing her milky white chest.

"But you know how the rest of the story goes, there would be little need for me to bore you with details now, would there?"

Her words, designed to torment as much as distract, gave him little in the way of information but told him without a doubt that who he was speaking with was, indeed, the person who all but ended his life on a stone bridge just outside his village over a decade ago.

"You disgust me," he said in a firm voice, as he levelled an accusing finger at her.

The woman who stood before him hung her head slightly and pouted like a scolded child, placing her hands behind her back and twisting her body gently from side to side.

"Why do you say such hurtful things to me? I, like you, am only doing what I must to survive. Is that a crime to simply want the right to exist like others around me?"

Her voice was heartfelt and trailed off on the brink of tears.

It was a compelling statement, one he himself had used many times to try and justify, to no one but himself, the murders he had committed, and for a brief moment he felt a strange kinship with someone he hardly knew but whom he loathed nevertheless. As his resolve wavered slightly in light of her words, his own hard-learned lessons fuelled a growing feeling of compassion for the assailant who had stolen from him all he ever held dear in the world.

He softened his stance slightly and took a small step forward, with half a mind to attempt some form of consolation. He felt that if anyone could have the ability to understand her situation, it was he. But as he did, his first step barely taken, she slowly raised her head, revealing a smile most evil.

"You see how easy it is, even after all the years. Years in which I am certain you have entertained the thoughts of meeting me again and ending my life. Yet, when presented with that very opportunity, you crumble. Can you imagine all the hapless men who do not know me as you do? How they, of their own free will and devices, seek me out, only to have their lust be the vehicle that delivers them to their own demise?"

She straightened up and leaned against the fence, as she had been when he first set eyes upon her. Then, taking a quick evaluation of her outwardly appearance, she addressed him as though she was meeting him for the first time, complete with an unsettling authentic accent.

"Fancy some lovin' before you make yer way home, good sir?"

A tiny girl-like giggle punctuated her final remark before falling deathly silent.

Enraged by all he had heard, and having been played for a fool on top of it all, he lunged at her and in one quick movement had her pinned to the wooden fence, his hand clamped over her throat. He squeezed with as much pressure as he could, a force that had incapacitated men twice her size, but for all his effort, she just laughed, staring back at him with eyes void of contrast, single pools of red filling each eye socket.

"Please, I am touched by this show of affection but I am not really sure of your intentions, dear sir. After all, I do have my reputation to think about."

"Your reputation!" he growled as he pushed her even harder against the fence, "You have no such quality within you, you demon, you abortion of life, I shall kill you this very night, I swear!"

It was then, without warning, much like a chameleon, her mannerisms suddenly changed once again. Her voice now carried within the words the sound of fear and uncertainty.

"Now please sir, I do not wish any trouble with you. So if you not be havin' the money then I kindly ask that you please release me and be on yer way."

Staring at her, confused by her words and tone, he watched her eyes slowly return to normal green, her razor sharp fangs receding until they were no longer visible, hidden by pale trembling lips.

"Another trick, another one of the Devil's deceptions! Is there no end to your evil?"

He was all but shouting at her, even though he held her tightly but a few inches from his face.

"I'm afraid I'm not understanding you, sir, perhaps you mistake me for another. Please release me, yer frightening me."

Her voice trailed off as tears began to well up in her eyes.

A series of taps on his right shoulder, applied with far more force than necessary to get his attention, were delivered in firm succession.

"That will be quite enough of that now, sir. Remove your hand from the lady and be on your way, else I'll be running you in."

Aremis turned to see who it was that was addressing him in such a manner, all the while retaining his grip over his quarry's throat. He had not even set eyes on the yet unidentified man behind the voice when he realized that it was a police constable out on the beat.

He loosened his grip slightly as he came face to face with the stern looking policeman whose height and stature easily matched that of his own.

"Let her go now or I'll take you down a peg or two. Do you hear me?" the constable ordered firmly.

Caught between what he knew to be true and what it must look like, he tried to explain the situation best he could without looking like someone quite mad.

"Constable, please, a moment if you will. This is not as it would appear. This lady, as you refer to, is nothing of the sort. She has killed many a man, you must believe me."

The well-seasoned lawman glanced at the woman Aremis had pinned against the fence, then brought his steely eyes to rest on the man who held her there.

"Is this so Miss?" he said with more mirth in his voice than any single ounce of seriousness. "Is it true what he says about you? How many men have you killed then?"

She tried to laugh, but cut herself short, as though the hand that was now loosely over her throat had prevented it.

"Release her now, or I will beat you down where you stand!" the constable demanded as he pounded his nightstick hard on Aremis' shoulder.

Even though the blow was delivered with much force he barely felt it, but faked the discomfort just the same, so as to avoid further suspicions on the part of the constable. Releasing his hold completely, he stepped back with his hands raised up in front of his chest.

"That's more like it. Now, see here, I've had a quiet night up to now, so you just make your way to wherever it is that you might be going and I'll forget this little indiscretion for this evening, do you understand me?"

Mary went and stood by the constable, holding her throat and quietly thanking him for coming to her rescue. The two exchanged a few hushed words interspersed with muted laughter as Mary began to play with the brass buttons on the front of the constable's uniform.

Starring back in disbelief at what he was now witnessing, Aremis was at loss as to how to proceed. He could not bring himself to simply walk away when faced with the very real possibility that the object of his quest, or more accurately the reason the quest existed in the first place, would simply disappear and not be easily found again. After all, he had lived in the city now for years and several of those years in the very vicinity to where those like her plied their trade and he had never once crossed her path.

His frustration at the situation must have played out upon his face as he stood there in a forced stalemate, his wrongdoings for the right reasons thwarted by one put in place to uphold the righteous but who had obvious and quite familiar ulterior motives behind his intervention.

The constable, noticing that his order to move along had still not yet occurred, levelled his billy-stick towards Aremis and again warned him to be on his way.

With little choice left to him at that moment, Aremis relinquished any further idea of finishing that which he had started before the constable's arrival and turned to go, his reluctant departure coming on the heels of still more ill gotten laughter.

He had only gone about ten paces when he heard Mary call out to him, the Irish accent once again in place and sounding as natural as anyone who had been born there.

"Oh, sir, please before you leave, I've got somethin' fer you t-see."

He turned to face the pair who remained standing side-by-side, Mary's hand slowly creeping up the front of the policeman's chest. She slipped just behind him and to one side, letting her other hand fall loosely onto his shoulder, slowly running her fingertips over the constable's neck before playfully caressing his earlobe.

Then, without warning, she looked around the officer's shoulder, her green eyes replaced with the blood red orbs, her mouth open, porcelain-like fangs long and sharp, protruding from within as she locked eyes with him.

"No!" he shouted, his warning coming far too late to be of any use to the constable who, until that very moment, had no idea that he was in any peril whatsoever.

What had been a nothing short of sensual caress had, within the span of a heartbeat, turned into a vicious attack as she dug her nails deep into the lawman's neck. With her fingernails secured firmly in his flesh, she cranked his head hard to the left, leaving the right side of his neck open and vulnerable. Buckling his knees and continuing to pull, she dragged the bigger man down to where his unprotected neck was mere inches from her mouth. Then, with a most deliberate hesitation, she paused to make sure her apprentice was still watching.

In shock, unable to look away, he found himself paralyzed by that which he was witnessing, incapable of helping the constable or even shielding his eyes.

Satisfied she had his full attention, she sank her teeth deep into the neck of the struggling constable, tearing a gaping hole from which a river of blood erupted, raining a crimson spray over everything within a 6-foot radius.

As the blood shot forth from the doomed man's neck, Mary quickly corralled the geyser, taking most of the bubbling torrent into her mouth and swallowing it as fast as it emerged.

Near the point of unconsciousness, with no trace of fight left in him, she released her grip, letting his body slip from hers and fall into a heap on the ground. Blood continued to pour from the wound, pooling in the cracks and crevasses of the secluded laneway. She placed her foot over the hole she had made and pressed hard against it. The pressure and the pain it was causing could be heard in the man's gurgled pleas.

Covered nearly head to toe in blood, she placed a finger into her mouth and slowly sucked it clean all the while never taking her eyes off the only other person within the tiny corner of the lane.

Momentarily terrified, perhaps for the first time since their last meeting, he stood frozen to the ground, not sure of what was going to happen next or whether he would be alive long enough to be worrying about it.

Pulling her second finger slowly from her ruby stained lips she addressed him,

"Would you like a taste, my dear?" she asked in a voice that had within it words that offered up dessert but with a sultry sound that would be more appropriate within the privacy of one's bedroom than it was in the space and horror of the situation.

Despite his best efforts over the course of the last few years he still had difficulty in controlling the physical changes that would take place when feeding time grew close. He had discovered that, at times, even when he did not need to feed for several days he could still will the teeth to grow. The eyes were another problem all together, one he could do little about, and so remained vigilant to his time schedule. Even though he still had several days to go before he would need to drink, the sudden appearance of blood flowing freely had brought about those changes within him, and as hard as he tried he was unable to control his thoughts enough to prevent it.

"I know how you feel," she continued, her voice making that which he was feeling all the more difficult to control. "We are not that different from one another, you and I."

"I am nothing like you," he said in harsh rebuttal.

She laughed but for a moment at his words.

"Oh no? So you have not killed before?" she quipped, "I dare say that I do not believe it. You would never have survived this long drinking only that which animals can provide." She paused, her harsh words thrown back at him, trailing off with a pensive look about her otherwise cocky attitude.

Seizing the opportunity to try and regain some ground, he pressed her for knowledge, even though he knew well he might only have a matter of minutes before she turned on him as well.

"How do you know this? How can you possibly know what I did and still do to survive?"

She looked back at him. Her eyes still red, solely without contrast or feelings.

"Because I tried to live that way before I could no longer hold that which I am at bay."

Her words were as void of feeling as her eyes were of contrast.

There was an awkward silence that followed her confession, and even though he knew well not to trust the voice that came to his ears there was something in her words that told him that, at least for the moment, she was telling the truth. Whether it was her words or something else entirely, it had him reassessing his original plan of simply destroying the thing that had attacked him and instead try to form some sort of alliance. If he could somehow accomplish this, then perhaps together they could find some way of defeating that which held them both hostage to the force within their own bodies.

He was about to try and reach out to her with carefully, albeit hastily, thought out words when the wounded constable grabbed her ankle in a futile attempt to dislodge her foot from his neck. With his hand weakly clamped around her leg it broke whatever contemplative state she may have been in and returned in its place the sadistic predator Aremis was all too familiar with.

Unaffected by the feeble retaliation, she pressed her boot even harder into the constable's neck, the pressure of which produces several bone-splitting cracks. The man's hand dropped back to the ground and remained there unmoving.

She knelt down and brushed the blood-covered hair from the man's ghostly white face.

"Tisk, tisk, tisk, you should know better than to touch a lady like that now. What would yer Mum say if she knew of ya behavin' in such a manner?"

She looked back at Aremis,

"He's not a gentleman like you were, or do you still believe yerself a gentleman when yer taking another person's life?"

"Mary, please," he pleaded, but he was no longer reaching the human side of her as his words fell upon deaf ears.

"Would you care to have a drink with a young lady, sir, or am I to be finishing this one meself?"

When her request went unanswered she removed her boot from the mans neck, clamped her lips over the wound and took in the last of his life's ruby current until the dying man's heaving chest ceased to move.

In the stillness that followed his passing, with her lips still dripping, long syrup-like stalactites slowly forming, then under their own weight, dropping from her mouth onto her chest, she pulled back and adjusted her position slightly. She took a seat upon the corpse, straddling his chest while she fished through his pockets, pulling out some loose change and a brass police whistle.

"A whistle," she exclaimed triumphantly, holding her prize high within bloody fingers. "What a lovely trinket. I do so love them, you know."

Her voice was near child-like in tone and expression and Aremis found it difficult to keep track of who exactly was speaking to him moment to moment.

Feeling as though he had lost his opportunity for dealing with what might be left of her rational mind, he reverted back to the original plan of killing her despite the fact that he was unsure of how he was going to accomplish this necessary evil.

Without a weapon of any sort and with her strength near or perhaps greater than that of his own, this poorly planned idea might easily see him the one lying dead and not her.

Either way, he felt he might never get another chance, so with a bold new plan; he began to make his way toward her. At the same time he scolded her for what she had just done, much in the same manner as a parent might do with a child who had broken a dish though nothing more than foolery.

"Mary!" he said sternly as he moved slowly towards her, "Look at what you have done to this poor constable. You are a very naughty girl. The police are our friends. They help us and here you have hurt him."

Mary looked down at the face of the dead constable for a moment then looked back towards Aremis. Her eyes were again normal, her fangs no longer visible, and if not for the blood that all but covered her, one would not think she had just committed a most unspeakable act.

"I am sorry," she began, her voice now normal and shaking.

"You apologize to me?" he replied harshly in order to keep the charade alive "I am very disappointed in you, my child."

Mary looked away, then buried her head in her hands, her sobs coming not a moment later.

How he felt at that exact moment was indescribable as he watched his nemesis reduced to nothing more than a whimpering girl, no more than eight or nine years of age. It was at that precise moment he could not help but wonder if the mind disorder she so obviously displayed was a direct result of whatever it was that infected them both.

At first, he thought it might be best to let her carry on with this outpouring. However, he quickly dismissed the idea, for if time was of the essence then giving her too much of that precious commodity might prove detrimental. Changing his approach from one of scolding parent to that of understanding consoler, he continued to close the distance between the two of them.

"There, there, sweetheart, everything is alright, you shall see. No need for all those tears now." His voice was warm, caring, and far from an act as he had used it many a time with his two younger sisters when they had caught it from their mother for whatever they had done collectively or individually.

The sobbing began to ebb and her breathing returned to a more controlled state.

"Am I in trouble?" she asked, her voice still trembling.

"No, no, not at all. It was a mistake, an accident, nothing more. We all make them. It is how we learn. I have made many, I can assure you of that, my dear."

Mary pulled her knees to her chest and pressed her cheek against one knee, rocking slightly as she hugged her own legs tightly, looking like a child sitting there in the dim light of the laneway.

He was nearly within striking distance. His plan now was to take her by force while her back was still to him then, with his weight on top of her, use her own hair as a hand hold, driving her head repeatedly against the cobblestones until she either died or she killed him in the attempt. He felt more than ready to accept either possibility but had not prepared himself for what happened next. Before he could lunge she spoke, so quiet and faint that it could have easily been missed had any other noise been present within stillness.

"Do you think that my father will still love me?"

Her soft words stopped him in his tracks, words that may easily have their roots in a time long since past but ones that still carried a human need, the longing for a parent's love and acceptance. Her question had him searching for an answer, one that he would have to procure from the myriad of personal feelings pertaining to his own family, and one that would keep the monster within his adversary at bay for a few moments more.

"Of course, sweetheart, I feel certain he shall always love you."

His best heartfelt assurances were not to be believed, however, as she slowly stopped rocking and remained motionless upon the dead man's chest.

"You are mistaken, my dear Aremis, my father did not love me, nor would he help me," her voice suddenly lacking any childlike characteristics as she told her tale. "If I had not killed him when I did I would have certainly been hanged, or worse, for my crime, the crime of wanting to live. The night that I took my own family's lives, they had plotted against me with members of the church and the landlord of our village, a representative of the King himself, or so I am to understand. I was to be taken to a place far from my home and there I was to be questioned about what I had become. All of this because my own little brother found me as I drank from a cat that I had found injured from a fight with some other animal, a drink which I needed to survive as they themselves need water. Frightened by what he saw he ran and told our father all of what he had witnessed."

She paused and looked away but for an instant before continuing.

"Can you imagine my fear, my own family turning on me?"

The truth be known, he did not have to imagine it. With little effort he could easily recall the horror of staring down the barrel of his father's rifle in the hands of his sister who was quite prepared to end his life on the spot.

His mind darted from thoughts of family to the night he had, without thought, killed a criminal on a deserted back street, a night before he knew how to manage the thirst. He challenged himself to be truthful: that if he had been in the same condition the night that Temperance had threatened to end his life would he have acted in a manner similar to that of the confession he had just heard. The answer that came to him did not sit well, and despite their obvious differences he empathized with the creature before him.

"How did you come to be like this?" he inquired in a matter of fact voice that belied the gravity of the situation.

The answer he was waiting for was not forthcoming as she suddenly turned her attention from him towards the corner of the laneway from which both he and the constable had arrived but a few minutes before.

"Shhh," she said, a bloody finger raised to her lips.

He strained to listen to what had her so intently focused on an area that lay beyond the maze of turns and overshadowed by tall stone buildings.

It took a moment or two but he could, at last, make out the sound of a faint footfall coming up the stone laneway, the walls that made up the narrow passage amplifying the plodding progression to make it seem closer than it might actually be.

"I must leave now, my friend, and I feel that it would be prudent if you did the same."

He felt that he was so close to actually making some meaningful contact with this creature standing before him that he could not bring himself to simply let her walk away, but he was not going to get a chance to debate the options with her.

Walking the few short steps to where he was standing she stood before him, her height far shorter than that of his own, she placed her bloodied hand upon his jacket.

"You seem to be a good man, truly, but it will ill serve you in the end, of that I can assure you."

She coughed and pulled back, clutching her stomach as she continued to cough.

Before he could help or inquire as to what was happening, a fountain of blood spewed from her mouth, covering his face and chest in a red paste.

Aghast, he pulled back, wiping the blood from his eyelids with his fingers before regaining enough of his composure to focus his attention on what had just happened and why.

"Mary, are you all right, are you ill?" he asked urgently as he pulled a handkerchief from his coat pocket and began to try and wipe the blood from his face.

Mary never answered him but slowly doubled over as if in the grip of a terrible stomach cramp.

"Mary," he shouted, as loud as he dare without running the risk of alerting everyone within earshot to the situation that was unfolding within the confines of laneway, "we have to leave here, now, someone is coming."

She raised her head slowly, a faint smile upon her blood-covered face.

"It is you who must leave this place." she said under her breath as she held up the police whistle, its polished brass finish looking as though the very metal from which it was constructed was bleeding.

"Everyone knows me here. They will believe what I tell them to be true. But as for you dear sir, I've not see you round these streets before now and I would be willing to wager, if I was partial to that sort of thing, which I am not, that the police would take my word, the word of a well-known whore over that of a blood soaked stranger, especially one big enough to take down poor constable Davis like that."

He looked over at the policeman as he lay in his own blood upon the cobblestones and, despite her sarcasm; he knew well that which she spoke of was true. No one in their right mind would believe that this slight, meek-looking woman would have within her the ability to render a fit and capable man, a policeman at that, defenceless to the point of his own demise. Even though it may well be true that she, and her kind, were seen as the lowest of the low by her fellow neighbours, she would have more credibility than that of himself. For the first time since its conception, his plan of constant anonymity, had turned on him, for there would be no one that would be able to vouch for him.

"Run," she whispered as she placed the whistle between her lips, the look of the devil in her eyes.

"I beg your pardon?" he asked, not entirely sure what she was alluding to.

With the whistle clenched between her teeth she repeated her previous one word statement then blew hard on the whistle. A shrill high-pitched note pierced the still of the laneway as she continued to blow rapidly, in short bursts, into the tiny instrument.

From somewhere in the darkness, still beyond view, came hails in response to the sound.

"Police! Police!"

Dropping the whistle down the front of her blood-soaked blouse, she let out a shrill ear-splitting scream that reverberated off the walls, sounding as though several people were in distress.

There was no more time for talk or negotiation as the urgent hails from the approaching constable grew closer and more frantic following the nightmarish scream.

Quickly removing his overcoat he tore the shirt that had been drenched in blood from his body, then turning the coat inside out he pulled it back on, clutching it up around his neck in order to conceal the fact he was not wearing a shirt.

He took one last look at Mary, having crawled from the body over to a wall where she lay huddled in bloody clump against the bricks, with a look most shattered upon her face.

He held out his hand in one last silent attempt to have her to join him and make good their escape together, but there was no reaching her. Her glazed over eyes told him she might well be completely unaware of his presence at that moment and so, without any further attempts, he turned and ran with all his speed towards the end of the laneway, his bloodied shirt stuffed into the pocket of his coat.

He rounded the corner at the top of the lane and continued down the street, the sound of numerous police whistles and shouting filling the air behind him. If there could be a single ounce of saving grace within any of this, it was that the hour was quite late and he did not encounter another person, either on the streets or looking out of any window he passed. So for moment, his trail would be well covered.

When he had put several streets between himself and the horror that lay within that laneway he slowed his pace to one more suited to someone not being chased. Luck and good fortune had seen him this far without incident or pursuit. It would be foolish now, being so close to home, to have someone identify him and report to the police a mysterious man running in the middle of the night who then ducked into the rooming house near the end of Thrawl Street.

His more relaxed pace allowed him to take control of the frantic thoughts that, until then, were running rampant through his mind. With the fear of being caught not an immediate concern, he began to go over the entire scenario, scrutinizing the smallest detail for anything that may yield some new information about her, or the evil that they both seemed to share.

The first thing, possibly the most important thing, beyond the mere fact of encountering her again after all this time, was the way in which she controlled her physical features. Was it something that she had mastered over time or did it develop through its own natural evolution? This was something he would have dearly liked to know more about, for it was the one aspect of his life he had the most difficulty managing. The sudden appearance of red rings that orbited his irises, that if left unchecked, would become like Mary's, single uniform pools of red, the unnatural eye colour slowly growing; consuming all natural shades and definition until only the scarlet hue remained. This, along with canine teeth that would gradually grow until they could not easily be concealed, were two things that could easily be his undoing if he were not completely vigilant to his needs.

Mary, on the other hand, did not seem to share the same difficulty controlling her ungodly attributes, as he saw them manifest and disappear several times, apparently at will.

Arriving at his door he paused in order to check his coat, pretending to be in search of his keys while instead taking careful note of his surroundings to ensure that he was indeed alone within the quiet confines of his backstreet apartment.

After several minutes of imaginary fumbling he removed the keys from a pocket, made a last careful survey of the area, then mounted the two steps of the tiny porch, unlocked the front door and disappeared from view, leaving the street and all the unpleasantness that had been born that night to the darkness, hoping as he did that, like the darkness itself, those same horrors would themselves disappear with the coming light of day.

Chapter 13

Dear Diary,

The news I bring to you today is one of violently opposed feelings for it comes within the pages of a letter sent to me by my brother. It has been some time since I have heard from him, and I had grown somewhat accustomed to his letters coming on a less regular basis of late. Although I still worry when I do not hear from him, I try and understand that it is his way and the long periods of time in between his writing is not a result of something tragic. In fact, he has never relayed to me anything to indicate that he is involved with things that would lend themselves to being insidious in nature or design, even though there are times I feel most sure that he has to be.

His letter today came earlier than I had expected and so with its arrival I held much trepidation within myself as to what might lay inside.

So many times when reading his letters I had secretly wished for a confession of sorts, words that would tell me that he had taken another's life or been arrested for acts deemed unnatural by both God and man alike, but no such wording ever appeared on the pages of any letter or small notation he had written.

Although these words were again not present in his latest letter, those that did appear disturbed me just as much, and the truth be known, perhaps more so. For he tells me of meeting the one who attacked him in the woods that borders our village, a person who, for many years, I refused to believe could exist, despite my most earnest efforts. He has described their chance meeting and of their interaction, all in terrible detail. Such things, the like of which I shall not repeat within these pages, for the very idea frightens me. Even though what he describes could be summed up as fantasy or delusional, I discount both of these possibilities based solely upon what I have witnessed firsthand. That, along with the fact it is simply too outrageous to be anything but the truth, for what purpose would it serve to tell a tale so preposterous it could not possibly be believed?

He has told me of his plans to attempt locate this woman (if that is indeed what she is), again and, if successful, to attempt to form some sort of alliance with her. The idea behind this plan, one of which scares me to death, is the hope of finding the answers, which have eluded him since returning from near death. He feels strongly that this person may very well be his only link to those answers. If that fails, his intention is to see to it that she cannot do to another that which she had done to him, and in that I can only assume he means to end her life.

In his closing to me he wrote: "If my plan ends in failure then you will, in all likelihood, not hear from me further."

I find myself praying to God that He will find it in His merciful heart to spare my brother's life. Even though I know, not from fact but knowing just the same, that he has done unspeakable things since my nursing him back to health, I cannot help but feel in some way responsible. For had I not been so attentive to his wounds, unwittingly interfering with God's plan, he may have simply passed on and his passing would have prevented all that I feel certain he has done from ever having taken place.

Temperance, the 10ᵗʰ of June in the year of our Lord, 1888

The police had spent the entire spring and summer of 1888 looking for the man responsible for killing of one of their own in a back laneway near Buck's Row, a small side road within the seedier East End. Even with a concerted effort by all levels of the police, and having an eyewitness description of the killer, they were making little headway in apprehending the culprit.

The murder made the front page of every newspaper throughout England for days following the grisly crime, and it was all one could do to avoid hearing gory details no matter where you might be.

Police had canvassed door to door throughout the entire area and surrounding neighbourhoods, posting an artistic rendering of the wanted man in several popular drinking establishments and in local shops, with the word REWARD written out in bold letters beneath the sketchy drawing.

Aremis had looked at the picture many times and could find no resemblance within the lines and shading to that of himself, all the while knowing full well it was he the authorities were mistakenly searching for. He had no other choice but to assume it had been Mary who had been the so-called eyewitness, the one who had been taken in for questioning and who subsequently gave a deliberately inaccurate description of the killer to the police artist.

The whole thing was a quandary and he could not come to terms with whether she was continuing to play her sadistic game of cat and mouse with him or if it was something more along the lines of a mental illness that had her believing, that which she was describing, was actually factual. Logic would dictate the simplest answer would be the correct one but he knew better than anyone that logic and reason had no place within this realm claimed by the unnatural.

He, like the police, had spent the summer in search of someone he very much wanted to meet again, but just as with his law-enforcing counterparts, his search was yielding little in the way of results.

For the first few weeks after the attack he had remained in his room for the better part of each day, making little in the way of noise and only venturing out in the wee hours of the morning to get food. He had reverted back to drinking only animal blood for the time being as he felt it was simply too risky to try for anything else. People in the area were scared and with the police not having made any arrests, it meant the killer was still on the loose.

As the weeks wore on, however, life in and around Whitechapel slowly began to return to normal and he too began to resume, what for him, amounted to a normal life as well. Failing to show up for work during the weeks he had been in hiding had, most certainly, cost him his job; of this there could be little doubt. So, without work, he informed his landlord he would be moving, packed his things into one small suitcase and went off to find both new employment and accommodation, something he had become quite comfortable doing on a regular basis.

Well practiced in the art of winning over those whom he needed, it was not very long before he had found suitable accommodation within one of the many flats that seemed to be always available along the numerous narrow streets that bordered the harbour front. With a never ending parade of new dock workers, shipmen and transients finding their way to the water's edge then just as quickly taking their leave of the place, there was never a shortage of either a room to rent or menial labour being sought by tight fisted employers. It was also in one of these waterfront businesses did he also find his next line of work. Having been raised on a farm and used to running a team of horses around, he had quickly negotiated a position of one that saw him starting as nothing more than a dock hand to that of couriering crates of goods from the various warehouses to the ships docked in the harbour with a flatbed wagon.

That summer had been one of the coldest and wettest on record, even by English standards. Scarcely a day went past that rain did not make an appearance, dampening everything, including the spirits of London's growing, impoverished population.

It was already well into August, and with the coming autumn looking to be every bit as miserable as the spring and summer had been, patience was in short supply while tempers were even less so. It seemed everyone was on edge over one thing or another and crime was once again on the rise. Everything from petty thievery, to brawls, and right the way up to murder, there seemed no end of it being reported within the pages of the morning newspapers.

Although appalled by the violence within the city he now called his home, he could not claim he had not contributed his fair share to the escalating number of unsolved crimes involving premature loss of life.

As always, however, his victims were selected for their own particular assortment of criminal behaviour. Attributes and activities that would always ensure there would be little in the way of a formal investigation, especially with the more influential people putting pressure on the local constabulary to apply their efforts in the well-to-do areas of town, of which the little area of Whitechapel most certainly did not fall.

It was a Thursday night, August the 30th and he was out in search of just such a person. There was certainly no shortage of drunken fools out on the streets that night, despite the driving rain and lightning which continually lit up dark skies with flashes of blue and white. In addition to the weather most foul, there were two separate fires burning out of control at the Shadwell Dry Docks, the flames of which had turned the overcast skies an angry orange/red that could be seen from any street that neared the wharf.

These wandering drunkards, braving elements thrown at them from a sky that looked as though it would be better suited to Hell than here on earth, were in the company of others, all of whom seemed to be equally debilitated by the effects of alcohol. Even though it would be a matter most simple to take on two or perhaps even three individuals while they were in such a state of inebriation, there were simply too many risks associated with such an attack, risks that, even if the plan could be executed properly and went off without any unforeseen complications, were not worth taking. For when the light of day eventually broke it would it bring with it the police investigators. Sadly, single murders had become somewhat commonplace, whereas a multiple homicide would most certainly grab the headlines as well as the attention of the higher ups within the police force.

No, he would have to bide his time and patiently meander the laneways and back streets until the right miscreant came his way. To rush would be careless and being careless carried with it a penalty most severe.

As time wore on without yielding any success, he decided to make his way down Osborn Street towards the waterfront in the hope of finding better pickings. The dock fires had been creating somewhat of a stir, and even though the weather was still less than welcoming, people had been making their way to the water's edge in order to see for themselves just how bad the situation was. Making his way along the rain-slicked cobblestones, his collar pulled up around his neck in an attempt to keep out the chilly damp wind, he noticed two women who appeared to be in their 40's standing together not far from the lone gas lamp at that end of the street.

As he approached he could easily make out the tell-tale signs indicating, without question, that one of the women was quite drunk whilst the other remained with her wits about her. Taking in some of their conversation as he approached, he heard the more sober of the two stating she had just come up from the docks where she had been the last hour in the hope of finding some late night trade due to the fires.

A faint smile crested his lips as he thought it interesting that two people, this prostitute and himself, so different in many ways and yet both having the same idea as to where to find people who might well serve their own particular need that evening.

As he passed the two women the church bell struck 2:30 a.m. and he tipped his hat to them as he passed. The common reply immediately ensued, to which he waved off the offer and continued on his way towards the waterfront, leaving the women to their dealings.

The docks that were ablaze were located across the Thames and seemed to be very close to one another, and so at first glance, one could easily make the mistake of thinking the two fires were, in actuality, one giant inferno. The men who had been dispatched to try and contain the blaze had withdrawn and taken safety some distance away, choosing to let the rains take care of extinguishing the flames rather than risking life and limb. There were still several people on the wharf, all huddled in groups, watching the early morning display as it sent flames and sparks skyward only to be snuffed out by the wind-whipped rains. He joined the ranks along the edge, watching the colourful display and taking in the idle chatter of all those around him.

It was not long before, like the prostitute he had passed earlier, he realised there would be little to be gained by remaining with those gathered there. So without formal pleasantries needing to be exchanged, he took his leave and made his way along the waterside before taking a connecting laneway up to Whitechapel Road and, eventually, home.

The following morning gave up little in the way of being a fresh new day as the rains from the previous night continued to pelt down on the world below. The prospect of spending another day soaked to the skin atop a wagon was not sitting well with Aremis as he rose in the predawn darkness. His morning routine was simple and lacked any sort of fanfare. As with every other morning since taking the keys of his first floor apartment at the back of an old brick house, he splashed his face with cold water, checked his eyes and teeth for abnormalities, and then began to get dressed for the day that lay ahead.

It was at this point he noticed something different. An envelope lay upon the floor, having been shoved beneath the door. Aremis was not particularly worried by this odd finding, for he knew his rent to be paid, and, he was quite certain his landlord would not waste time addressing matters concerning his property in such an indirect means.

Looking at it momentarily, as it lay there, he could tell there was no name or identifying mark upon its face, and little did he realise as he plucked it from the floor that the note within would bring nothing in the way of good tidings. Turning the tiny envelope over, there appeared on the paper flap, a place where a seal of closure would often be placed, not a seal of stationary, or stamp, but an image of lips pressed against the page as if to mimic a kiss, its shape and texture having been reproduced not in ink but in blood.

The bloody kiss, areas of which were still moist, had soaked through the envelope to the paper note hidden within, making some of what was written there difficult to read as it had been scribed in red ink.

Hello luv,

I must tell you that the way you tipped your hat to them whores gave me fits.

Me, I am not as fussy as you luv.

The drunk one was very nise, never made a sound.

Seems that you cannot find me luv. Yer as bad as them old cocks looking for you, you is.

I found you pretty as you please. <u>ha ha</u>

There will be quite a to do this morning on Buck's Row but they have not seen half over my games, I have not but started and you know better than any that I am not codding, luv.

You will soon hear of me and laugh, for the police will have no clue and I shant stop until you find me or till I get buckled proper.

Catch me if you can.

Holding the note in his hands, an overwhelming rage came over him as he thought back to the night before and the two women whom he passed, of his nemesis who stood watching from the darkness, perhaps not more than fifty feet away while he remained oblivious to her presence. If let run unchecked the anger that was quickly building inside would soon consume his rational thought and undoubtedly have him running headlong on a fool's errand straight into dangerous waters.

He touched the bloodstained lip print with the tip of his finger and brought it to his lips. It had the taste of gin within its body. Gin being the popular drink amongst the ladies of questionable professions, and remembering well the intoxicated stupor of one of the prostitutes the night previous, it certainly seemed to support the note's grim message.

To the wording itself, it seemed as though its author was to be in some manner of speaking 'not quite right'. For even though it was well penned, like that of one well schooled, within those finely sculpted lines were found to be words most crass in nature, the likes befitting a common street person. The two dissimilar traits entwined within each other upon the same page, was as though two separate persons had a hand in its composition simultaneously.

It was still early morning and with the note held tight within his grip he began to make his way the four or so city blocks to Buck's Row to see what, it anything, was to be found there. It was approximately a 10-minute walk, which would allow him another ten minutes once he had arrived to have a good look around before he would be forced to leave in order to make it back in time to start work.

Leaving his flat, he quickly made his way to Whitechapel Road and followed it east to where it passed Bakers Row, taking it north the short distance to where Buck's Row intersected it, the plan being to investigate the street's entire length.

Keeping to the right as he entered Buck's Row, he peered over the small stone wall that prevented one from falling some 20 feet to the railway lines that ran below. Peering over the wall, he quickly took stock of the dimly lit surroundings, and upon seeing nothing peculiar, he continued on past the large warehouses that were just beginning to show signs of life.

Approaching the old school council building, its windows to a large extent broken out, the missing glass allowing both birds and the elements to claim what lay beyond the staunch brick exterior, Buck's Row split into two smaller lanes, Buck's Row continuing on the left while Winthrop Street took to the right. Remaining to the left, taking the narrow laneway past the derelict building, he had only just passed the back edge of the property when, through the rain and fog, he could make out a small crowd gathered near the far end of the street. It was still too distant to make out anything more than the crowd itself, so with caution being his guide he calmly pressed on towards where they had gathered.

The crowd was made up of what appeared to be mostly locals, some of them still dressed in their nightclothes, a coat or blanket wrapped over them to fend off the elements and a scattering of police all gathered around a gateway. In addition to the police keeping the small gathering of curious onlookers at bay, there were also several uniformed as well as plainclothes policemen going door to door, apparently seeking out anyone who might have seen or heard something during the night.

As Aremis continued his approach, a man, having had his fill of whatever had taken place there, left the group and, with a satchel over his shoulder, he adjusted his cap and began making his way toward him.

As he drew to within earshot Aremis made inquiry to the approaching stranger as to what all the fuss was about.

"So, what's all this in aid of?" he asked bluntly.

The man looked up then back over his shoulder at where he had just come from.

"Some woman was killed last night. Police ain't saying much, but I'm bettin' it was one of them filthy whores, bitches all of 'em."

The two men stopped and both watched the slow movement of people mingling about in the street, some trying to converse with police while others jockeyed for a better vantage point.

"What makes you say that? Why do you think she was a prostitute?" he asked the man.

"Don't be daft. What respectable woman be out here in the middle of the night, especially on a night like the one last, if she ain't a whore?"

Aremis did not bother with an answer, but nodded his understanding just the same.

"Are the police letting anyone through or is the street blocked off?" he asked changing the subject.

The man chuckled at the idea proposed before replying.

"No mate, the street's wide open, as I said, it weren't the blumin' Queen that was killed now, was it? And this ain't what you would call High Park, now is it?"

With sarcasm closing the conversation the man took his leave, heading off in the direction Aremis had just come from, most likely on his way to work in a warehouse or factory that might well be beside the one he himself was so employed in.

Aremis took out the small pocket watch and after a quick glance continued on his way towards the crowd, joining their ranks quite anonymously.

He could tell, even with the morning's lighter rains, that there had been a body laid upon the ground, the silhouette of drier payment marking where the person had been lying during the heavier rains. In addition to dry pavement, there could also be seen a quantity of blood pooled at one end of the dry patch, a trail of which led away towards the gutter, an amount he calculated to be not more than a glass full.

"What's gone on here then?" he asked a woman in her late forties, wrapped in a tattered shawl as she stood shivering in the misty morning.

Looking up briefly to see who it was who had addressed her, she quickly turned her attention back to the crime scene as she answered.

"Some whore got beaten down but good, she did. Charlie found her on his way out to work this morning."

She pointed discretely in the direction of man in tan coat and hat standing some distance away. He was standing with another fellow in a blue work shirt and pants topped off with a dark overcoat. Both men are talking with another man whom the lady believed was an inspector or perhaps one of the many newspapermen that had been by already that morning.

He was about to inquire further when another woman of similar age and dress joined their conversation.

"She weren't beaten. Had her throat cut right across she did. I seen it for me-self before the men came'n took her away. She was cut from one side t'other," the woman dragged her finger across her own throat to better aid in describing what she had seen. "Yup, right across and another one going down the side just below her ear it was. I seen it all when the bobbies showed up with their lanterns. They let me come close on account I told 'em I might know the girl."

"And did you, did you know this woman?" Aremis asked, curiosity getting the better of him.

The woman smiled somewhat sheepishly, her lower teeth missing completely.

"Naw, I just wanted a look see is all. Not every day you gets to see a dead person."

He did not share her enthusiasm for wanting to see the dead up close. He himself had seen quite enough of it since coming to London. He turned his attention back to the blood stain on the ground, his gaze narrowing as he tried to estimate how much blood should have been on the ground given the nature of the wound as it had been described to him and things were, simply put, not adding up.

"You say her throat was cut clean, in two places, is that right?" he asked still studying the blood pool.

"Aye, I seen it for me-self I did. Bit gruesome it was."

He casually strummed his fingers on his chin as he contemplated the two things he knew for certain: if it was indeed Mary who had killed this woman there would be no need whatsoever for her to require a knife, and a wound like the one the toothless woman had described would have seen blood spread all over the wooden fence and ground, far more than was currently present.

If the woman had indeed been killed where her body had been discovered then the question of why there was so little blood upon the surroundings surely needed to be asked.

"I should be off less I catch it from my boss," he said as he prepared himself to leave.

"You seem to know a great deal about this crime, good lady. Do you think the police would want to speak to you as a witness?" he asked as he readjusted his collar.

"Me? Naw, they're not interested in speaking with the likes of me, only asking the bloke what found her and the well-to-do up the block."

"I see. Well then, I will ask you one last question before I take my leave and that is: do you think this woman was killed here or merely left here already dead?"

Pleased to be taken so seriously, the woman took to telling her thoughts, few as they were.

"No, she weren't killed someplace else. I heard Charlie telling that constable, over there that she was still warm when he found her, that he even thought she was still breathing some. They all say she was killed right here and no one saw nothing."

"Interesting," he said, turning to go.

"How's that then?" the woman asked after him.

He returned to her and, in a voice just under his breath so that only she would hear him, he said his final words on the matter.

"Where did all that blood go?" he asked. "If she was indeed killed here, with two cuts the likes of which you have described, where is all the blood?

He paused just long enough to ensure he had the woman's interest before continuing.

"Surely there would be more from wounds such as those, would you not agree?"

With that he pulled the brim of his hat down and took his leave, heading back the way he had come, cutting short at Court Street and taking the bridge back to Whitechapel. He hoped that the toothless busybody would take it upon herself to point this observation out to those in charge.

The rest of the day went by in a routinely uneventful fashion even though his thoughts were far busier than his body would lend credit to. Atop his buckboard, teaming his horses through the busy dockyard district, his mind trying to formulate both a plan to find Mary as well as attempting to figure out what it was she was up to. Answers to both were in short supply.

That night, and the nights that followed, found him wandering the back streets in the hope of finding the one who had penned the note foretelling the murder of Polly Nichols, a local prostitute, discovered on a deserted street in Whitechapel's east side.

The papers had printed in detail all the facts, along with much of the hearsay about her murder, sighting her death as the work of the Whitechapel Murderer, while at the same time faulting the police for not having caught the fiend before now.

It was in those moments, having seen the articles and having heard the gossip on the streets, that he began to wonder in earnest if the woman, Nichols, was not, in fact, the first prostitute to lose her life at the hands of his creator. It seemed more that feasible that she had been killing these poor souls all along and only now, after finding his whereabouts, had decided to turn the murderous spree into some sort of morbid game.

As nights of fruitless searching continued to accumulate, he was forced to pursue alternate means of investigation beyond that of his solitary, covert missions carried out under the cloak of darkness, and that was something he had hoped he would never be faced with.

Unable to find even a shred of evidence that Mary even existed, much less that she lived and worked the very streets he himself called his own, he began to make inquiries of those who plied the same trade in the hopes of uncovering some clue to her whereabouts. Walking the streets and laneways, which in the past he would have sought to avoid, he no longer simply dismissed the calls and queries directed his way from the women who worked the streets, but instead, took to engaging them in polite and sometimes even humorous conversation. But despite his best efforts, little in the way of tangible information was gathered. The closest clue being that of a woman matching Mary's description and going by the same name, (which he was told could very well be an alias, as most woman would not choose to use their actual name given their profession), was seen from time to time at The Frying Pan Public House. He had followed that lead, discretely taking up outside the establishment on several afternoons, staying there throughout the evening until the arrival of morning, the only result being somewhat lighter on funds for having purchased a meagre meal and a hot tea.

It had been nearly a week since receiving the letter telling of what grim finds would be discovered on Buck's Row, and as another work day came to an end, his plan was go home, wait for nightfall to thoroughly descend upon the city, then make his way through the neighbourhood in search of a woman who was seemingly more a ghost that that of a physical being. At the same time, he would seek out an undesirable from whom he could satiate his own dark need.

His plans were not to be, however, for as he entered his tiny room from the backyard entrance, he found another envelope, much as the first one he had discovered, lying on the floor having been slipped beneath the door.

Leaving the door ajar for the time being, he dashed back through the yard and out into the laneway that ran behind all the properties, searching in both directions for any sign of the woman he felt certain had left it. Several minutes of wandering its length, his eyes and ears straining for any movement that could aid in the spectral chase, he succumbed to the nothingness that was becoming very much commonplace in he quest.

Returning to his doorstep, he snapped up the letter from the floor and with a quick glance about the secluded yard, he sat down on the stoop and began to inspect it. The paper envelope was the same as the first note that had arrived, although this one was void of bloody lip prints pressed over the flap.

Removing the single folded sheet of paper from within the envelope, he carefully unfolded it exposing the red ink to the fading light of a day in retreat.

Hello luv,

No luck as yet I see, never mind now,

I must tell you that you look very much handsome atop that cart with them fine horses and all.

Clever use of the knife on that foolhardy thief, was he your first? I should thank you for that tip, how to hide the bite. In fact, I use a blade most every time now.

Police talk about being on the right track but have no clue that it is me they seek.

Some days I laugh right out loud. I rip them whores' throats only half a block from them old cocks and they still can't catch me.

I took a couple of lads the other night, two of three. The sods robbed and raped my next whore before I got her, mistreated her something awful they did. It was hard to watch ha. ha.

I hear the papers tell she died the next day, I would have been quicker had they not got her first.

Not to fret, though. They are both quite dead. The little one actually cried when I tore his friend's throat open, I will have the last one by Monday morning.

I dumped em in the Thames, be long away now I wager.

To our game, I'll give you tip here, I have a new friend, Annie, all this nasty business 'as all us poor whores in a terrible fright, I told her we could work together tonight.

If you can find me this eve, then they won't find her come morning.

You will know my work because I'll pull her innards out and hang em round her neck.

Good luck.

"God damn you!" he shouted, as he crushed the note into his hand. "Why do you let such vile creatures as we walk amongst your flock?"

The elderly woman who lived on the second floor poked her head out the window to see what the ruckus was about.

Catching sight of her looking down at him, a quizzical look upon her face, he merely waved her off as he stuffed the crumpled note into his pocket and stormed into his apartment, slamming the door behind him.

Inside he paced around the cramped quarters like a caged animal as he tried to figure out what he should do next. The old law-abiding, God-fearing man would have simply gone to the police with the notes, telling all he knew, but he was no longer that man.

The anxiety within him was mounting exponentially, and as it grew so did it bring about the physical changes that divided him from the rest of humanity. The now familiar pain within his gums and nail beds as human teeth grew into dog-like fangs, and fingernails now long and as sharp as any knife, told him without so much as having to look into the mirror that the monster hidden within would be easily identified should he venture beyond his locked door. It would take the better part of an hour before he was able to regain his body, if not himself.

The twilight that had graced the skies upon his arrival home had been swallowed up by the unrelenting darkness, a shade that by its very nature encouraged and even nurtured things deemed most deplorable by those who lived within the light of day.

Sitting upon the edge of his bed, the heels of his work shoes resting on the bed's wooden side rail, he ran his thumbnail up and down in the small gap between his lower front teeth. Even though his thoughts were very much preoccupied, he could not dare lose sight of a more pressing matter, that of his own need, a need that if left unchecked could see him no better than the author who had scribed the taunting notes.

There would be little time for a careful meandering through the promising docks spaces and places where the excrement of humanity went to forage and prey upon the weak or foolhardy. He would need to coax what he needed into finding him.

Changing quickly, he tossed his work clothes onto the chair and in its place pulled on somewhat finer looking trousers, shirt and a long black overcoat. Even though everything had been purchased second or maybe even third hand from a local vendor in the marketplace, they instantly transformed his appearance into someone having loftier means.

"I can only hope that some stupid soul is in as much need as I on this night." he said, as he grabbed a well-worn top hat from the dresser.

Popping the topper onto his head, and with walking cane in hand, he locked up and made his way with as much refinement as his urgent timeline would allow.

Cutting through both laneway and dismal street alike, he arrived in the fog-shrouded alleyways that serviced the wharf. There he began to wander about aimlessly, looking every bit the part of someone quite lost, all the while checking his pocket watch so that anyone watching from the shadows would easily catch sight of it.

He had not been there but ten minutes when he heard the approach of two men coming down the narrow strip of dock between the brick wall of the bordering warehouse and the water, their voices, undetectable to any ear of human characteristic, telling of the men's intentions, none of which were kind in nature.

Turning to face them but not looking in their direction, he waited and, unlike the uncontrolled manifestations, which had taken place back in his tiny apartment, those very same changes were now willed into being. Brought on by a hunger that may have been thousands of years in the making, teeth slid long and sharp beneath the cover of pale skin and muted blue lips, just as nails became claw-like at the end of fingertips, their unnatural appearance hidden well by both the fog and the night. The deadly trap set and well camouflaged, it was not until the two men were practically on top of him, too close for any hope of a safe retreat, did they realize the error of their choice that night.

Just as the larger of the two men raised his fist to deliver what he thought would be a stunning blow to his intended victim, his fist was deflected harmlessly away with the walking stick, while at the same instant, a vice-like grip took hold of his throat, nails like talons, long and sharp, pierced the skin down through muscle, tearing out the entire front of the man's throat with a single fluid motion.

Ducking beneath the blood that gushed forth from the crater he had just created in the assailant's neck, he threw his shoulder hard into the dying man's torso, sending him off the wharf's edge into the black waters below while simultaneously driving the end of the walking stick into the other man's soft abdomen, winding him considerably and forcing him to collapse on the old boards of the pier.

Shocked, lying on the ground and unable to catch his breath, much less call out for assistance, the accomplice to the botched robbery was powerless to prevent the continued attack. Grabbing the man's hair, winding the dirty strands around his fingers to ensure a good grip, he wrenched his head backwards, violently exposing his throat. Then, without a second thought or moment lost, he sank his teeth deeply into the flesh.

Unlike the first man, whose lifeless body had already slipped beneath the icy water of the Thames, the warm torrent within his partner's veins would not go to waste.

The whole murderous interaction was over in less than a minute, and with the one-sided confrontation now at its end, his need again satisfied for the time being, Aremis remained quietly crouched over his victims lifeless body as he carefully took in the world around him, listening for any tell-tale signs that someone may have witnessed what had just taken place. Without having any of his concerns confirmed by noise or action, he quietly wiped his hands and face on the sleeve of the dead man's coat, before fishing the loose coins from his pockets. Then, without prayer or remorse, he dumped the body into the water, the splash entirely concealed by the peal of bells striking the hour.

The fresh blood brought about a new light within him, a familiar warmth that would become conspicuously absent as the days grew in number from the time of his last ingestion. Like water to a plant that has been parched, the leaves quickly retuning to life, his senses seemed to come alive immediately upon swallowing the last mouthful. As the warmth permeated his being, he became keenly aware of not only himself but all around him, as though it were not reality played out minute by minute but rather some meticulously painted picture, where every detail was painstakingly recorded and preserved.

With his immediate surroundings deemed clear of any threat, he took stock of his outwardly appearance, adjusting his coat, pulling at both the collar and sleeves so they regained their more professional façade. Removing a small pocket mirror from within an inner pocket of the garment, he carefully checked his face for any evidence that might have been left upon his skin during the quick altercation.

Satisfied that any such evidence did not exist, he retrieved his cane from the spot near where the body had been, then taking a few more steps he plucked his top hat from the ground where it had landed in the scuffle. He gave it a quick dusting with his hand then placed it back on his head, tapping it down slightly to ensure a proper fit. Wandering off down the wharf with a manner that belied what had transpired but a few moments before, his mind was clear and precise, unlike the fog that now drifted in off the water, even thicker than before, swallowing his tall dark form like a willing accomplice, making good his escape.

Continuing on through the veil of fog he turned his full attention to the task of finding Mary and, with luck, preventing the death of another innocent woman. The plan was simple enough. He would make his way back towards the Fry Pan and other well-known haunts of local working girls and then, by observation or subtle interrogation, locate either the murderess or her intended victim.

Arriving at the Fry Pan, he wasted little time in idle chatter as he had done during past visits but instead went straight to the point, asking some of the women there whom he had befriended over the last few days if they had seen or heard any further of the woman going by the name of Mary.

By nothing more than mere coincidence he had come upon the only person who had given up any information at all not more than a week ago, telling him then of a woman who matched both name and description of the person he was seeking, She told him that she had not seen the woman in question this particular night, nor the last few in actuality. His only real lead, as faint as it had been, came from a woman in her late thirties, dressed in a long black coat with tattered bits of fur around the hem, most likely pressed into prostitution in order to make her way. He felt compelled to run the risk of losing her as a contact altogether in order to find out if she might know another woman named Annie.

With a relaxed voice and unhurried manner being his closest ally on a street that saw all manner of ill repute, he broached the subject as he casually looked about as though the answer, whatever it might be, mattered little one way or the other. Using the ruse that Mary, the woman he sought, had often mentioned through written correspondence another woman whom he knew only as Annie and he had to only assume that they might be friends.

"Do you mean Dark Annie?" she replied casually.

"I am not entirely sure what name she might go by other than Annie," he began in a voice similar in volume to that of his female counterpart. "Do you know where I might find her this evening? If she is Mary's friend, then she may know where I might best find her. Perhaps, if luck is with me this night, I may even find them together."

The woman looked about, eyeing other potential clients as they passed before answering his query.

"Not sure to be frank, she usually works a bit north of 'ere, you could try Brick Lane if you was so inclined."

"I see. Might I enquire as to why you call her Dark Annie?" he asked while he fished about in his pockets for something that seemed quite set on not being found.

The woman took on a quizzical look to his question and shrugged.

"I dunno, it's what we call her is all, she's got a bit of temper when she's been into the drink."

Pulling three shillings he had taken from the man he had just killed, the going rate of a prostitute in Whitechapel, he gently took hold of the woman's wrist and placed them into her hand.

"What's this for then?" she asked, quite confused by the gesture offered for services not yet rendered.

"For helping me, and perhaps, that you might consider going home early tonight."

She smiled as she hiked her skirt up placing the coins into her waist purse.

"Yer a gentleman sir, but with yer generosity I might make enough for a bit of dinner as well as me bed tonight, thank you kindly."

She straightened out her skirt and coat over top then gave him a quick curtsy.

He bid the woman a good evening and began making his way north along Osborn Street to where it turned into Brick Lane.

Several hours had passed and he had searched numerous streets several times over without success. It was now nearly 4:00 a.m. and although he had not had any luck he hoped that with morning only two hours away, a time when most prostitutes retired to their meagre sanctuaries, leaving the rest of the city to go about their lives in a more acceptable fashion, Mary had also come up empty in her search as well.

The streets, which had been occupied by women soliciting sex for money earlier in the night, were now beginning to be travelled by those on their way to more conventional means of employment. Even though the morning that approached would be a Saturday, most were still expected to show up for work, Sunday being the only real day of grace granted by employers. This would have be the same for him if the wagon he teamed was not in for routine repairs, this due in large to the ship scheduled in Friday having not arrived, probably due to bad weather. The weather that summer had caused the delay, as well as the sinking, of many a vessel, small and large alike. Owners of the shipping yards and warehouses would waste little time on a ship that was late more than half a day, instead using the time to make repairs or simply laying the workers off until the vessel arrived.

Whatever reason was behind the ship's delay, he was glad to have the extra time to apply to his search. Not tired in the slightest, he planned on carrying on throughout the day, into the following night and straight onto Sunday morning if need be.

At just past 4:00 a.m. he entered Hanbury Street from Brick lane, the bells from the Black Eagle Brewery striking the hour. A solitary figure of a woman making her way west along the north sidewalk, probably on her way to work in Spitalfields Market as her smart-paced step was not in keeping with someone soliciting their body for hire, was the only other person on the otherwise deserted street.

Watching her as she crossed the road and until she turned the corner onto Commercial Street where she disappeared from view, he pondered his next move.

Standing, his back against the brick wall that made up the row of old housing, he took a deep breath and closed his eyes. Not unlike a man who is blind, his other senses becoming more keen in order to compensate for the loss in vision, the world that surrounded him suddenly became alive with sounds and smells, some of which were so subtle they would most certainly be undetectable to anyone not giving it their full attention and perhaps not even then. In this self-imposed darkness, so did arrive, the scent of blood, carried to his nostrils on the early morning breeze. It was not uncommon to catch wind of such things with the market place being but a few streets away, and he could have easily discounted the distinct odour if not for the fact it was human blood. To most, the scent was completely indistinguishable from the blood of other animals. So much so, that even the most practiced physician or butcher alike would be hard pressed to tell the difference through scent alone. But for one such as he, there was no mistaking it. Not allowing the sudden aroma to startle him into haste, he relaxed and let it wash over his senses, its subtle fragrance having within it a flavour he could actually taste.

He took in another long breath through his nostrils, trying to get a sense of which direction the smell might be coming from, but with little in the way of wind that morning it was proving to be a difficult undertaking. It was then, just as he exhaled, did he see it. There within his mind, like waking from a vivid dream, the images foggy and unclear and yet existing just the same, two women talking quietly to one another, their forms shrouded in the darkness then fading from view all together.

He let his body slide down the wall until he was crouching, his long coat folding up on the ground around him, as he pressed his fingers against the side of his forehead. He took another breath, slowly and more deliberate as he tried to bring back the fragile image within his mind. As the scent of blood again filled his senses, the ghostly images also returned, but this time he could make out more than just the two people. He could now see that the pair was standing by an old fence, within a backyard of sorts, and they were still talking with one another, even though he was unable to make out what it was they were saying. He continued to probe the delicate image, gently pushing forward through the cloudy veil, in an attempt to glean more from what he was witnessing. For whatever the reason, he felt this waking dream had to be of some importance. Although there was no evidence to support this other that his own feelings, he was not about to dismiss anything that could possibly give him the upper hand. It was at that moment he thought of his sister and what she had referred to as her other sight, something she had only shared with him since his unsolicited journey into this hell had begun, and he wondered if he too might be privy to such a gift, if such a thing did in fact exist.

With time being his enemy in every possible way, he had to, for the moment at least, push that notion from his mind with the hope of revisiting it at some later date. He could ill afford compromising the intricate images that hung so precariously within a vision he could barely comprehend, much less control.

He settled his mind and cleared all other thoughts so that only the single image remained. Then, like a voyeur to his own thoughts, he peered through the veil until he was standing but a few feet behind the two women. In this dream-like state, his movements were painstakingly slow, as though he was moving through water and try as he might to control them, to hasten them, he could not.

Standing now perhaps only one foot from the phantom woman closest to him, her back towards him, her face not visible, he could only make out her clothing. Beyond that, he could see the face of the other woman who looked to be in her mid to late forties, short and heavy-set with blue eyes and brown hair. The conversation between the two women was still mute and very much one-sided, making it impossible to understand what was being said. It was obvious, though, that they knew and were comfortable with one another for the look on the face of the woman he could see was one of casual indifference occasionally marked with a smile and even restrained laughter, not something one would expect from adversaries.

Still convinced that the images had, within their existence, some importance, he turned his attentions to the woman he was unable to see and, with careful thought, began to move within the vision so he might better see who she was speaking with, even though by this time he was nearly certain who it would be.

The unknown woman put her hand on the other woman's shoulder and drew her close, kissing her cheek, and then hugging her warmly, not unlike the way sisters might behave. The two remained like that but for a few moments before the tender embrace turned into a predatory hold.

Unable to make out what was going on at first he reached out towards the women, his hands passing through them as though they were nothing more that water vapour, their images wavering slightly as his hand passed through them before they returned to their previously pristine form. The woman whose face he could make out earlier now pounded her hand down hard on the back and shoulders of the other who held her tight in an attempt to get her to relinquish her hold with little, if any, effect; her blows becoming less and less violent with each passing second. As the final weak blow glanced off the shoulder, her arm falling limp at her side, the struggle slowly came to an end. The woman who had held her tight now moved her away from herself, revealing for the first time the reason behind the struggle. Her hand still clamped tightly around the other woman's throat, effectively cutting off both air and blood flow to the brain, as well as silencing any attempt at raising an audible alarm, she pressed her nearly unconscious victim against the fence with enough force to cause its length to buckle slightly under the impact.

Now, apparently certain the woman who was completely incapacitated could no longer put up any further resistance, she let the woman's own weight pull her down the fence and then laid her out on the ground face up.

Pulling up her own skirt and petticoats, the attacker pulled out a long knife that had been tucked into the top of her boot, the blade thin and slightly curved measuring ten or more inches in length. With the weapon in her grip, she wasted little time. Grabbing the fallen woman by the hair, she pulled her head to one side, and then drove the blade deeply into her neck, pivoting it slightly then dragging it straight across her throat. There was little doubt that the injury inflicted was most certainly a life-ending wound, so there was little point behind the second slash, delivered in much the same manner and with as much ferocity as the first. The second cut, approximately one half-inch lower than the first, instantly extinguished the flow of blood from the first incision and sent a second fountain of blood towards the fence. As she ripped the razor sharp blade across the woman's throat for a second time she rocked the woman's head back and forth violently, as though trying to tear it loose from its muscular attachments.

The whole scene was hideously violent, grotesque in every sense of the word, and even though he himself had killed many a man, two as recently as a few hours ago, this which he was silently bearing witness to, if only in his own mind, made him nauseous.

It was at that moment the illusion within his mind, one that had seemed so real turned to dust and blew away into the darkness as something quite external from that which he had been experiencing took him quite unawares. A steady rhythmic tapping, of which was quickly growing in intensity, was being delivered to his shoulder as he remained in a huddled heap against the wall.

"Move along now. You can't be sleeping here." Came the voice from somewhere above him.

Feeling as though he had in actuality been in a deep sleep for days he had to force his eyes into movement. As they finally answered his command his first visual intake, being that it was still dark out, told him that time had not passed more than a few minutes at best, and that there was a man standing before him. He looked up quickly realising that the person before him was a beat constable making the rounds and must have, and rightly so, assumed him to be asleep in the street. With the whole district on edge, and the police being faulted for the lack of presence and action with respect to the number of vicious crimes that had been taking place, he had no wish to provide the policeman any further reason to think him more than a law-abiding citizen.

"I am not sleeping constable," he began, but was cut off by the gruff lawman.

"Asleep or drunk in a public place, it's all the same offence." he stated flatly.

Annoyed at his tone and still trying to maintain both a civil manner as well as holding onto the memory of the fragmented images, Aremis replied in the best manner he could muster.

"I am neither drunk nor have I been sleeping, sir. I merely fell faint from my walk, the air is chilled this morning and my lungs do not take kindly to it, I fear."

The constable ordered him up, then looked him up and down for any sign that what he was saying might not be the truth. After several moments of questioning regarding his evening's whereabouts and place of employment, the constable's tone changed ever so slightly as he bid him a good morning and went off in an easterly direction.

"Very well, then. I suggest you might take more care should you go walking in the future."

"Yes, yes, I shall, thank you. It was careless of me."

He watched as the policeman, his lantern in hand, continued down Hanbury Street and rounded the corner onto Brick Lane, heading in a northerly direction.

With the police presence no longer an immediate threat, and the images within his mind gone, he returned his attention to the blood, the scent of which had grown considerably stronger.

He began walking west, his eyes half shut, letting his sense of smell be his guide, and as he passed a wooden doorway he stopped, the scent suddenly much reduced. Backing up he found himself at a door that covered a walkway that passed to the east of number 28 Hanbury. Trying the door's handle he found that it was not bolted.

Checking both directions to ensure no one was present, he pulled the door open and slipped into the dark passageway, closing it behind him.

The smell of blood was now so strong he could actually taste it on the air more than he could smell it, and as he cautiously made his way along the narrow passage, his eyes better suited than any mortal could be in such conditions, he began to notice blood droplets upon the ground that led to the property behind the row housing. Crouching on one knee, careful not to take his eyes off the dim light that was coming from beyond the entrance to the backyard, he dabbed a finger into the blood. It was cold and congealed, certainly not fresh, but not fully dried either, which meant whatever the reason behind it being there was most certainly the result of a recent event.

The droplets increased in number as well as size the further down the dark passageway he went, but even with the increase it still could not account for the plentiful aroma. As he arrived at the entrance to the secluded backyard he gingerly removed his hat, then, cautiously poked his head around the corner. At first glance the yard appeared to be empty, with the exception of some lumber and the privy at the far end of the tiny property. Not until he had actually entered the yard and was making a second sweep of the area did he notice the body of a woman lying on the ground next to the fence that separated the yard he was in from the neighbouring one.

It was in that instant, looking at the fence that he realised it was the same one he had seen, not but a few minutes earlier, in the dream-like vision. The way the woman was laying, the blood upon the vertical planking, it was all the same down the smallest detail. About the only aspect that was not familiar was the way in which the dead woman's legs were arranged. Her knees were up and bent, the legs falling outwards to her side, her skirts pulled up and over the knees leaving her legs bare. At first glance, taking into consideration both the location as well as the distance he was from the woman, she looked like someone who was positioned for childbirth.

There were few places within the barren yard for someone to hide other than in the privy, but he already knew by the silence that the yard and the toilet were both void of occupants.

All the windows within the house were dark, and the cooler temperatures of late had ensured that those same windows were closed as well. The only other accesses to the secluded yard was by way of a basement door and a single back door, both of which were closed, the door to the basement having had a padlock through its bolt. As he made his way to the body, his earlier hopes that Mary had, like his search for her, not been successful in finding her predetermined victim faded from wishful thinking into a harsh reality.

Reaching the body, he quickly discovered that the poor woman had not only her throat cut clean through but her abdomen had been roughly laid open, a wound that ran from just below her ribs continuing down her torso and disappearing between her thighs, leaving only an empty cavity pooled with clotting blood. And just as her note had promised, the woman's intestines had been cut clean away from her body and were laid over her shoulder and her neck.

He had witnessed and had even been directly responsible for some of the most brutal murders London had known in recent times, but nothing he had done could compare to the butchery he was now witness to.

From within the blanket of darkness, a protective covering that would shield the horror from the rest of the world for another hour yet, he quickly checked for anything that might help him catch his enemy. For if this was but a mere game to her then perhaps she might have been careless, leaving behind a clue. Or maybe, she may well have left one with deliberate intention.

It was obvious that she knew where he lived, and with that knowledge, she could easily lead the police to him by simply placing that address in the dead woman's coat pocket. That would be something he could ill afford, so, with as much care and speed as could be managed, he began checking around the body and then checking the body itself in the hopes of finding something that might not even exist.

He had gone through her waist purse and coat pockets, finding both empty of anything more than the meagre belongings someone such as her might own, and was about to begin checking the yard when he heard the bolt on the backdoor of the neighbouring home being drawn back.

Ducking down quickly he stumbled over the legs of the dead woman losing his balance and falling with a thud against the fence.

"Allo?" a man's voice enquired from the next yard.

Holding his breath, Aremis hoped that silence and pitch darkness would be deterrent enough. However, if it was not, then he would have to face the hard reality that would dictate the need to kill this unknown person in order to save himself from being connected to this sickening crime.

After a few seconds, seconds that felt like minutes, he heard the man exit the back door and make his way across the yard that was on the other side of the wooden fence, and then the sound of the privy door opening then subsequently closing again.

Letting out the breath he had been holding since the sound from the neighbouring yard sent him ducking for cover, he knew he was now most certainly on borrowed time and it would be most prudent to beat a hasty retreat. He was about to do just that when something caught his eye. From his crouched position against the fence a dark line between the woman's lips could be seen, as though she was holding a button or the like.

Quietly he reached over the body and carefully opened her mouth, sweeping a finger around the inside for what might be there. Having been dead for some time, all the saliva had dried up causing whatever was in her mouth to stick to her tongue. As he pulled on the foreign object, it caused her tongue to momentarily come with it until the force of the extraction broke the friction between the two surfaces and a key was collected.

Holding it in his hand he turned it slowly over in between his fingers, studying it as though he had never set eyes on such a thing before.

Just then the door to the privy in the neighbouring yard opened, and once again he heard the foot fall of the man as he made his way along a familiar track back to his house, bolting the back door once he was inside.

When no further noise was heard from either household, he made one last look about. Then, tucking his prize into his coat pocket, he made his way across the yard and down the passageway. Cautiously opening the lane's doorway but a crack, he peered out onto the still deserted street.

With the way clear he slipped from the darkened passageway that led from a scene most gruesome, and began to make his way home. There was little point in remaining out on the street for the evil deed he had been trying desperately to prevent had already been carried out. With her plan having been completed, he could only assume that she herself had retired for what remained of the night, and any hopes he might have had in finding her were now removed from his mind.

As he walked along the streets, most of which were still void of pedestrian traffic, he passed the key he had found back and forth between his fingers all the while contemplating its significance, which he felt certain, had to exist.

Only a short distance from Hanbury Street, it took him but a few minutes to reach the laneway that led into the backyard of the house his apartment was part of. Choosing to take the lane over the main street reduced any risk of being seen by those who might be on their way either from the house he shared or any number of others homes on the street.

He cut across the yard to the stairs that led to his back door flat and as his fished about in his pocket for the key to his door he noticed that the door was slightly ajar.

Even though he had left in haste several hours previous, he had, without a doubt, locked the door behind him. Seeing it now in a state other than the way in which he had left it had him motionless in the growing light of the predawn. Suddenly, without any warning, he leapt up the steps and burst into the tiny room; ready to confront whomever he might find inside, only to find it quite empty.

Relieved but still somewhat concerned as to why his door had somehow come to be open, he went to set his hat and cane on the small table before removing his coat, and in doing so discovered another note, this time set upon the table.

Picking it up from where it lay, he unfolded the small paper and in the dim light he read the words that had been penned.

I must apologise for the intrusion, luv, but I had a gift for you and I did not wish to leave it outside. You should see to it that your landlord makes repairs to your door, it would not keep out a stiff wind in the state it's in.

It would seem that others are taking credit for what I am doing, little sods. The papers say that letters have been sent all telling of my doing. They are lies all, but soon they will have the real thing as I will post my own letter shortly.

I do so love games.

Them coppers all think themselves so smart and they know who I am, but they have no clue. They still think I am a man, ha ha.

I doubt that you have been with a woman in some time so I brought the cunny from the whore I ripped last night, no need to thank me.

You will know which letter is from me when you see it,

Jack the Ripper

The words that had obviously been penned whilst in his own flat burned into his mind. He let the note fall back onto the table as he took in his room anew, its familiar setting now cast in the cool grey light of dawn. At first glance nothing seemed to be amiss, and it was not until his eyes fell upon the bed for the second time did he notice the small irregularity in the bedclothes, a small bump beneath the blankets that suddenly had him feeling quite ill. Taking a deep breath in order that it might somehow block what he was about to see from actually penetrating his being, he grabbed a corner of the blanket and yanked it free of the bed.

There, in the middle of the sheet, lay the genitalia, which he could only assume had been cut from the woman he had seen in the backyard that same morning. His stomach muscles wrenched, but nothing would be forthcoming for he had not eaten anything in the way of a real meal in many hours, the blood he had taken back on the wharf having long been digested, its life force absorbed into his own being.

With the dawn almost upon the city, he had no time in which to ponder a course of action, and acting on instinct alone, the drive that is within all of us to survive, he pulled the sheet loose from the bed and in one quick motion gathered up the bloody organ within the once white cotton bed covering and took the bloody mess to the door.

Peeking out through the door, opened but a crack, he surveyed the back yard for an indication that any of the other residents were about. Feeling fairly secure in the knowledge that he shared the house with drunkards and the like, it would be unlikely anyone else would be about at this early hour. So, with the morbid parcel tucked under his coat, he made his way quickly to the privy and once inside dumped the remains through the opening in the seat. The depth of the hole and the lack of light, accompanied by a smell most foul, had him feeling reasonably safe that no one would be spending any more time in there than was necessary.

Back inside, he quickly flipped the mattress over to hide the near two-foot diameter blood stain, then tossed the sheet into the small stove, watching as it was slowly consumed by the red embers that still lay glowing in the grate from the evening before. When the sheet had completely turned to ash, he lay back on the bed. There was little he could do at that moment other than try and get some sleep. It would be nothing short of a fool's errand to rush and attempt to engage in this morbid game of cat and mouse with anything less than a mind that was alert.

He grabbed the note from the table and read over it again, not sure of the meaning, if any, behind the sudden appearance of the signature: Jack the Ripper. It struck him as peculiar that a female, for lack of a better term, would coin the name of a man, especially when he felt certain she must already know he was well aware of who was behind the notes and the murders. Perhaps it was nothing more than the workings of a mind suffering from mental illness, something he was sure existed within his adversary.

Having reached yet another dead end, suitably pointed at the end of her last correspondence, unable to see any possible reason for having odd signature at the close of her letter to him, he let the paper slip from his hand onto the floor and closed his eyes.

Forcing the last few hours from his mind, he turned his thoughts to his sister back home and the gift she had, for years, hidden away from everyone. As he drifted off to sleep, his thoughts wandering the fields and woodlands of home, he thought he must inquire further of this other sight the next time he wrote to her, if indeed he would be fortunate enough to be granted a next time.

It was early afternoon when he awoke to a commotion coming from somewhere in another part of house. Alarmed, his thoughts turning immediately to the grim depository that lay in the ground below the privy, he leapt from his bed and dashed to the small window. Drawing back the edge of the curtain slowly he could see that the backyard was still quite empty. Relieved, he took a shaky breath to try and settle his nerves and grabbed his work coat from the chair where he had laid it the previous night. Throwing it on, he ventured out into the yard and then re-entered the house through the main back door that opened into the kitchen. Upon entering the kitchen, its tiny space crammed with other tenants, all of whom were in a heated discussion with one another about the discovery of another prostitute murdered not a dozen streets from where they now stood.

Not having been in the habit of casual conversation with any of those with whom he shared the common space, he simply made the appropriate inquires of interest as though he himself was hearing the news for the first time and then, with a look of disgust upon his face, he left them to their discussions.

Out on the street it was a busy Saturday afternoon as he made his way towards the business district in the hope of acquiring more information about what had happened, or more specifically, the common belief regarding what had taken place the night before.

As was the case within his place of residence, the talk on the street was largely one of outrage and concern. Large groups of people stood outside store fronts discussing what had happened, while others could be overheard as they made their way past him on their way to take care of their daily affairs. In every case the sentiment was the same: anger, directed mostly at the police.

Continuing along, it quickly became obvious that the horror and magnitude of the crime had already reached the public, either by the press or through some unauthorized source. Either way, the word was out that this murder was the work of the same diabolical mad man that had killed Polly Nichols; known by her friends as Penny.

Taking Brick Lane, as it would provide the quickest way of getting to his destination, he passed the entrance to Hanbury Street. A large crowd had already gathered outside the gate that led to the backyard where the body must have been discovered, the same yard he had been in but a few hours earlier. He could see a number of police officers keeping the crowd back and in some semblance of order while, he presumed, investigators were carrying out their grim task within the confines of the property's rear yard.

He pulled the key he had taken from the dead woman's mouth from his pocket and held it between his fingers, studying its features in the diffused light offered up by an overcast morning.

"What is your significance?" he asked the tarnished and worn key.

His question left unanswered, he tucked the mute key back into his pocket, gave the crowd a final looking over, then carried on his way.

With no way of knowing if and when she would strike again, all he had to work with was the note he already had and try and gather as much additional information as he could in the hope that it would lead him to her whereabouts.

Unfortunately it would be nearly two full weeks before anything useful would be forthcoming.

Chapter 14

Dear Diary,

There has been no word from my brother. Neither I, nor our parents have heard anything from him and I must confess that I fear the worst may have happened.

Temperance, the 2ⁿᵈ of September in the year of our Lord, 1888

The days and nights following the gruesome murder and mutilation of Annie Chapman passed at an agonizingly slow pace, where the nights that followed the days did not seem to have much division between them, until, it felt as though the week itself had been nothing more than one continuous day.

His once tidy, and what one could easily describe as barren, room now had a resemblance to that of a newspaper's cutting room. Papers from all the local news agencies lay discarded upon the floor, any articles pertaining to the Whitechapel murders having been carefully removed and pinned to the wall above the table. The table top was nearly covered by four sheets of paper, on which were drawn a map of the entire area, including roads and laneways right down to even the smallest of passageways. A tiny almost insignificant X marked the spots where the bodies of the two prostitutes had been discovered. An equally small question mark showed the position where a prostitute alleged she had been attacked by three young men, and who had subsequently died in hospital the following day.

In addition to this collection were articles pertaining to missing persons, both male and female, the times and dates carefully circled then transcribed into a ledger of sorts that sat beside the hand-drawn map. The crowning jewels in this macabre puzzle were the notes he had received from Mary. They, too, had been pinned to the wall, directly above the newspaper clippings.

He had replaced the lock to his flat's door the Monday following the murder of Annie in order to keep his little investigation a well-guarded secret and hopefully thwart any further attempts by his adversary at gaining access. The unsolicited installation of the lock had also procured considerable favour with the landlord, Mr. Huntley, who had, up until that time, been less than cordial with him. He had told Mr. Huntley that someone had broken in, taking several personal items. As a result of the robbery he was going to change the lock, promising to give the new key to him upon his departure. The good turn obviously struck a chord within the gruff homeowner for from that day onward he would always say hello whenever he caught sight of Aremis, either coming or going.

The papers had provided him with quite a bit of information but as he began to take in the bigger picture it became clear to him that most, if not all, of what was being said could not be taken as the truth. The cases in point were the so-called eyewitness accounts pertaining to the Chapman case. Two individuals, one claiming to have seen the dead woman alive well after the coroners established time of death, while the other stating he had not seen anything unusual in the backyard at a time when the body would have been there. The collaboration of separate information that alleged the body had not been in the backyard as late at 4:45 a.m. were nothing sort of outright fabrications.

Incredibly, these fabricated accounts were not only being taken seriously by the public but were also looked on as credible leads by the police. So much so in fact that public opinion was being taken as accurate over the findings of the coroner.

The only semi-accurate story being told seemed to be that of a young carpenter who was living next door to where the body had been discovered. Albert Cadoch, 27, told both the police and the papers that he had heard something in the neighbouring yard about 5:30 that morning that sounded like a woman saying "no" followed by what he believed to be something falling against the fence.

It was not long before the murder of the Chapman woman had been officially deemed the work of the Whitechapel Fiend, as the killer had so been dubbed, and the findings made by the medical examiner quickly found their way into various newspapers. Dr. George Phillips stated that, with respect to the Chapman case, it was his belief that whoever had carried out the crime had to have considerable medical knowledge given condition of the body, the time constraints, and the lack of light. Some papers had taken that assessment a considerable step further, stating in black and white that the police were now looking for a doctor or a student of medicine in connection with the ghastly murders.

It was a challenging task for police as well as for Aremis, sifting through the so-called sightings by countless persons, all claiming to have seen something or someone who would, with near certainty end up taking on the appearance of a short, shabby Jew. Of course his job of separating truth from fiction was made that much easier as he already knew who the murderer was, whereas the police were still groping through the dark in search of the wrong gender and quite possibly the wrong species.

True to the words written in her last note, letters were indeed arriving at local newspaper buildings, police stations, and the post offices with daily regularity. Some of these were hostile letters by concerned citizens aimed at the police and the police commissioner directly for their incompetence in not having apprehended this mad man, while other notes and letters were said to have been written by the killer himself, taunting the police to try and catch him. These letters, some having been smeared and spattered with blood, were often supported by inaccurate descriptions of the murders aimed at adding credibility to the missive, which instead only condemned the note to being nothing more than a morbid hoax.

Saturday September 29th was a cool but bright morning, well over three weeks since the murder committed on Hanbury Street and, despite his careful collection of information and nightly reconnaissance throughout the streets of Whitechapel, Aremis had not managed to locate Mary. The absence of her red-inked correspondence and, mercifully, a subsidence to the brutal murders had him wondering if she had grown weary of her own game and simply moved on. As pleasant as it might be to entertain such thoughts, something told him that it was nothing more that wishful thinking on his part.

Unable to make any progress, beyond pouring over the same information and walking the same streets without success, he had taken a break from it in order to write a letter to Temperance. It was the first time in all of his letters to her that he had actually included his mailing address in the hope that she might write him back. In it he had made inquiries about her other sight, asking if she would share with him all that she knew of it. He went on to explain that he, too, was experiencing such visions but did not elaborate on what it was he was actually seeing.

It was on this afternoon, returning from the post, that upon entering his yard from the laneway he spied a boy standing at his door.

His suspicions immediately aroused, his senses heightened, he pulled back into the laneway. Remaining concealed by the fence, he took in his surroundings all while observing the boy who was now knocking on the door and seemed to be peering through the old keyhole. After a few moments, quite certain there were no other persons beyond that of himself and the boy in the immediate vicinity, he stepped from the laneway into the yard and called out to the boy in a harsh tone.

"What, might I ask do you think you are doing?"

Catching him off guard, the boy jumped back from the door, spinning around in the direction the voice had come from.

"I'm sorry sir. I don't mean no disrespect. I was just seein' if someone was at home is all."

The boy looked to be about ten or eleven years old and his voice was shaking from the sudden start.

"Who are you?" Aremis asked as he approached the boy, "What is it that you want?"

"My name is Timothy, and I was told to bring you this letter right away, that it was very important."

The boy held up a letter to show that he was sincere.

"I ran all the way here, never stopped once," he continued, having not received any sort of acknowledgement from the tall stranger who was still advancing on him.

Feeling fairly certain the lad posed no real threat, Aremis softened both his stance and his tone if but only marginally.

"I see. Well, that would make you one fine delivery boy then, would it not?"

The young lad smiled nervously at the words that were only slightly more accommodating than the ones heard previously.

"Who was it that sent you on this errand deemed so urgent?"

The boy shifted uneasily, adjusting the small hat that was pulled down over dirty black hair.

"Dun-know, to be truthful. She was a woman, is all. She said you'd know her."

Aremis bit his lower lip as he looked about the yard with hardened eyes for anything that might be amiss. There could be little doubt who had penned the letter the boy now held in his hand, but even with this knowledge he had an opportunity here, and he had to be careful on how to best put it to good use without endangering the boy's life. So with an air of one quite pleased at the news that was being presented, he hid away his true feelings in order that he might persuade the boy to divulge as much as he could about the woman who had solicited him to this duty.

"Ah, a pretty woman, about this high," his hand levelled just above his chest, "Brown hair, long at the back," he said in a voice that well belied his true feelings.

The boy nodded, "Yes sir. That would be her, indeed."

"Well, that is some good news then. I am relieved that you have shown up. She was correct in telling you that which you carry is most urgent and you have done well to get it here so smartly."

The boy beamed at the accolades that were being bestowed on him.

Retrieving two half pennies from his coat pocket, he motioned for Timothy to bring him the letter.

Following the hand instruction Timothy jumped from the back steps and ran with the letter, presenting it as he arrived.

"Thank you," he said, taking the letter from the boy and giving him in exchange for it the two half coppers.

Taken quite a bit by surprise, the boy thanked him repeatedly.

"That's fine now. You did well and your efforts should be rewarded."

Aremis turned the letter over in his hands, its envelope unmarked in any way that might indicate who it was from or what might wait inside. He slipped his thumb under the paper flap and gently tore the seal along its edge. Opening the top he could make out the now familiar red ink. He pulled the double folded single sheet of paper from its sleeve. Opening it, he quickly glanced over the words. Then with a smile, one most forced, he thanked the boy again for a job well done.

"Ah, it is as I was hoping, a letter from my sister. She was coming to London next week. From this note, I can only assume she has arrived early. I am indeed pleased. I must ask you, Timothy, you seem like a quick lad, did you happen to recall what street my sister was on when she gave you this letter?"

Timothy pondered a moment or two and then with a look of recollection he answered the question put to him.

"Yes sir, I do. It was on Osborn at Whitechapel. She was coming out of the store on the corner."

"I see," he said in a concerned voice that matched the worried look that seemed to grow out of the boy's words.

Seeing the sudden change in the man who had just given him such a grand amount for something he would have done for much less, he inquired as to what was the matter.

"Is everything all right, sir?"

Playing on the boy's concern he carefully set his next words into play in the hope of getting the one thing he needed to know more than anything else.

"No, not so much per say. As I said, I had expected her next week and now I am set to wondering where she might be staying and why she did not come here directly. I do not imagine you might know where it was she was staying now, do you?"

Timothy shook his head, his lips pressed tightly together before speaking.

"No sir, I'm afraid I dunno that. She never told me and I never took to followin' her. I didn' see the need to. You might want to go there yerself and wait. You might be lucky an' see her there like me."

Aremis smiled and nodded at the young lad's eager suggestion before the boy put forth another option.

"If yer too busy, I could go for you. I could wait and when I see her again I can tell her that you have the letter and are worried after her, and the like."

The little plan of information gathering had suddenly taken a potentially deadly turn. He knew if Timothy did go back and did in fact encounter Mary for the second time the meeting may very well end in the boy's death, particularly if she thought he had tipped her whereabouts to him. Now he had the delicate task of having to tell the lad, without alarming him or having him thinking, that something sinister may be afoot, especially at a time when just about every man in the city had the potential of being a suspect. At the same time he had to ensure the boy did not attempt to make good on his idea of locating and conversing with someone he could not possibly visualize as cold-blooded killer of demonic proportions.

"No, no that will not be necessary. You have done more that enough," he began in a soft voice that had almost a melodic quality to it. "I did not wish to discuss this with a stranger, my dear Timothy, but you seem like a trustworthy lad and I feel that our conversation will not leave this yard."

The boy nodded without speaking, privileged to be trusted in adult matters as yet undisclosed.

"Good, well, you see, my sister is somewhat ill, a sickness of the mind, so I have been told. It is the reason for her coming here, so I might take her to London Hospital. I want her to see a doctor specialising in such matters with the hope that something can be done for her."

He paused but a moment to ensure he still had the boy's attention before continuing.

"I will go myself and look for her. I am certain she will, in good time, make her way to me. It is obvious she knows my place of lodging as she managed to instruct you well as to how and where I would be found. However, I must ask that you not to try and talk to her further for she might find it to be unsettling, and although she was quite nice to you today, she may not even remember speaking with you should you see her again. I do not wish for you to be made a fool of or called a liar, for her memory fails her more often than I care to say. Do you understand me, Timothy? It is very important that you follow what I am saying to you."

Again the boy nodded his understanding.

"Yes sir. I will not bother your sister. And if I happen on seein' her again, what should I do?"

"Just be yourself, if she makes inquires about the letter you may tell her that you gave it to me in person and left without exchanging anything more than simple pleasantries."

Timothy removed his hat and smoothed down his hair before replacing it on his head, readjusting the shabby cap until it sat much as it had before he had removed it.

"All right then, don't you worry about her." He said enthusiastically, "I'm sure she will be just right as rain when you see her, I am sure of that. My Mum used to tell me, before she died, that good things come to good people, and you and yer sister are both good and kind to be sure."

Aremis shook the boy's hand, slipping another half penny into his hand as he did so, then bid him a good day. He watched as the boy left through the side gate that led between the houses out to the front street, all the while thinking on the boy's last words.

"How mistaken you are young Timothy," he whispered under his breath. "I only hope you never come to realise the error of your trust."

Back inside his apartment he reopened the letter this time taking the time to read over it properly.

Shorter in length than all the others had been it was unmistakably written by the same hand.

Hello luv,

Forgive me for my lack of writing but I must confess to having been a tad busy of late.

I was relieved to see your door repaired the last time I was by. Can never be too careful these days. As your door was repaired I decided to send the letter along by way of the boy, I thought him a tasty treat, I do hope you enjoyed him.

Tonight I will make up for lost time and unless I can be caught there will be two dead whores come the morning light.

JR

PS, I see they think me a doctor now, a woman, ha-ha. The real doctor here is Phillips, and he is right, the time is not, you know as I how well we can see in the dark.

He carefully read over the note several times looking for anything that might give him the edge he so desperately needed. The medical examiner, Phillips, who had been called in to look at the body found in the backyard of Hanbury Street had declared that the time of death lay somewhere between the hours of 2:00 a.m. & 4:00 a.m. and not the reported 5:45 a.m./6:00 a.m. time frame that had been reported in all the papers.

This note, as brief as it was, was the first real piece of evidence that could possibly tie her to the crime. But even though she made clear reference to the reported times being incorrect that could easily be cast aside as most of London already knew of the debate that was being waged between the various investigations. To any outsider looking at the note, it would look no more authentic that any of the other letters that had been received by the authorities since the onset of these bloody crimes.

Unable to get anything more useful from the note, he plucked a stickpin from the tiny tin box then pinned it on the wall along with the others.

Taking a step back in order to better assess the collage of paper set upon his wall, he pondered what his next move should be. No longer rattled by the note which contained what could easily be described as a predetermined death sentence for someone, and in this case perhaps more than one, he returned to the table. Moving his meal plate and cup from the morning's breakfast to one side he studied the map that he had created. After a few seconds he placed his finger over the corner where the two lines that represented Osborn Street and Whitechapel Roads intersected, tapping the spot lightly.

"Where are you hiding?" he said aloud as he continued to study the streets and laneways, which led from that spot to the two points on the map where the murdered prostitutes were discovered.

"Easily negotiable on foot," he muttered to himself, "especially if no one suspects you, but why so far apart from one another?"

He continued to tap his finger softly as he narrowed his gaze, as if somehow that might allow him to see more than the myriad of intersecting ink lines that stretched over the papers.

It was obvious to him, given the note he had received, that the Chapman woman was a planned attack. But what of the first woman, Polly, was that murder also planned, or was it more a crime of opportunity?

From what he had witnessed firsthand, the only thing he could really count on was that Mary was unpredictable, thoroughly vicious, and nothing short of insane. To try and put any form of social edict or logic on her would not be helpful. If there was any hope at all of finding her he would have to think like her, and perhaps in some ways, even become her.

He sat on the edge of the bed and let his head fall into his hands as he tried to imagine being of ill mental health, of having no regard for those around him, of thinking of no one beyond himself and his next meal. To live in such a manner as to have no respect for life and little fear of retribution for the atrocities that lay before you, a direct result of your own action, and to know that those whom you walk amongst believe with all their hearts that creatures, the like of which you are, cannot possibly exist.

They were terrifying thoughts all; to be so far removed from humanity that the life that surrounded you on a daily basis had little, if any meaning, beyond that of sustenance. To walk, the predator among the prey, disguised so perfectly as to blend with the flock; to strike down any one that so tickled your fancy at any time of your choosing, then disappear back into the masses without so much as a trace, that was truly frightening.

And yet, as frightening as it was, he could not deny it was by that very design that he, too, had managed to survive and elude capture all these years without a single soul thinking him any more or less than that which he presented himself to be.

The evening that followed an otherwise bright day was turning out to be like most of the evenings throughout the summer past, with scattered showers moving across the city, driven by stiff winds. With the light having long given way to the darkness, he grabbed his long coat, his hat, and with his cane in hand he left for town through the back lane, locking the door tightly behind him as he did so.

It was not long past the stroke of eleven when he cut through an alleyway that led from Thrawl Street through to Brick Lane. Walking slowly along the street, he had already resigned himself to the idea that no matter what he did this night there was a better chance than not that two women were going to end up dead before tomorrow's sunrise. The only thing he could do now was to do as he assumed she was doing, and that was to begin the search for her first victim.

Similar to what he had done on previous nights, while in search of the ghost-like adversary, he wandered the streets that were well-known areas for prostitution, the difference being that this time he was going out as the hunter and not the saviour.

Having not taken blood in just over a week, with plans for doing just that over the course of this very weekend, he hoped that the heightened senses brought on by the need to have new blood would help him in his hunt. The only thing he had to absolutely keep in check was to ensure that his body and mind, both still human, as well as the other thing that lurked relentlessly just below the surface, understood that this hunt he was on was to locate suitable victims and not actually make victims from those he did happen upon.

It would be a difficult challenge at best as he already felt the need growing both metabolically as well as physically and, whatever the outcome of the night, he knew someone or something would have to die in order to quell the monster within.

Making his way down Brick Lane to where it turned into Osborn Street, he stopped outside the grocery store where Timothy had told him that Mary had given him the note. Standing there, just back of the corner bathed in the amber glow of the lone gas lamp, the chilly damp wind blowing the tails of his coat around his legs, he looked up at the three floors of windows that topped off the brick grocery store, wondering if within one of those flats his nemesis did reside. Turning his gaze from the windows to Whitechurch Lane located on the south side of Whitechapel Road, he tried to put together some direction that might lead him to her whereabouts. Turning his thoughts inward in the hope of finding there in the darkness a similar vision to the one he had two weeks earlier, something that might yield even the smallest glimpse as to her whereabouts. To his disappointment, nothing more than fragmented memories of death and pain, answered his mental request.

From within the shadows of a secluded passageway not a hundred yards north of where he stood, she watched him while she wondered what his next move might be. After several moments, taking in all that surrounded him, he continued in a southerly direction, crossing Whitechapel and disappearing down the laneway that bordered the church.

Mary quietly slipped from her hideaway to give chase while maintaining a safe distance. She was curious to see where he might be headed, and if stopping outside the grocer's small shop was merely a coincidence or if the boy had given up the spot where she had commissioned his service that very afternoon. She felt certain she had not been followed earlier in the day but now, having witnessed the one she had been taunting the last few weeks heading off in the general direction of her flat, she simply could not be certain.

"My little friend, if I find that you have tipped the scale I will be most unhappy with you," she said, in not much more than a whisper, the very words whisked away on the chilly night winds.

She followed him down the lane, ensuring she kept herself well hidden as she did so, the idea that she indeed may have been betrayed by her choice of errand boy growing stronger the closer he came to reaching the lane's end.

The tiny laneway finished up letting out on the north side of Commercial Road and there, as he had done outside the store situated on the corner, he stood and took in his surroundings while she remained quite concealed by a section of wall that jutted out into the lane. Several minutes passed as she watched him through critical eyes as he slowly paced back and forth across the mouth of the south entrance to the lane.

"Are you lost, my dearest Aremis, or is it you who now toys with me?"

Her hushed words barely out of her mouth, he suddenly stopped his slow pacing and stared up the laneway he had just negotiated, freezing her as though she was nothing more than the stone and brick she was pressed against. Even in the dim light that came from the lamps on Commercial Road she could see his eyes, glowing red, as they searched the darkness. She knew all too well that even the slightest movement made by her, even within the near pitch darkness, would most certainly spotted.

Barely breathing, her own eyes not open more than slits, she waited out the tense stand off at more that 80 yards until at last he turned, rounded the corner and went off in an easterly direction along Commercial Road.

After several moments of stressful anticipation she let out a slow quiet breath, all the while not talking her eyes off the end of the lane.

The rain had again begun to fall more heavily now and after remaining against the wall for several more minutes she pulled away, opened a black umbrella and slowly meandered back up the lane towards Whitechapel Road.

Having seen him head off in the opposite direction to where her flat was located she felt there was little to be gained from continuing the pursuit, especially when it was obvious he was far more aware of his surroundings than she had previously thought.

She had much to accomplish this night if she wished to keep her word to both her adversary and the papers. She would have to seek out someone engaged in such activities as those whom she masqueraded as, on a street somewhere south-west of where she had last seen her pursuer. There she would, without remorse, end that person's life, the first of two, if she were to remain credible.

Generally speaking, the weather did not deter those seeking sexual favour or those willing to provide, for a fee, that which was being sought but, for whatever the reasons might be, this night there were few people of any trade or social status on the streets.

Having walked numerous streets in a westerly direction, she had turned south traveling several more blocks again until she had reached Fairclough Street. Here, the rains having relented for the time being, she closed her umbrella and waited on the corner, all the while keeping a keen eye out for his familiar silhouette should it suddenly appear from out of the darkness. Several minutes had passed and she was about to resume her southerly trek when she caught sight of woman crossing over Fairclough Street, a man following closely behind. The man called out to the woman just ahead of him for her to hold up whereby she did as he had requested.

Too far away, even with her acute hearing, to make out what was being said in hushed whispers, she began to silently make her way towards the couple.

Not quite half way to where they were, the woman, her back to the wall of the building that bordered the narrow sidewalk, the man standing in front of her holding his weight with one arm supported by the same wall, she noticed another man emerge from a small chandlers shop and cross the road. He passed the couple and as he did he looked over his shoulder at them, but beyond that, he continued on his way, disappearing into a doorway set in a long row of housing.

Continuing her unhurried approach she began to take in what was being said, and in those words, words separated by long pauses, she could make out a familiar voice. It was that of a woman she had met, not far from the street where she now walked, outside The Bricklayers' Arms on Settles Street. She was known as Elizabeth by those close to her, but she had always called her Liz anytime she had cause to address her in the short time she had known her.

As she closed the distance between herself and the couple, the sound of Liz telling the man that that his lust-fuelled affections would have to go unsatisfied this particular night seemed to be falling on deaf ears.

"No, not tonight, perhaps some other night, luv, I'm really tired now and I am off home."

Not taking her repeated requests for a meeting at some date in the future, the man, dressed in a long black coat, leaned in whispering something to her about saying her prayers or something to that affect.

It was at that moment Liz looked up from the ground, catching eye of a woman standing beside them. Seemingly arriving from thin air, the sudden appearance of another person within a conversation that was obviously intended for two and not three made her jump slightly.

"Hello Liz, having some trouble?" Mary inquired.

Hearing a familiar voice there in the dim light had Liz take a breath in relief.

"Oh, Jacquelyn, you did give me quite a fright, you did, sneaking up on me like that."

The stocky little man in the coat, quite annoyed at having his advances first thwarted and now interrupted, reacted with hostility at the intrusion.

"Look ere' you's inertuptin' my business ere, so push off or I'll muck up that pretty face fer ya!" the man growled under his breath.

"Is that so?" Jacquelyn replied with little, if any, concern to the threat, stepping even closer and placed her hand upon the man's chest.

"It is quite obvious that my friend here has had enough for this evening, but perhaps you might find me a suitable substitute."

She let her hand slid down the front of the man's coat and finding a space between the buttons she slipped her hand beneath the woollen outer shell, letting it come to rest upon his groin.

The once confrontational situation, for the moment defused, she continued to caress the man's genitals through his trousers as she waited for his response, which was quickly forthcoming.

"Well, since you's willing enough I have no issue with it, so long as the price be the same." he stated in a voice that was a far cry from that of his first angry protest.

"My price?" she asked softly moving in closer, "It is always the same for a gentleman such as yourself."

The man chortled softly at the lies being whispered to him from common whore, knowing that anyone of them would say anything to get a coin or two.

"You's as bad as she is," he said though bated breath.

"Oh, and how might that be then?" she replied.

The man took a deep breath, lost in the caresses beneath his coat, before finally answering.

"You and er, you's both would say just about anything, anything but yer prayers."

Jacquelyn smiled and let out a little giggle at his words.

"And why would *I* need to pray? God has not seen fit to help me thus far."

With that she clamped her hand down tightly on the man's testicles, while at the same time, pressed her other hand tightly over his mouth to stifle the painful scream that erupted not a moment later.

Increasing the agonising pressure it was but a moment before the struggle was over, the man laying face down in the gutter, the painful cries of protest silenced through unconsciousness.

"Oh Jac, you shouldn't be about doing such things, when he comes 'round he's going to be out for the both of us."

But her heartfelt words seemed to have little effect as she watched as Jacquelyn stooped down to retrieve her umbrella from the puddle filled sidewalk.

"He's drunk, Liz. The only thing he's going to remember when he comes 'round is that his bollocks are going to be hurting something awful."

Still fearing reprisal at some future date, Liz again tried to appeal to her friend but she had hardly begun when Jacquelyn placed a finger over her lips.

"Shhhh, now, that's quite enough. With any luck at all one of them beat coppers will pick him up for being drunk."

Despite being both worried and tired, that idea in of itself made Liz laugh out loud.

"That's more like it, lass," she said placing an arm around Liz's shoulder. "Come-on, I'll walk you part way home."

"That would be good of ya," she replied, "could I put on you for a sweet?"

"Sorry luv, all I have with me is a packet of Cachous."

"Oh that would do nicely, so long as you can spare one."

Jacquelyn pulled up her skirt from the side to access her pocket and produced the small packet of breath sweets handing it to Liz.

"Keep them, I have another packet at home."

"Oh, you really are too kind to me, Jac."

The two women left the man in the gutter and headed off together up Berner Street. They had only managed to get about four doors up when Jacquelyn pulled Liz though a wicker gateway.

"What the Hell?" Liz protested loudly.

"Shh, hold your tongue! I fear I may know that man at the end of the street.

Jacquelyn eased the gate open slowly and poked her head out to investigate further that which she had just seen from the safety of her hiding place.

Having not seen anyone at the street's end, Liz inquired in a whisper as to who the man was that had her tough, self-assured friend suddenly in such a worried state.

"Who is it? I never noticed anyone there. Are you sure it was not just a shadow or the like?"

Bent over at the waist while still peering out of the tiny opening in the gate, Jacquelyn gently eased a long knife from within her boot top.

"I think he went the other way," she said, letting the gate slowly close, plunging the two women into complete isolation and total darkness.

"Well that is a relief," Liz said, as she turned away from the gate. "I guess I really should be making my way home then. It is really getting on."

Her words, left without response, disappearing into the inky stillness, her final statement punctuated by the sound of razor sharp steel slicing through her flesh, her attempted cry for help producing nothing more than a gurgling expulsion of air as her last breath exited her throat through the deep and gaping wound that was cut well below her vocal cords.

Reaching out into the night air, clutching for someone or something to help her, she staggered a mere three feet before crumbling into a heap upon the ground in front of the large main gates that let into the yard.

"Sorry luv, But you see, I may be in need of a new place to stay, since no one can apparently be trusted these days. That, and I have made a promise, and you know well a promise must not be taken lightly. I do hope that you can forgive me."

Her words fell on deaf ears for Liz had already expired from her injuries.

"Oh don't be like that Liz," Jacquelyn went on, in almost a playful manner. "It's nothing personal, you understand. It just has to be this way, it has always been this way, well, sort of..."

She trailed off, her own words being lost in the night, consumed by the blackness that engulfed the area between the two buildings. She brought the blade up to her face then ran its length over her tongue cleaning the bloodstained steal of its crimson coating.

"Mmm, now that is nice," she whispered to the corpse that lay still upon the ground. "But unfortunately my dear, I will not have the time to enjoy you in that way for I have much work that needs to be done and precious little time in which to accomplish it."

Taking hold of Liz's coat Jacquelyn rolled Liz over onto her back pulling her legs up, bent at the knee then letting them fall open of their own weight.

Taking a rose she had pinned to her own coat she carefully attached it to Liz's, along with the piece of fern that had been coupled to the stem of the rose.

"I know you won't have many flowers at your funeral luv, so you can have these. The sweet man that gave them to me won't mind you having them. Perhaps you two can even share a cup of tea in heaven."

A small giggle followed the cruel words, then only silence.

With the tiny corsage pinned in place she had begun to tug at the skirts that were wrapped around Liz's legs when she suddenly stopped, forced to hold her breath as her ears strained to make out a noise emanating not far from the gate. As she remained silent and in the dark it quickly became apparent that it was a horse and wagon making its way down the street. When she heard the elderly driver order the horse to a stop she knew her plan regarding Liz would have to be abandoned. Without so much as a sound she darted off into the darkness and waited there in the shadows for an opportunity to make a casual escape.

Watching from her hiding place, she saw the gates proper open and the man begin to guide the horse and small cart through the opening. Not more than a few feet inside the gates, the pony suddenly shied and pulled back against the lead, refusing to move any further.

With the dark entranceway now only marginally lit from the gates having been opened, it wasn't initially obvious to the driver why his pony was refusing to enter the familiar courtyard. Thinking there might be some unseen obstacle barring their path he began probing through the darkness with his folded whip. It was not long before he came across the reason laid out face up on the muddy entranceway.

Nudging the body of Liz with his foot several times while commanding that she right herself immediately was to be no avail, and he finally gave up, leaving his horse and wagon so he might enlist the help of anyone who may still be at The Working Man's club, the building that neighboured the cart building yard where the body now lay.

Seizing the opportunity, Jacquelyn made her move, running though the darkness and out onto the street where she slowed her pace and began walking north, opening her umbrella as she did so.

It was only a few moments later, as she reached the corner of Commercial Road and Berner Street, that she heard the first cries of murder ringing out from Dutfield's Yard.

Not two streets south east of Dutfield's, the cries of murder also found another pair of ears, and still another pair beyond that.

The multiple hails for assistance and cries for police soon followed as Aremis ran up Christian Street and onto Fairclough in time to see a police constable rounding the corner from Fairclough headed north on Berner Street.

Composing himself he hurried along the street, all but following in the constable's footsteps, until he had reached the corner of Berner and Fairclough where he cautiously peered around the corner of the building.

There was already a crowd of about fifteen or more gathered outside the gates of the Dutfield Carriage works which told him that, in all likelihood, whatever the attraction was it, was not likely to be anything good.

Two more men suddenly passed him and made their way over to the crowd and, like debris caught in the wind of a passing train, he tucked in behind them, quickly mingling with onlookers.

There were already two police constables on the scene, and as one shone his lamp light on what appeared to be a body lying in the driveway of the yard, the crowd pushed forward in order to get a better glimpse of what or who it might be.

The constable nearest the body warned the crowd back and then ordered the other constable, obviously his junior, to see to it that the crowd held their distance.

The younger policeman held his hands out wide and moved towards the crowd, ordering everyone to move back several feet. It was in that moment the first constable again shone his light on the body, revealing a woman dressed in black, her throat covered in blood, so much so in fact that it trailed off through the mud like rivulets making their way towards the side door of the club.

A few gasps went up along with more hushed words of murder, both of which were soon lost in the cacophony of voices all vying for a chance to speculate on the cause and perpetrator.

"It's him, the fiend's struck again!" one man shouted out.

"These coppers is useless!" another woman stated angrily.

As more police began to arrive from all directions, Aremis quickly realized he would not be afforded a closer look at the body or the area surrounding it, not that it really mattered at this point. The woman discovered was obviously dead from what appeared to be a slashed throat, but beyond that, he was unable to make out much else. Even if he could reach the body, there would be no guarantee he would find anything that would lead him to the killer. He had spent considerable time with the body of Annie Chapman; the only piece of evidence was the key, its purpose, and the meaning behind why it was in the dead woman's mouth, still remained unclear to him

With more people and police steadily congregating in the street, he inconspicuously slipped from the crowd and made his way north towards Commercial Road, leaving the body that now lay in entrance-way of an abandoned carriage works to that of the police and the various men of medical science.

Unlike the body he had found some two weeks ago, her insides cut out of her, this poor soul, although most certainly cut down in a vicious attack, was apparently not mutilated, at least as far as he could ascertain, given the lack of time he had for which to view the corpse and the limited descriptions being offered up by those who had been first on the scene.

This somewhat second-hand observation put him to wondering, if it had been Mary, why did she not disembowel the woman as she had done with Chapman?

Suddenly it dawned on him that if this murder was committed by her hand, and not the hand of someone else, then maybe she had been interrupted. If this was the case, then it could stand to reason she had been forced to flee before she could finish that which she had started there in the dark, isolated courtyard.

The blood that still flowed in the gullies of the driveway could attest to the time of death being nothing much beyond thirty minutes, for it would have long since congealed if the time had been any much more.

Entertaining the idea that she had, for whatever the reason, been interrupted; he cast a glance back towards the growing crowd near the south end of the street.

"You must have walked this very road not long before I," he said aloud as he searched both directions of Commercial Road for any sign of her.

Just two streets to the west, and unaware of exactly how close her pursuer actually was, she had only entered the narrow lane that led to Buckle Street moments before he had reached the corner. Had she been but a minute slower he surely would have caught sight of her.

Now on the street where her tiny one room flat was located on the second floor of small row of shabby townhouses, she stopped momentarily outside the steps that led to the home's front door, contemplating on whether or not to call it a night or keep to her word and find another prostitute she could lay waste to.

Spinning around within the sprinkling of light drizzle that was falling from the overcast night sky, she let her umbrella catch the air as she held it at the end of her outstretched arm, her face turned to the heavens, the misty droplets of water settling like dew on her alabaster skin.

When she finally stopped her solitary pirouette, her umbrella coming to rest appropriately on her shoulder, she stared without expression towards the end of the street.

Her eyes slowly misted over in a blood red hue until nothing more than a singular colour remained between her eyelids. Fangs, long and pearl white, slowly became visible, the tip of one tooth piercing the skin of her lower lip, causing a ruby pearl to bubble up from the wound. Balanced in the tiny self-inflicted crater like a gemstone, there it remained, unmoving in size or position, until the moisture of the rain that lay upon her skin diluted the droplet enough to cause it to run over the edge of her lip, disappearing down her chin in a thin red line.

She ran her tongue over the break in the skin, feeling the irregularity in her otherwise unblemished skin. Bringing her fingers to her mouth, she wiped the blood that had escaped onto her lip and chin. Holding her hand out in front of her she could see that she had blood smeared across two of her fingers. She watched as the rain began to wash it from her skin before she placed them into her mouth, stealing the treat from the night. Suddenly, as if responding to a voice heard but unto her, she pulled her fingers from her mouth, tilting her head slightly much as a dog might do in order to better hear the sound that had caught her attention.

"Yes Momma," she said softly, as she inspected her fingers for any traces of blood that might still remain. "Yes, I understand the importance of being punctual."

She swayed back and forth like a bored little girl. "Yes, and of keeping my word, I know all of this." She let out an uninterested sigh to punctuate her unhappiness at this voiceless line of spectral-like questioning.

Then, as if dismissed, she uttered her final words to the night and the blind cobblestone street, walking towards the point where it let out onto Leman Street. "Good night Momma," she said cheerfully, and vanished around the corner heading north.

Dressed all in black, she moved quietly along the rain-slicked streets and laneways not unlike a shadow. She stayed close to walls, using sidewalks well darkened by surrounding buildings, and avoiding the lamplight wherever possible. Even moving as she was, it was not long before she found herself outside St. Botolph's Church, more commonly referred to by locals as the prostitute's church, located on the corner of Houndsditch and Aldgate. It was often the place many of the women in that trade found themselves when they had either not made enough money to cover their lodging or had consumed I through drink.

Given the late hour and the inclement weather Jacquelyn had thought the location would lend itself nicely to the task of finding her next victim. But it was the same at this unassuming house of God as it had been throughout most of the East End with precious little in the way of human activity on either the streets surrounding the church property or within the grounds themselves.

Slipping though the wrought iron gates, she quietly wandered around the old churchyard, looking for anyone who may have simply sought shelter from the police more than the weather and had found sanctuary beneath shrubbery or against the back wall. But after making one complete round of the building she had discovered nothing more interesting than the odd rat that scurried along the laneway between the church and adjoining building.

Abandoning her plan, she left the churchyard and continued west along Aldgate, past a block of mostly empty row housing. It was there, at the foot of Duke Street, she caught sight of a man and woman making their way across the street, not far from where she presently stood.

The distance too great given the wind and the drizzle for her to be able to listen in on their conversation, their obvious mannerisms combined with the late hour had her convinced that this was a couple brought together through mutual business interests and not anything of an actual relationship.

Standing, her body mostly concealed by the brick wall of the row housing, she continued to track their movements until they disappeared into Church Passage, a shortcut that led from Duke Street through Mitre Square, letting out on Mitre Street.

Mitre Square was a dark and foreboding place by night, with only three gas lamps to shed light over a relatively large area that was all but enclosed on four sides by high warehouse walls. The only really entranceway of any meaningful size at was off Mitre Street, the only other means of entrance were through two long and narrow covered walkways.

She had killed an old man in one of the empty houses that lined Mitre Street several years back and she had all but forgotten the place until that exact moment.

"The night may not be lost after all," she said to herself as she started to make her way up Duke Street towards the passage she had just seen the couple disappear into not but a few moments earlier.

Inside the passageway, she could easily tell it was clear of anyone as it was a straight line from one end to the other. As she made her way along its length she stopped her progression as a sound, reverberating off the bricks walls, reached her ears. Motionless in the darkness she could make out the sound of a heavy footfall, running, a quickened pace that was just as quickly fading until she could no longer hear any trace of it. It was then, in that silence that ensued, she heard a sound, one of which she found most intriguing, that of muffled whimpering.

Emerging from the passage into the edge of the square she casually took in the surroundings, searching for the source of the discomfort. Even with her eyes accustomed to seeing in the dark, it took her several moments before she could actually make out the form of a woman lying on the ground near a wall located at the most westerly point of the square.

Making a secondary visual sweep of her surroundings to ensure that she was indeed alone, she quickly made her way across the cobble stone courtyard to where the woman lay, one hand clutching her stomach.

"He stabbed me!" the woman announced in a panicked voice as she caught sight of Jacquelyn's approach.

"Who did?" Jacquelyn replied, her voice mimicking the urgency of her injured colleague.

The woman on the ground pulled her hand from her abdomen, pointing off in the direction of Mitre Passage, a laneway that led north from the square, then quickly replaced her blood-covered hand back over her midsection.

"A man, he went that way, through the passage. Bastard took my whole night's work!"

By this time, Jacquelyn was at the woman's side attempting to see how bad the wound actually was.

"Now then, I think your night's dosh is the least of yer worries luv," she said, as she tried to coax the woman's shaking hand away from her stomach. "Yer going to need to get that looked at by someone at the hospital."

The news of having to seek medical attention did not seem ease the woman's worry in the slightest as she continued to struggle against having her hand lifted from the wound.

"Come on now, it surly ain't that bad or you would have slipped away by now."

Jacquelyn's voice was reassuring, and after a few moments of gentle persuasion the woman relented, letting her have a better look at the gash in her stomach.

"There you see," she said, gently pulling back the clothes around the wound, "it's not as bad as all that, not much more than deep scratch is all. You'll be fine in a few days, you just see if I ain't right."

The woman smiled, albeit faintly, letting her head fall back to the cobblestone ground but brought it back up with a jolt.

"Please, I beg of you, do not leave me here. Promise you will stay with me until someone else comes along. Promise me!"

"Shhh, it's all right. Of course I will stay with you. No need for you to be worrying yerself about that now. One of them old beat coppers will by soon enough."

Jacquelyn looked about as if in search of such a policeman before continuing.

"Never around when you need one, are they?" she said, trying to pull another smile from the injured woman. When that failed, she changed the subject, inquiring what her name might be.

"Kate, you can call me Kate." she said, "It's short for Catherine but no one calls me that."

"Well, not exactly the best way to make acquaintances, Kate, but nevertheless, my name is Jacquelyn. You may call me Jac. It's sort of what I go by these days.

The two women exchanged formal greetings as best one could, given the grim circumstances, before the injured woman posed a more serious question.

"Do you think it was that mad man that's been attacking us women?" she asked in a shaky voice.

Jacquelyn looked a bit taken back at the woman's inquiry but replied in her usual matter-of-fact voice, seemingly unaffected by the query.

"The Ripper? Here with you? Nonsense? You was robbed, luv, that's all. If it were the Ripper, I can assure you that you and I would not be having this conversation."

"The Ripper?" the woman asked, an air of confusion in her voice, "Is that what the papers are calling him now?"

It was at that moment that Jacquelyn realized her slip. She had told the paper service to hold back the letter she had sent in order that she might have chance to kill again. It was her way to prove to them that she was indeed the one behind the murders, as well as the author of the letters true. No one but herself and the news service had seen the name she had penned at the bottom of her letter.

Since neither the letter nor its contents had found their way into any of the local newspapers, she felt it safe to assume that it had either been held back from both the police and public, as she had requested, or it had simply been dumped in with the rest of the mail from those claiming responsibility for the crimes. Either way it mattered little to her, for she knew that by tomorrow's light that same letter would have more validity than all the other fakes combined.

"No, no luv," Jacquelyn replied. "It's a name I thought up myself on account of how the bodies are all 'ripped' open."

The woman lying on the ground turned her face towards the wall, letting out a disgusted protest as she did so.

"Oh dear Lord, that is simply awful. How can you speak in such a way about the dead, especially when any one of them could have easily been you or me?"

She thought about what the woman had said as she quietly pulled the knife from her boot.

"I guess I ain't quite sure to be honest," she replied, suddenly clamping her hand firmly over the woman's mouth, "I thought it was somewhat humorous."

With that, she forced the woman's head back and with one quick flash her blade cut deep through the soft unprotected flesh, severing muscle down to the bone.

With the fatal wound delivered, Jacquelyn let the knife fall and quickly covered the chasm with her hand, preventing the blood from spraying out. Gradually she eased up on the pressure, allowing the woman's dying heart to slowly pump its last few contractions and letting the spoils pool in her cupped hands.

As Kate's heart stopped and she slipped from this world into the Reaper's hands, Jacquelyn raised her hands to her lips and drank back the warm liquid.

"Mmm, Kate you *have* been drinking tonight." She said after swallowing the last of what was in her hands and licking the ruby red syrup from her skin.

The rain had stopped for the time being but the night air was chilling as she collected her knife from where it had fallen and began to perform the brutal invasion of Kate's now dead body. There, in near complete darkness, she opened up the woman's abdomen, cutting out her intestines and laying them to one side before carrying on.

"You see Kate, it wasn't the Ripper who robbed you at all. He was just some poor old thief out to get his drink money from a defenceless woman. Not to worry though, luv, his kind soon meets their maker, if such a being truly does exist. In fact, it might even be I who sends him on his way."

She giggled to herself at hearing her own words as she moved the knife around Kate's insides, removing the woman's kidney in short order.

Taking a moment to examine her prize, the blood from the organ running between her fingers, she playfully tossed it up into the air, much as a child might do with a ball, catching it as it returned to earth, only to send it aloft once more.

"You know something, Kate? I'll let you in on a little secret here tonight."

She looked around to ensure no one else would be privy to that which she was about to disclose. Drawing in close to the dead woman's ear, she whispered, "They all think me to be a doctor, can you believe it?"

She burst out laughing at the very thought of such a thing, her, a woman, to be thought of in such high esteem as that of medical practitioner.

"Those pompous fools! A common butcher could have done this, and better, I am quite sure. They think they know me. They have not yet even discovered that I am female, a common whore at that."

She paused in the delivery of her lone soliloquy, gently squeezing the kidney in her hand as she let the thought that was manifesting in her mind come to fruition.

"Perhaps they need help. Perhaps they need to be shown that they are looking in the wrong direction," she said in a most serious voice, a voice that was a far cry from her previous statements that had easily bordered on being gay. "And you know what, Kate? You are going to be the one who is going to tell them."

Setting the kidney down for the moment, she straddled Kate's body, sitting well up on the dead woman's chest so her own skirts and petticoats would not be sitting in the pools of blood that were forming around the body.

Using the tip of her knife she carefully cut small slits into both of Kate's eyelids, then sat back as if to admire her careful handiwork. Her own eyes narrowing, a frown creeping across her face, it was obvious she was not satisfied with that which she was viewing, and so she started anew, just below each eye, cutting in what appeared to be triangles, the upper tip of which pointed towards the cuts she had made in the eyelids.

"Open yer eyes, old cocks. Look past what you believe you know and see what is actually before you."

Her words were cold and quiet, more befitting that of a teacher or tutor than a methodical killer.

Studying her work anew, more satisfied in with what she was seeing, she carried on.

Moving to the woman's nose, she cut most of it off in two quick passes of the blade, tossing the severed nose to one side. It bounced twice before falling through a gap in between an old basement window and the steel grate that was set in the ground just before it.

"Yer on the wrong track, old dog. You have picked up the wrong scent. Stop following yer nose, else I'll cut it off."

In a trance-like state, she cut the lower part of the woman's left ear clean off with such force that it sent the severed piece into the folds of her victim's clothing.

"You must stop listening to those around you; use what you have before you. I have given you many clues now, the key to my lodgings for one. Pay close attention, old cocks, look carefully at that which I have given you."

She slashed her blade across the woman's face, down and over her cheek towards her mouth. "And above all else, stop dispensing the lies that I am a man!"

The cut would have certainly separated the lower jaw from the upper pallet had she continued but she suddenly stopped, the blade still in the flesh several inches from the corner of her mouth.

Remaining still and near breathless, she listened closely to the chill night air, the wind blowing the dried leaves mixed with scatterings of garbage around the brick-lined courtyard. There, subtly mixed in with the muted rustlings of nature and mans discarded refuse, she could make out the sound of a heavy footfall, still far off but definitely coming closer. Too heavy for a woman to make and too uniform in pattern to be that of a drunk, the steady slow pace, could only belong to one sort of person at this late hour, a constable on the beat.

"They are a nuisance tonight, they are," she said under her breath as she tucked the knife back into her boot top, retrieving the kidney along with a small selection of disembodied bits which she had severed free from their dead host.

"You be sure to tell 'em Kate, tell 'em all that they've not a clue," she whispered as she got up to leave. Then, with the her bloody collection wrapped in cloth torn from Kate's clothing, she tucked the lot into her small handbag and darted off through the darkness disappearing into the passage that let out onto Orange Market, a small courtyard on the other side of the warehouse that made up the north side of the square.

She had barely made Duke Street when she heard the shrill police whistle sounding from somewhere behind her, its single piercing note reverberating off the many brick walls.

Tilting her head slightly, she listened to the lone note being played continually for almost a minute before it fell silent. In the ensuing silence that followed, she opened her umbrella and slowly made her way towards home, fresh blood still gathered in between her fingers.

"I do so love whistles," she whispered to herself, a smile upon face, her lips red as though having been painted with rouge.

Once again, and for the second time that night, the sound of a police whistle found him nearly a half mile from where the sound was emanating. So far away was the sound, in fact, that he felt sure he was the only one that would have been able to hear it from where he now stood.

Having witnessed the result of the previous use of the policeman's call for assistance, he felt his heart sink and wondered if there was any real point in making his way towards where he had first heard the sound. There would be little likelihood, if Mary had indeed struck again, that her victim would be found alive. He knew this not simply from his previous encounters with her, but from an understanding regarding himself, as he would not be as careless as to leave someone alive who could, at some point, be able to identify him. She herself would be no different, and of this, he was never more certain.

Nevertheless, he made his way along the darkened streets until he was at the foot of Mitre Street where, for the second time that night, he came upon a crowd being held back by police.

It did not take him long to get most of the gruesome details from those in the crowd and he was, in short order, convinced that it had indeed been the work of Mary. Not long after arriving on the scene rumour began circulating that a man had been arrested not far from where the body had been discovered, and for a moment he held fast to the idea that it may have been someone else. But as more and more details regarding the condition of the body began to find their way out of the crime scene, it was an idea that could no longer sustain this hope.

With little else left to do but stand around in the damp night with an ever-increasing crowd that was also growing more unruly the larger it got, he decided his time would be better served elsewhere. Taking his leave, he separated himself from the crowd and made his way north on Mitre Street to where it intersected with King Street and began to make his way towards home, unbeknownst to him that his enemy had walked that very way herself and was not but a mile ahead of him.

Chapter 15

Dear Diary,

I realize that writing takes time and the post is slow to arrive, but with all that has and is going on right now I would dearly love to hear from Aremis. The lack of contact spawns the fear in me that even though I have had his reassurances that the murders of which we hear so much about in London are not, as I had originally feared, a result of his doing, I cannot rule out the possibility that he may simply be lying. Other than his reassurances, he tells me little of the actual deaths, for which I am grateful, for even out as far as we are, safe from what has been going on in London, we are not spared from hearing the dreadful details regarding the murders of those unfortunate women.

I do have some good news from within all of this horror and personal doubt. Aremis has, for the first time, included his return address within his letter to me. I thought I would not live to see the day when I would be able to write to him as he does to me. I hope the letter I have sent this morning gives him strength and that he finds what I have said pertaining to my other sight useful. I must confess, however, to knowing little about how it works, only that when it does come to me it has always been correct in what it has shown me.

I would like very much to visit him for I know it would do him good to have someone from his family by his side, but I am too frightened to entertain even the mere idea for longer than a moment, much less put the idea into motion.

I feel ashamed of my own cowardice as I sit safe and warm by the fire. My husband is talking with neighbours in the adjoining room, his low tones finding their way to my ears, reminding me that I am not alone. I have my baby in the bed beside me, and all with our family is good, while many miles away my brother is far from home, perhaps face to face with the demon that stole him from us. These thoughts alone terrify me. I cannot imagine what it must be like for him.

As always, I pray that God can find it in His infinite mercy to keep my brother safe so that he might again return home to us as I remember him to have once been.

Temperance, the 29th of September in the year of our Lord, 1888

The days and weeks that followed the brutal double murder of two prostitutes in London's East End were anything but "business as usual" for those living and working there. The police had been dealing with no shortage of angry protests at both locations where the murders had taken place. Public outrage was also commonplace in front of the police stations, the people of the community demanding to know why the police were unable to bring such a brutal killer to justice and seeking the resignation of the police chief. In addition to the daily slurs levied at the police and government officials alike, letters continued to arrive in abundance, all claiming to have been penned by the killer himself. However, only two of these many letters had actually caught the attention of the investigators, so much so in fact that the authorities had taken photographs of them, distributing them to the local constables. All of this effort having been carried out in the hope that someone would be able to recognize the handwriting and lead the police to the person behind the worst murders in anyone's memory.

Despite not having any real leads come from the hand printed bills, someone was able to identify the handwriting for he had in his possession, pinned upon his wall, several notes penned by the killer, all of which were scribed well before the two letters, now of interest to the police, had ever been public knowledge.

Although the police had received letters via the news agency telling of the grisly double murder, what they did not know was that Aremis, too, had also been the recipient of just such a letter. More disturbing than the letter, however, was the parcel that the letter had been attached to, for inside the small package was discovered a small portion of kidney. Both the note and the portion of human organ were delivered nearly two weeks after the double murder, a time in which it seemed that the horrific killing spree had come to an inexplicable but welcomed end.

The note, stained with dried blood, told him that she was deeply saddened that her previous gift was not well received and so to make up for her poor choice she was enclosing something she felt everyone can appreciate: good food. She then went on to describe how best to cook it and that because the woman it had come from had been drinking hard that night, there would be no need to marinate it.

The new letter joined the others on the wall while the kidney was deposited where he had disposed of her last disgusting gift of human flesh, out back in the privy.

One thing was certain, she had been correct in her last letter to him. He pulled the pin from the note last received and took it down from the wall, reading it over as he held it in his hands.

She had written that he would be able to tell her letters from those who could only claim to be the one responsible. The first one the police had made post bills of was, at least in part, because of the second letter that had been sent to the press, which not only made reference to the first notation but also described, in brief, the latest two murders. Now that in of itself would not lend much to the credibility of either note as actually being from the killer except that the second letter arrived at The Central News Agency several hours before police had released any details of the gruesome double murder to the press.

He had obtained copies of the actual letters, as many curiosity seekers had done, and added them to the wall of hand written notes. He kept the copies off to one side so as not to confuse them with the others and to have them more easily accessible to his reach.

Pinning the note he had previously taken down back on the wall, he then looked over the two copies he had placed side by side. It was plain to see, reading over the words, the similar dialect, penmanship and grammar that had been used in both the letters to the press and the ones left specifically for him.

Dear Boss,

I keep on hearing the police have caught me but they won't fix me just yet. I have laughed when they look so clever and talk about being on the <u>right</u> track.
That joke about Leather Apron gave me real fits.
I am down on whores and I shan't quit ripping them till I do get buckled. Grand work the last job was. I gave the lady no time to squeal.
How can they catch me now? I love my work and want to start again. You will soon hear of me with my funny little games. I saved some of the proper <u>red</u> stuff in a ginger beer bottle over the last job to write with but it went thick like glue and I can't use it. Red ink is fit enough I hope <u>ha. ha.</u> The next job I do I shall clip the lady's ears off and send to the police officers just for jolly, wouldn't you?

Keep this letter back till I do a bit more work, then give it out straight. My knife's so nice and sharp I want to get to work right away if I get a chance. Good Luck.
Yours truly

Jack the Ripper

Don't mind me giving the trade name

PS Wasn't good enough to post this before I got all the red ink off my hands curse it. No luck yet. They say I'm a doctor now. <u>ha ha.</u>

The first letter overlapped the second one slightly, and after having read it over for what seemed like the hundredth time since having picked them up, he carefully moved it to one side so he could see the full page that had lain under and off to one side of the first.

I was not kidding dear old Boss when I gave you the tip. You'll hear about Saucy Jacky's work tomorrow, double event this time. Number one squealed a bit couldn't finish straight off. Had not the time to get ears for police. Thanks for keeping last letter back till I got to work again.

Jack the Ripper

Letting the first note fall back over, he let out a laboured sigh. True enough, she had not sent the ears of the Eddowes woman on to the police as she had indicated she would, but it was an interesting fact that the portions of the woman's ears had been clipped off and thought to be lost until the body was moved to the morgue whereby the investigators discovered them in within the dead woman's clothing.

"Why Jack?" he asked himself as he turned his attentions from the notes to the map. He had added two additional Xs to indicate the spots where the two women had been killed soon after the night they were discovered. Pouring over the map for several minutes, he still could not make out any significant pattern, other than they were all within a fairly close proximity to one another when taking into consideration the vast area of the greater city.

He tapped the centre of the table where the four sheets of paper that made up the hand drawn map came together.

"You must be here somewhere or why else would all these killings be so concentrated."

Although these deplorable acts most certainly were centred within the area of Whitechapel, that in of itself presented somewhat of an oddity as there was no shortage of prostitutes throughout the entire city of London. While Whitechapel was most certainly notorious for being a seedy neighbourhood, it still could not lay claim to holding the market on the selling of illegal sexual favours. If someone was actually hunting women based entirely on their line of work, then they could easily have their choice on most any London street once the sun had gone down. It would be foolhardy to continue on with this morbid obsession in an area that was now flooded with police and vigilante groups, all with the single-minded purpose of apprehending this killer. It would seem logical and far less of a risk to simply move on to another location where there would be less of a police presence.

A few more silent minutes passed with the only sound being that of his fingers, as they gently ran over his whiskers, a trim beard that framed his jaw line and mouth.

"No, you live here, somewhere close by at that. But why have you stopped? What are you up to in your absence?"

The newspapers and posts that arrived daily upon the streets of London during the days that followed the double murder had confirmed the thoughts he had about the culprit being interrupted. The body that had been discovered in the entranceway to Dutfield's Yard had been identified as a local prostitute known as Elizabeth Stride. Unlike her sister in trade, Annie Chapman, who had been killed almost three weeks earlier, Stride had only sustained the single life ending slash across her throat, thought to have been delivered from behind with a razor sharp blade. The other woman killed that same night, however, was not so fortunate.

Catherine Eddowes had been found in Mitre Square, several streets to the west of the Berner Street carriage works, her throat cut in a similar manner to that of Stride, Chapman and Nichols. But unlike Stride and Nichols, she had been badly mutilated much in the same manner in which Chapman had been discovered, having had most of her insides removed and laid about her body. The parts of her body removed but not arranged in a grotesque frame about the upper body included one kidney and some of what was described, 'as the poor woman's reproductive tissues'. They had, as yet, not been recovered by the police. The most striking difference between Eddowes and all of the other victims was that she displayed horrible and, from the coroner's report, quite deliberate facial disfigurement.

In an interesting, yet equally disturbing turn of events, a similar letter and parcel as the one he had received was reported to police as having been delivered to a one Mr. George Lusk. Mr. Lusk had formed and was head of the local Vigilance Committee, set up due to what was described by Lusk as the complete incompetence by the police to catch this fiend who still remained on the loose. Police had reported that Mr. Lusk had indeed received a letter, as well as a portion of what appeared to be a human kidney. However, the contents of the letter, and whether the kidney in the box had really come from a human being, were not disclosed. The only thing that was revealed was that the hand writing in the letter delivered to Mr. Lusk was similar to that of two other letters, and so they were not discounting the letter or the organ as being genuine.

Pinning his own letter back on the wall from where he had removed it, he sat down on the bed and retrieved another envelope, its closure having already been opened, from the small table beside the bed. Removing the folded paper from within, he let his body fall backwards onto the covers with it in his hand.

It had been the first letter he had received from his family since having arrived in London so many years earlier.

Although he tried to return home at least once a year, he had not allowed anyone to know of his exact whereabouts since having relocated to the city. This was done, in large measure, for their own protection, but it was also because he knew in his heart that it would be too painful for his family to see him making his way at a level not much above that of someone in poverty. The risk of having any member of his family, individually or as a group, arrive unexpectedly on an afternoon he was planning to end someone's life was simply something he was not prepared to accept. Even though he had managed to gain control over when he would need blood as well as some of the physical manifestations that came along with the need, it would simply be too dangerous for them to be in his company during those times.

To lie there with the words written by his sister on paper that she had held made him again long for a life that was no longer his to have.

Sitting up suddenly, he quickly tucked the letter back into the paper enclosure it had first arrived in, shaking off as he did, the feelings of loneliness.

He had hoped the letter, if it would arrive at all, would contain within it more useful information about his sister's other sight, but to his disappointment it held no such insights. She had only touched on the topic, saying she had little idea how it worked other that its accuracy was without fault. Beyond that she had no idea how to conjure it forth on demand, and that it seemed to come to her by its own choosing, far from anything brought about by her own conscious thought.

The rest of the communiqué was filled with worry for his safety and a hesitant desire to know more regarding things, things he knew well were better left to the realm of ignorance.

Chapter 16

Dear Diary,

Two more horrid murders involving prostitutes fell on the heels of posting my last letter to my brother, but since then the news pertaining to women being brutally killed in London's East End seem to have drawn to a close, along with the letters from my brother.

I sent my first letter to Aremis nearly a month ago with hopes of having more frequent communication with him, but so far I have heard nothing from him.

The newspapers, once full of horrific details pertaining to these ghastly crimes, are now all but void of them, with the exception of those reporters who seem driven to keep the murders of these unfortunate souls in the headlines.

My thoughts continually wonder if my brother's lack of writing and the sudden end to these horrible murders are not, in some way, connected.

I feel wicked to think such things but I have good reasons for doing so.

My son is currently teething and is most unhappy about the process. He calls to me now so I must close for the moment.

Temperance, the 26ᵗʰ of October in the year of our Lord, 1888

In a clearing near a grove of poplar trees some ten miles from the Scottish border, Jacquelyn sat on a small grouping of rocks that looked more as though they had been created by man and not of nature's hand. Sitting bathed in the cloud-filtered sunlight, the late autumn breeze blowing her brown hair about her face, she gently twirled a late blooming daisy between her fingers as she stared off absentmindedly towards the mist-shrouded hills that lay beyond the trees.

Humming softly, a lullaby of sorts, she remained there for some time before at last finishing her quiet melody unto herself. Sitting there, momentarily lost within the silence, she let the flower slip from her between her fingertips to be swallowed up and lost within the tall weeds that covered the entire area. Hopping off the large, moss-encrusted stones that had served as her seat, she slowly wandered through the weeds, seemingly without much direction until she came upon a parting within the line of old stones, a space where the wall of sorts ended and then began again some two feet over.

Approaching the gap, she put her hand out before her as if to test for something that might be there but was, in actuality completely unseen. Then, leaning forward slightly, she called out to the wind.

"Momma, are you here? I have come home."

The wind blew through the opening, pushing her hair back from her face as the sun disappeared behind a thick bank of clouds, the air suddenly growing chilly, the scent of rain being carried on its stiff current.

"Momma?" she called out again as she passed through the opening in the stones and into a thicket of sumac, their once-green leaves now having been replaced by their autumn hue of crimson, the intertwined branches reaching skyward some four feet above her head.

"Momma, it's me, Jacquelyn. Please forgive me. Can I come back home?" she asked in a meek voice.

Once again, only the rustling of leaves could be heard in answer to her query and so, in silence, she made her way through the thicket until she stood before a dishevelled pile of stone that was located at the far end of the condensed thicket of sumacs. The stones, some of which were charred black from years of smoky fire, had long since crumbled from what had once been a carefully made fireplace.

Kneeling down before the rocks, she held her hands out in a fashion similar to that of someone warming their hands at a fireside. Her hands trembled slightly as she held them before a flame visible only unto her, bringing them together on occasion and rubbing them so she might distribute the imaginary heat through her skin.

Tears began to well up in her eyes until the weight of the tiny droplets could no longer be held back and a slow trickle of salt water made its way down her cheeks.

"Momma, why will you not speak to me? I do not understand," she began, her voice cracking with emotion. "I was in love, like you and Father were. Is that my crime, to fall in love?"

Another long silence followed her address to the ghosts of the long derelict home, her tears continuing to fall, punctuated by soft sobbing.

Brushing the water tracks from her cheeks with her sleeve, she spoke as though in response to a voice uttered by a person unseen, who at last, had finally responded to her questions.

"But I did not know. How could I have known?" she said sharply, then pressed her lips tightly together and hung her head slightly. "Forgive me, I did not mean to raise my voice, but I still do not understand why you and Father will not forgive me?"

A dark formation cloud drifted over the sky, casting the valley and hillside into more muted shades of daylight. A cold breeze accompanied the cousin of night, its icy fingers touching her skin and setting a shiver upon her. She pulled her coat around her, clutching it tightly to her chest, as she listened to the silence that was speaking to her and to her alone.

Angered by what she had heard, sounds that lay hidden beyond that of the wind which whistled through the trees she spun her head around sharply and stared with harsh eyes at a spot not three feet from where she still knelt.

"And how was I to know that, how could I have known that?" she shouted, apparently no longer concerned about the volume of voice and how it might be perceived by the spectral party of this conversation.

"When you look on me now is that what you see? Do you see a monster or only your daughter?"

"Look at me!" she screamed, as she stood up suddenly, her arms out to her sides facing full on the spot she had been addressing.

"Do I look like a monster? Can you tell from how I look that I am not solely what I appear?"

There was a momentary pause before she continued.

"Momma, please look at me," she begged, in a tone far removed from the previous outburst. "Please, please look at me." She paused again, waiting for her plea to be acknowledged before continuing.

"I could not see more than what was there, and what I saw was a man, a beautiful man, a hard-working man, one with property and standing, one who said he loved me. He told me he wanted to marry me, for me to be his wife, like Father had said to you. Did you think Father to be evil when he courted you, Momma?"

She paced around beneath the crimson canopy wringing her hands together while trying to formulate the words she next wished to convey, but before she could put into words that which had only been thought, she stopped and stared at the emptiness that had been her focus of conversation.

She shook her head, slowly at first, then more frantically, the tears flowing over her cheeks.

"No... No, you do not understand me. I cannot remember. I have no recollection of that time. I can only recall dreams, horrible dreams. Have we not gone over this time and time again?

She paused but a moment, "Do you not think if I could have come home I would have?"

She fell to her knees, curling up into a ball, her hands over her face as she cried openly, the tears finding their way through the tiny gaps between her fingers and falling into the soil she was kneeling on. Pulling her face from her hands, her cheeks wet and red from crying, she spoke with a voice that was cracked with grief from a time long forgotten by most and yet one that was still brutally vivid within her own mind.

"I awoke in his bed. I was covered in blood. I was terrified. He told me I had not been harmed, that everything would be all right. I thought I had been attacked or injured in some way, but I could not remember how this could have happened. I wanted to come home but he would not let me leave. He told me it was no longer safe for me to see you or any of my family again."

The grove fell silent; the desolate location reclaimed by the wind and remained so for the better part of an hour, until a week and fragile voice of humanity spoke up from within the overgrown living room.

"When I was told what he had done to me, what he made me into, that he had taken the blood from my body and consumed it, and that I too would need to feed on the blood of the living if I wished to sustain my own life, I refused to believe his words. However, I was soon shown the words he spoke were not lies, and if I did not soon obey my need, I would kill the first living creature that I lay eyes upon. Anything that had within its body the one thing my own body craved."

She slowly pulled herself to her feet and stood on trembling legs before the stones that had once been her home's hearth.

"When I could no longer deny what had happened, I told him a lie, telling him that I had accepted this 'new beginning', as he called it, and wished to celebrate this life anew together. Then, when he was asleep, taken from the day by wine and spirits, I lashed him to his bed, and with his own sword I drove it through his chest with a force not that of my own but something beyond anything I could myself produce, a force that was sufficient to penetrate not only his body but the bed upon which he lay drunk and lodge it firmly into the boards of the floor beneath." She paused, looking over her shoulder to ensure that she still had the attention of her ghostly audience, then returned her eyes to the hearth and continued.

"His scream was one most painful, and most certainly nothing God himself had created. The wound, which I had inflicted on him, would have surely ended the life of anyone human, and yet he did not perish, but pleaded with me to pull the weapon from his body and release him. I did not do as he begged of me, instead I doused him in spirits and set him on fire."

She paused again but did not turn around, a shiver running though her body, her shoulders quaking as it ran its course.

"I walked from his home, a place I once thought I would be happy in, a place where I thought you would visit your grandchildren, and I sat on a pile of fire wood watching the flames consume my dreams along with my husband-to-be. His screams continued on until the fire was so hot I was forced back to the trail that led through the forest to the stream. Soon after that I could no longer hear his cries."

She wiped her face with the back of her hand, sniffling as she finished recounting the tale.

"I thought, not being of much education and such, that if I killed him, that somehow that which he had done would be erased from within me. Failing that I thought that God, in all His kindness, would remove that which evil had placed upon me..." her voice trailed off to not much more than a whisper. "God, too, had forsaken me."

The sun was beginning to set and the shadows were quickly growing long in the dying embers of the afternoon sunshine, the lack of light much more apparent under the canopy of trees. The leaves, with their vibrant red colour back lit by the sun, took on the appearance of ornate wallpaper, the likes of which would never have adorned such a simple abode. The wind seemed to settle, along with the last glimpse of the sun, leaving the landscape dressed in the still blueness that was the precursor to the veil of darkness that would soon swallow up the land.

"Tell you?" she said suddenly, and with as much surprise in her voice as there was annoyance. "How could I tell you of this? It happened to me and

I myself could not believe it. How could I expect someone to believe such a tale?" She turned from the rubble to face into the room, her hands outstretched to either side in an appeal for understanding.

Then, oddly, she laughed and looked away over her shoulder, perhaps though a window that may have once been set into the south wall, a point that when looked through would have, at one time, looked out over most of the valley towards where the road now followed the stream.

With her voice weak to the point of being near that of a whisper, she pointed to the earthen floor that had both rotted away the wooden floors and filled in any evidence that there might have once been a hollow beneath where she now stood.

"I tried, Momma. The day Father locked me away below this very floor; I did try to tell you. Do you not remember? After little Daniel had come upon me in the woods, having discovered me with the cat, my face covered in blood, he ran to tell Father. I tried to catch him, but I was too afraid I would hurt him in doing so. So I let him run away. Father did not want to hear anything I had to say, but called me a child of the devil and locked me in the root cellar."

Taking another break from what was obviously tearing her up inside; she took in a ragged breath. Not taking her eyes from the hearth, she prodded the ghostly parent for recollection of that which she was retelling.

"Do you not remember me crying to you through the door, pleading with you to let me out, to let me seek an answer on my own? Do you not remember leaving me there, alone, cold and in the dark with a hunger I could not control or understand?"

She stared blankly into the darkness that was quickly engulfing all that was around her while she waited to see if the nothingness that she looked upon as her mother truly could recall that which she was asking of her before continuing.

"Do you not remember, Momma?" she asked again. "I spoke to you through a locked door of the man who did this to me, the man who everyone came to know as George Pratt, the man, who in fact, was a Roman soldier, Gorgonius, who along with his legion, travelled into the far reaches of countries that had not yet been explored by civilized men. In one of those Godless countries, he encountered a beast; a beast guised in the cloak of man, and this creature inflicted upon him a disease more terrible than any army he had ever faced. Left for dead, he awoke, starving and near death to discover his legion wiped out, the bodies of his comrades rotting where they had fallen. He remained in the woods for years, living off his wits, driven by his hunger until he had come to master it. Returning to Rome, he was heralded a hero, his reward, to be dispatched to England where he eventually settled, retired from fighting but not from killing."

"That was nearly one hundred years after the birth of Jesus Christ, Momma." She said at last, unable to believe her own words as they left her lips and disappeared into the night.

"You thought me ill of mind and that I had killed an innocent man, where I had done no such thing, I had killed a monster, just as Father intended to do to me." she said firmly, her back now towards what remained of the ancient fireplace.

"No, do not tell me such lies. I know the truth. I overheard everyone talking in the yard. Father had gone to get Reverend Kinsley and the soldier at arms for the village. Not one person would even speak to me directly for fear I would put them under some spell, but instead spoke to Daniel and to you, and you both told them what I had said and done."

She levelled an accusing finger into the darkness.

"They were going to take me out and hang me and you did nothing to stop them. Nothing!" She screamed hysterically, shaking her head so that her hair took flight and flew about her face as though it were caught in a whirlwind.

"I was starving, not from lack of food but from a need far deeper," she began in a trembling voice as she regained some control over herself. "I had tried to keep my hunger to myself, drinking from small creatures, ones that would not be missed, but I did not understand how not having enough of what my body required would affect me."

She was about to carry on with her tale when it suddenly took a sharp turn.

Agitated by the conversation and the terrible memories it conjured up, she brought a shaking hand to her face and with trembling fingers she rubbed her forehead in a fashion that was far more severe than would be necessary to alleviate any minor tension or provide a momentary distraction from the difficult conversation.

"When the door opened that morning and I saw the men and the ropes, I was terrified, but that terror only lasted for a moment."

She began to cry as she continued on.

"I do not remember much of what happened next, only fragments. There was blood everywhere, and the screaming. Oh God, the screams. I am still unable to purge them from my thoughts after all these years..."

She raised her head towards the heavens, her tear-filled eyes catching glimpses of the occasional star, its twinkling white light passing through minuet spaces between the leaves, a light made more significant by the water within her eyes. She swallowed hard, choking back her tears as she tried to continue.

"When I regained my thoughts, the pains I had felt within myself for so many weeks were gone, and for the briefest of moments I felt human, as though I was again myself. I thought that perhaps the whole ordeal had been nothing more than some terrible dream or an illness that I had recovered from, but as I took stock of myself I became aware of the horror that surrounded me. The things that greeted my eyes on that morning I have not been able to erase from my mind, and I do not believe that I shall be able to do so no matter how long I may carry on in this life. As I walked from the root cellar, I found the bodies of the Reverend and two soldiers; their throats ripped open, flies thick upon their wounds. Beyond that I found our neighbour, Mr. Campbell, in the same condition, face down in yard."

Weakened by what she was reliving, she slumped to the ground in a heap and remained there, unmoving beyond that of several body tremors that shook her violently.

"I found Papa at the front door. I knew it was him only by his shirt," she sobbed into her hands, which muffled her continued confession. "He had no face. All the flesh had been ripped away."

It took several minutes before she could regain her composure enough to continue.

"Stepping over his body, I made my way through the house looking for you, calling out to you but you were not there. I called to you several more times but you did not answer me. I ran from the house towards the barn and that is where I found you. You were still holding Daniel, his shirt soaked through with his own blood, your arms covered and caked in blood, some of it his, some of it your own... I had killed both of you where you had taken refuge, huddled against the wall behind the hay... My little brother, whom I adored and my own mother whom I loved and cared for deeply, yet I cannot remember having killed either of you other than to know in my heart that I did."

Now in a darkness so complete, accompanied by a silence such that is found within a place long void of the sounds made by the living, she remained still within its tomb of stone and trees until a single sound snapped her from a past. Out of a history most would find too horrendous to bear she was brought, with single-minded focus, into the present in less than a heartbeat.

With eyes now red and canine teeth protruding over her lower lip, she stared towards the broken remnants of the eastern wall in coiled readiness for whatever might be foolishly forthcoming. A fox suddenly crested the small wall that remained and atop the moss-covered stones bared its teeth and snarled at her. The adversarial confrontation was met quickly with a flashing of teeth pearl white and a screeching growl. The sound, terrifying and penetrating, something that did not seem to have even remote similarities to anything within the realm of nature, quickly dispatched the fox in the direction it had come.

With the threat having been dealt with she settled back, resting her full weight on one arm, propping herself up as her teeth and eyes gradually returned to normal, any remnants of the ordeal she had been reliving no longer apparent in either her face or voice.

"I could have been our family's protector had you all not conspired to take my life," she said solemnly, as she stared out through the opening in the rocks where the front door had once been.

"No, you are the one who is mistaken. No one would have ever known. Gorgonius, or George as you had come to know him, had lived amongst you all, amidst all of us and well before our time, in fact for hundreds of years, and no one knew. And still no one knows of my curse, not even now after all these years..." her words falling off as a tiny smile slowly crept over her face, "save but one kind man."

She stood up abruptly, brushing the debris from her skirt and pulling her small coat around herself.

"Soon I shall be well known, more so than even the highest men in power. If one is to believe that which is currently written in the newspapers then perhaps I have already achieved that. It would be quite an achievement, better than most of our humble beginnings, would you not agree, Momma?"

She waited but a moment for an answer, which from her facial expression was not to be forthcoming. In those fleeting seconds, she took one last look around the darkened homestead that had once been her home, a place where the passage of time had reduced it to nothing more than a scattering of stones. This was all that remained of what had once been a place where she, along with her family, did once reside.

Making her way through the gap in the stones, she stood in what once might have been the front yard. Turning back to face the sumacs she whispered something, but her words were lost, swept up by the night's own quiet language.

Without further lamentation or words to those unseen, she made her way down the hillside on a pathway that, like her home, had been lost in time. A place long forgotten and completely unseen by those who now lived in the village but two miles away, a village that came into being right upon the very border of this fifteenth century farm, all without ever knowing anything beyond rocks and weeds had ever been there.

Chapter 17

Dear Diary,

(Continued)

Matthew is now asleep and comfortable, the discomfort of his teething subsided for the time being, so I will take this opportunity to properly close out my last entry to you.

Without word from my brother, it is all I can do not to worry. I know it serves little purpose and he would not want me to waste my time in such a manner, but I must confess that I find it difficult at times to think of anything else, especially during the hours of nightfall.

I have loosely spoken with both John and with my father of visiting Aremis for Christmas. I was saddened and relieved that neither one of them seemed particularly keen on the idea. I shall not mention it again, and would not venture the trip alone, in fact, not at all, if we do not soon hear some word from him.

I will share something with you I cannot tell another and that is I feel that he may well have passed on. I have no real explanation for this, and perhaps it is nothing more than my mind trying to find closure to a terrible wound. But if this has come to be, then I hope he has found peace and is finally rid of what had so unfairly cursed him.

Temperance, the 26th of October in the year of our Lord, 1888

With an uneasy calm having settled over the area of Whitechapel, things cautiously began to return to something resembling normal. This in and of itself was miraculous considering all the unsavoury business pertaining to the as yet unsolved murders involving local prostitutes, which had all but taken the community hostage throughout the final weeks of summer right through into autumn.

Aremis, too, had gone back to what for him was now a normal existence as well, working during the day taking cargo to and from the various docks and warehouses while at night he would casually take to wandering the streets, quietly searching out his next blood supply.

It was on such a night, while seeking out a suitable person whose meaningless life he could quickly extinguish without fear of retribution, did he found just such a lost soul. He had seen him many times before, a homeless old man making his way along Christian Street near its end where the lines of railway tracks severed its southerly continuation. He followed the man down the hill and onto the railway lands well beyond the eyes and ears of anyone who might bear witness to what was about to take place.

It was over in a less than a moment, the elderly beggar hardly a match for his attacker. He had not even the time to put out a cry before his life was taken from him through a single traumatic neck wound.

The rail yard, with its many lines of steel stretching out for hundreds of yards in either direction, was completely desolate. Seizing the opportunity afforded by the weather and isolated location, he plucked the lifeless body of the man he had just killed from the wet ground and carried him to one of the many rail lines. There in the dark, he laid him over the tracks so that he was face down with his neck stretched across one of the rails.

"My apologies friend," he said in a grim voice, "but it has to be this way. I truly hope that you are now in a better place than here in this Hell with us."

He checked his watch, then his surroundings, before heading off towards home, feeling somewhat safe in the knowledge that no one was likely to find the homeless man's body before one of the many trains that entered and left the city almost hourly did so happen by. It was nearly a certainty that the engineer would not easily spot a man in dark clothing lying across his path. If by some miracle, coincidence, or good fortune he did manage to see him, it would be at such a close distance that it would be impossible to bring such a weight already in motion to a complete stop before striking the body. The steel wheels were sure to be a most trustworthy and mute accomplice, making the initial cause of death quite undetectable.

He had just reached the foot of Christian Street when he heard a faint noise that at first sounded like a woman talking.

Stopping abruptly, concerned that someone may have indeed seen what he had done, he stood there motionless in the falling rain, straining his ears in an attempt to locate the source of the muted sounds. The light rain, which had been falling most of the evening, was now coming down more heavily now, accompanied by low rolling thunder, a combination that quickly blocked out the snippet of verbal exchange he had been privy to but a moment earlier.

Unable to make out any sound beyond that of the rain, he took in the deserted street, looking for anything that might seem out of place or could provide a clue to the origins of the voice. He strained his senses one last time for anything that might exist beyond that of nature's torrent but came up empty.

With nothing more out of the ordinary than that of the storm and occasional passing vermin, he was left to assume the voices had been nothing more than an audible trick brought on by the weather. That, or more simply still, whoever had produced the hushed words he had picked up on had merely moved on.

He was about to do the same when he again caught wind of the female voices. This time it took but a fraction of a second to realize that what he was actually hearing had not been coming from anywhere within his surroundings but from within his own thoughts.

Taken aback by the sudden discovery, he tried to focus on it rather than dislodge it from his mind. Seeking shelter from the deluge he ducked into in a covered doorway, and there he sat on the stoop in order to better listen to that which made no sound.

As the fragmented whispers and broken dialogue began to take shape so did a translucent image that, like the conversation, was visible unto him alone. Closing his eyes and letting the images unfold in time with the voices, he began see and hear more completely until, after several minutes, he could observe in detail that which was neither visible nor audible anywhere within his current physical location.

In the centre of the shadowy imagery lay a small area of clarity, like the stillness that exists within the centre of a hurricane, a small space that lies quiet and calm while darkness consumes everything beyond its perimeter. He could tell from what he could see that he would be standing across the street front of *The Horn of Plenty*, a public house at the corner of Dorset and Crispin Streets. From this vantage point, he could make out two women standing together under the main doorway to the public building, taking shelter from the storm. Staring through the rain, completely unseen by those whom he watched, it took but a moment for him to realize that one of the women standing in the doorway was Mary.

Without thinking, he shouted out a warning to the other woman who did not, and could not, possibly hear him. As his urgent words, intended for another, entered his ears, the sounds penetrated his mind causing the oscillating waves to warp the image like ripples on a still pond. The once clear picture now moved with the symmetry of the waves, eventually losing cohesion and disintegrating into nothing more than loose tones of grey and white which were all but obliterated by dark, shifting clouds which moved like chimney smoke cast adrift by the wind over an otherwise blue sky.

"No, no, no," he whispered under his breath, his hands reaching out into the air before him as he tried to coax the image back into clarity before it disappeared completely from view.

Quickly taking hold of himself, he began to breathe with calm regularity as he composed his thoughts and allowed himself to relax. The steady rain, now made worse by a stiff wind, pelted down on him, and even though partially shielded by the covered doorway, he was soaked to the skin in no time at all. Blocking out the elements and his surroundings, the black fog that had threatened the delicate imagery within his thoughts slowly began to recede until it had once again formed the dark circular perimeter that framed the porthole, a window that looked in upon another place and time.

"I am so sorry that I set such a worry on you, luv, I should have told you that I was going off to visit with my mother," Mary said, touching the other woman on the arm in a comforting manner.

"Well that would have been a thought," the woman who was standing with her replied curtly. "Everyone's been in a fit, what with all this business of murder around the city. Honestly!"

The woman stopped her somewhat scolding lecture as she took in the street and a male passerby before continuing.

"I'll be telling you somethin' else as well. I'm not the only one who thought you to have met your end at the hand of the Ripper."

Mary brought her hand to her lips covering her mouth, feigning shock at the very idea that was being put forth by her compatriot.

A few moments of mutual silence passed in which time the rain that had been falling hard began to subside slightly, allowing the two women to venture out from their makeshift shelter and take refuge under Mary's umbrella.

"Not much chance of us making any money on a night like this," the unknown woman said, peering from under the umbrella, her hand stuck out, palm up, testing the force at which the heavens were delivering the rain to the street. "I think I'll be calling it a night then. What about you, Jacquelyn? Why not have an early one and go on home?"

'Jacquelyn?' he thought, repeating the name quietly in his mind, 'Why do you address her as Jacquelyn? Is that your real name then, or is it just another thread within your web of deceptions?'

Then, like a hammer, it struck him, a mental blow that suddenly sent multiple pieces of a puzzle that had been nothing short of illusively infuriating to him crashing together in perfect alignment with one another.

"Jacquelyn," he whispered, afraid of upsetting the delicate image within his mind.
"*JAC*-quelyn, you are using a shortened version of your own name to sign your letters. You have been giving us your name all along but with a different spelling, damn you!"

Jacquelyn, as it would seem her name might well be, smiled back at her companion as she spun her umbrella, the water spraying off its edges creating a pinwheel-like effect, the tiny droplets of water catching the glow of a nearby lamp so they looked like amber gemstones being cast onto the street.

"No, not tonight, Mary Jane, I cannot," she began in melancholy voice. "I fear that I have been away so long that the deputy of the house I reside in has already let my bed out to someone else and I have not the money to find another place to stay. I shall have to work a bit yet. Not to worry though, there is bound to be some poor sod along looking for some cunny even on a night like this. Bad weather never stopped a horny dog, now has it?"

The two women shared a moment's laughter before Mary Jane carried on her conversation with her friend.

"You know, if we were to be quiet, I'm sure I could sneak you into my room for the night. Not supposed to, you realize. I only give the landlord, McCarthy enough for one but the hour is late, and if you was to be gone early, before anyone was about, then no one would be the wiser now."

Jacquelyn smiled at the offer and gave her colleague a quick kiss on the cheek.

"You are a dear thing, truly you are, but I would not want you to get yourself into any trouble on account of me. You go on home now and I shall find my own way."

Mary Jane would not hear of it, however, and pressed her point further, trying to reassure her friend that no harm would come through the implementation of the plan.

"Nonsense, I shall not get into any trouble so long as no one found out." Laughter again erupted from beneath the umbrella. "I'm being quite serious now, take the night off. You is only just back from visitin' with your Mum now. You should not be tempting fate your first night back."

Before Jacquelyn had even a chance to reply, the other woman took hold of her arm and stepped out from beneath the umbrella pulling her along as she walked.

"Alright, alright, I'll come with you. Stop pulling at me as though I were a three year old." Jacquelyn stated, knowing that to fight her further on this would be useless.

Stepping back beneath the cover of the umbrella, the two set off along Dorset Street, and without moving a muscle he too, silently followed their meandering progression along the dark and rain slicked street.

"Where is it that you live now?" Jacquelyn inquired as they made their way along the deserted street.

"McCarthy's Rents, in Miller's Court. It's just down the street, not a hundred yards. I have the first room off the street. It ain't much, to be truthful, but it has its own stove and decent enough bed, but..." she paused for a moment, unsure of whether to continue on with the description of her humble abode, but then decided it was best to finish that which she had already begun, "I do hope yer not of a superstitious nature because it is room number 13."

Jacquelyn laughed out loud at the very idea of being put off by such foolish things as superstitions.

"My dear, I do not believe in such things as superstitions, tell-tales of monsters, ghosts or even God for that matter. It is of little consequence to me what number has been nailed to a door. Far more important is the latch on that door be a sound one."

"True enough, true enough. You are right, Jacqui. I do fret over needless things at times."

Jacquelyn put her arm around Mary Jane's shoulder and pulled her close.

"It sounds a might bit better than being out here the rest of the night but I must be frank with you."

The couple stopped under a lamp near the middle of the street.

"I will be along, and in short order if I can manage it, but I really must find some money before the night is out. I promise you though, that I will meet you by your room as soon as I have made a little."

The other woman frowned and was about to put up a rebuttal to the change in plans but found a finger gently placed over her lips.

"Now, now, you know our lives and how they are. I need for you to understand and trust that I will be along shortly. I very much appreciate you being willing to share your space with me. It is most kind and I will take you up on it, but I must try and make even a little tonight so that I might buy my bed back at the lodge. I feel certain that if I get back there before 3 o'clock and slip the deputy a bit, he shall do right by me come tomorrow night. Certainly you can appreciate this?"

The rain had slowed to nothing more than a slight drizzle when Mary Jane reluctantly nodded that she did indeed understand what her sister in trade was conveying to her. She, more so than most, knew all too well that life on the street was a life without mercy. It might well be true that on this night in particular she had a place to call home but it would not remain so if she could not soon make good on the back rent she owed. She had promised the landlord, Mr. McCarthy, she would have it by the first of the week and here it was Thursday night and she was still well shy of the amount owing. In addition to this, she had an outstanding fine, which she still had to reconcile with the courts for being drunk and disorderly in a public place a few weeks prior. Pondering her financial predicament, she suddenly felt that she too should do as Jacquelyn was doing and try her best to solicit some money despite the weather. It would be far better to at least make good on a portion of the rent due rather than continue to run the risk of being evicted the next time she happened to run into the landlord or one of his cronies.

"Alright then, but I warn ya, you best be careful, and take care not to be too long."

Mary Jane stepped out from beneath the shelter of the umbrella. Pushing the thoughts of working further that night from her mind, she pulled the collar of her coat up around her neck to ward off the chill night air and headed off alone. She had only gone a few feet when she stopped, turned and called back to her friend.

"I may do as you once I've warmed up a bit, else I might find myself housed at the jail tomorrow night for not having paid McCarthy his due. I shall leave the door unlatched for you should I not be home when you stop by."

Jacquelyn waved her acknowledgment, dispensing with any further communication and carried on in the opposite direction.

Standing in the dream-like state, Aremis found himself suddenly torn as to which person he should pursue. Almost before the decision had been consciously made he found himself once again quietly drifting along some fifty feet or so behind the woman he had come to know as Mary, silently hoping the other woman would find her way home in good order.

He began to close the distance between himself and his adversary when the darkness that cradled the image suddenly caved in, wiping it out completely. Momentarily shocked by the disappearance of something that had been so intensely real that it felt as though he had actually been a part of it rather than merely a spectator; he was completely oblivious to the man who was angrily addressing him from the doorway in which he had taken shelter. Not until he felt a heavy blow to his back, one of which was delivered with sufficient force to send him sprawling into the street, did he actually come to realize where he was and what was taking place.

Laying face down in the gutter, the full force of the storm pelting down on his already sodden clothing, he could hear the man cursing him and referring to him as a vagrant from someplace within the darkness of the night and his mind.

Momentarily confused and trying desperately to hold onto the fragmented images in an attempt to determine if what he had witnessed had been real, and in current time or was it something that had already taken place. His unresponsive reactions to the man's demands for him to move on brought the irritated homeowner out from the shelter of the covered stoop and down into the street whereby he delivered another severe kick into the side of the man he found hunkered down in his doorway.

"Get moving else I swear I'll wipe the street with yer face, you hear me?" the man shouted so as to make himself heard above the storm.

The painful kick that had been delivered effectively snuffed out any remaining imagery that had been left within the darkness, sending the tiny dots of light within his mind scattering like flecks of sand blown about the seaside on a blustery day.

Aremis let out a frustrated cry, pounding his clenched fist upon the cobblestone street. To be so close, to have the possibly of gaining the advantage over his enemy only to have it snatched away over something as petty as loitering enraged him.

Taking his single blow to the ground to be that of a threatening gesture, the man again ordered him to be on his way and was about to punctuate it with his boot when he suddenly had his feet swept out from beneath him as Aremis lashed out with his arm.

Taken completely off guard by the retaliation and the speed in which it was delivered, the man was helpless to do anything but fall backwards in an uncontrolled manner, striking his head on the stone surface of the street. Rendered unconscious by the impact, blood slowly running from his head and swept away with the torrent of rainwater that ran down the spaces in between the cobblestones, he lay unmoving in the middle of the street. Aremis knelt over his attacker to access his condition. Reasonably satisfied the man's injuries were not to be life ending in nature; he retrieved his hat and quickly made his way up Christian Street, leaving the man and his injuries to the storm.

Slipping his hand beneath his coat while stepping along smartly, he gently massaged his ribs where he had been kicked. He tried to recall some of the details that he had seen in his vision, with little, if any success. It was not until he had nearly reached the intersection of Christian Street and Commercial Road did the first detail at last reveal itself.

The Horn of Plenty was located at the corner of Crispin Streets and Dorset, more than a dozen blocks north-east of where he now stood. From what he could recall, Miller's Court was at the eastern end of Dorset on the north side of the street. The vision he had seen had the two women parting company and then going off in opposite directions, Jacquelyn heading off in a westerly direction, perhaps back to the public house or further west in search of someone more suitable to kill than the woman, Mary Jane, with whom she had been conversing.

Either way, he had to get to Dorset Street in short order. With thoughts of confronting his maker more than babysitting a prostitute, he thought it best to try and come up on Dorset from the west and run into her head on rather than take up a position of following.

With the hour now approaching half past two in the morning, he sprinted up Commercial Road towards Whitechapel Street, dashing across the all but empty thoroughfare. Continuing north at the same pace for several blocks, he did not slow down until he had reached Whites Row where he turned left onto the street and took up a pace more suited to that of a respectable walk than that of a hurried mad man.

Hardly winded by the run, he carefully took in his surroundings; mindful of every shrouded doorway or secluded alley he came upon. Making his way about the darkened streets for the better part off an hour, he searched every laneway and backyard, anything that had access to the roadway, all with the hope that he might find her. Unfortunately however, as it had been with all his past attempts at locating her, he was unsuccessful.

Frustrated and feeling that time had never been more of the essence than it was at that moment, he stood on the sidewalk outside Providence Row Convent. There, leaning against the wrought iron fencing, he stared at the public house that sat on the corner across from him, its detail obscured by a blanket of fog that had rolled in on the heels of the rain.

The Horn of Plenty did not appear to be especially busy this particular evening which was odd given the inclement weather conditions. Crossing Crispin Street, he made his way quickly to the front door. There, taking a last quick look about the fog shrouded street and upon seeing nothing unusual, he entered the establishment. Inside, out of the chilly night air, he slowly made his way around the dimly lit interior searching out the dark recesses in the hope of finding her tucked away somewhere within the gloom. His sudden appearance and agitated manner was beginning to attract unwanted attention from the few patrons who were quietly looking his way and whispering amongst themselves. With only a scattering of lodgings located on the second floor he abandoned his search, returning to the anonymity offered by the fog and the night.

Back on the street, essentially swallowed up by the fog, he pondered his next course of action in quiet isolation. He had already searched a small area just west of Crispin Street and had found not so much as a trace of her. Beginning to doubt what he had seen, but not willing to run the risk of abandoning his search based on that uncertainty, he began making his way east along Dorset. His plan now to find room number thirteen in Millers Court and wait for her there, this of course providing that both his vision was accurate and his adversary was true to her promise made.

The rain had once again begun to fall from a dark overcast sky as he approached the entranceway to the court. Still several yards from where the entrance let into the dank and secluded courtyard, he saw a couple enter Dorset Street from its easterly approach. Crossing the street almost immediately, they made their way slowly towards him, arm in arm laughing, and joking between themselves. It was obvious that the woman was quite the worse for the drink, so much so was her inebriation that it had become necessary for the man in her company to hold her in order to keep her from falling flat into the street.

He slowed his gait considerably, and as the couple drew nearer he could tell that the woman was, without a doubt, the same woman that he had seen with Jacquelyn. Her clothing was exactly the same as that which he had seen her in earlier. This observation lent credence to the possibility that his vision had indeed been seen in current time. Holding up on his progression altogether in order to see what might unfold between the couple, he took up a casual position in front of a door as though he were calling on someone residing within.

The pair arrived at the entrance to the court, apparently unaware or not bothered by the tall stranger standing not one hundred feet from them. There, they continued to chat and laugh quietly with one another. From his conspicuous vantage point he could clearly see the man who appeared to be about 35 years old, only about 5'6" tall and had a moustache. He wore a long dark coat and a hat that could have been made of felt or possibly velvet. His outer attire gave him the appearance of someone quite well off for both the neighbourhood and the hour.

Mary Jane began to look for something in her handbag then proclaimed that she had lost her handkerchief. The man chuckled at her drunken mannerisms and produced a red one from within his coat pocket and handed the silken hand cloth to her.

It was at that moment another man standing at the corner of Commercial Road and Dorset caught his attention. He was tall and partially concealed by both the building and the fog.

He took his eyes from the couple he had been observing to see if this man might pose a threat or could be in some way connected with the woman he was desperately seeking. It could easily stand to reason that she was working in conjunction with an accomplice. She had, after all, enlisted the help of the young boy, Timothy; in order to have her letter delivered to his flat without being intercepted herself. The police had also entertained the idea the Ripper was not working alone, and even some of the so-called eyewitness accounts spoke of two men having being seen scuffling with Stride near the entrance to Dutfield's Yard the night she was murdered.

But after several moments had passed, and without having noticed anything particularly strange about the man other than an unusual fascination with the couple standing near the entrance to Millers Court, he returned his attentions back to that of Mary Jane and her companion, occasionally casting a glance towards the stranger at the end of the street.

Mary Jane, obviously intent on getting her gentleman back to her room before he could possibly reconsider whatever might have been the terms of their agreement, looped her arm though his, pulling him towards the entrance to the court.

"Come on, you will be comfortable," she said, kissing his face and tugging at his arm. Finally consenting to his temptress, he gave in to her repeated requests and put-on affections, allowing himself to be pulled along behind her. The darkness of the tight entranceway swallowed them up, leaving no visible trace that any living person had been standing before it not a moment before.

The clock tower struck 3:00 a.m., and as it finished its final chime, the man on the corner began to cautiously walk up Dorset but only carried on with this action but a few yards before stopping and turning around. Crossing Dorset quickly he continued on to the opposite corner from the one he had been standing at and disappeared from view, heading north on Commercial Road.

With his secondary interest having moved on, and not sure whether his departure had been brought about by suddenly catching sight of a man watching his approach, Aremis again had to make a choice. Follow the stranger who may or may not be an accomplice in the Ripper murders or stick by his original plan and wait near Mary Jane's apartment.

He decided that it would be a better choice to stick it out at his current location rather than try and follow the stranger. If Mary Jane was to be the next victim then she was, for the moment at least, still alive and that was enough reason to remain close by.

Standing with his back pressed against the brick wall, occasionally peeking around the corner, he could make out the silhouette of the two people standing below the lone gas lamp which hung off the wall of the laneway just inside the court. Their bodies were so close to one another as to make their shape seem like that of a singular object rather than that made by two individuals.

In the dim yellow glow cast by the lamp he could see that they stood before a doorway, which lay in the east wall just beyond where the tunnel-like entrance opened up into the courtyard.

"No, we cannot, I have let my room out tonight," Mary Jane said in a hushed voice that, even though low in volume, still managed to echo off the surrounding walls.

The man whispered something into her ear the content of which sent her into a fit of laughter. She tried to slap the man's chest but in a fashion more belonging to that of playfulness than one born of anger or insult.

"I will have part in no such suggestion not even for twice the money, good sir," her words so slurred by the affects of the alcohol they were nearly incoherent. "But I know of a house at the end of the court which is empty. I have slipped the lock before and..." she trailed off into hushed whispers which he could no longer make out.

Whatever was said in those final whispered words must have agreed with her male companion, for he put his arm around her and together they disappeared from view, heading deeper into shadows of the courtyard.

The night had turned much colder than it had been earlier in the evening, and even though the rain still drizzled down through the fog, it was the stiff winds that made the damp chill in the air feel far worse than the temperature might have one believe. Waiting outside the entrance for several minutes to ensure those he had been observing would not return unexpectedly, he pulled his wet coat around himself and flipped the collar up against the inhospitable elements.

A brisk breeze blew down the tunnel from the court towards the street, caressing his face with the icy fingers of an approaching winter. The night's cold wind did not only deliver to him an icy shiver but something far more chilling than the temperature alone could instill. As the stiff breeze subsided, the forerunning gust having been spent, its force being followed up by softer curling currents, they brought with them the unmistakable scent of human blood.

He felt his body stiffen slightly as the scent penetrated his senses and told him without a word or a doubt that she was close by or, at the very least, the remnants of her handiwork most certainly were. He was about to investigate the source of the sweet aroma when he caught sight of a woman turning onto Dorset from the Commercial end of the block. Her head was down, her coat drawn up around her neck, held in place by her free hand in order to keep out the chill night air.

Not wishing to seem out of place or to rouse suspicion as to his loitering, he began to make his way slowly towards her, his hands buried in the pockets of his coat, his head mimicking hers in posture.

He felt her pass by more than he saw her, and when he could barely hear the fall of her shoes on the walk behind him he glanced backwards just in time to catch sight of her disappearing into the same entranceway he had just moments before been standing in front of.

He slowed his step slightly but continued in the same direction until he was certain the woman who had passed was not simply on an errand of sorts to be returning from whence she came in short order.

When he was about as certain as he could be that she was but a resident and not merely a visitor he quickly made his way back to the tunnel. There, with the briefest of visual inspections having been carried out, he ducked from the street into the tomb-like passageway. He darted through the blackness towards its end, past the side door of number 26 Dorset, to where the lone gas lamp illuminated the spot where he had seen Mary Jane and the unknown man standing but a few minutes earlier.

Inside the courtyard, free of the claustrophobic confines of the tunnel, the surroundings were not much better. The dirty brick walls having at one time been painted white in order to lend some light to the enclosed area did little in the way accomplishing the intended purpose, the darkness being only marginally brighter than it was in the enclosure of the passage which led into it.

Taking a deep breath in order to calm his nerves, he took in the length of the court to its end ensuring no one was out, as he felt his heart rate slowly returning to a calmed state within his chest. The scent of blood was still all around him, and with the wind constantly changing direction and velocity within the confines of the court; it was all but impossible for him to focus in on where exactly the source was coming from.

With his back to the outside wall of the building, he was about to weigh up his options when he became aware of a woman's voice softly singing from within the room that lay on the other side of the wall directly behind him. Turning slightly, ever vigilant of his surroundings, he quietly pressed his ear to the wall while not taking his eyes off the far end of the entrance that opened out onto Dorset.

The soft words being expressed in quiet song were muted, both by the singer's quiet voice as well as by the mortar and brick that made up the walls of the apartment. Even after several seconds it became apparent that he would not be able to distinguish either the song or the voice behind it. The last thing he could afford was to be mistaken in his assessment and burst into the room only to have his error in judgement punctuated with screams from a terrified young mother.

Choosing for the moment to stick with surveillance, he ducked past the single wooden door, its faded green paint having for the most part peeled and fallen away, and rounded the corner into the blind east end of the court. Taking stock of his new surroundings, he found himself beside a curtained window, a window from which no light could be seen, a window which also had one pane of glass broken from its frame. The missing pane of glass providing a means of escape for the quiet voice that lay beyond the paint-bare casing, the soft words slipping easily from within the darkened confines and into the court. It was at that moment he knew without a doubt that the person behind the sweet lullaby was that of his enemy.

Preparing for what could easily end up being his last moments on this earth, he said a silent prayer to a God he felt had abandoned him long ago. When he had finished, alone in the shadows, his canines grew long, their tips as sharp as any man-made blade, his eyes losing any trace of humanity, his final thoughts being that of his family and a life that had been so cruelly taken from him.

Pushing the comforting thoughts from his mind so that they would not cloud his judgment, he slipped back around the corner so that he stood squarely before the door that let in on the tiny room. The faded outline where the number 13 had, at one time been nailed was barely visible. Sizing up the exterior dimensions he took some solace that the space within those walls could not possibly contain more than a solitary room, which meant there would be no place to run, no other avenue for escape once he was inside.

Taking one last breath, he grabbed the handle of the door and then, in a violent rush, he threw it open. Bursting in on the room with such a force that the door crashed into something hard and then, like a rubber ball, bounced back, slamming shut again, leaving him inside and in total darkness.

Within the tiny domicile, he found himself in a room so dark that no one person would have been able to make out even the faintest of shapes, never mind being able to pick out any defined detail. But for him it was not the case for he was well suited for functioning within places that light refused to enter. He could see as though the room was filled with sunlight, the only thing abnormal being the total absence of colour.

Through this precisely defined world of black and white, the sights that assaulted his eyes were beyond belief. Like something from his worst nightmares, he stood looking across the tiny room at the body of a woman lying motionless on the bed, her entrails pulled out and dumped on the night table, the same table the door had in fact crashed into a moment earlier. Her breasts had been removed and her face was hacked beyond anything recognizable as being a human being.

Just beyond the gruesome discovery, standing between the bed that had been pulled out and the wall, was Jacquelyn, her eyes glowing red, the long steel blade still in her grasp.

"Well, my friend, Mary you most certainly are not," she said with much disappointment in her voice as she returned her attention back to the task of removing muscle and ligature from the bone of the woman's right thigh.

Completely taken back by her nonchalant statement and mannerisms within what was nothing short of a macabre setting, he shot back with something that he felt certain would get her attention.

"Neither are you," he said flatly.

"Oh, is that right?" she replied, an over exaggerated air of sarcasm in her voice at his brazen accusation, "And who exactly do you think me to be then?"

He had anticipated that her interest would most certainly be piqued, even if she had disguised it well within mocking sarcasm. He knew before even setting the bait that he had no intention of letting her in on how he had come to know the things he did and answered her inquiry with words and a tone that were as cutting as the edge of her knife.

"Perhaps you are not as clever as you would have fooled yourself into believing, Jacquelyn." His statement was cool and delivered with an unhurried confidence, placing emphasis on her name at the end.

She stopped her work for a moment, letting the neatly severed piece of meat fall away from the bone onto the blood soaked sheets between the dead woman's legs. She remained motionless for a few seconds, and then turned her head slowly to face him, her hair falling softly over one eye as she gave him an innocent smile, the like that one might expect to see on the face of a child.

"Well, are you not the clever one," she said softly. "You should go to work for the Commissioner. Seems not one of them under his charge presently can find their own cock with both hands and a mirror."

She laughed at her own analogy but was cut short by his sudden outburst.

"Enough!" he shouted, his words taking her by surprise and actually startling her slightly. "What in heaven's name is the matter with you? Have you taken leave of your senses?"

He waited but a moment before charging on with his verbal assault.

"Look at this place," his words only slightly diminished in volume from those of his previous statement. "Look at it!" he demanded.

She looked around, not sure what exactly she was supposed to be seeing that had him so agitated.

"Really, Aremis, there is no need for this level of conversation. People will still be sleeping."

Unable to comprehend that which she was saying in the light of what they were surrounded with, he rubbed his one eyebrow, trying to fathom her way of thinking.

"Are you telling me that you are actually concerned for those in neighbouring homes, that their sleep might be disturbed?"

She nodded, but said nothing more.

"And what of this grand mess you have created here? Do you not think that this might well disturb them once they find out what has taken place within their own backyard?"

Again only silence came to his query, his adversary only shrugging slightly in response.

"I can accept what I am, what you have made me into; that I must take human life in order to survive. But I do it quickly, and I take life from those who squander it, who bring misery onto others. I do not relish or take delight in what I must do, what I must do because of you, I simply do what I must."

A long silence followed his accusations and self-proclamations to the point he felt the room itself might very well explode from having to contain such wretched things within its walls.

During the deafening silence, he weighed up his next move. Not quite sure how to go about maintaining a conversation with an unstable, unpredictable predator, he knew it was a better option than that of a physical altercation in tight quarters; especially being surrounded on all sides by dwellings, all of which contained within their walls potential eye witnesses.

"You on the other hand," he finally continued, "you seem to find elation in the pain and suffering which you inflict on people, never mind the terror that you have instilled in this community. What has happened to your sense of decency? Surely to God you were not always as you are now. You, too, must have once been like I, human, with a family. Does not some of that which you were still exist within you?"

She snorted, then laughed, but it was anything but humorous.

"You are naïve," she said calmly. "You stand before me with this air of righteous arrogance when you yourself freely admit to killing men then justify it because of the way they lived out their lives. I could easily say the same."

She directed the point of her blood covered blade towards the corpse on the bed and continued.

"This woman lived her life selling her body for money. She, like all the whores in this wretched place you so quaintly refer to as a community, take for granted their so-called *God given right* to have children. They spread disease to the men that frequent them, who in turn take it home to their wives and infect them. These wretched creatures spread misery every time they open their filthy legs."

Like that of a mother displeased with her child, chastising him for some punitive wrong doing, she pointed the knife towards him, shaking it as though it were an extension of her own finger.

"And then, you have the gall to speak to me of God. Surely by now you must admit, if but only to yourself, that He cannot possibly exist."

She waited a moment to see if a response to her rebuttal would be forthcoming, and when only a continued silence ensued she continued.

"Where was God when I attacked you, mmm? She asked bluntly, "Where was the most merciful, the most powerful being in all the world when I was taken from my family, my life destroyed? Where was this magnificent loving God when I butchered my own family, and where is he now?"

She stood in the darkness, her arms stretched out to her sides in an appeal for a response or perhaps, at the very least, his understanding.

"I walk these roads and laneways, no different than any other street or passage I have travelled in any other town or village, preying on who I wish, when I wish, all without fear of an almighty God striking me down."

She let the once accusing knife point fall to her side and hung her head with a tired sigh escaping her lips.

"I had prayed to Him for so many years, first to cure me of my affliction, then later to end my life. I cried to Him, pleaded with Him, on my knees. I begged of Him, all of which went unanswered. How could a God, who I have been led to believe loves all of us so much, not help me in my plight? I had done nothing to bring about this which had been thrust upon me."

She raised her head, her flame red eyes burning into his.

"Do not speak to me of God and His divine existence. He is nothing more than a fantasy created by clever-minded men to control the masses and quell their fears by leading them to believe that things the likes of you and I do not exist."

Her point was well founded and he could find both truth as well as familiarity in all of what she had said. If not for the desecration of human life that surrounded him, and the ordeal she had put him through the last two months, he thought himself easily swayed to her way of thinking.

"You make valid points on all accounts, I will grant you that," he said, in a voice that now matched that of her own calm delivery. "But if you have issue with these women then end their life so that you may continue. Why go to such lengths? Why the need for such horrible mutilations? It is this action you have taken up that I do not understand."

Jacquelyn brought her leg up and set her foot upon the edge of the bed. She wiped the blood from the blade onto the sheets then hiking her skirt up, she tucked the weapon into the top of her boot.

As she let her foot back to the floor, straightening her skirt as she did so, she explained her actions in a manner completely removed from the well-spoken woman that had put forth such a remarkable argument against such damning accusations.

"Because it entertains me," she said flatly.

Shocked by the bluntness in which her answer was delivered as much as the answer itself, he stood astonished and in disbelief at what he had just heard.

"Entertains?" he replied, his voice again elevated.

"Shhhhh," Jacquelyn urged as she placed a bloody finger to her lips, a moment later bringing both hands together and placing them to the side of her head, shutting her eyes briefly, so as to give the appearance of someone sleeping.

"Yes, life can be so boring at times, would you not agree?" she said, opening her eyelids so the glowing red pools could once again be seen.

He shook his head slowly from side to side as he spoke.

"No, no, I would not agree. Life can be tedious at times, yes, for everyone, but to look on this," his hand passed before him in a sweeping arc that took in the contents of the room, "as a way of relieving that is nothing short of insanity."

"Ha," she snorted, blowing off his statement. "Talk to me in another two hundred years and we shall see if you still feel as you do at this moment."

Her words echoed though his mind, her offhanded statement hinting at measurement of time, one of which could not possibly be correct. A timeline that, by its very length, challenged both his beliefs as well as accepted rules governing all life. Left momentarily stunned by what he just heard, he tried to gage whether the words within her reply were nothing more than another ruse designed to confuse him, or was it her way of emphasizing her plight through exaggeration? He was prepared to accept either possibility, but if what she had said was even remotely true, then his idea of killing her may be far more difficult than anything he had considered, if it was possible at all.

The idea that someone could live for hundreds of years and yet still remain youthful was something that had fascinated mankind for as many centuries as time held record of. If he was now faced with the reality of a lifespan that would see him outliving his normal sum of mortal years, carrying on into the future some two hundred years, it would be prudent for him to understand as much as he could about what pitfalls lay in wait upon this uncharted path. This of course would only be possible from one who had, themselves, traveled such a road. Only by navigating its course could anyone ultimately know the answers. All of this being assumed that words expressed in idle threat were actually true.

With time still not his ally, he frantically pondered the situation and made one last mental observation. It had suddenly occurred to him that perhaps her mental instability could be a direct result of outliving one's own biological timeline. It was conceivable that even though she remained youthful in appearance that her mind had deteriorated, and thus produced such wild unpredictability within her. If this was to be the case then the prospect of living out beyond one's due time did not sit well with him. Of course the more obvious conclusion to any rational being evaluating such a situation would be that the idea of one living some two hundred years was the product, and not the cause, of her mental disorder.

The time was growing late and soon their escape, if there were to be one at all, would be effectively cut off by the arrival of daylight. Now was not the time for further debate, either within himself or between himself and his female counterpart.

"So then, what happens now?" he asked bluntly, breaking the deathly stillness that had, until then, enveloped the room.

"I am afraid I do not quite follow you..." she replied, folding her arms over her chest.

"In your note to me, you said that you would stop once I caught you. I seem to have discovered you, in the act, as it were, so I suppose I am asking if you intend to turn yourself over to police."

A failed attempt to stifle a giggle into silence quickly grew into a full out laugh as she leaned against the wall to steady herself.

"I cannot believe that you just asked that," she said, as she tried to compose herself.

Annoyed and feeling as though he had once again been played as the fool, he took a step towards her, his finger raised in accusation.

"You said you would not stop until I had found you. Well, I have found you, and you will stop this madness one way or another!" he demanded harshly.

Jacquelyn raised her hands up in a defensive posture, a wide smile still across her face.

"Now, now, no need for all of this," she said calmly, but with much mirth still in her voice. "You are most correct and I will stop with my game, you have my word on it. But as to your query regarding turning myself in, you were the one who found me, not them. The police did not win the game, so justly, they do not get the spoils."

"I could hold you here until the police arrive and then we could let them draw their own conclusions." he shot back angrily.

"Yes, let's do that, it sounds as though it might be jolly good fun." She said sarcastically, traces of her humorous outburst at his expense still very much present. "And what do you think they will do when they arrive?" she asked.

He did not have time to formulate an answer, much less actually annunciate one, before she provided what could very well end up being the truth if they were to let this stalemate play out beyond this time and place.

"The police already believe, without question, much to my annoyance I might add, that the person they are seeking in these murders is a man, and you, my dear sir, are most certainly a man. If you wish, we can do as you suggest and wait for the local constabulary to arrive. I can assure you they will take us both into custody. I can also assure you with equal confidence that I will be released in short order, whereas you will stand trial for these crimes, not forgetting the crime of murdering one of their own in a laneway not far from here."

She paused just long enough for what she had said to begin to take root before delivering the deciding blow.

"How long would you estimate that you could maintain this pleasant outwardly appearance of yours while locked in a jail cell? How long would it be before your need for blood consumed your thoughts to the point of insanity, driven to tear open the wrist that brings your meagre dinner plate, condemning yourself by your own actions to dance at the end of a hangman's rope?"

She paused and reflected, her hand brought to her face, her index finger tapping her lower lip in contemplation.

"Although, I am truly doubtful as to whether that would actually finish you off, it would be a situation that would prove to be most interesting upon them cutting you down, would you not agree?"

To agree or not was pointless for he knew she was most likely correct. Even if her scenario did not play out exactly as she had scripted it, the end result would be devastating, and most certainly life ending.

"Sadly, that which you state so bluntly, is probably all too accurate," he said holding back the contempt he had for her. "But to this game of ours, it has concluded then?"

She nodded, her eyes closed, her arms once again over her chest.

"And of this mess here, am I to understand we are to simply walk away from this?"

She opened her eyes abruptly, but otherwise remained unmoving.

"That is precisely what we are going to do, unless you wish to remain here by yourself. If not, however, I would humbly suggest that we make our way from here for it will soon be light."

He turned his attention towards the bigger of the two windows, which still gave no hint that the morning light would soon be upon them. Both windows looked out onto the blind alley, the same one he had only moments before been standing in. Its small area was surrounded on all sides by high brick walls that made the light at ground level dim at best. Unless it was close to the noon hour with a sky free from cloud, one would be hard pressed to see much, if any, sunlight, through either window, even with the curtains opened fully.

Within a relatively calm mind, he carefully plotted his next move, compiling all he had learned this night and combining the information with all the other encounters he had had with her, in person or through written contact.

He brought his hand to his chin and tugged at his short beard with his fingertips, then posed a question.

"So then, if I am the victor of this game, what are to be my spoils?"

"Your spoils?" she asked curiously. "I will not butcher another whore. I thought that was clear enough."

"Ah, I see. So my victory is a hollow one in as much as it nets me nothing of a personal nature? It would seem to me that you have had your *entertainment,* as you so put it. You have given you word that you will not take the life of another prostitute in Whitechapel, so in some way these unfortunate souls have become somewhat of a winner as well. It would seem that the only one who goes uncompensated for his efforts in this pastime of yours is I."

He turned to face her, his hand upon his chest, his fingers spread wide in a humble physical plea for her to see his point of view.

She paced a two-foot square at the foot of the bed, her one hand supporting her elbow while she ran her thumbnail around the point of her fang, while pondering that which he had presented. After several minutes of mindful contemplation, she turned to face him.

"You are correct. It is hardly just that you should receive nothing for having won my little challenge." she said, her voice somewhat sheepish. "What would you think is fair compensation, keeping in mind I shall not be turning myself in?"

He already knew exactly what he wanted, but stalled in his response, so as not to seem too eager or give the appearance that he had it planned all along.

"Fair enough then," he said. "What I want from you is information. I want to know everything you know, everything that you have experienced in as much detail as you care to offer up."

A sly smile crept across her face, one fang becoming more visible as the smile grew.

"My life story, then? Is that what you are requesting as your winnings?" She responded quietly.

"Yes, give that to me and I will feel adequately compensated."

He stood with his arms crossed over his chest in a stance that effectively cut off her access from the door.

He was prepared to fight and, if need be, die in the process in order to prevent her from walking out of this room. She was either going to agree to his terms or she would have to face a fight which would end in the death of one or both if she chose to do otherwise.

Not flinching a muscle, he stood his ground and awaited her response. After only a few seconds, seconds that felt more like hours, he finally received his answer.

"I am flattered and would be delighted to tell you of my life. I will grant you your just rewards."

He felt a trickle of sweat run down the centre of his back as her words settled into his mind, slowly defusing the coiled predator within. He was about to discuss how this transfer of information was to take place when she interjected with a verbal representation of the thoughts he himself had only just begun to contemplate.

"I doubt that we will have the sort of time required to carry out such an involved and long tale while here, though. I think it would be best if we took this elsewhere, unless you have an objection."

He shook his head slowly, indicating that he had no such disagreement with her suggestion of abandoning this room full of horror in order to fulfill her obligation to him in a place where time would not be such a factor.

"No, I have no objections. Do you have a place in mind?"

She shrugged slightly to his query suggesting at the same time that they could make their way to her flat located on Buckle Street, but a few minutes' walk from where they now were.

'Buckle Street' he thought to himself, suddenly recalling her note both to him and the one she had sent to the police where she stated that she would not stop until she was buckled. 'My god, it could she have simply been playing on words? Was she so bold or without fear as to have practically given her very location away?'

The more he thought about this, the more he was leaning towards the latter.

Still momentarily lost within his own thoughts, his focus turned to that of Sister Jillian and her words that had shown him the answers we seek are so often right before our eyes if we only choose to open them.

"Clever," he said quietly under his breath, the hushed words nothing more than the culmination of private thoughts never intended to be verbalized had, however, caught her attention just the same.

"What is?" she asked, her interest now piqued.

"Your clever use of words in the notes you had sent to me and the police."

Her face lit up like that of a child at Christmas.

"Do you think so, do you really think me clever?" she asked eagerly.

"It only stands to reason," he remarked casually, his hands out to his sides. "You all but gave your address away and it is only now that I come to understand it. I am convinced that this observation is only due to you having just told me of your lodgings. I strongly doubt I would have noticed it or discovered your whereabouts otherwise."

Jacquelyn clapped her hands quickly before her face, her excitement too large for her to contain.

"Marvellous! I am so pleased that you thought to share this with me. You are so very kind, truly you are."

Aremis forced a smile in support of her jubilance.

"It is the truth," he said solemnly while maintaining the false countenance upon his face.

Her own smile beamed while she twisted from side to side, her hands placed loosely behind her as she did so. It was something he had witnessed before, a long time ago now, on that first night outside the town hall where he had the greatest of misfortune in meeting her and thus setting into motion the whole series of unbelievable events that had led him down a nightmare-filled road to the place he now stood.

Feeling confident that he had won her over and that, at least for the moment, she posed no threat to his well-being; he thought it best to make the most of the delicate truce. Extending his hand towards her, speaking softly as he did so, he encouraged her to take what he had offered up.

"Come then, we should do as you suggest and make haste."

Momentarily suspicious, she cautiously hesitated but then took his hand, letting herself be drawn towards him until they were but inches from each other. Looking down at her face as it was turned up towards his, he watched her eyes slowly lose their scarlet hue, returning to their human characteristics.

She placed her free hand onto his chest then let her head come to rest on top of it, the damp fabric of his coat setting a cool sensation through her skin.

"You are soaked though," she said softly. "You must be chilled to the bone."

In spite of all his feelings regarding this vile creature now softly resting against his body, a hatred he had painstakingly polished over the years, he could not help at that moment but feel a fraction of comfort within her words and her touch.

"I find myself to be cold most days now. I cannot say in earnest that this damp that is upon me now is any worse than any other day, warm or otherwise," he replied quietly.

He felt her head moving up and down softly against his coat as she answered.

"I know. I do believe I despise the cold above all else. The only thing that seems to keep it from me is the blood, and then it is but for the shortest of time."

He had also discovered this through his early experiments, and it was as she stated: the warmth collected from another's life lost did not seem to last much beyond a day at best. For him to actually try and maintain his own body temperature as he remembered it to be would require him to kill more than once each day and that was something he was not prepared to do. But to the person now pressed against him, he felt certain it was easily within her ability and mindset.

"We must go," he whispered, gently rubbing her back in the hope of moving her into motion. "It will soon be light and with its arrival will come the people. We must make our way from this place."

Apparently not willing to heed his gentle warnings, he pulled back from her, leaving her momentarily out of balance. Quickly regaining her stability as well as her focus, she grabbed for something on or near the small night table where she had dumped the woman's entrails. Fishing around beneath the grotesque heap until finding that which was in search of, she held out her blood-covered hand, in between her fingers, a key.

"I think it best if we lock up before we leave," she said, any trace of the soft tender voice of but a moment earlier no longer evident. "I would feel dreadful if something were to go missing on account of my carelessness."

She giggled, then quickly covered her mouth, as if suddenly realizing that her humour might be in bad taste.

"That would be wise," he said, looking back over his shoulder, "not so much regarding the loss of property as affording us more time to distance ourselves from this place."

His words were so fluid, so relaxed, that he could have easily convinced himself that he had become a willing partner in this nightmare of hellish design and proportion.

She put the blood covered key into his hand, placing a small bloody kiss upon his cheek as she did so, happy that he was again in agreement with her suggestion.

Her lips stuck to his skin, the tacky blood momentarily acting like an adhesive before finally releasing its bond as she withdrew.

Touching his cheek with her sleeve, she carefully removed the sticky lips print from his face.

"Now that simply would not do now, would it?" she said as she inspected her handiwork.

"No I suppose that it would not." he replied, touching his own cheek and inspecting his fingers to ensure she had indeed removed all traces of bloody evidence.

He pulled the door open and took a quick look about the dark courtyard. Satisfied the area was void of inhabitants, he slipped from the apartment into what would soon be the dying last minutes of night. Following his lead, she quickly exited the room then waited by the wall while he pulled the door to, securing the lock fast with the key.

"There, it is done," he said, dropping the key into his pocket. "I will discard this on our way to your flat, once we are a safe distance from here."

He turned towards the arched entranceway and began to make his way along its length when he felt her take his arm, slipping hers neatly under his.

"We may as well look the part of a respected couple, or at the very least, a whore and her paying gentleman." she whispered.

He felt his legs grow weak beneath him, her words suddenly overriding the initial mental request to keep moving, replaced instead by a sickening feeling growing in the pit of his stomach. But just a he had done in the room, producing a smile when it was the farthest thing from his mind; he had to force his limbs forward. Even though it bothered him greatly to have her on his arm like she was, and yet there was another part that still held on to her words, a touch and a kiss upon his cheek, all given within a room ill suited for any such feeling to have ever come into existence.

Exiting the tunnel onto Dorset Street, the rain was still falling but with less force than it had been throughout the night. It was just then, as they rounded the corner onto the sidewalk, did they run into Mary Jane nearly bowling her over in the process.

"Mary Jane!" Jacquelyn exclaimed, as Aremis grabbed hold of the woman's coat in order save her from falling, "Are you all right?"

Mary Jane was far worse for wear due to her drinking, more so than she had been earlier in the evening, her words being all but incoherent. Despite this obvious impairment, she still managed to convey that she was indeed quite fine.

"I did as you, Jac, I found me a nice gentleman who paid me well, he did. Even bought me a drink when we was finished, a real gentleman he was."

Somewhat assured that she could stand on her own, Aremis released his hold of her as she showed the couple her earnings for the evening of illegal loving, a small handful of coins.

"Now I shall have my rent for last week and McCarthy can kiss my bottom, he can!"

Mary Jane patted her own bottom, emphasizing her wishes towards that of her landlord.

"That's wonderful Mary, good on you," Jacquelyn said hugging her tightly, ensuring her blood stained hands did not come into contact with Mary's coat.

For Aremis, this display of mutual friendship and even affection was something of an oddity to observe, to see the two women before him, in a warm embrace, one completely unaware of the other's intention to kill her but a few hours prior. He felt that had it not been for her good fortune in having gone out earlier in the evening she would, in all likelihood, be the one laying disembowelled in her own bed. That or there would have been two women found dead come the morning instead of only one.

"Did you take your gentleman to my room?" Mary Jane drunkenly asked, finally having taken notice of the man standing with her colleague, but quite unawares that that it was he who prevented her from stumbling to the sidewalk but a moment before.

Jacquelyn smiled and shook her head,

"No, I went there but the door was locked tight. I knocked several times, and then a woman who somewhat resembled you came to the door. She told me you had not returned and that you had offered her lodgings as well. I did not wish to intrude so I waited outside for a little while to see if you would be returning, but when you did not I went walking. I have only just met my man but a moment earlier and he has been kind enough to offer me lodgings until I can make my own way again."

Mary Jane slapped Aremis on the arm in a fashion that was often done between men for such things as congratulations and such, telling him as she did so that he was a kind man. After that she apologized to Jacquelyn for not having been there and on top of that neglecting to inform her of her roommate. She went on to explain at length, more than what would have been necessary for the situation and information, that she had taken in the female stranger a few days earlier in order to attempt to ease the dire rent situation.

"I wish I had a bit of good fortune come my way for I would most surely leave this place and this life behind me."

Jacquelyn gave her another hug and whispered into her ear.

"I know love, I know. But sometimes good fortune comes on the heels of misfortune and you must be able to distinguish when it is at your door, for it will only knock once and if you do not answer it will be lost forever."

Mary Jane looked at her friend bewildered by her odd statement.

"You do say some peculiar things, you do honestly, Jacqui."

"I know, but some of what I say has its foundation in truth. Opportunity takes on many faces. Do not be afraid of it."

"Yes, yes all right, opportunity and fortune, all right. I cannot think straight any longer, I must go to my bed." Mary Jane slurred as she pulled away from Jacquelyn and began to stagger down the dark tunnel towards her room, searching her bag for the key to her door.

"Should we not stop her?" Aremis asked urgently under his breath.

Jacquelyn re-established her hold of his arm and began to lead him off in the direction of Commercial Street.

"And tell her what?" she asked.

He thought for a moment as they continued to make their way towards the end of the street. It was a conundrum of grand proportions, for if they did warn her then there would be questions raised as to how they knew of the horror that lay in a room beyond a locked door. On the other hand if they did nothing, if they simply walked away as they were doing, then she would soon be greeted with a sight the likes of which no person should ever have to witness. He was about to suggest an alternative, that being the idea of having Mary Jane come with them or have her join them at the Horn of Plenty, but the plan would never get the opportunity to be put into action as a cry of murder echoed out from the passageway that led into Millers Court.

The couple stopped momentarily in anticipation of another cry or, worse yet, the sudden appearance of Mary Jane running from the scene. As they waited, however, neither event came into being, and the silence of another damp morning quickly overtook the area.

"She may have fainted," he said as they started off again.

"Possibly, or perhaps she saw an opportunity and held both her tongue and resolve."

"What are you going on about?" he asked, a trace of annoyance in his voice. "How can what lay in that room in any way be viewed as an opportunity?"

She did not answer his query straight away but continued along the sidewalk in an unhurried pace that did not lend itself to that of one who had just committed such a violation of human life.

"I suppose you would have to live her life in order to understand it," she said at last as they turned onto Commercial Street. "Mary Jane wanted a chance to leave this place, a chance to have a life far removed from the one she is now so hopelessly trapped in."

He pulled her to a complete stop as the first grey light of dawn began to be seen advancing from the eastern sky on the darkness that had blanketed the city.

"I still do not follow what it is that you are trying to say here."

She turned to face him making a brief indication with her finger in the direction from which they had just come from.

"That woman, the one I found in a room that was supposed to be empty, although you never saw her, she did, in fact, have an astonishing resemblance to Mary Jane. Now, granted, if the two were standing one beside the other then the differences would be obvious, but given the current situation I doubt that anyone would be able to perceive those differences now. They were about the same height and weight, and even had similar hair colour. If Mary Jane can keep her wits about her, then she may see the *opportunity* for escaping her landlord as well as her outstanding issues with the police and start anew someplace far from here."

The very idea that someone, a woman, of an age not much different than that of his own mother, was now standing in that room where he had been not fifteen minutes earlier, confronted with the horrors that lay contained within its four walls, brought forth feelings of which could have easily made him nauseous. Despite these feelings, he knew that there was nothing he could do to reverse what had already taken place. He could neither save the woman slain in a stranger's bed nor spare Mary Jane's eyes, which by now had most certainly been visually assaulted by the revulsion within her own home, quite possibly scarring the woman for life. There was little else left to do except ensure his own existence by taking the advice of a merciless killer and simply walk away.

He held out his arm and silently encouraged Jacquelyn to take it. When she had, the couple continued on their way as though nothing was more out of the ordinary that damp morning than the impending daybreak.

The walk from Millers Court to her humble place of residence, situated in a line of row housing on the north side of Buckle Street, was uneventful and they made the short journey in good time as well as in complete silence.

Releasing her loose hold on his arm, she began to ascend the stone stairs towards the front door when she realised that he was not following her. Stopping her advancement, she turned slightly to see what might be holding him up.

"Are you going to come upstairs or would you prefer to remain out on the roadway?" she asked somewhat playfully.

He looked away, towards a small lane; the only exit letting out onto Commercial Street.

"This is where you live?" he asked as he took in the street and the dwellings that lined it, all the while thinking to himself that he had walked past this street and house many a night and never knew that which he so desperately sought was in the very house he now stood before.

"Yes," she replied. "Is there something the matter?"

He shook his head. "No, not really." Then, after a slight pause, he carried on. "Well, actually yes, yes there is."

He turned his attention from his survey of the street and focussed it towards the staircase where she was standing,

"Why should I trust you?" he asked bluntly as he stared up at her.

Jacquelyn shrugged her shoulders slightly and made an odd face at his query.

"I give in, why?" she replied quietly.

Frustrated by her yet another flippant answer, he hopped up the few steps so that he was standing beside her.

"Do not play the fool with me," he said angrily, as he took hold of her coat sleeve at the shoulder. "I am through with playing games with you. Do you understand me?"

He shook her slightly as he punctuated his final words to her.

She slapped his hand free of her coat with a casual but forceful backhand, straightening her coat where he had bunched it up.

"I have no idea what you are going on about. How can you trust me? How can I trust you?" she shot back, her harsh reply taking him by surprise. "It is I that should be wary of you, not the other way around."

She narrowed her gaze placing her hands squarely on her hips. "I am quite certain that you have more than entertained the thought of ending my life many times over, just as I had done with the one who..." she trailed off rather abruptly, quickly looking away. Then, without warning, she turned and continued up the steps to the front door, not bothering to finish her address to him.

Left on the steps, his thoughts free to wander, he watched as she fumbled through her bag while he weighed up what she had just said, and more so, to what she had deliberately chosen not to. His mind was suddenly filled with questions, one upon the other, so fast that he barely had time to ponder the answer before the next question was already upon him. Did her sudden end to an otherwise powerful statement come at the hand of some long departed ghost, one she may have dispatched from this life? Had she been created as he had been, or was she born that way, a victim of some sort of terrifying deformity? If she had met a creature such as he had done in meeting her, did she actually succeed in killing the one who had made her into what she now was? And if she did manage to end the life of such a being, then he most definitely wanted to know how she accomplished such a feat. These questions and the like quickly filled his mind, gradually shutting out the world around him, including the woman standing not more than a few feet away.

The morning had taken back the skies from the fleeing spectre of night, and although drizzle and heavy cloud cover obliterated the sun's rays from actually reaching the ground, daylight was well upon the city. He knew that with its arrival it would not be long before the police would be at Millers Court, if they were not there already, and would subsequently be out canvassing anyone on the streets for information regarding what would soon be reported as the latest Ripper killing.

Her brief search within her handbag at last yielding success, she produced that which had momentarily eluded her and she pushed her prize, a rusted iron key, into the tarnished brass lock of the door. The latch reluctantly opened with a loud clack, and she pushed the heavy door inwards until it was open only enough to allow her access. Standing in the narrow opening that separated the light of a new day from the dim interior of an old household, her dark shape was all but lost in the background of the gloomy interior.

Her voice broke into his thoughts, scattering them like autumn leaves blown about by the early winds of winter.

"Would you care to come in, or would you prefer someone more suited to your level of trusting?" she asked, her voice so void of emotion that it could have belonged to death itself.

The silent stalemate stretched out over some fifteen feet of shoe-worn steps before he took up the offer in earnest and ascended the remaining few steps until he was standing directly before her. Almost face to face, her shorter stance having been made equal by the height difference between that of the landing and the threshold she was standing upon, he took in her features from a new perspective. Her light brown hair pulled back and tucked up under her hat, her soft green eyes set in pale silken skin, well-defined cheekbones above her jaw-line that curved to frame her mouth, lips smooth and sensual. It was all he could do to cling to the fact that she was a ruthless, unpredictable killer and not some unfortunate by-product of a society that was seeing hard economic times fall upon the lower working class.

"No, I would prefer no other such company," he began softly. "I confess to being overwhelmed by all that I have seen, all that I have done. It disturbs me so, fills my mind until I cannot think straight."

She readjusted her weight to better hold the door open as she nodded, her lips pressed tightly together as she reached out to touch his shoulder.

"It would appear that the rain is not about to be letting up anytime soon," she said, in an attempt to ease some of the weight within his mind. "I think that it might be prudent for us to remain indoors for the remainder of the day, until the rains have passed."

She stepped back and held the door open so he could enter.

Feeling as though he was entering the living room of the Devil himself, or at the very least one owned by his daughter, he with reluctance in his mind and a heavy step took up her offer and passed though the doorway.

Inside, the hallway that led to the back of the house was dark and narrow, while an equally narrow and somewhat precarious staircase climbed the wall leading up through the darkness to the second floor.

She closed the door and latched it tight before slipping past him in the tight confines offered by the home's main thoroughfare.

"Come on then," she said, holding up her long skirts as she began to make her way up the gloomy staircase. "My room is on the second floor at the front."

He followed her lead up the stairs and along the hallway that separated the second floor rooms from the dilapidated banister, its obvious disrepair most surely affecting its ability to support anyone who might, by chance or need, lean against it.

Passing two doors and another staircase that led up even higher to a third floor, they arrived at the last door, set directly at the end of the hallway.

"It's not much really, but then I do not require much," she said as she entered the flat, its interior as dark and unwelcoming as the rest of the house.

The one-room flat was furnished in much the same fashion as his place of residence, with the furnishings being both sparse and well worn. The two small windows situated directly opposite the door were covered with thin lace curtains, a fabric that, by its very appearance, had seen better days.

In addition to the standard items one might expect to find in such a room, a table with chairs, and a bed with a night table, there was also was a large wooden wardrobe standing against one wall, its hinged doors long having been removed, leaving her meagre belongings on display inside what once might well have been an ornate cabinet in its day.

Warmth from a small coal stove, which stood in the corner, could still be felt even from across the room. On the floor lay a round rug, most of its decorative fringe gone. Its once vibrant pattern woven in various shades of green over a white background was now mostly hidden by the room's furnishing, anything still visible was soiled into a uniform grey, its former beauty lost through the years of wear and neglect.

The only thing in the way of nonessential items was that of a borderless oval mirror that hung on the wall overlooking the table, most of its silver backing having come off the top and bottom edges giving it a look of glass frosted by winter's icy touch.

"Please, come in. Make yourself at home." she said, as she set her handbag down onto the table. "Would you like a cup of tea? I have no milk but I do have a little sugar if you fancy it sweeter."

The way in which she spoke and acted had him fighting to keep what had just happened, not much more than an hour ago and less than mile away, at the forefront of his mind. As he watched her go about her business within her familiar surroundings, she looked like any average woman, coming from meagre means, having returned home from an evening of respectable work, and yet he knew she was anything but that.

She opened the door to the stove and carefully placed a small lump of coal into the red embers, stirring it slightly with the poker to ensure it would catch.

"Tea?" she asked again as she closed the door and stood up.

Her words, reiterated, snapped him from his mindless observations and attentive thoughts.

"Ah, no, no thank you. I am quite fine for the moment."

She smiled and brushed past him, closing the door that led to the hallway but not latching it.

"Here, let me have your coat. I shall hang it to dry." she said, as she stood behind him with her hands at his shoulders, gently lifting the water-laden garment from him.

Initially not wanting to give up his protective outer shell, he quickly relented and let her slip it from him. He watched over his shoulder as she placed it on one of two hooks that were attached to the back of the flat's door.

"What of your work?" she asked as she picked up her umbrella and placed it inside the wardrobe. "Are you not supposed to be working today?"

"No, I gave notice last week." he replied.

"Oh really. Why did you do that? Were they not treating you well?" she asked, looking momentarily concerned for his well-being.

"No, it was nothing like that," he began but elected not to finish.

"Oh? What was it then?" she continued as she placed a small amount of water in the tin kettle then set it on top of the stove to warm.

He let out a long sigh before he responded to her.

"I resigned my position because I needed to devote more time to the task of finding you."

His words had her turn from the stove, her hands raised in prayer-like fashion pressed against her lips. She remained like that, motionless, her eyes wide and not blinking as she stared in his direction.

"I am so terribly sorry that you had to do that because of me," she said at last, her words somewhat muffled by her hands that were still over her lips. "I had no idea..."

Her apology was cut off by his casual wave and calm words that accompanied it.

"Please, there is no need. It is done. I have changed homes and employers so many times over the years it feels odd to remain at one place for more than a few months."

Her concern amused him, in a macabre sort of way. Aremis was fascinated by the idea that she would be so worried about something as trivial as his employment and yet did not exhibit even the slightest concern or remorse about what she had done over the last two months.

"What will you do now?" she asked, her hands lowered slightly, her fingertips resting against her chin.

He tilted his head slightly in contemplation, pushing his lips out slightly until he looked as though he might be pouting.

"Well, I suppose that would depend on you. You have promised to tell me of your life and I wish to hear of it. Beyond that I have no specific plans, at least not at present."

"I see," she said in a subdued voice, as she turned her attentions back to the stove. "Well, I have indeed promised to tell you of my life and I assure you that I will make good on that promise. Mother is always reminding me of the importance of keeping one's word."

"Your mother?" he asked with some confusion in his voice.

"Yes," she replied, "she is always on me about things like that, anyone overhearing her would think I was still a child."

She removed the kettle from the stove and set it on the small iron trivet in the middle of the table, the water having not yet boiled or even warmed sufficiently to wash with.

"Do you no longer wish to have tea?" he asked, still somewhat puzzled by her last statement as he watched her cross the floor and sat upon the edge of the bed.

She shook her head but said nothing to his query, obviously still bothered about the circumstances that had forced him to give up his source of income.

Her mannerisms and posture took him back to times he had spent with Temperance when she would sit in a similar fashion after having had some disagreement with their mother over something-or-other that, in the end, would turn out to be quite trivial. Even though he had seen for himself, first hand, the trickery that the person who now sat before him was capable of, he felt that, in this instance, what he was witnessing was indeed genuine.

He went over to where she was seated and sat down beside her, his hands set squarely on his knees. His mind taken back to the laneway in which some time back she had stated, with conviction, that she had killed both her mother and father. Again, he was faced with having to sort out what was real, real in her mind, and what was complete fiction. Not wishing to upset the delicate balance within the new liaison, he decided to simply follow her lead.

"Do you still speak with your mother?" he asked, trying to draw her into conversation in the hopes it might lift the mood.

She nodded slightly, following it up with a verbal response.

"Yes, sometimes, but she is far away from here."

Her words were still solemn and quiet.

"So then do you write to her whilst you are away?"

She gently shook her head, her hair falling over her face. "No, my mum cannot read and father is always working. He can read a little if he tries, but he is always too busy for it. I visit with them when I can, with mum mostly. I talk with her then."

Aremis nodded but did not reply. The room falling silent, the only sounds being that of the world which lay beyond the tattered lace window coverings, muted and dissimilar noises mixed with one another, rising from the street below as it slowly came to life with people either on their way to or returning home from work.

Beyond the statement she had made in the lane, her response was still interesting but from another point of view entirely. The sarcastic rebuttal she had made when they were both in Mary Jane's room, one that alluded to her being far older than she appeared, if it were true, it would dictate that her mother to be even older. Not able to trust her, and unable to imagine the idea of being so aged while remaining so youthful looking, he found it far easier to accept the idea that everything she was saying was simply fabricated. Although it was easier, by far, to accept they were nothing more than stories, it did have him beginning to question the reasons behind why he was seeking answers from someone such as her.

Jacquelyn stood up slowly and made her way to the wardrobe, unbuttoning her black dress as she did so. With the dress partially undone she bent down and released the laces to her boots, pulling the knife out as she did, laying it on the floor of the dressing closet. Removing her boots, she set them carefully over top of the weapon so as to conceal it from view. Peeling the dress from her shoulders she let it fall from her body, the garment piling up on the floor around her ankles, whereby she stepped out of it, shaking its clingy grip from her feet. She plucked a hanger from within the cabinet, then retrieved the dress from the floor, placing it on the hanger and setting it onto the wooden rod that ran between the two walls of the wardrobe.

"I am so tired." she said in a sleepy voice, as she ran her blood-stained fingers through her hair whilst making her way back to the bed and taking up on the spot where she had previously been sitting.

As she passed by, he could see her cream-coloured chemise, its original colour almost secondary now, overpowered by the bolder stains of blood, heavy in the front and covered in spatter just about every place else. It looked as though the dainty undergarment should have belonged to a butcher and not that of a lady. Looking from the corner of his eye, he could easily see that some of the staining was old while other areas were still wet, most certainly a result of her actions earlier that night. There could be little doubt that if her underlay looked as it did then the dress she had just put away would be equally coloured. In fact, he felt that, if not for the dark shade, the amount of blood that would be visible on the fabric would surely have caught the attention of someone before now.

He had learned early on how to best avoid being covered in blood during an attack, but it seemed by what he was witnessing that she either did not employ a similar method or she simply did not care whether she wore her victims' blood upon her clothing.

Not wishing to discuss the state of her delicate attire, or have the room fall into another awkward silence, he was about to inquire as to how long she had been in London when his thoughts were interrupted, not by words, but movement.

Jacquelyn slid herself along the bed towards the headboard and pulled her legs up so that they were on the bed, her bare feet pressed against his thigh, the flimsy bloodstained undergarment having risen up exposing her thighs, as well as a portion of her bottom.

Feeling immediately uncomfortable, he removed himself from the bed and went over the table where he pulled out one of the chairs to sit on.

He watched her through a series of uncomfortable sideways glances as she stretched out, fidgeting on the bed in an attempt to find a comfortable position. The whole thing, beyond the obvious fact that she was a cold-blooded murderer, was quite disconcerting, for he had never been in the company of a woman beyond that of his family and never in such circumstances. If this had been any other woman he would have simply left, returning later once she had awoken. But he was not about to run the risk of losing her again, not after so much human suffering.

He tried to make himself comfortable in the straight back chair, using the table as a support for his arm, which in turn supported his head. Although, he too, was feeling more the worse the wear from lack of sleep, he refused to give into its demands. He had gone without sufficient sleep many times over the last two months, and today was simply going to have to be another one of those days.

He was just beginning to formulate the first of many questions he wanted to ask her, when she stirred. Her voice lost somewhere between the realm of sleep and that of the waking world.

"So cold..." she murmured, pulling her thin covering down over her legs.

A shiver ran over her skin and shook her shoulders slightly, but she seemed to be unaware of it as her breathing settled back into a rhythmic rise and fall. A second unconscious wave shuddered though her lower limbs, and she drew them up close to her chest, also completely unaware that she had done so.

Looking about the room, its interior bathed in the dismal light of an overcast morning, he spied a blanket tucked away above the wardrobe. With as much stealth as he could manage, he quietly crept across the floor, the old wooden boards doing nothing to aid in his plan, and retrieved the heavy woollen bed covering from its hiding place. Unfolding it, he gently laid it over her, turning down the leading edge so that it covered her shoulders but did not touch her face. Carefully, he tucked her feet in then turned away, intent on making his way back to the chair when he heard her voice soft and low from behind him, her words stopping him cold in his tracks.

"Lie with me..."

He could barely comprehend his most recent actions, having just tucked into bed, the individual responsible for what could easily be described as the worst string of murders in the history of London and quite possibly the modern world. To now have that same person make such a request of him was utterly inconceivable.

"I think it would be best if I remain in the chair..." he began, with no real idea how to finish that which he had started.

"Please," she pleaded, her voice gentle and meek. "I have been alone for so long, both night and day, for so many years. Is it too much to ask that you hold me for a little while?"

"I am not sure that would be wise." he stated, his voice firm.

"Please, am I so horrid?"

In truth, he knew that she was, but then he was as well. If he were to be honest with himself, there was precious little that separated them one from another, and in the eyes of any court of law, the two would be charged equally for the atrocities they had committed. More importantly, however, was the truth no one could possibly know or he himself could easily deny, and that was that he felt as she: that on many a lonely night he also longed for someone to lie with. Often he had thought of what it might be like to be with another, to be loved, but not as a mother loves her child or the way in which siblings care for each other but to be cherished and loved in an intimate way, to express affection through physical contact. He had all but lost hope in ever knowing of such things.

Now, in this room, all of which he had given up on, and yet at some deep human level still craved, was offered up to him by one who lay before him. Most beautiful to look upon, while at the same time being someone for whom he had held nothing but contempt.

In the seconds that ensued, he entertained the idea that the whole thing might be nothing more than enticing bait to a deadly trap whereby, if he agreed and took up beside her, she would simply end his life at the first opportunity. A notion that would have set fear into the heart of many a man only served to calm him further. For although it was true that he craved the touch of another, it was also true that he yearned for death with just as much passion. To be free of this life and all that he had done would be as welcome as being normal again.

He sat on the chair and removed his boots and shirt, setting them near the stove so that they might dry. Staring back at her across the small space within the tiny apartment, her green eyes barely visible through heavy eyelids, he weighed his choices one last time. Then, without further deliberation, he crossed the floor and stood by the bed.

She slid over towards the wall, then held up a corner of the blanket for him.

Taking it from her, he slipped beneath it, settling down on his back beside her.

The two lay there quiet and still, the sounds of city life outside filling their ears for several minutes before he felt her move slightly beside him. A moment later her cool hand lighted upon his chest, then moved to his arm. She took hold of it gently and encouraged him with a gentle upward pull to move it. When he did, she slid beneath it, placing her head on his chest, letting his arm fall down around her shoulders.

"Thank you." she whispered and kissed his chest.

He listened to her breathing, the ebb and fall of her breath growing more regulated as her subconscious mind took over the matter of her well-being as she slept.

Even though he had wanted her dead for years, and had even fantasized about doing the grim deed himself, he could not refute that at that moment he was glad he had not been afforded the opportunity to put his dark dream of retribution into reality.

Chapter 18

Dear Diary,

It is almost Christmas Day and everything here is wonderful. John had found us a lovely tree and had secretly brought it into the house two mornings ago. He had brought the decorations down and had it looking beautiful before I even awoke. It was a lovely surprise. It will be our son Matthew's first Christmas, a joyous occasion to be certain. Father has come to spend a few days with us, and having him around the house has done us both good. Iris is to come by on Christmas Day and I can hardly wait. It almost feels like days so long ago now when we were all a family, whole and together under one roof.

It has been snowing more than it has in the past few years, and the landscape around our little village looks as though it has been covered in sugar. The fields and rooftops sparkle in the light of day, while at night the moon's soft light reflecting off the snow covered ground would have me believe it is day and not night.

I have not heard word from Aremis since his last letter to me asking about my other sight, and I must confess to still being very much fearful regarding his well-being. Even Father asks if I have received word as to whether he will be joining us for the holidays, and for Father to be asking is something indeed. For him to make such inquiries of me I have only to assume that he, too, has not had word from his only son.

The sudden end to the string horrific murders that had besieged London throughout the late summer and into autumn has compounded my fear further that something terrible must have happened. The newspapers, once full of the horrors, now carry only occasional reports which, in many cases, are very much conflicting. Reading one report might have you believe that the police are baffled, both by the murders themselves as well as with their sudden end, whilst another would tell of the police having apprehended a man and questioning him in connection with the murders. What the truth might be is unclear at this point, but what is certain is the case or cases, remain open still.

I will say truthfully that I am relieved that the killings have come to an end no matter the reasons why, but I would be a fool if the thought did not cross my mind that either Aremis made good on his promise to stop the person responsible or, the harsher of realities, he had been keeping the truth from me all this time, that he was, in fact, the architect behind these terrible crimes and is now in custody or has himself been killed. I had witnessed first hand the end result of what he was capable of in the woodland of our family home, and all whilst seemingly unawares of his own actions. Perhaps he carried out such things in London in a similar fashion, oblivious to all that he was doing, a terrible monster hidden away inside a man.

I will hold out hope that he is not as I imagine him to be, and if he has been taken by death's cold hand then I pray that God can find it in His mercy to forgive him for the things he may have done while condemned by this affliction.

Temperance, the 22ⁿᵈ of December in the year of our Lord, 1888.

The weeks that followed the grim discovery of his adversary in the throes of her latest killing, a finding which had effectively put an end to a murderous streak that had become known, perhaps the world over, as the killings committed by one mad-man calling himself Jack the Ripper, had passed quickly.

It would seem from her conspicuous absence that Mary Jane Kelly had made good on the grim opportunity fate had presented her, for she had disappeared sometime that same morning and had not been heard from since. Even though there had been two eyewitnesses who had come forward to swear to having seen Kelly on the morning the mutilated body was discovered in her tiny room, both accounts were quickly discounted. The police had already been given a positive identification that the body that lay butchered in the blood-soaked bed was indeed that of Miss Kelly. This identification having been provided by the landlord, Mr. John McCarthy and Mr. Joseph Barnett, the man with whom Kelly, on occasion, resided with.

As it was told to the police, Thomas Bowyer, McCarthy's assistant, had gone to Kelly's apartment that morning in order to collect the back rent. After receiving no response to his knocking, he had gone to the side window where he managed to move the curtain aside by putting his hand through the broken pane of glass in the window. It was at this point he saw the body. He informed McCarthy who ran to the police station on Commercial Road and reported the finding to Inspector Walter Beck who returned to the room with McCarthy.

Unable to unlock the door, it was several hours before Police Superintendent Arnold arrived and ordered McCarthy to break down the door. Although the men at the scene that morning had all seen the body from within the room, the official record would state that identification was accomplished by looking through a window while a police constable, inside, pulled back the curtain. This report also concluded that both men, McCarthy first and Barnett some time later that day, were able to make a positive identification despite the horrific wounds inflicted to the woman's face, wounds that had effectively removed any recognizable features. The main factors in establishing that the body in the bed was actually Kelly were the length and colour of the woman's hair, which matched that of Kelly, and clothing, identified as being Kelly's, found neatly folded on a chair. Officially, no one other than the police and the medical examiner had been allowed to see the body or the room in which it had been discovered.

Without further credible evidence to support that the body found in room 13 was not that of Kelly, and since no one had reported another woman matching the description of Kelly missing, the true identity of the woman would not likely come to light.

The body bearing Kelly's name was taken from the coroner's office on November 19th and buried in a public grave at St. Patrick's Roman Catholic Cemetery, Langthorne Road, Leytonstone.

During this time, Jacquelyn had made good on her promise, providing Aremis his reward for having beat her at her own game. She told him at length of her life, from as early as she could remember. The days and nights quickly began to accumulate as the stories and accounts continued in a vivid living history. Conversations, mostly one sided, sometimes shared over a cup of tea or on other occasions while out walking. The tales beginning from a time when she was a little girl, a time before her life had been stolen from her, carrying on through the years into decades then, unbelievably, into centuries. So detailed were her accounts, so dramatic were the images she spoke of, that it was all but impossible not to believe that which she was conveying could be anything but the truth.

Aremis had retained his small room at the back of the house on Fowler and Dean but was rarely seen there, choosing instead to remain with Jacquelyn in her apartment on the second floor in a run-down house on Buckle Street. He had given his landlord December's rent in full, telling him that he was going home to see his family for Christmas but would see him upon his return in the New Year. He thought it best to keep Jacquelyn distanced from his life, especially from those who knew him. There was no reason to expose them to the risk, nor did he wish to be presented with uncomfortable questions pertaining to her sudden appearance, and quite possibly a similar disappearance should he be forced to take lethal action against her.

Life for the couple, most unlikely to be such, carried on in ways that for anyone looking in on the world they portrayed would see nothing more than a life that was predictably normal. Aremis had once again found work, putting in hours at the convent on Crispin Street, doing an assortment of odd jobs that ranged from night watchman to custodian. Jacquelyn had sworn off prostitution and had managed to acquire a position in an upper class home tending the domestic needs of Mr. and Mrs. Abbott, a well-off elderly couple on the more respectable Upper East Side. The work was easy and the pay was more than fair for what was asked of her. Aremis had cautioned her on several occasions that if she gave in to her desires and murdered this couple, there would most certainly be an investigation, one that would surely find her a suspect of notable interest. Even though his warning carried with it substantial weight, he never could rest easy when he knew that she was at the Abbott's home.

During their hours when they were not working they would spend time much as any other couple might do, walking together to the market in order to fetch a few groceries, or meandering along the streets, providing the day permitted such a stroll without the need of numerous layers of clothing to ward off the bitter chill of an unusually cold winter. Although quite normal in both daytime appearance and activity, it was at night, during the hours in which most of the city slept, leaving the streets to the vermin of society, would their activity, if viewed, be seen as something entirely unnatural and completely unholy.

Walking the quiet back streets together, predators of humanity, one for survival, the other for sport, conversations conceived in civility would quickly break down into conflicting points of view.

Many an evening Aremis would argue with her, sometimes right through until daybreak, attempting to have her understand that there was little purpose beyond that of her own selfishness, to kill as often as she desired to. Using himself as the example, he tried to convince her that she could learn to live as he had done, taking only what she needed to survive, to prey on only those who would not be missed by an untimely death, but it was difficult task at best. By early December, however, he had grown cautiously optimistic that he was actually making some progress, and together they remained vigilant, committed to the task, as she kept track of how long she could go without the hunger returning. The best she had managed was a full five days without her physical appearance showing any signs of change. The mental and emotional symptoms, however, were harder for her to control, and more difficult for him to help her overcome. She would often complain of feeling chilled to the bone, pleading with him at length to join her in the streets so that she might find warmth in another's lifeblood. His understanding and sympathies were often insufficient to keep her at home and he would, on occasion, hear the latch of her door as she crept out to find that which she could not be without.

During these nights, he would lay awake and wonder if she would return home, having instead met her demise or simply grown tired of trying to learn a new way of being. There was no denying that he had feelings for her, even though he knew well all that she had done and, despite his best efforts, he found himself entertaining thoughts of a relationship lasting longer than a few weeks.

However, dreams that are born of one person's ideal are not always shared by two, and on a night but three days before Christmas did she go off into the night. As it had been during their short time within each other's company he heard her get up, dress quietly, then slip the latch, her footfall vanishing, swallowed up by the darkness as she made her way down the stairs and onto the street.

The following morning when she did not return he told himself that she was late, that perhaps she had wandered farther than was her norm to do. But as the hours slowly wore on and morning became afternoon, he had taken to the streets in search of her. By nightfall he had not found even a single trace of her, nor had he heard word of her handiwork. He had gone to all the known establishments, as well as a few that were not so well frequented, all in the hope of finding her, but his efforts went unrewarded. Discouraged and growing fearful, he was forced to remember a time only a month previously when he had looked for her without success, consumed with the thoughts of killing her. It seemed ironic to now be searching for the same person, his thoughts, not of death but preoccupied with the hope she would be found alive. But as the hour grew late, his memory of weeks of futile searching playing on his mind he came to realize that if she was indeed alive and did not wish to be found then he had little hope of locating her.

He remained in her room for nearly a month into the New Year, a small present that he had bought her for Christmas sat unopened upon the table. Numerous notes lay piled one on top of the other, all of which stating his whereabouts should she return whilst he was away, all of which remained unanswered.

He had been back to pay his rent as well as to collect mail, mostly letters from his sister Temperance, all filled with worry and dread for his well-being. Reading them one afternoon as he walked back to Buckle Street, he felt a horrible sense of guilt for having not written, but it paled in comparison to the loss he was feeling within himself. It was difficult to understand, to experience a feeling of pain and loss pertaining to someone who had once taken from him everything he had ever loved or cared about. There was a time, not that long ago, when this would have been inconceivable and yet the fact remained.

He had ensured her rent up to and including the month of March, but had abandoned his stay there towards the later days of January, returning to his own tiny flat at Flower and Dean.

In the later days of April 1889, some four months after he had last seen Jacquelyn, the district of Whitechapel was again rocked when the bodies of two prostitutes were discovered. Both had been brutally murdered and mutilated, one so badly that only her torso remained, the limbs and head were never found. The police were quick to discount any rumours that Jack the Ripper had struck again, instead calling the murders nothing more than duplicate killings done in order to divert their attentions away from the search for the real killer.

It seemed like a foolish reason to most who heard it. Why would someone other than Jack the Ripper kill two women in order to draw the attention of the police investigators away from Jack while at the same time putting themselves at risk? Very few people were subscribing to the theory being offered up, instead remaining steadfast that Jack had returned.

When the news of the murders had surfaced, Aremis found himself, like those of his neighbours, seriously considering whether Jac had in fact returned to her old ways. Those thoughts, however, would be vanquished on April 29th that same year when a letter arrived by regular mail to the house. When the landlord told him of the its arrival, his immediate thoughts were that it was but another letter from his sister however, when he saw the handwriting that was scribed in red ink upon the envelope, those thoughts quickly vanished.

Returning to his room, he locked the door behind, and sat on the edge of the bed as he had done so many times before. All the letters she had written to him, as well as copies she had sent to the police, had been taken down and placed in a small cardboard box, which he had tucked under the bed in the hope he would never again need look upon the contents. But as he opened the letter he wondered if those were just foolhardy fantasies.

Inside the envelope there was, as before, a single sheet of paper folded neatly into three equal parts. As he unfolded it, revealing the message, the first discovery made was that it had been penned in black ink, something quite different from what he had become used to seeing. At a glance he knew without a doubt the letter was from Jacquelyn.

My dearest Aremis,

I am truly sorry for having left in the manner in which I did but I felt there was no other way. I knew if I told you of my plan to leave you would try to convince me otherwise and very well may have succeeded, I simply could not have that. You are kind and for that there can be no denying. I know you meant well for me and had hoped that I would change. I truly wanted to, to be that which you could see in me. The fact is I could not, as much as I told myself that I could, I knew it was a lie. I have been this way far too long now and as much as it will pain you to read this you must know it, the girl I once was is gone. I enjoy killing, I do not make excuses for what I do. You, as would others, see it as wrong, whereas I do not. I did not wish to endanger either of us by remaining with you even though a part of me very much wanted nothing more than that.

I would like to thank you for the pendant you left me; I assume it was for Christmas. It is quite lovely, and you are most sweet, I wear it all the time. I retrieved it along with some of my things a short time after you had returned home; you are either loyal or stubborn to a fault.

In closing, I want to tell you that I have heard tell of two murders in Whitechapel and I wanted you to know that it was not I that ended the lives of those women. I gave you my word that I would stop my game and I have.

I must confess to having found it flattering, to have someone attempt to mimic my handiwork.

Perhaps one day our paths will again cross,

Jacquelyn the Ripper,

PS, forgive my signature; I could not help myself for wanting to see what it should have looked like all along, ha- ha.

The letter still in his hand, his feelings awash with conflicting emotions, in some ways he wished he had never seen or knew of its existence, for that way he would never be certain that she had not simply met her end that night before Christmas and yet there was another part of him that was glad she had contacted him. He was relieved to know from her own hand that she had not resumed her hunting and mutilation of prostitutes, for he felt strongly that if she had, the police would have little to do other than tend to the mess come the morning.

Folding the letter neatly into its original state, he tucked it back in the envelope, then, turned it over so that the postmark could be seen. The stamp was nothing of a local origin and to his untrained eye he thought it might be German, but there was no way to be sure without having it checked by someone who knew more about such things.

Entertaining the notion of going to the post master's office located but a few streets over to do exactly that, he quickly extinguished the thought, deeming it to be pointless as he was not about to give chase. He had not had much success locating her within a five-mile square of familiar streets and alleyways; the chances of finding her in an area that had been expanded beyond that of England's borders would be impossible at best. Instead, he retrieved the box from its hiding place beneath the bed and placed it on the blankets beside him. Unwrapping and removing the strings that held the top closed he opened the lid. Not bothering more than a moment with that which had been so hidden away within the cardboard walls he, without emotion of any kind, added the newest letter to the pile of papers and closed the top, tying the strings back together so that it was as it had been.

He went to slip it back under the bed but stopped half way, returning it back to the bed. Sitting there a moment, he strummed his fingers mindlessly on the top of the box, the action making a soft almost musical sound until he got up, the strumming having been replaced by a slow mindful pacing within the confines of the tiny room.

If it had been a conversation he had been engaged in, his current actions would seem to be those of someone lost for words, but as there was no such verbal exchange taking place, it could be said that he was simply lost within his own thoughts.

He drew back the single curtain from the window and gazed over the empty backyard while he slowly pulled on the whiskers that made up the short beard on his chin.

Then quite suddenly, almost as though something in the yard had either startled him or caught his interest, he turned, letting the curtain reclaim the window. Fetching the lighter spring coat from the hook he threw it on, not bothering with the clasps. He collected the box containing the letters and newspaper cuttings, tucking it under his arm. Forgetting for the moment that he had not worn the coat since late in the summer of the previous year, he absentmindedly fished through the pockets in search of his keys pulling out, not his familiar keys, but instead a single key. He held it up as he studied its features, his mind flashing back to the grisly find in the backyard of Hanbury Street when he had pulled it from the mouth of Annie Chapman as she lay in a pool of her own blood, her entrails having been ripped from her abdomen.

"Never did ascertain what you were for," he said to the key as he spun it slowly between his fingers, much as he had done so many nights before. "Guess I shall never know, will I?"

He dropped the lone key back into the pocket he had retrieved it from and pulled his keys and some money from his heavier winter coat that hung on the hook but one over from where he had taken the coat he now had on.

This day was the first where the temperature was actually comfortable, the sun warming his back as he locked the door to what had been both his sanctuary and his prison throughout the better part of the last twelve months.

Taking the shortcut through the house and out the front door, he met his landlord as he sat on the front steps not far from where he had first given him the letter some thirty minutes earlier.

"I will be off home for a couple of weeks. I should be back well before the rent is due"

Obviously lost in his own thoughts and enjoying a more spring-like day than the city had seen in months, the heavyset man simply waved a casual acknowledgement of the statement.

"That's fine lad".

So with arrangements having been made, albeit somewhat loosely, he topped his head with a top hat, placed the cardboard box back beneath his arm, and made his way down the street smartly, walking cane in hand.

It had been nearly a year since he had been home, and from the tone carried in the words written in the numerous letters his sister had sent, he thought it best to make a conscientious effort to get there rather than try to explain the last year to her through paper correspondence.

Settled into his seat, much-belated Christmas gifts stowed beneath him, the train slowly began to pull out of the station, the gentle vibrations finding their way through the train car to his body making him feel incredibly tired. The conductor slowly made his way down the narrow aisle checking tickets. Aremis handed him his ticket, and after having it stamped and returned to him, he made himself comfortable, closed his eyes and drifted off to sleep.

Chapter 19

Dear Diary,

The days preceding my letter to you have been nothing sort of strange to say the very least, and I am most certain that I will not be able to convey all that I wish to tell you in a manner befitting the events.

Aremis arrived at my house quite unexpectedly, and to my shock and surprise I was so happy to see him that I threw my arms about him and hugged him so hard I thought later I might well have injured him. I say surprised as I had no fear of him at that moment, and although I have had some of that fear return to me, it is nowhere near what it has been in the past.

He seemed older than I remember, last time I saw him which, in fact, is only a year ago, but yet he remains unchanged. This is confusing, I am sure, but it is difficult to explain. Perhaps it is all that he has witnessed that has aged his soul more than it has his physical being.

I can only imagine what I will have to tell you in the coming entries as my brother wishes to share with me all that has happened to him these years whilst he has been away.

He has already told me in moments when we have managed a minute from family and friends that Mary, or Jacquelyn as I am to understand her true name to be, has gone on to places far from here. I feel for the people who may reside in such places.

To be truthful, although I desperately wish to know all he has to tell, at the same time I am apprehensive of what I am to hear.

In addition, he has given to me a box, the contents of which I have no idea. He entrusted me with it when we were alone and has instructed me to safeguard it, as what is contained within is most important and, as such, not safe within his possession. I have since put it in a small storage trunk Father had made for me some time ago. I keep my writings of years past inside and it sits in a corner of the attic. I can think of no safer place in which to keep it. He has asked me not look inside and for now I will abide by his wishes. However, I cannot promise that I will hold fast to that over the course of time.

Aremis has since returned to London, apparently unwilling or unable to spend more than a few days with us. He had gone off to the cemetery that same morning shortly after breakfast to visit Mother's grave. I had offered to go along with him as it will be the first time, to my knowledge, he had even been to see her since her passing, but he kindly requested of me that he go alone.

Upon his return, he had asked if I would take him to the train station. This was a bit to sort out, as I had to all but plead with John to mind little Matthew. He is a good man, just not with womanly things.

I took Aremis to the station in our carriage, a far different trip than the first time we went to that station, so many years ago now. I must confess that I still do not know how much of the brother I grew up with is still there.

I waved to him on the platform, a much happier goodbye, one that had promises made on both our parts to see each other again soon.

As I write this, I can honestly say that I am looking forward, with anticipation, to that day.

Temperance, the 5th of May in the year of our Lord, 1889

Aremis sat on the stone foundation of Tower Bridge looking out over the Thames. Many people in the community thought it was high time the city officials had a proper bridge built in the East End, and from the look of it she was certainly going to outshine the older London Bridge but a few miles upriver. He stared out over the black water, its calm stillness a near perfect reflection of how he had been feeling since having seen his family. It was difficult to leave after only such a short visit. But he knew the reasons behind his departure, and even though he could not explain them to those he loved, he knew better than to trifle with them. Jacquelyn had moved on to parts unknown, but the danger she posed could easily be played out with as much carnage through nothing more than his own carelessness.

It was well after midnight and he was about to set off for home when he heard someone approaching from behind him. He cast a casual glance over his shoulder then looked back out over the water.

"Alright mate, all yer dosh and be quick about it, and no one gets hurt"

Sitting as he was, the shabby thief had no way of knowing what was about to happen, as all traces of humanity slowly disappeared from his intended victim's eyes. Aremis continued to stare out at the cold water and the lights of the opposite shoreline, seemingly unaffected by the demands just made of him.

"You are mistaken my friend," Aremis replied quietly. "Someone is indeed going to get hurt this evening."

The End

www.waynemallows.com

CPSIA information can be obtained
at www.ICGtesting.com
Printed in the USA
LVOW04s1426190816

500904LV00001B/3/P